SUNSET OVER THE YUCATÁN

Gateway to Atlantis

Deborah L. Cannon

Copyright © 2023 Deborah L. Cannon

All rights reserved.

This book is a work of fiction. Names, characters, businesses, organizations, places and events either are the product of the author's imagination or are used fictitiously. Any similarity to real persons, living or dead, is coincidental and not intended by the author.

No part of this book may be reproduced, stored in a retrieval system, or transmitted in any form or by any means, electronic, mechanical, photocopying, recording, or otherwise, without express written permission of the publisher, excepting brief quotes used in reviews.

ISBN-13: 9798854822244

Cover design by: Aubrey Cannon

Printed in the United States of America

For those who believe
And for those who don't

My dear Lucy,

When your mother told me she wanted another child I was frightened of the whole idea. All of my plans would be put on hold; and you have no idea how long I have been making these plans. Although she does not understand, I hope that when you are grown up, you will. I can already see by the way your face screws up when you want something and the way you pummel the air with your tight little fists that you will be a force to be reckoned with.

I asked my lawyer to deliver this letter to you on your wedding day. Whether I will be there or not only the future knows. If I am not there—then I will be dead. And you will receive this letter in my place. Know that I see something special in you and I have high hopes. Promise me you will finish what I began. In my safety deposit box, you will find all of my research notes. Notes to what, you ask? I have one word for that.

ATLANTIS

Every one of us is blind to our destiny. We cannot predict the future, only guide it in the direction we wish it to go. Every obstacle that you will face is just a stepping stone to where you will end up. Remember my baby girl, courage cannot be measured by comparing yourself to others. Courage can only be measured by comparing yourself to yourself. Only when you face what you most fear do you show true courage.

Your loving father

CHAPTER 1

I only meant to go for a short excursion into the countryside.
Excitement propelled me, and here I was skimming over the highway until I reached the offramp and pulled onto a lonely road. The town was a mere hour outside of Paris. Little traffic tangled the rural routes this early, and if worse came to worse, and for some reason I was delayed, Johnny Sayid could rescue me in Luke's helicopter. I patted my handbag where my trusty iPhone lay beside me in the passenger seat of the rental. Despite the unreasonable hour, the hotel had been accommodating and ordered me a car.

A small sign came into view.

Bienvenue à Chevreuse

I continued driving.

Some people would say I was crazy to head out of the city on such an important morning, and yet what could I do for five hours? My hair would take, what, thirty minutes? And at most forty to primp and dress. Hanging around with my mom and sister, fussing, could only make me nervous, and I had no desire to be nervous. I was marrying the love of my life.

The clock on the dashboard read 6:45 a.m. I had showered and dressed on waking, and Norman was totally oblivious of my plan. We had agreed to sleep in separate rooms the night before. Oh, to catch the look on his face when he saw me for the first time as his bride!

I know, I know. It really was dumb to arrange a wedding in thirty days. The past two weeks had been stressful. Being close friends with the billionaire Luke Trevanian was a Godsend, as he had pulled a million strings to get Norman and I our perfect venue. It was done, and now all I wanted was a couple of hours quiet reflection before we exchanged vows.

I pulled up along the main street. My side window was open and the early morning sights and sounds, and smells of the village enchanted me. Colorful flowers in earthenware pots on every doorstep. Birdsong and the rustle of leaves in green spreading trees. And the aroma of newly ground coffee and fresh-baked bread. People were just opening their shops, all under the protective gaze of the castle on the hill.

The Château de la Madeleine brought magic. It hovered on the skyline above a swirl of dawn mist. The gray stone fortress poked through a sea of trees atop a rolling green mound and oversaw the quaint and colorful scatter of houses and businesses at its feet.

Chevreuse was a favorite retreat of my ancestor Jean Racine, who supervised some of the earlier modifications of the castle keep. He was one of three important playwrights of 17th century France. Until a month ago I had no idea of my illustrious pedigree.

As I hiked the road to the plateau the sun—just rising over the tor—formed an ethereal glow on the turrets and parapets. A parking lot lay next to the Château. I had chosen to park on the street though because I felt like a walk.

It did not strike me as unusual when I saw the white unmarked truck, one of only three vehicles in the lot. Many cars in Europe had foreign license plates, as the EU allowed for free movement across borders. True, the plain, white van stood out among the dark-colored sedans, and had I looked closer, it might have aroused suspicion.

Too overcome by its beauty to care, the age-worn structure with its sturdy ramparts and enormous towers and arrow-slit windows drew me like a magnet. Was anything open to the public? I had arrived much too early and would have no access to the interior. The guard tower was open, however, and I followed my instincts and climbed the steps. At the very top a lookout rewarded me with a breathtaking view.

Every shade of green and pink flooded my vision as I absorbed the undulating valley of trees and flowering shrubs. Here a red, brown or blue roof peeked through, and there, a church steeple. The buildings followed a picturesque pattern that traced a branch of the lazy Yvette River, crisscrossed by stone, iron-railed footbridges.

"*Bonjour*," someone said. "I am sorry, but there is no food allowed inside the buildings."

"Good morning!" My bluster was also in French. I swallowed the mouthful of baguette in my mouth, brushing away the crumbs and apologized for my improvised breakfast. The irresistible aroma of new bread in the village center had literally led me by the nose to the boulangerie. How could I resist fresh bread? Besides I was starving.

"Our *spécialité—la baguette.*"

The remains of the crusty loaf broke in half in my nervous grip. I almost offered him some, but surely a bribe was inappropriate. Instead, the bread went inside my carryall, an action performed self-consciously. A bad idea perhaps, or at the very least, messy, but why discard a perfectly good (and delicious) baguette?

Amusement creased his eyes, and he resisted confiscating the food. "I am afraid the Château does not open to visitors until 11:00 am."

Eleven a.m. was precisely the moment I would be standing at the altar.

My sight lowered to the phone in my other hand where the time was displayed—I had meant to take a photo—and noted my visit to Chevreuse had stretched to forty-five minutes. Another hour and I must go.

My French was fluent. "*Je sais.* But this morning is the only opportunity for me to see your beautiful village, and of course, the Château de la Madeleine."

"You know it? The Château?"

"*Ah Oui.* Eleventh century, *non?*"

"*Oui.* She has had many keepers over the centuries."

This was one of the Château's security guards. It was early, and there were few on the premises yet. The guard was holding a lidded paper cup of coffee in his hand (the aroma delectable and making my mouth water), and his jacket was partially unbuttoned. So, he wasn't even officially on the clock yet.

My gaze bounced off the coffee again. One rule for tourists and another for security guards? I curbed the impulse to tease. What if he misunderstood? Instead, my free hand lifted automatically, and puffing a lock of unruly hair out of my mouth, I introduced myself. "Lucy Racine. Pleased to meet you."

His brow arched. "Pierre Lemieux. *Enchanteé, mademoiselle.*" A hard pause followed. "You are related to our local celebrity, Jean-Baptiste Racine."

"I am," Pleased that he had noticed.

"Then of course, I must allow you inside. Monsieur Racine was very famous in Paris. He came this way, often, to the countryside, you know... the road between the castle and the village, it was named after him."

Before making the trip to Paris, my Internet research had led to the famous playwright. Stunned to learn that Chevreuse was one of his local haunts, I was also delighted to see that the town had his name on one of its roads.

"Come." He led me down the staircase and out to the main doors. "I will give you a guided tour myself."

The interior of the castle was cold. That was expected. It was impossible to heat a structure this size without the village going bankrupt. But the numerous bodies that daily flowed in and out gave it a tolerable ambient temperature. It was only now, in the fresh hours of the morning, without the sun to warm the stones, that the interior had cooled to cellar temperatures.

"Ordinarily," he said, "visitors are prohibited from certain areas. You are allowed only in the exhibition gallery where it is explained the history of the Château." He showed me this space and left me alone for several minutes.

It was a large room with displays presented in chronological order in the form of decorative signage, didactic text and restored photographs, and period objects such as tools, household items, clothing, and some of the spicier relics of a thankfully bygone era. I would not want to be the victim of some of those scary-looking contraptions. Which I am sure were recovered from the castle's dungeon.

From the building of the Château as a fortification against pillagers, through its numerous aristocratic owners, to its capture by British troops during the Hundred Years War, and on up to its renaming after the local chapel Sainte Marie-Madeleine, the visitor was eased into the present-day where the Château now operated both as a museum and headquarters to the Regional National Park of the Chevreuse Valley.

When the guard returned, I asked for clarification on a few details of the Château and he patiently explained.

"I see you have many of the original artifacts." I indicated the 'rack' that took up much of one display case. A method of torturing prisoners, it was meant to stretch a human body to agonizing lengths. Hanging on the wall above it was a metal implement called a 'pear' that was inserted into a victim's anus or vagina after being heated to excruciating temperatures.

To account for my peculiar interest in these barbaric instruments, I explained that I worked as head illustrator at the Royal Ontario Museum in Toronto. Years of exposure to these types of artifacts had steeled me to the cruelty of medieval man.

He chuckled. "I see you do not need a guide."

"Oh, but I do. My knowledge of French history is poor."

"Not so poor," he contradicted me. He paused. "Would you like to see the dungeon?"

I immediately nodded.

"Generally, the dungeon is forbidden to the public. It has not been refurbished and has been used as a storage room for many years."

I could see that by a sign labeled EMPLYOYEES ONLY strung across the landing of a stairwell. Call me morbid or simply curious, but I was excited to see it.

After descending a number of stone steps and winding through a tunnel of similarly worn rock brick, we arrived at a rusting iron portcullis. The smell in here was dank with centuries of seeping moisture. And black mold or algae crowded the corners and edges of the ceiling and floors. No wonder visitors weren't allowed down here!

We ducked under the semi-raised iron gate and entered a room, dark, except for some windows near the top, barred with iron spindles and open to the river breeze.

A few raw lightbulbs had been hung across the room and he switched these on, immediately transforming the horror of the dungeon to something more bearable.

There were iron-barred cells for holding prisoners, recently filled with stacked plastic storage boxes, the locks on the gates removed to avoid accidental confinement. There also existed an interesting system of drainage built from rock to remove human sewage. A stone well, long since unused, was there to provide water, and on the filthy walls were the original hooks for tools and equipment, and empty antique lamps and lanterns.

"Creepy," I said in English.

He laughed and agreed.

"Shall we?" He indicated the rusty portcullis and preceded me to the exit. I am assuming the notches that kept the portcullis in position were secure. How horrible it would be to be trapped down here. Yes, indeed.

Monsieur Le Security Guard and I returned to the upper floor. Still early. Just after eight. None of the staff had arrived, although apparently there was one other guard somewhere in the massive labyrinth of towers and bastions.

"Thank you so much for the tour, M. Lemieux," I said.

"*Mon Plaisir, mademoiselle.*"

In a nearby office a telephone rang.

"*Excusez-moi,*" he said.

"Of course. I'll see myself out."

He waved and turned to scuttle towards the persistent sound.

Through the large passageway I spotted the main entrance, and started to head in that direction when an open door to my left caught my eye. Glancing back, I saw that the guard had disappeared into an office, and a second later the ringing of the phone stopped.

Should I risk it? No one else was around and the guard was engaged with his call. What could it hurt? If I was caught, I would just say I thought this was another public gallery.

It was indeed some sort of gallery. Although I doubt if the public was welcome. The space was small and the display cases held unusual objects, objects that appeared to be unrelated to the medieval castle theme.

One glass case held Greek pottery and another had a Roman statue. Here was a Chinese dynastic vase, and there a small portion of an Assyrian fresco. There was also what appeared to be an ancient manuscript, a scroll illustrated with something that might be a Sea god in his chariot drawn by six winged horses and accompanied by—what—nymphs? Riding dolphins. It struck a chord in my mind. But slipped away when something else grabbed my attention.

The oddest item on view was something I had definitely seen before.

Oh my god. Was that…?

What was it doing here?

Now, this is going to sound strange, and look even stranger. I felt like a criminal and if I was caught, I would have no chance to explain.

Why did a French medieval castle house a Mayan artifact? Because there was no mistake. That large round mosaic object, decorated in turquoise tesserae, pyrite, gold and mother-of-pearl was an almost perfect Mayan ceremonial shield.

I recognized it.

Because I was the one who had discovered it.

CHAPTER 2

Only four weeks ago today I had fallen into the subbasement of the Cádiz Cathedral in Spain during an earthquake. Obviously, I wasn't hurt or I wouldn't be here today, but neither was the shield. Hurt that is—or more precisely—damaged.

The beautiful, magical mosaic, the thing that had cost several peoples' lives, had hung, unknown to anyone, on the wall of that cavern beneath the cathedral for centuries. Until *I* found it. And now, it was in Chevreuse.

I was well aware that when the treasure was confiscated by Interpol, they had brought it to France. France was the headquarters of the International Police who were in charge of pancontinental thefts. A mystery surrounded this artifact as no one was certain why it had ended up hidden in the subbasement of a famous Spanish cathedral, or who it belonged to. One thing was for certain; it was of great value. The authorities had no idea what to do with it. And until they could determine some kind of history for it, and thereby ownership, Interpol had taken the precious object into custody. But to store it here? In this tiny village? How odd.

Well, maybe it made sense. It was a treasure and a lot of people were after it. Who would ever think to look for it here?

I stared, thunderstruck by its presence. Except for a roughly rectangular piece missing from the bottom, it was perfect, and exactly the way I had discovered it in that subterranean hiding place.

A lovely round shield.

And fully decorated in the Mayan tradition.

How should I describe it? The turquoise represented the sea. The two-headed serpent at the bottom signified renewal. The white conical teeth. Could they be mountain peaks? And in the center of the shield was an irregularly shaped golden circle with concentric rings. An island. I had no doubt it symbolized an island. Or perhaps a continent. And the semi-crescents of mother-of-pearl were boats. From the top, bottom and sides of the shield, pyrite and gold shapes—bridges, I decided—radiated from the island. I pondered over it for a while. Come to think of it, for the first time since seeing it in Spain, it reminded me of a map.

My right hand went to the strap of my carryall that crossed over my chest. My left hand moved to the satchel by my hip. I felt the hard rectangular object nestled in bubble wrap hidden within. It was the same object. It had to be.

What was it doing here?

"Mademoiselle!"

I jumped, startled out of my thoughts.

My arms instinctively crossed in a protective gesture.

"Excuse me, but this room is off-limits to visitors."

"*Desolée desolée*," I mumbled. "I am so very sorry…

the door was open. I thought it was a public gallery."

"*Non.* Monsieur Armand, my partner, must have left it open when he went to the loo. Sloppy and very irresponsible of him." M. Lemieux's English was very British (although accented with heavy French) and he had reverted to this when he caught me trespassing. Was this the tone he used for bumbling tourists? Those without a scrap of French? Under his breath, he muttered in French—clearly forgetting that I was fluent —most of which I'd rather not repeat. Suffice it to say, the words were meant for Armand and not me.

Of course, M. Armand had no way to know that his partner had brought in a guest. It was not exactly visiting hours.

He grabbed the doorknob and pushed wide the door. A clear gesture for me to exit. I threw one last anxious peek at the Mayan mosaic and complied. He closed the door with a jerk. I heard a jingle of metal as his right hand fumbled about for the set of keys in his pocket, withdrew the ring, located the pertinent one—and— and then something really strange happened.

Just as I got up the courage to ask him about the Mayan shield, M. Lemieux crashed to the floor. His head smashed the door as he fell.

The keys rattled away. I dropped to my knees beside him. "Monsieur, *monsieur.* Are you alright?"

The security guard had fallen forward against the door. Was he having a heart attack? A stroke? Some sort of seizure? And now he was going to have concussion.

He seemed too young for it to be cardiac arrest or stroke. His looks were those of a fortyish man. A seizure then.

And then I saw it. Blood.

There was a small hole in his back. A bullet wound. I had missed it at first because the jacket of his uniform was dark blue. The blood made no impression on that color of fabric, until the blood flow increased. And then it gleamed like thick oil.

Nightmares of what had happened in Cádiz flooded my brain. No. Not again. I had watched one man shot to death only four weeks ago. I refused to witness another death. Not on my wedding day!

I fumbled in my handbag for my phone to call Emergency. A hand came down from above me and stripped it out of my fist. A heavily accented voice, coarse and muffled warned, "You scream, you will be like him."

The body that I was kneeling beside began to slide away from the door. I looked over and saw two men disguised in ski masks, both armed, and with sneakers on their feet to erase the sound of their approach. One in black; the other in blue.

The one in blue dragged the unconscious security guard facedown by the ankles, leaving streaks of blood on the stone floor.

When he was clear of the door, the man who had taken my phone (he too had a gun, and wore a dark green ski mask) hauled me to my feet. "What should we do with the woman?"

The question was asked in Spanish. The only reason I understood was because I knew the Spanish word for 'woman' And… who else could he be asking about concerning a woman—except me?

Black mask responded. It seemed he was the ringleader. "Tie her up."

"Where?"

"In there." He pointed with his gun at the treasure room. So, they knew about that?

They were speaking a mixture of Arabic and Spanish. I understood almost nothing. Only the bare minimum. But it was enough for me to know that my brief employment in multiple countries—and the effort to learn the different languages—was paying off. I might not be fluent but I could just make out the gist of their dialogue.

Blue Mask patted down the semi-conscious security guard and removed anything from his body that might help us prisoners escape. These included his cellphone and a Colt 1911 pistol.

When the things were firmly stashed away inside his jacket pockets, Green Mask kicked the door open. It hadn't been locked yet and he forced me inside. His arm was like a vise, his forearm stiff against my chest and his hand cupped onto my left breast. There was nothing between his gloved hand and my skin as he shoved his hand under my loose sweater. Whether this was an accident or on purpose I'll never know. I had left quickly this morning and hadn't bothered with a bra. I had expected to be back in my hotel room by now dressing for my wedding. No matter either way. The look in his eyes told me his thoughts. Pervert!

Blue Mask followed dragging the wounded security guard upright, smearing blood everywhere, and onto one of three metal chairs. There was also a wooden desk. But that was irrelevant. Except for the complex telephone with its numerous old-fashioned buttons, there was nothing for these criminals to worry about here.

Black Mask ripped the cord of the phone system

from the wall just as it started to ring. *"Rápidamente,"* he hissed.

Something about me had caught his attention, and he gave me a doubletake. Then tugged his eyes away.

Green mask hugged me against him, forcing me to feel the hardness inside his pants. But Black Mask, seeing how his minion was distracted, jerked me out of his arms and slammed me down on one of the free chairs.

"No time for that!" he barked.

Green Mask glared at him.

At this moment I was ready to kill. If I had any hope of saving the security guard's life, I would have to put up with this pervert a little longer. I had a small pistol inside my carryall. But dared not go for it. Lest they find my secret package. And the last thing I wished to do was draw attention.

So, I played dumb and suffered the harassment. And watched as Green Mask dug out some packing tape from the desk drawer. With that he bound the wounded guard's wrists and feet, while Blue Mask kept his gun aimed on me. A Ruger P89. They were all carrying similar models.

The body jerked with each rough motion and finally the security guard was secured.

It was packing tape, I thought. It would be easy to cut through if I got the chance.

Now it was my turn. Green Mask did a quick job of it, not even making me hold my hands behind my back, but permitting me to clasp my hands together over my handbag on my lap like I was praying. The tape was tight, but not too tight.

He didn't bother to do my feet. Didn't even bother to

pat me down. Why would he? He already knew I carried nothing on my person, and that I wasn't even wearing a bra.

Then he did the thing I was most desperate to avoid. He lifted my bound hands to check my handbag. My heart started to beat fast. If he found the gun that was one thing. He would simply take it away. But if he found the other thing…

The beats escalated and then subsided.

What he found was bread. Three quarters of a baguette broken into two pieces and filling the top of my handbag.

He laughed, said something rude. Although I didn't quite catch the words. They were in Spanish and I recognized their vulgarity in his tone. What did a baguette look like to a pervert? Lemme guess.

He rubbed his crotch, and dropped the bag on my lap.

Thank goodness for that. He was so distracted by what my body had done to his, he wasn't thinking straight. Another victory for womankind.

Black Mask yelled at him. He turned with a coarse utterance. He looked like he wanted to grab at me one more time, but Black Mask, patience exhausted, catapulted over to us and twisted his accomplice's arm up his back. The man screamed, growled some unintelligible words as Black Mask turned his accomplice towards the glass cases.

I swear they would murder each other. Black mask surely appeared to be intent on breaking the other's arm. But that would be stupid if they intended to escape with the goods. Finally, the one with the advantage gave the other a sharp warning. Whatever he said worked.

Green Mask swore and yanked his arm free.

I stared at the figure in the black mask as the one in green turned away. Overkill, maybe? Since when was a thieving crook a gentleman. Why would he care what his accomplice did to me? I could swear that altercation had something to do with me. And not just the fact that the man in the green mask was wasting precious time.

Oh, the hell with it. What did I care? The thieves had my phone, and that was all that mattered. Without a link to the outside world, calling for help was impossible. They thought me an unfortunate tourist. Wrong place, wrong time. Weak and frightened. Nothing for them to worry about. And maybe that was all the heroics was about. Did he have a soft spot for women? If he thought me weak and vulnerable maybe I could use that.

Green Mask returned and when he was satisfied that the security guard and I were bound side by side with no chance of escaping, he sealed a piece of packing tape over our mouths. I should have pleaded to Black Mask when I had the chance. He seemed like he was the only one with a conscience. So why would they make him the leader? It hardly made sense.

Green Mask turned back. My heart started to beat wildly... If only I could see his face... He pressed his fingers to his lips then against my sealed mouth as though planting a kiss. I jerked my head away in disgust. I felt the tape loosen.

Like I said. It was packing tape. It wasn't going to hold.

And did they care? Seemed not.

All they wanted was... was what?

I had my answer before I could guess. Of all things...

they were after the Mayan shield.

I heard a smash as Blue Mask raised the third metal chair and shattered the glass of the display case. I twisted, lowered my head, raised my bound hands to my face, and shut my eyes as shards splattered in all directions. I turned to see if my companion had been hit, but we were both out of the splash zone. Besides, he was already unconscious from the shot in his back and the bump on the head when he fell against the door.

The thieves wasted no time. The black-masked leader yanked a large cloth sack out of his jacket front and opened it for the other two to heave the mosaic shield inside. The blue-masked one, the largest of the men (don't get me wrong; they were all tall and muscular) hugged the treasure to his chest and exited without speaking. The others followed, but not until Green Mask had blown the thumb latch from the deadbolt before closing the door.

My ears were still ringing.

Then silence descended.

The entire heist had taken fifteen minutes.

CHAPTER 3

I rolled out of the chair and ran to the door. The thumb latch was gone. All that was left was to try turning the knob with my wrists still taped together. No such luck. The thieves had locked the door from the outside.

I twisted my lips and raised my hands to peel the tape off my mouth. I two-fisted the door with rhythmic beats and then listened.

"Hello! Is anyone out there?"

I hollered for about two minutes, pounding until my fists ached, and then collapsed to the floor in exhaustion.

No time for this. M. Lemieux would die if I didn't get help right away. I ran to the desk and found a pair of scissors to saw at the tape. Once freed, I checked my companion for life signs. A pulse. He was still breathing. "Hang on, monsieur," I whispered. "I'll get you out of here."

How? How was I going to get help. I no longer had a phone. The thieves had stolen it. I removed the tape from his mouth. He didn't flinch, didn't even wake up.

I cut the tape from his wrists and ankles and he still

remained unconscious. I pressed up close to his nose and mouth and felt air subtly flowing in and out. Now what?

The office phone. Could I reattach the wires? I had witnessed Norman attempt this very thing with enormous success. But could I do it with no experience of wiring or telephones or anything technical? Had the thief really ripped the cord or simply unplugged it? I dropped to my knees, scrunched in between the desk and the wall, and reached for the cord.

Dangling wires.

So that option was out.

No help was coming from the outside. Did Lemieux still have his cellphone? I was confused by all the activity. Maybe, maybe not. I think not. I think one of the masked thieves had taken it from his pocket. Did he have a museum security-grade, two-way radio to communicate with his partner?

Where was M. Armand anyway. That was his name, wasn't it? My frustration was growing by the minute. Security at this castle was pathetic.

But I was being unfair. In general, no one came to museums at the crack of dawn. They weren't open. Which was probably why the security had been so lax. And, also, the reason the thieves thought it was a good time to break in. Furthermore, castles on principle had few or no valuable objects, generally not the kind you could sell on the black market.

Instruments of torture were not high on their wish list.

Clearly, the Château was an exception. My eyes were at this moment roving over the antiquities the thieves had passed over. I stopped at the blue and white porcelain. That Ming vase must be worth a penny or two. And those Greek and Roman objects. What were they doing here anyway?

I went to examine the objects more closely. These were authentic artifacts from what I could see. But I was no expert. Neither were they anything special. Museums worldwide owned specimens like these. There must be another reason they were here.

But how could I get into the displays without breaking the glass? My vision sailed around the room. Too much was broken already.

Time was a-wasting. Plenty of opportunity to puzzle this out when I was free and my wounded companion was safely in the care of a doctor.

M. Lemieux was counting on me. Where was his radio? Had the thieves swiped that too?

I seemed to recall Norman mentioning that radio, not cellphone, was how most professional security guards communicated with one another. Contact was instant, hence more efficient. Norman was Luke's official bodyguard. He would know.

Speaking of which he was going to kill me if I left him standing at the altar.

Shit, shit, shit. I was desperate.

On the outside of the security guard's belt there was a holder where the radio should have been. It was empty. Those masked men were definitely pros.

I still had my gun. I ran back to my handbag that I had left on the chair, tossed the bread aside, giving it a silent blessing for distracting the thief from a more thorough search of my belongings, and rummaged through the bag's contents.

Pistol in hand, I returned to the door.

I could blow the lock off. Or could I? Was that something that was only possible on TV? I had never used my pistol for anything but target practice and self-defense. Was it possible to open a locked door that way? Or would I simply fuse the mechanism and trap myself and my injured companion even further?

Norman would have been able to do it. I had seen him in action.

What about the ricochet? What if my firing a shot sent the bullet flying wild and killed the security guard or even myself. Yeah, I know. No self-respecting hero spends anytime thinking on stuff like this. They just react. But hey, I never said I was a hero.

Voices came from outside the only window. I raced towards it. The window was small and stood near the ceiling. In order to look out, I needed a boost. I seized the chair I had been bound in, and pushed it against the wall and climbed up. There they were. The crooks. Still masked, all three of them. And heading for the white unmarked truck. I *knew* it was suspicious!

The parking lot remained empty except for the three vehicles. The two sedans obviously belonged to the security guards.

The blue and green masked men entered the back of the van with the Mayan shield, careful not to damage it. So, they knew what it was. They were treating it with kid gloves. That meant something. And it got me to thinking that they had to have a boss. The thief in the black mask was not the head honcho. He was just in charge of the heist.

Black Mask got into the driver's seat.

License plate; memorize it! Generic letters and numbers. Nothing easy to remember. Crap, I wish I had my phone so that I could just take a picture of it. On the right side of the plate: white cross on red shield. It was Swiss. On the left side of the plate: red, black and gold canton. So, it was Geneva. The coat of arms had a black crowned eagle on a gold background on one side and a golden key against a red backdrop on the other. I suddenly registered why Swiss, why Geneva. Switzerland had the largest freeport in the world for the storage of antiquities and it was located in Geneva. A perfect place to hide stolen objects until the heat cooled off.

Miles of identical corridors with faceless locked metal doors housed priceless treasures in the freeport. While there, the object and its purported owners enjoyed anonymity and prison-quality security. No questions asked. For a price, users were guaranteed confidentiality and the use of aliases or false names— which enabled tax advantages.

That meant, whoever had ordered the heist was rich.

I shoved my pistol against the glass. If I took aim, maybe I could blow out the tires. But it would be stupid to fire through the glass. Again, sharp splinters flying everywhere. More likely I'd take my eye out.

And these were unopenable windows. Safety measures. For what? The window was so high and the pavement below so close, that a person could hardly commit suicide from here. And from the outside, no one could break in without a ladder. Okay, so a professional thief, like these assholes (pardon my French but I was really ticked off) who had just stranded me here with a dying man, would likely have rope or a ladder.

I decided to smash the window with my gun and take a shot. But what good would that do? If I blew out their tires and stranded them, they'd only come back and kill us both. But I was damned if I let them get away with this.

They were making me miss my wedding!

The engine of the white van started up. I raised the butt end of my pistol and crashed it against the window. The glass webbed, and split. I cleared a hole while the van rolled out of the lot crossing over the yellow lines of the parking spots and I still hadn't made a fix on the tires. I fired several shots blind. Missed.

The driver stared at me through his window and for a moment I felt a flash of recognition.

It was only a momentary sense of familiarity. No face or name came to mind. Who *was* he? In that split second, I was certain he would stop and finish me off.

There was no return fire. No need to kill me. I couldn't identify them. They were all dressed in black, every inch of their skin and hair covered except for their eyes. I couldn't have given a description if I was tortured. Unless you counted the slight differences in mask color.

The van headed fast down the switchback hillside road. Dipped low beyond the curve. And was gone.

CHAPTER 4

"Monsieur, Monsieur, are you alright?" I shook the security guard gently by the shoulder.

The thieves had stripped us both of our cellphones and Lemieux of his sidearm. I had heard nothing when they fired the shot. They had used a silencer.

Who had done the actual shooting? That, I had not seen. By the time I realized what had happened, all three of the culprits were holding guns.

The guard murmured something, and his eyes opened vaguely.

"M. Lemieux. You'll be alright. Please try to stay awake."

He had lost a lot of blood. He was a corpulent man, around two hundred pounds despite a stature of maybe five feet seven. The way he was seated made it awkward for me to dress the wound or put any pressure on it to stop the bleeding. I had no medical training, none whatsoever, unless you counted what I had learned from instinct in the field. If I moved him, I might make things worse.

I pounded on the door and shouted. Lemieux

had said there was one other security guard on the premises. By now Armand must be headed back this way if he'd only gone to the bathroom. This castle was enormous and its hallowed halls would either absorb the sounds into the rock or broadcast it in giant echoes. I had no experience with castle acoustics.

No response. No footsteps racing towards our door. No anxious voices.

No one at the other end would expect a hysterical woman to be screaming for help. So why would he hurry? No one was supposed to be here.

What time was it? I was starting to feel hysterical. *Get a grip. Think!* Surely, the rest of the staff would arrive soon, and someone would hear me. I must do something about the bleeding. I went behind my patient to study the options. The bullet hole in his back was visible just below the back rail bar of the chair. If I maneuvered him ever so gently, I could do something about the bleeding.

Could I somehow use the packing tape to strap a compress to the wound?

I had a better idea.

I took off my belt but it was too short to be useful. The guard was also wearing a belt and I removed it from around his waist as carefully as I could without hurting him. If I attached the two together it might just work as a tourniquet around his ribcage. But I needed something for a bandage.

There was nothing in this room and I was eating up valuable time searching. If worse came to worst I could take off my sweater and use that, but I preferred to try something else first. Being caught with your top off by strangers, half-naked, was not exactly the memory I wished for my wedding day.

Besides, that sweater was white cashmere, a gift from my beloved.

I finally removed my shoes and stripped off my socks. I did the same to him. His socks were bigger. With two pairs of socks, I formed a thick wad, hiked up my sleeves, and went to the back of his chair. The wound was small. And the good news was, the flow of blood was slowing.

I plastered the sock bandage against the seeping wound and struggled with the belt, now double length, and wrapped it securely around his ribcage and fastened it.

Lemieux gasped as I jerked it tight. "I'm so sorry," I said. But I was glad he was still awake. "You rest. I'll be right back."

I returned to the window to see if anyone else was in the parking lot. If I hammered my pistol on the cracked window… I could try to widen the gap big enough to crawl through.

No need. Cars were arriving. Several black vehicles that all appeared alike.

This looked suspicious, too. Surely, all the museum employees didn't drive the same dark-blue model.

Hadn't they seen the getaway car and tried to stop it?

Then reason sank in. Naturally they hadn't. Why would they stop an apparently innocent truck leaving the premises?

Fifteen minutes later, a team of ten men broke into the office to find me and the wounded security guard barefoot and relieved to see them.

"Your name, mademoiselle?"

"I told you. I am Lucy Racine. And I don't have time to hang around here. Please. Tell me. What time is it?"

"It is nine fifty-six," the officer said glancing at his cellphone. He had a thick French accent and was interrogating me in English. He was dressed in civilian clothes, slacks and pressed, monochromatic shirt. All of the officers arriving were dressed alike. "Now please, the longer you resist, the longer this will take. I need some identification."

"How did you know we were trapped in here? Did M. Armand call you?"

"You are not answering my questions, mademoiselle."

"I'll give you a statement and answer whatever questions tomorrow, but right now I have to get back to Paris. I am getting married in an hour." My voice was threatening to escalate into a desperate squeak. If they didn't release me soon…

The interrogating officer raised his eyebrows. He was from AID, the Antiquities International Division, a special branch of Interpol. "Then what are you doing here in the midst of a crime scene."

"I told you." I once again recounted the tale of my imprisonment. How we had been taken by surprise, how the security guard was shot in the back and both of us bound. How I had freed myself and attempted to blow out the tires of the getaway van with my personal firearm, which the authorities now had in their possession.

"Please," I implored, straining to control my exasperation, and fetched my passport from my handbag. "Let me talk to someone in charge."

He glared at me. Somehow, I had insulted him by assuming he was an underling. And that made me realize that I had just cut my chances in half of getting his cooperation.

He took the passport from me as though it were diseased. He studied the pages and his facial muscles twitched at the multiple international stamps.

"If you have a heart at all, let me call my fiancé, and his best man, who is one of my closest friends. Luke Trevanian."

When he raised his head from examining my passport, his eyebrows were arched even higher. I clarified. "Yes. That's what I said. Luke Trevanian. The globetrotting billionaire archaeologist. Surely, you've heard of him? He was just on the news last week for announcing his intention to search for the lost continent of Atlantis."

He laughed. He tucked my passport under his notepad and scribbled something down.

"Did you hear me?" I demanded. "Have you not heard of Atlantis?"

"I heard you. And what does his search for a mythical island have to do with this theft."

"Did I say it had anything to do with the theft?" Then it occurred to me. What a coincidence. Some people believed that the Mayan shield—

"Again, Mademoiselle Racine. Explain to me how you came to be tangled up in the middle of a theft."

I had omitted the part where the security guard had expected me to leave the premises while he went to answer the phone. I explained how my curiosity, being a museum employee in Canada, had caused me to enter the office lured by the sight of exotic objects. *Wrong place, wrong time!* I wanted to shriek at him.

Surely, they didn't think I had anything to do with the heist? Oh God. Now I needed Norman and Luke more than ever. And perhaps a lawyer?

I rose from the chair I had been sitting in. "Please. Call Luke Trevanian. He'll vouch for me. He's staying at the Hôtel Plaza Athénée in Paris. He's in one of the penthouse suites. He's my fiancé's best man."

I think he meant to ignore me but then a man in a black suit and tie, with a beige overcoat approached. Now, this was probably the boss.

"Ms. Racine," he said in English. "I am…" Curiously, he hesitated. "I am John Moz—" His underling gave him a startled look. Then turned away. "—Superintendent of the Antiquities International Division."

He had taken his time about approaching me and I intended to give him a piece of my mind. Something stopped me. It wasn't just the way he had introduced himself, and the fact that he spoke perfect English.

Why did he look familiar? I had never seen this man in my life.

He was maybe fifty-nine or sixty, hazel-eyed and brown-haired, lean and pleasant-looking in a nondescript way, and of medium height. Five nine perhaps. In spite of the fact that he wasn't a towering giant, he had an imposing presence. Clearly, everyone in this room respected him.

I tasted his name and tumbled it around in my brain.

Moz? I gripped the offered hand. What kind of a name was that? If I'd had my phone, I would have looked it up. From the sounds of it that word sounded like it could be equivalent to a hex or magic spell. *"If you don't watch it, I'll moz you!"* He certainly had the power to influence.

"You wish to contact Dr. Luke Trevanian?" he asked, releasing my hand.

"Yes. Yes, please. He'll explain that this was all an unhappy coincidence."

He nodded at the official who had been questioning me, and the man scrolled over the links of his phone to find the hotel. Good thing they didn't ask me for the number, but then I suppose they were used to the fact that no one memorized phone numbers anymore. All they would have to do was contact the hotel to page Luke or Norman and the boys would be at the desk in a flash if they knew I was in trouble.

The superintendent gestured for me to sit on one of the cold metal chairs that I had earlier vacated. He would have taken one of the other two except that the one holding the security guard was still smeared with blood. Forensics was taking samples just to be sure whose blood it was. The third chair was bent like a pretzel from smashing the case where the prize mosaic had been housed.

"While Agent Toussaint contacts your friend and your—your fiancé, please tell me exactly what the thieves stole from that case." He shoved a thumb in the direction of the broken glass.

"It was a round object," I said. There was something prickly about my instincts regarding this official. I cannot describe it. But I thought it best to answer in generalities. To tell the truth… but not the whole truth.

I stretched out my arms to emulate a large circle. "It was decorated," I said. "With a mosaic in mostly blue and white."

"Turquoise? Mother-of-pearl?"
Uh-huh.
"And pyrite?" he asked.
I hesitated. Nodded.
"And gold?"
He knew it?

He removed his cellphone from his pocket and swiped left, then right until he came to a photograph. He turned it to face me. "Did it look like this?"

I struggled to keep my face blank. The object in the photograph was the spitting image of the Mayan ceremonial shield. It had been photographed and documented by Interpol before being brought here for safekeeping.

"Ms. Racine." His voice was queerly soft as he addressed me.

I nodded. "Why did they steal that, and not the other things?" I asked.

Superintendent Moz glanced over at the display cases housing the Greek ceramics, the Roman statue, the Greek scroll and the Assyrian frieze. He ignored my question.

"I see from my assistant's notes, you work at the Royal Ontario Museum in Toronto. You are an illustrator? A professional scientific illustrator? So, you have knowledge of many types of ancient artifacts."

This wasn't exactly a question, so I merely dipped my eyes.

"You have seen the Mayan mosaic before."

If I shook my head, he would know that I was lying. Why was he asking me these questions when he already knew the answers?

"You are the person who found it."

"Yes."

I stayed silent. He knew that too. How did he know I was the one who had discovered it?

Was he going to accuse me of enabling the theft? I didn't even know it was here. My heart started to tick. Anymore accusations and it would go into overdrive.

"Did you recognize any of the thieves who broke into this office?"

They were all wearing masks. I had already told Agent Toussaint my story. They were all strangers to me… except… I almost mentioned that flash of familiarity concerning the man in the black mask. But I had no idea who he was, so mentioning my strange feeling was pointless. "No," I finally said.

"I see."

"Well, *I* don't," I snapped. "I had nothing to do with the theft… if that's what you're implying."

"I am implying nothing, mademoiselle. I simply wish to get the facts straight… Stretch your legs. Get out of that chair and come over to the display case for a moment."

We skirted the broken glass, and a female agent who was photographing the scene of the crime. Superintendent Moz dismissed the two men who were dusting for fingerprints and collecting any possible forensic evidence. I doubted there would be any, as the thieves were covered from head to toe in clothing—unless one happened to lose an eyelash and that guy with the tweezers happened to find it. He was picking up bits but I couldn't imagine what they might be.

The only hair and blood were from me and the security guard, and *he* had been taken away immediately for medical attention. I could still hear the sirens in the distance.

It was I who had been left the burden of facing the authorities and answering all of their questions. "Please," I begged. "Let me speak to my fiancé Norman Depardieu. He'll be worried sick. I should be at the chapel by now." I was on the verge of tears.

Toussaint came up from behind us. I could tell from the look on his face he wished he could say I was lying when I told him the billionaire was a dear friend. But I wasn't lying.

"Messieurs Trevanian and Depardieu are on their way by helo."

Superintendent Moz sent him away with a nod and returned his attention to me. What a peculiar person he was. He was a most unlikely character to exude power, and yet he did. His gaze returned to the display case and now I noticed what had stolen his attention. It was the strange Greek scroll. Was that Poseidon escorted by Nereids riding their dolphins?

"How much do you think these objects are worth?" His hands gestured at all of the artifacts behind the glass, not just the scroll.

"I am not an appraiser," I warned.

"But you have seen—handled—objects like this before. Surely, as a museum illustrator such objects have come into your hands. Tell me, please. How much were they priced?"

"It depended. From the thousands to the millions. It depended on their condition. And I was not allowed to physically touch them if they were worth that much." No amount of insurance could replace a priceless piece of history.

"And would you say, these items fit the same

category?"

"Maybe."

"And you question why they were left behind."

I nodded. "If they meant to sell the Mayan shield, why not steal all of the goods and make an even bigger profit?"

He agreed, deep in thought.

"Monsieur Moz," I said.

"Superintendent… Moz."

"Superintendent. There was another security guard somewhere in the castle. His name was M. Armand. Have your men found him? M. Lemieux was not alone on duty."

Five of the ten agents with Moz's team had been dispatched to search the Château for further evidence and other witnesses. They had touched base five minutes ago by text, just before Moz came to question me. "I am afraid my people have been unable to locate him, Mlle. Racine."

"So, how did you know to come here?" I asked. "How did you know the shield was stolen and we were trapped in this room?"

He watched my face and then answered. "I received a tip."

"A tip? From whom?"

"It was anonymous. The voice was electronically garbled so we could do no recognition tests on it. But I suspect it was a man. Do you know of any man who might wish to harm you Mlle. Racine?"

"I don't know of anyone who would even know that I was here," I replied irritably. "I came on a whim."

"Then they came specifically for the Mayan shield… Mlle. Racine, what can you tell me about the shield."

"It's Lucy," I said. For some odd, irrational reason, I was beginning to feel more comfortable with the superintendent. "I prefer Lucy."

"Lucy," he said softly.

The peculiar way he spoke my name caused shivers along my arms.

"Tell me about the shield."

CHAPTER 5

The whop-whop-whop of helicopter rotors told me that my ride was here. And unless the superintendent had ordered a helicopter, it had to be Johnny Sayid, our pilot landing in the parking lot amidst the commotion of the AID agents left outside. The account of my adventure with the Mayan ceremonial shield would have to wait. Although I suspected Superintendent Moz knew more than he was saying.

Sayid remained with the chopper while Luke and Norman were vetted before they were allowed into the château.

Norman was the first through the door when their escort finally gave the green light. I could hear the pattering of expensive Italian shoes following on the stone floor. Norman wasn't waiting for Luke. As soon as he saw me, he backhanded an approaching officer and I ran to him.

Superintendent Moz gestured to the officers to permit our reunion.

I plunged into the powerful arms of my fiancé and he tugged my hair back to glare into my eyes. "What happened."

I yanked my head away and he released me as I buried my face in his chest before I answered. "I thought I'd go for a quiet drive in the countryside."

"Why?"

I peeked up at him. His dark eyes were fiery; his French accent thick. He was not Parisien but Montréalais. Born and bred in Canada, not France. His mother tongue was the same, but different. "I couldn't wait five hours with people fussing over me."

He shook his head. "*Chérie*. You will be the death of me."

My chin jerked up. "Is that anything to say to your bride on our wedding day?"

"*Merde.* When that phone call came, I thought I no longer *had* a bride."

Norman peered past my head to see that Luke had made his way past us and was talking to the superintendent.

"What's this about the Mayan shield," Norman asked.

"Toussaint told you about it?"

"Of course. When he asked for Luke, he wanted to know what Luke knew about the mosaic."

"What did he tell him?"

"The truth."

Ah. I paused. "So—nothing."

He laughed and kissed me on the forehead. He dug his hand into my hair and kissed me violently. He didn't care that the agents from the Antiquities International Division were watching. Although they did turn away when we broke apart and stared back. I thought nothing of it. I was used to voyeurs. Being in the Trevanian social circle meant you were never out of the limelight. The only thing that was unnerving about all the ogling was that Moz seemed to find me fascinating. God knows why. Other than the fact that I once dated the most notorious and wealthy archaeologist in the world—and was now about to marry his bodyguard—I am actually pretty ordinary.

"Why does the superintendent keep on staring at you?" Norman asked.

I shrugged. "I think he believes I was in on the heist."

Norman grinned. Despite the grave situation. "Were you?"

"If I was, do you think I would have left you out of it?"

"*C'est ma fille.*"

I hugged his hard body against me, and he released his grip on my hair and rubbed my back. "Ça va, petite? Those rogues, they didn't hurt you?"

"No. But they shot a security guard. He's been taken to the hospital. I hope he's alright. I couldn't perform any first aid until the crooks had left. I might have been too late. He looked pretty bad."

"Don't worry, Lucy. You did your best."

A few minutes later, Luke joined us.

I swung my attention to him. I was so grateful he was influential due to his billionaire status that he could get me out of a jam almost instantly. But what did that say for all us little folk, huh? *No doubt about it, money speaks.*

"Okay. We're free to go. Moz says he'll be in touch, but for now he's got all he needs. Hope you don't mind that I invited him to the wedding. Seemed like the most expedient thing to do... He wants to keep an eye on us?

Now he can." Luke smiled at the concern on my face. "It's fine, Lucy. There will be a hundred people at the reception. You won't even notice. Besides—" he lowered his voice. "—I want to know what he knows about the Mayan shield."

"Oh my god." It suddenly struck me. "Are my mom and Colleen aware I'm missing?" They must be having a fit. Especially Colleen. The truth was simple. Of course, they knew I was missing. I was a no-show at my own wedding. My sister would have come barging into my room by 8:00 am when I neglected to show up for breakfast. And when I failed to make my nine thirty hair appointment…. How long had she waited before raising the alarm?

She would have gone to Norman first. What did he tell her?

"I said you went out for a drive," he said, answering my question before I even asked. "Your family knows nothing official, and certainly not that you were MIA."

That was good. My hand went to my head, felt my straggly hair. And then it really struck home. I was supposed to get married today!

Would I even have time to do much about this rat's nest? I combed the tangled strands between my fingers; like that was going to do anything. "What time is it? I'm a mess. And we should have exchanged rings by now."

"Stop fussing, Lucy," Luke said in his holier-than-thou voice of authority. "I sort of made up a story to appease everyone when we knew you were okay, and had to take off to rescue you. I've pushed everything forward to this afternoon. You realize we almost called the police?"

"Thank goodness you didn't. The crooks took my

phone."

He snorted out a snicker. In the short acquaintanceship I have had with Luke Trevanian I must have lost ten cellphones.

"Never mind that now," he said. It's time to go."

By the time we returned to the Hôtel Plaza Athénée it was twenty minutes past noon. Luke had asked Shaun, my brother-in-law, to delay the ceremony until four o'clock. All of the guests had been sent emails, texts and phone calls to inform them of the time change. That gave me two and a half hours to get ready. And an hour to get to the venue early.

Lucky for us, Luke had booked the venue for the entire day and evening. The ceremony was to take place in a modern space, the famous tourist apartment in the sky, also known as the *Tour Eiffel*. The tower apartment had been converted into a chapel by the request of our one and only Luke Trevanian, who enabled the transformation with a generous e-transfer.

It took some convincing, but I finally made Luke realize that our wedding was not *his* wedding so no point in inviting three hundred people I did not know. Besides the capacity for the restaurant was one hundred and twenty. The maximum number of guests at the ceremony would be thirty.

I couldn't wait to see the chapel garnished in peach satin bows and white baby's breath, and pale blue roses. Luke had hired a professional to do the entire venue. The space was surrounded by glass that overlooked the lattice architecture of the exterior and was situated near the top of the tower. Even the ceiling overhead had a skylight and the latticework outside resembled metal lace.

The reception would occur in the Jules Verne restaurant, an elegant Michelin-starred dining spectacular with a breathtaking view of the river and the city. Along with the thirty from the ceremony, another ninety guests were invited to the reception.

Milo, the hotel's beauty shop stylist, charmed by Luke's request, returned willingly to my room to do my hair after I had a quick shower. Mom and Colleen were ecstatic to see that I was not the Paris version of *The Runaway Bride*, and hovered about just to prevent my pulling a fast one on them.

Mom went to the enormous closet to remove my wedding gown and hung it on the brass stand that the hotel had provided for that very thing.

I gasped every time I saw it. Pure satiny white, the dress had a plunging V-neckline pairing romantic soft tulle with lace appliques on either side. The bold bare back, framed with delicate lace, had wide-set sheer straps and small, sweet, fabric-covered buttons from waist to bottom in a vertical row. The sexy fit-and-flare silhouette, paired with stylish fluted lace, fanned out mermaid-style at the knee to a dreamy, flowing skirt.

Lace appliques were strategically placed throughout the slim gown to cover the bits that required modesty and to reveal the bits that did not. Intricate details above the skirt and embroidered motifs along the train gave it an understated elegance. Luxurious streamers hung on a separate satin hangar to attach at each shoulder in ethereal, translucent chiffon.

A knock came at the door.

I glanced over. "Mom, can you see who that is? If it's

Norman, tell him to get lost. He's not allowed to see the bride in her wedding dress."

I actually wasn't wearing the dress yet. I was in a white satin robe.

"Don't worry," my mother said. "I'll deal with him."

Colleen was painting my nails. I'd had them professionally done yesterday but after this morning's escapade they needed a touch up, and she was still admonishing me for making her worry.

"When are you ever going to grow up, Lucy, running around in the countryside on your wedding morning! Good grief. You must take after Dad. Mom and I would never do anything as foolhardy as that."

Foolhardy? Who used words like that?

But then I remembered she was a school teacher. She started every class by having the students drum up one word they never used or knew the meaning of. Then she required that they look the word up and use it in a sentence.

"Sit still, Lucy," Colleen ordered. "Or it won't just be your nails that get painted."

In the enormous vanity mirror I could see my mom Eleanor open the door to a man in a black suit and beige overcoat... Superintendent Moz?

She took one look at him and cupped her mouth.

What? Why?

I swiveled, but Colleen slapped my hand and Milo seized me gently by the jaw and turned me back to face the mirror. "Mademoiselle," he said. "Please. It will only be a few more minutes. If you do not remain still, all is wasted."

"I'm sorry, Milo." I glanced quickly at my reflection. Had I ruined my hairdo? No. it was lovely. Swept up to one side with tendrils spiraling from my forehead over my ears. A pearl comb was snuggled into the smooth chignon that matched the multi-roped pearl-bead necklace and dangling earrings that Luke had delivered as a wedding gift.

Milo twirled a tendril in his finger and sprayed it lightly with a medium-hold mist. Then did the other side.

Behind me, I saw that Mom had recovered from the sight of the superintendent. She must have worried that he had come to arrest me. But then I realized that couldn't be it. She knew nothing about my encounter with the police

"What are you doing here?" my mother gasped. The silver strands from her earrings rippled, as her hands clapped her breast over the dove-gray beaded neck of her silk gown.

"Eleanor," Moz said. "How are you?"

Eleanor? How are you? What the—how did he know my mother?

I pushed Milo's hands away from fussing with the tendrils. By this time, Colleen had finished with my nails. She had risen and turned to stare at the stranger in the doorway. But now I realized that to my mom and sister, this man was no stranger.

CHAPTER 6

Colleen was in first grade when our father John Racine died. I was a baby. Now I learned that his full name was John Mozley Racine. Moz was a nickname that his colleagues called him. And guess what?

He wasn't dead.

John Racine pushed his way through the door.

Colleen hurried over to him. How could she even recognize him? The last time she saw him was thirty years ago.

I got up from the seat at the vanity and moved towards them. Then I saw it, John Racine aka Moz, had the same blue eyes as my sister. I had the mud puddle eyes of my mom. Not to say that Eleanor Racine wasn't attractive. Ted, her second husband, certainly thought she was. But river-blue eyes vs mud-puddle brown? Okay, some people call it hazel. But which is more eye-catching? No pun intended.

Speaking of which. Holy crap. Did this mean my mom wasn't legally married to Ted? They had tied the knot five years back.

"They told me you were dead," Eleanor accused.

"I *was* dead," Moz answered.

He turned to my sister. Admittedly, she was a beauty. Despite having had a baby her figure was perfect. She wore a gorgeous silver blue dress that accentuated her attributes and perfectly suited the plunging neckline and lowcut back. "You must be Colleen. I would recognize you anywhere."

How? She was six years old when he vanished from our lives.

I felt oddly detached as I stood halfway across the floor. I had no real feelings for this stranger I had met just an hour ago. Only a strange familiarity. I observed the interaction between the man called Moz and my sister. And this, *this* accounted for it.

He was our dad.

Eleanor grabbed her former husband by the arm to separate him from Colleen. "You have three decades to account for. I suggest you do it or get out of here."

Moz's eyes looked across the room to me.

"Lucy." His deep voice grew soft, as did his eyes. "When you said you were getting married… when Toussaint told me your name. And then when I saw you, I knew."

Knew what?

"Your appearance. It's exactly the way your mother looked when I first met her."

Despite her frustrated anger, Eleanor blushed.

For some reason I had lost my voice. This wasn't happening. How could this be happening? First the horrific incident at the Château de la Madeleine, and then this? My errant father, my *dead* errant father suddenly appears out of nowhere to rescue me?

"Where have you been all these years, John?"

Eleanor demanded. Her eyes were filled with tears of rage—or joy? It was hard to tell.

"I was on a mission—"

"A mission! A mission for whom? You worked at a museum!"

He did?

Like father, like daughter. I was hoping for an explanation. What did he do at the museum? Which museum? And why had he vanished and left his family thinking he was dead?

"We're waiting," Eleanor said. She tapped her fingers impatiently on the sheer sleeves of her crossed arms.

Moz glanced from her to Colleen and then to me.

This was going to take some time. How do you explain why you disappeared for thirty years. And then I had a heartrending thought. Colleen's husband had done the exact same thing to *his* wife. Not the disappearing act, but the lies. Well, not lies exactly. More like omission.

Shaun Templeton was a curator of classical collections at the Royal Ontario Museum where I was head illustrator. But he secretly worked for the antiquities rescue organization called ISORE, the International Save Our Ruins Effort, headed by the director of the museum Arianna Chase, Luke's ex. All of this was hush-hush. We could get in deep trouble if the authorities learned that we had taken it into our own hands to rescue endangered artifacts from terrorists and art thieves.

Yes, I said 'we'. Because I had also been recruited in the last two years. Neither Shaun nor I had told Colleen or my mom. And although Shaun had recently broken down to his wife and confessed to the dangerous side-job, Mom remained ignorant. I was not about to reveal the truth to her on my wedding day.

"You have nothing to say?" She glared at him.

"Mom," I begged. "I think he's going to need more than a few minutes to enlighten us."

"I—" Moz glanced over at me. He fussed with his tie and glanced away. "I shouldn't have come. But when I saw Lucy—"

"No, you should not have come," Eleanor cut in. "Lucy is getting married in an hour. Get out. We have to get ready."

Silence followed.

"Ellie…"

"Don't call me that. You have no right to call me that."

The door suddenly pushed wide and Shaun, in a navy-blue suit and tie and monochromatic blue shirt, stood on the threshold with my niece Maddy.

My brother-in-law sensed the tension between the four of us. He shifted Maddy in his arms and extended his free hand. If he had any idea who Moz was, he hid it well. "Shaun Templeton, Colleen's husband," he said.

He introduced himself out of politeness and in an effort to abate the awkwardness.

"Just call me Moz," my alleged father said. "Superintendent Moz."

Shaun raised a brow. Apparently, someone had mentioned the name to him. He had heard of my antics at the castle. Now he was wondering why the man from AID was back to interrogate me.

"Whatever this is about, it has to wait," he insisted.

Shaun could be authoritative when he wished. "This young lady is about to get married as you can see. And unless you have evidence that she has committed a crime, I think you should postpone your inquiries until a more convenient date."

Moz sent Shaun an appraising glance. This was his son-in-law—if Moz was indeed who he purported to be. And the little girl in his arms, all decked out in sky-blue lace and satin, with precious wheat-colored ringlets twined with tiny blue cornflowers was his granddaughter. "Of course," he acknowledged.

He gave Colleen a remorseful yet approving smile and nodded at me. "I'll let you get dressed."

"You'll be at the wedding?" I asked as he turned away.

He swiveled back with a hopeful smile.

I watched the struggle in my mother's body as she wrestled with her voice. "Lucy. He was *not* invited."

I switched from studying my father's reactions to my mother. "Luke invited him."

Her attractive and expertly made-up face creased with impatience. "This is not Luke's wedding."

"Well then, *I'm* inviting him."

My mother fell silent. Clearly, she was unhappy, but I needed to hear this man's story... Didn't *she*?

Moz smiled. "I'll be there, Lucy."

CHAPTER 7

A familiar shape against the Parisian skyline the Eiffel Tower is iconic. Completed in 1889 and opened to the public at the World's Fair it was the tallest building in the world until the construction of the Empire State building in New York City. It was designed by structural engineer Gustave Eiffel to commemorate the French Revolution.

How and why it became a global symbol of love and enduring romance, is largely unclear. It just is. Perhaps it was because, when first conceived, three hundred of the city's most celebrated artists and intellectuals declared the radical design an insult to Parisian culture. The protest was published in a prominent newspaper on Valentine's Day:

> "We, writers, painters, sculptors, architects, passionate lovers of the beauty, until now intact, of Paris, hereby protest with all our might, with all our indignation, in the name of French taste gone unrecognized, in the name of French art and history under threat, against the construction, in the very heart of our capital, of the useless and

monstrous Eiffel Tower..."

The mob was so enraged that they declared the Tower a 'gigantic, black factory chimney' so despised that even industrial America did not want it.

And yet the Tower remained even though it was meant to be dissembled a few years later by the French government who intended to use it for scrap metal. Against this threat, Gustave Eiffel built an antenna at the top of the tower for experiments with wireless telegraphy, which led to invaluable advantages for the French military.

In fact, during World War 1, the wireless station intercepted enemy messages from Berlin enabling the French to organize a counterattack in the Battle of the Marne. It also intercepted a coded message that helped the French capture the dancer/seductress Mata Hari for her alleged role as German spy.

Well, if that wasn't romantic, I don't know what is!

There was a private room for me to dress. Luke had thought of everything. Colleen deemed it best for me to change into my wedding gown at the Tower chapel because knowing me, I'd get the delicate lace train run over by a truck. Or caught in the elevator as I was going up to the venue.

So here I was finally dressed and appearing totally unrecognizable in my own eyes. But as they say, 'All brides are beautiful.' It doesn't matter what you look like in your everyday persona. The moment a woman dons a wedding gown, a magical transformation takes place—and she becomes a queen. Or at least a princess.

That's exactly what happened to me. The image in

the mirror looked like something out of a fairytale.

There came a knock at the door. My sister went to answer it.

I heard Luke's voice.

Was something wrong?

No, no, I heard him say. But since Norman wasn't allowed to see me in my wedding dress, and he normally played bodyguard—it was his profession after all—the groom had sent him to check on me.

No more than I deserved after that caper I'd pulled early this morning.

"Let him in," I instructed.

Luke stepped inside the dressing room, dapper in a deep blue tuxedo and white shirt with a peach-colored boutonnière.

"You look gorgeous," I said.

"You should see the groom."

I literally could not wait.

"Just wanted to wish you luck and love, Lucy. I can't tell you how much you mean to me."

I gripped his arms and gave him an air hug. Didn't want to mess up anything on my person or his.

"Have you heard from Aras?" I whispered. "Is he coming?"

Luke shook his head. "Sorry." I could see the frustration in Luke's eyes. His younger brother or should I clarify—Syrian half-brother—had been a thorn in his side for decades. But I knew Aras. Despite his impulsive nature he had a good heart. If he wasn't here, he had a good reason.

"And the rest of the team?" I asked hopefully.

"All waiting to see the beautiful bride."

I punched him playfully in the arm.

"You look like a dream, Lucy."

I felt like I was *in* a dream. A wonderful dream that included the two men I loved most in the world, and I was marrying one of them. And my team: Alessandra Piero, Johnny Sayid and Arianna Chase, our boss and Luke's ex-wife, were here to celebrate with our families. If only Aras would show up, things would be perfect.

My mother stepped up beside us. "Plenty of time for compliments later, Luke. We have a wedding to attend."

And then there was Mom—Eleanor. And let's not forget—Moz... my dad.

Oh my god. This was going to be one special day!

I had long ago decided that, if ever I was lucky enough to get married, my mom and sister would walk me down the aisle. They were the two people who were consistent in my life. They were my rocks. It was only fitting. And while both Shaun and Luke had offered, it didn't seem right. Shaun was my brother-in-law, and Luke was my ex and Norman's best friend. We had ties that were unbreakable. But it was nothing like the bond between a mother and a daughter, or the intimate relationship between sisters. And without a father in my life... Well, why did it have to be a man anyway?

I peeked out at the scene in the chapel. Luke, as Norman's best man, waited off to one side of the altar. On the other side was Alessandra in stunning pearl green, looking like a supermodel or maybe an elegantly dressed superhero, my maid of honor. I had had to twist her arm to make her agree to be part of the wedding party. Alessa did not do girly things. She was more comfortable in khaki with a Sig Sauer sidearm in her shoulder holster than she was in silver and lace. The thing that convinced her was when I refused to get married if she turned me down.

Seated in the family row were Norman's mother, Colleen's husband Shaun, our helicopter pilot Johnny Sayid and boss Arianna. Yes, the latter two I considered family even though we were unrelated by blood. I glanced quickly around the room. If only Aras were here.

The music started up.

In front of me Norman's French-Canadian niece Evie and his Francophone half-Asian daughter Gigi, dressed in identical sky-blue satin, tossed peach-colored rose petals onto either side of their paths.

We followed with my arms looped in my mother's and my sister's.

I should have noticed that there was a cold draft coming from somewhere. But I did not. All I could see was the way my husband-to-be was gazing mesmerized at me as I walked down the aisle with Mom and Colleen.

The music I had chosen, in place of the traditional wedding march, was *All You Need is Love*, sung by Katy Perry in person accompanied by a violinist, a cellost, a saxophonist, a trumpeter and a trombonist. Yes, I know. Once I saw *Love Actually*, nothing else would do.

As we approached the altar, the little girls, Colleen and Mom joined the family in the front row. I linked hands with my groom.

The preacher smiled at us. Although neither of us was religious we had chosen a preacher out of respect for Norman's mother. The preacher, I did not know before this day, as he had been chosen locally. Curiously, I noticed his accent was not French.

As he began his homily, I heard the crash of glass come from the back of the congregation. We all spun to look and two armed, masked men, dressed identically with semiautomatic weapons, entered through the broken windows on either side of the room.

Superintendent Moz was seated in the third row, and I expected him to react, but he had no backup and was powerless to act without endangering all of the guests.

"What do you want?" Moz demanded. He spoke in French.

"Jewelry," the man answered, also in French. "He extended a bag and demanded that Moz drop his watch into it, then thrust it out at the nearest bejeweled guests.

"Do as they say," Moz ordered as the other man threatened with his gun.

When the guests refused to obey, the man fired his gun into the windows opposite and glass came spattering down. Norman and Luke had already started down the aisle when the first round went off. None of our team had their guns with them. Why would they? It was a wedding. Why would anyone do this on my wedding day!

In the chaos and shouting I felt something plunge from the skylight. I thought the sky had fallen, but instead I found myself lifted into a black-costumed man's arms and hauled up and away through the skylight in a harness with a hand clapped over my face, and the chiffon streamers and train of my gown flowing like angel's wings.

A smelly cloth—some kind of knockout drug—was forced into my nose and mouth.

CHAPTER 8

When I awoke the floor was trembling. My vision was foggy and my head pounded. I was neither bound nor gagged. That was a relief. And I was seated in a comfortable chair. When I say I was not bound I meant my hands and feet were free. My body, still clad in my now rumpled wedding gown, however, was secured by a seatbelt.

I was in a jet, speeding above the clouds, to God knows where.

How long I was out is a mystery. No one was seated near me. I unclasped the seatbelt and twisted around. The jet was small, capable of seating about thirty passengers. At the very back where the lavatory was, two men sat playing cards. They were unmasked, but I recognized neither of them.

This was bad. If they hadn't blindfolded me, it meant I could identify them. If I could identify them, they would have to kill me. After they had gotten what they wanted.

What *did* they want?

I rose and turned, catching their attention.

"Sit down," one of the men said.

"I need to use the bathroom," I lied.

The man scowled, muttered something that looked, rather than sounded, like 'women', since I couldn't hear his low tone against the roar of the jet engines.

He had a thick accent that could be Spanish. He shouted, "All right. Come here."

I rose and grabbed at my train to keep it from getting caught between the seats. I was also cold, and realized that I had lost the chiffon streamers somewhere during my transport to this plane. I tripped over something on the floor and saw that it was a blanket. Someone had placed a blanket over me while I was unconscious. How strange.

I picked up the blanket and wrapped it around my bare shoulders. I didn't really need to use the facilities. I really just wanted to get away from these men so that I could think. Also, if I was inside the lavatory, which was just behind where the men were playing cards, maybe I could overhear their conversation.

The more information I had, the better chance I had of getting myself out of this situation. There was a reason they had kidnapped me, and I understood now that the jewelry theft was meant to be a diversion. With everyone focused on the thieves, no one, including myself, noticed the kidnapper's stealthy descent above the altar to abduct me.

The question now was why?

I dragged the bulk of my wedding train and the blanket down the aisle, and squeezed past the men. They made no attempt to stop me from going into the lavatory. As I did so, I tried to get a good look at them. They were both tallish and fit. There was no possible way I could have a wrestling match with those two.

I closed the door and fastened the latch. The roar of the plane drowned out any conversation the men were making.

Was there anything in here I could use as a weapon?

Unfortunately, no. Just a bar of soap and toilet paper. And paper towels.

Break the mirror and use a sharp piece like a knife, perhaps? Smash it. But with what? My fist? That wouldn't work.

Maybe I could pry off the toilet seat and use that as a weapon? And then what? How many men were on this plane. I had seen two. And there had to be a pilot. Was there anyone else?

Still, three against one were impossible odds. I had no gun.

The best thing I could do was cooperate until I figured out why I was here. I silently unlatched the door and widened it only enough to hear. No one was talking. The only sound audible was the steady hum of the plane.

Okay. The sensible way to find out was to ask.

I flushed the toilet for effect and opened the door.

The two men looked up as I reappeared.

"Go and sit," one of them ordered. This man had two weeks growth of beard. The other one had a mustache. They were dressed in lightweight, dark pullovers and pants. And combat boots. They had automatic pistols in shoulder holsters.

"I need a drink of water," I said.

He glared at me.

"Whatever horrible concoction you knocked me out with has made me dehydrated."

Bearded guy scowled and something about his eyes

gave me the creeps. I hugged the blanket tighter around me and scowled back. "Water," I said.

He rose and went to the galley, opened the refrigerator and pulled out a bottle of Evian and thrust it at me.

"Now go sit. At the front," he ordered.

"First, I want to know why I'm here."

"I don't *know* why you are here," he answered in broken English.

"Well, then, who does? I want to talk to him."

"Go. Go sit. Or I will slap you around, drag you over my shoulder like a sack, and put you there."

Mustachioed Man must have overheard. He rose and grabbed Bearded Guy by the bicep.

"Not allowed to damage her."

"They won't know. I'll do it where they can't see."

"He could come out of the cockpit any minute. You want to risk that? He will shoot you."

"Not if I shoot him first."

"A plane full of holes.... Not a good idea."

I was glad Mustache Man had made that observation. Although he had it all wrong. Air Marshals carried guns with them all the time. And if they had to use their weapon it was no big deal if a few holes were left in the bulkheads. Maybe not a great idea to shoot the plane full of holes, but it wasn't like anyone could get sucked out of a tiny bullet hole when the cabin depressurized. The system would compensate and repressurize. And there was no chance of an explosion unless the engines or fuel tanks were hit. Good thing, he didn't know that.

I only knew it because Luke once told me that planes were full of little holes. He owned a small fleet of jets.

They were designed that way. You just couldn't see them. A few more would make no difference.

"Can you tell me how long we've been in the air?"

"Twelve hours," Mustache Man said.

That long? I was unconscious for that long? No wonder I felt like something the cat dragged in. I tried to think up all the possible places they could be taking me. We were still in the air. How much longer? Had they stopped to refuel while I was unconscious? What could our destination be?

Nowhere in Europe or Asia. The flight wouldn't take that long. The U.S.? Canada? Somehow, I didn't think so. We'd be there by now.

"And where are we going?"

"Enough questions," he said. "Go. *Sit.* Now!"

I decided I had tried his patience enough. Even if a few bullet holes in the fuselage didn't send us into a nosedive, I wasn't about to test it.

I pulled up the train of my now bedraggled wedding gown, cursing my abductors for destroying the most beautiful dress I had ever owned in my life, hugged the blanket around me, and waddled back to my seat with my water.

For the next few hours, I plotted how I was going to get revenge after I escaped. It was apparent they had no intention of killing me. Not yet anyways. So, was it a ransom they wanted? Or something else? Did they know Luke wasn't the groom? Because that would make more sense if they believed he was. A billionaire could pay a multimillion-dollar ransom. A bodyguard would have a hard time of meeting that demand. But they must have noted that the groom was the bodyguard, not the billionaire. They had no way of knowing that Luke would be willing to pay a ransom for his best friend's bride.

Money must not be what they wanted. What was it then? Why me?

I finished the last of the water and tossed the bottle aside. Hell, *they* could clean it up. I mopped my lips with the blanket and stared out the window. Nothing but clouds and ocean below. That meant we must be crossing the Atlantic.

I have been in some sticky situations since hooking up with Norman and Luke. And while I have been more afraid at other times than I was right now, I had no regrets. I knew Norman and Luke would never stop until they found me. By now they would have an APB or whatever they called it in Europe searching for me. But how could they find me when I had no way of sending them a clue? I have never been kidnapped from my own wedding, rendered unconscious and dumped in an airplane flying off to nowhere.

I mulled it over and over in my mind.

What was the motive?

So far, I still had not met the scary guy who 'could come out of the cockpit any minute,' and shoot his subordinates. He was keeping a low profile. If I could just catch a glimpse of him, I might understand why I had been kidnapped.

I kept my eyes peeled on the cockpit door. No one exited. The men who had been left to guard me knew there was nothing I could do in a plane. Screaming would get me nowhere—except maybe shot. I was not willing to risk that. I had no cellphone, so could not let Norman or Luke know where I was.

Poor Norman. He must be going crazy wondering

where I was. I don't think either of them even realized I had been abducted through the skylight. They were too busy being distracted by the staged jewel theft. But the preacher would have seen, although he'd been powerless to stop the act. The abductor had a gun. And he was a pro.

If I could figure out where we were headed, I'd have a better idea of why I was here. Despite my earlier fear, the boring flight with nothing to read or watch to occupy my mind had turned the anxiety into sheer weariness. If they weren't going to kill me, what were their intentions?

Must find out. I rose audaciously and with no regard for the men who were guarding me. I let the blanket fall from my shoulders, and dragged myself and my wedding gown to the pilot's cockpit door. I tugged at the lever but the door was locked. Dammit, my manicure was ruined. I rapped loudly with my knuckles.

An accented voice snarled. "What is it?"

I hesitated for a flat second. Was that voice familiar? I rummaged through my memory, through all of the scrapes I'd gotten into, since joining ISORE. Who among my enemies, or Norman's or Luke's enemies would benefit from my kidnapping. Most of them were dead.

My mind conjured up no one. "I want to know where we are going," I demanded.

I heard a smattering of Arabic and then Spanish. "You'll find out in due time. Go and sit down."

I banged on the door with the palms of my hands. *Come out and face me, you coward!*

Only silence came from inside the cockpit. I heard muffled voices. Then sounds from behind me. The morons they had left to guard me had finally noticed my antics.

They came up the aisle and Bearded Guy shoved his pistol in my face.

"Sit."

I was tempted to resist. Was it really true that their orders were to leave me physically unharmed?

But this guy looked like he meant business and that any orders from the higher ups were irrelevant.

I pushed past him and returned to my seat by the window, fuming. Nothing to do but wait. I refastened my seatbelt.

An hour later, I sensed the plane was descending.

Out the window I could see land approach. Thick, lush, jungle.

CHAPTER 9

"Okay, get up," Bearded Man said.

I turned from watching the plane land, and rose. He grabbed my bare arm and yanked me into the aisle. From behind me an accordion of white chiffon (probably torn from one of my streamers and gathered to make it opaque) dropped over my eyes and tightened like a bandana. Vision stolen, I tried to lift the blindfold off but my hands were caught behind me and the trailing end of the streamer was used to bind my wrists. There was nothing to do but walk. I took one step and heard the sound of tearing fabric. I turned to scream at the man for ripping the train of my wedding dress.

What was the point? They didn't care and by now, the dress was rags.

To complete the image, I felt one of them lower to their haunches and when I realized he meant to tear the train off, I kicked him.

"Shall we tie up her feet and carry her like a pig?"

"No." It was the voice of the man from the cockpit.

Oh, how I wished I could see his face.

"Cut off the train so she can walk."

The ripping started and I forced myself to stay still until it was done. No point in aggravating them further over a dress. It was in tatters anyways.

Besides I wanted to walk. I had to keep my muscles toned and flexible if I was to get away from these brutes when the chance came.

Were we at an airport? It must be a private one. Even in the most primitive of countries a woman bound and blindfolded would be noticed.

The first thing I sensed when I stepped out of the door was the softness of the air. I stood on the first step of a mobile passenger airstair.

One of the men was holding my shoulders from behind leading me down the steps. I hoped I had not too far to go because I was totally blind and was wearing the worst footgear possible for an adventure like this—my white, three-inch, pearl-beaded, open-toed pumps. As I hesitated at each step, certain that the next one would have me crashing to my doom, I felt a pair of hands cup my waist and lift me to the ground.

He was very gentle and this not only surprised me, but disturbed me. We walked for about five minutes, the man holding me by the upper arm to lead me. I should have shrunk at his touch, but for some inexplicable reason I did not.

It's true what they say that when your sight is taken away from you, the other senses kick in. I could feel the warm breeze on my shoulders and smell the dampness of the jungle. The terrain we crossed was hard—the airplane tarmac I presumed—and then it became softer, and I stumbled a few times because my heels sank into the earth and strange vegetation tickled my ankles and feet from my open-toed shoes. We had better be going a short distance because I was not going to make it in these heels.

There were also unusual sounds: parrots? Monkeys? I felt like I was in a Tarzan movie, except that this wasn't Africa. I was pretty certain we had crossed the Atlantic. We were somewhere on the east coast of southern Mexico or South America.

At someone's mention of Chichén Itzá—a world-famous archaeological site and one of the largest Mayan cities filled with pyramids, cenotes and strange ballcourts—I guessed we were on the Yucatán Peninsula.

My knowledge of the geography of this part of the world was weak. I have never been to Latin America, not even Mexico. While most people have been to some kind of Mexican tourist resort, I have not. The only reason I could understand a little Spanish was because of my tenure in Spain. Cádiz and environs to be exact. And Barcelona.

Was there a connection? These kidnappers spoke mostly in Spanish. Although occasionally I heard a phrase in Arabic. And that was another peculiar thing. Why was an Arab among my abductors?

I felt a chill ride my spine. We had made a few enemies in the Middle East while rescuing artifacts there. In fact, some local terrorists had declared eternal vengeance. Cham Nassar for one. Had my boss, Arianna, done something to rekindle the vendetta? Surely, there was no association between the two countries? Cham Nassar was the leader of an Islamic extremist group named for him—the Star of Baghdad. He was born in Iraq but when the Americans freed the nation from the grip of the terrorists, he set his sights on Syria. That was where we last encountered him.

"This way," my kidnapper warned. "Watch your head."

Watch? I couldn't see a damn thing.

"Maybe if you would take off the blindfold."

"Not yet."

A hand pressed down on my head and I was told to get into a vehicle. From what I could feel with my feet and knees, I figured they had put me in the back seat. It smelled of cigarette smoke, stale food, sweat and marijuana. It took several attempts at breathing normally to quell the urge to gag.

Someone got in beside me and dragged the seatbelt over my chest. So, they didn't plan to harm me physically and they wanted to keep me safe. That was interesting. There was also no inappropriate pawing of my body. That too was interesting. After all, having half my dress ripped away and the other half missing to start with (the gown was almost strapless as it was) I was, by any definition, half naked. In front was the driver and one other man. They spoke to each other in a flurry of Spanish.

The car trip was brief, the roads rough and bumpy, informing me that the suspension was bad or we were off the beaten track. The windows were up and the air conditioning was on. I could tell by the coolness of the air and the stiff breeze from the fans. Twenty minutes later the vehicle stopped.

A creaking sound, and car doors opened and the men got out.

"This way," the one who was in charge of me

instructed.

I had no choice but to follow. I felt his hand guide me down the street several paces, which I now realized was of concrete from the tapping of my soles on the hard surface.

The gentle hand was removed from my upper arm and I was left standing, hands behind my back. I turned to try and detect where he had gone.

A voice in Spanish (him maybe?) said, "Take off the blindfold, and bring her inside."

I'm assuming that was his request because that was exactly what happened next. The strip of gathered chiffon was tugged off my head and allowed to trail down my back from my bound hands. I blinked hard at the sudden assault of sunlight on my eyes.

It took me a moment to adjust to the sharp blue sky and newly defined white clouds. The thick humid air made everything on my body feel limp and clammy.

I was indeed standing on a sidewalk and in front of me was a house, an old, primitive, whitewashed plaster building, grimed with dirt and remnants of pink and turquoise paint on its stucco walls and decorative borders. There were few windows. And oddly, dwarf palm trees. None visible from where I was standing however. The windows I mean. But there had to be windows or it would be totally unlivable.

Only two men accompanied me now. The two creeps from the airplane. They had their orders to keep their paws off me, and whoever was their head honcho must be scary because they obeyed.

"*Adentro*," the bearded one uttered, and held wide the right side of the narrow, peeling, wooden double doors.

A musty smell greeted me as I cautiously stepped out of the sunlight into the dark interior. I was correct about there being almost no windows. Hardly any natural light found its way inside. And the windows that I could see were tiny and near the ceiling. We were inside some sort of living room with a shabby orange sofa and brown armchairs, some scarred wooden coffee table and end tables, and a colorful braided oval rug dyed in bright traditional colors. Bearded Guy untied my wrists and tucked the torn chiffon under a chair.

"Do not try to run away." He glanced at his mustached partner. "We will shoot you."

I highly doubted that. If they were allowed to hurt me, they would have done so. I had decided however that since I was an unwilling guest I would hang around and find out what this was all about. Even as I had these thoughts, I believed that Norman and Luke were doing everything in their power to locate me. I also realized I was in no immediate danger. Once I learned where I was, I could find some means of communication and let the team know.

"Where are we?" I demanded.

Bearded Guy snapped in broken English. "You are inside my mother's house. *Qué ocurre?* You don't like it?"

Could be worse. This could be *his* house. "I meant what town are we in?"

"Stop talking."

I had no intention of zipping my lips. "What town?" I persisted. I was pretty certain we were in the Yucatán, somewhere near Chichén Itzá. But where? There were probably a hundred small towns in the vicinity.

"You don't need to know."

"Then maybe you can answer me this. *Why* am I

here?"

He snarled. "Because until we get the word, we have nowhere else to put you."

An elderly woman came in from the kitchen and hollered in Spanish, "What is all the noise?"

She was in her late sixties or early seventies. Her dark hair, ribboned with gray was braided and wound into a messy coil on the crown of her head. She wore no makeup and about her stern, glassy eyes the brown skin crinkled.

"Nothing, *Mamá*. We have a houseguest. The *gringa* girl I told you about. She'll just be here for a couple of hours or so. Just until we can get her to her *papá*."

"And this is the way you treat her? Your boss's daughter? Shame on you Diego. Why is she in rags? And such a pretty dress it must have been too."

I understood, boss's daughter. *Jefe* was boss and daughter was *hija*.

Diego was obviously his name.

"She won't be here long, *Mamá*. *Ay*, she can clean up if you want her to."

Must be some kind of tall tale he was spinning for his mother so that she would allow me to stay here.

The woman clapped her thick hands onto her more than ample hips. "Your boss will be shocked to see his daughter like this. What happened?"

"She was in an accident."

Uh, hardly.

I wished my Spanish was better so that I could tell her the truth. But attempting to do so with him and his partner present could be dangerous. And there was no guarantee she wouldn't be on their side.

"Come, come," she said, taking charge. "You need

clothes." She appeared to accept her son's explanation for my condition and made no attempt to ask me any questions. Instead, she led me into a bedroom and pointed outside the doorway to a bathroom. "*El bāno.*"

Then she pulled out some drawers from a painted wooden dresser and rummaged through some peasant blouses and black fabric skirts. She removed a pair of pale blue jeans and a long white tank top. My brows shot up in surprise. Because, honestly, I thought she was going to put me in some weird traditional costume.

She must have got the joke. She gave me a gap-toothed grin and said, "*Si, si.* This—" she held up the clean garments "—belongs to my niece." I caught the word 'niece' and knew exactly what she was saying. She pointed to herself. "Adella. Mamá Adella." She pointed at me. "You are…? *Tú…?*"

"Lucy," I said, tapping my chest.

"Ah, Lucia."

"*Si, Gracias,*" I said, sincerely meaning it, and wondered how such a nice old lady could possibly have mothered my ill-mannered abductor. Well, I suppose, even crooks had moms. Was the niece a criminal as well? And was *Mamá* aware of the illicit activities of her family? And if she was fully in the know, was she complicit?

I lifted the jeans to check for sizing. Banana Republic for God's sake. Other than the length being two inches or so too long, the niece was practically the same size as me. Will wonders never cease.

Mamá Adella left me alone and I quickly changed out of my tattered wedding dress and went to the bathroom to scrub the filth off my face and hands. After drying off with a crunchy towel, smelling of last week's laundry, I removed my pearl comb from the side of my lopsided chignon and let the rest of my hair tumble down. The pearl comb went into my pocket, while I clawed my hair into a ponytail and fastened it with a coated elastic band that I found in the bathroom cabinet.

There was a pair of blue canvas, rope-soled espadrilles on the floor by the bed when I returned. A little loose, but better than the pearl-studded stilettoes. I tightened the straps, then folded up the hem of the jeans until my ankles showed, then I left the bedroom.

From what I could see, standing in the hallway, there was only one entrance to this house. That meant only one exit. No back door. Even if I wanted to escape it would be near impossible.

I returned to the living room.

My two jailers were seated in the living room drinking local beer from brown bottles. They were also eating taco chips with what looked like thick, chunky, homemade pepper and tomato salsa. I was starving, but there was no way I was going to eat anything they had touched.

The man with the beard, Diego, got to his feet, wiping his hands on his thighs. "We go now," he said in broken English.

"Go where?" I asked. I was starting to feel safe in Mamá Adella's presence.

He took my arm, not roughly in case his momma was looking from where she was rattling dishes in the kitchen.

He thrust me towards the open door and I had no choice but to follow.

We were in the car again, this time I could see it

was a beat-up Honda SUV. I was forced into the backseat with my guard while the mustached man drove. His name was still a mystery to me so I decided to call him El Peludo, which meant the Hairy One. Not only did he have a mustache but he had woolly hair almost the length of mine gathered into a ponytail which exposed his hirsute arms and neck.

The town was small, with a population of what I guessed to be somewhere between fifteen and twenty thousand. Most of the buildings were colonial style built from dismantled Mayan temples and former homesteads of plantation owners and governors. Now they housed government buildings, a school, a post office, and what might be a small hospital or clinic. The buildings were painted brilliant colors: hot pink, canary yellow and aquamarine. The main road was paved; the ancillary roads were limestone gravel.

I caught a Spanish sign that read: **'Leaving Espita.'** So that was where we were. A little town called Espita. I had never heard of it.

We came to a stop in front of a hacienda on the outskirts of the town. There were men on the property. With automatic rifles. Where were we? The hidey-hole of a drug lord? Who else would have their own personal militia?

The hacienda was large, long and ranch style. It had the typical covered stone terrace that ran the length of the house, and beyond that was an open mosaic patio with a ragged, drought-ravaged hedge. The nearby trees were cedar, guayacan, ceiba and chicozapote, which being indigenous were in better shape. What looked like vestiges of ruins poked out of the ground sporadically beyond the gardens. The sounds of exotic birds echoed from the neighboring jungle canopy. And I even thought I saw a deer peeking through the foliage. No, my mistake. The animal dodged into the open and I recognized it for a wild Mexican boar.

That was long enough to identify it. A terrific bang came from somewhere near the house and a black hole appeared in its tawny side. Blood. The boar collapsed.

Slinging an Ak-47 over his shoulder, a man dressed in army fatigues approached to inspect his kill.

I turned in horror but Diego who sat beside me grinned cruelly. "Supper," he said in English. And I tried not to gag.

What was this primitive hideout they'd brought me to?

The grounds had the appearance of once being immaculate and precisely designed, mostly due to the planted palms and urban flowers since gone wild. Only now was the estate giving way to nature. Weedy growth climbed most available surfaces. It seemed that recently, however, someone had been at great pains to keep it under control.

At one time the hacienda must have been magnificent. Currently, most of the exterior looked rundown and unlivable. The walls peeking between the invasive vegetation were of stained, once white stucco, and the roof of red ceramic tiles. Glimpses of faded painted murals were visible on several of the panels. Was that image of a bullfight? And another of a country market.

One part of the house exterior was clearly reworked, and this was the entryway. It had three high arches and was clean and new in appearance. The double entrance was clear and so was most of the terrace near the doors.

Was this an ongoing restoration? It was going to take a fortune to finish renovating it. Millions, I would say.

The car door opened, and a wild turkey scuttled away. I jerked back, half expecting a gunshot to scuttle the giant bird. The second course in this evening's repast perhaps? I sank back into the seat, collecting my nerve.

A man extended his hand from the opened car door and I refused to take it, drawing on all my powers of self-will and hauling myself out of the vehicle on my own.

When I stood up, I blinked the sun out of my eyes.

I was seeing things. The figure in front of me was tall, physically fit and familiar. When he spoke, I knew I wasn't dreaming.

It was Aras.

CHAPTER 10

Aras was Luke Trevanian's younger brother. Half Syrian and half American, he was born to a Syrian mother and American father—Luke's dad. He was also a freedom fighter. Last time I had anything to do with him, the team was in the Middle East rescuing statues from a terrorist. A pair of giant, stone winged bulls. And then, I almost lost the love of my life to that very same terrorist. Before tracking down the tomb of Cleopatra.

Aras was the leader of the resistance attempting to bring down the corrupt government and allow for change. He was not a terrorist. His intent was a simple coup. Topple the current government and replace it with a true democracy. But the plan had backfired. The conflict had allowed hardcore jihadists to take advantage of the situation and get a foothold in the country. Over a decade had passed. And still the terrorists had enclaves in Syria.

What was Aras doing here?

It was *his* hand that had appeared in front of my nose. And which I had rejected. I thought he was one of the kidnappers.

"Aras!" I exclaimed. "Have you come to rescue me?"

"Not exactly," he confessed. His voice was low, no longer disguised, and with a slight Arabic accent.

Suddenly I understood. This scene was all wrong. Aras wasn't holding a gun on my captors. And they weren't holding one on him. The only person who had a gun aimed in their direction was me.

"There's someone who wants to see you," he said.

"I am tired of being manhandled, pushed and shoved around with Modelo 4s in my face." Yeah, I knew my pistols. That was the Mexican equivalent of a Colt 1911.

Aras said something in Spanish to the bearded man, Diego, and he reluctantly re-holstered his weapon. "Just cooperate, Lucy, and everything will work out just fine."

"Nothing is fine," I snapped at him. "I'm in the middle of a Mexican jungle, when I should be on my honeymoon!"

He had the decency to wince.

"So—this is your excuse for bailing on my wedding?" I scolded.

"I didn't bail—"

With great horror, I suddenly realized that he hadn't. The whole nightmare replayed in my mind. The splintering glass as the masked thieves descended on my guests demanding their jewelry. Then the shadow dropping from the skylight, scooping me up as though I were a kitten and hauling me into a helicopter.

Aras was there at the ceremony. He was there when I was kidnapped. Because it was *he* who had done it!

I almost slapped him but his hand shot out and caught my wrist. "I won't let any harm come to you."

Are you kidding me?

"Multitudes of harm have already come to me!"

My face was flush with anger. The other two men clearly had no idea as to the topic of our conversation. By the way I was reacting though, and by the color of my face, they were quite aware of my rage. Malicious grins spread across their rough features. Like they were watching a comedy.

"You owe me a wedding gown. A wedding reception. *And* a honeymoon!" I exploded.

"I had no choice, Lucy."

"You always have a choice." *Unless you were tied up and blindfolded.*

He sighed. "Come inside. She's waiting for you."

She? Who the hell was *She?*

For a crazy second, I almost bolted. The jungle was ten meters away. I could do it. But where would I go? The fading sun was a reminder that I wouldn't survive even one night in that jungle alone.

I had no phone so even if I reached the safety of those jungle shadows, how would I call for help? That militia guarding the perimeter would hunt me down. Like that sad wild boar.

Through the double front doors, I followed. The foyer had been recently renovated. Immaculate white walls rose from gleaming red and tangerine tiles, replicating traditional floral designs like the yucca and dahlia and Mexican sunflower. You wouldn't think it was possible with such a color palette, but it was pleasing to the eye and quite tasteful.

Other than this front lobby and a large pillared entryway leading into what looked like an enormous recently remodeled study, the hacienda was old and in need of monumental repairs. Had the owner run out of money? Was this what my abduction was about? The crook needed funds to complete renovations? I snorted in disgust and secretly laughed. Diego and El Peludo glared at me.

The floors here were of plain red tile against ubiquitous, spanking white walls and the furniture white with accents of red, yellow and black in the pillows and throws. The grimy men who accompanied me looked ill-suited to step on these brand-new floors, no less enter the room.

My patience was tiring. Any moment now I would learn who it was that had orchestrated my abduction. I had a word or two to say to her. And they were not 'thank you.'

From where she sat behind a white lacquered desk studying some diagrams on a computer, she rose at the sounds of our arrival. She was dressed in white. A white, smartly styled, sleeveless blouse, cut low to expose her cleavage. And white, loose pants. Beneath the desk her red-sandaled feet were visible. It took me a couple of seconds to place her. She had gone to some trouble to alter her appearance. But there was one thing that gave her away. On her left side, just above the breast was a tattoo.

I make no apologies for staring. It was impossible to forget. Who else had a swastika tattooed over their heart?

"I hope your flight over was comfortable," she said, raising her head.

She was the last person I expected.

Her voice was not particularly distinctive and I

believe it might have gone unrecognized had I remained blindfolded. But I made a point of listening to anything particular to her speech. I never again wished to be blindsided as I had been with Aras. I should have recognized *his* voice.

Now that I knew who she was, I have to say she had done a lame job of changing her appearance. Natasha actually looked pretty much the same as when I last saw her several months back. Close to six feet in height, she was as tall or taller than her henchmen. Whatever workout she did (or maybe she just wrestled iguanas) her limbs were sinewy, just as I remembered, like an athlete. Her hair had grown down past her shoulders in a blunt cut, and she no longer sported bangs. Also, she was blonde. The look washed her out. I have to say, when she was a brunette, she was more striking. But she was showing her true colors now.

I just stared. To be fair, she stared back. *What?* My borrowed duds not to her liking? Surely, they matched her taste. The white top was something she would wear.

Her eyes left my apparel and landed on my face. Natasha Borg was one of the few adversaries that had escaped retribution in her dealings with the ISORE team. We rescued ancient relics, but we also put the bad guys away, or got ourselves in such precarious situations that it ended up 'them or us.' No one cared if a terrorist died in a situation of self-defense. Natasha was different. She was the former employee of a bad politician. A neo-Nazi. She had not only aided in a multimillion-dollar antiquities laundering scheme, but she had kidnapped a child (Norman's precious daughter), stolen artifacts and escaped without paying for her crimes.

"My apologies for disrupting your wedding, but it was the only way I could think of to get you here." Her smile was smug, more of a smirk.

"You could have asked."

She laughed.

I white-knuckled my fists to my sides. If I had a gun right now, I would have shot her. Instead, I sucked back the emotion and displayed a blank façade. "How did you know where I was getting married anyway?"

"That is an interesting question. Too bad for you that you were in the right place at the wrong time."

What did she mean? And then I saw it. Behind her. The unmistakable bright turquoise mosaic and white mother-of-pearl. The gold and pyrite glinting in the sun. On a large table behind her desk, in the alcove where the light came through tall latticed windows, sat the Mayan ceremonial shield.

Natasha Borg had stolen it. Or more correctly, she had sent her henchmen to France to steal it.

"What are you doing with that?" I demanded, deliberately moving forward so that I could view the shield more clearly.

Light suddenly dawned. I knew who her accomplices were. Aras was the man in the black mask at the robbery inside the Château de la Madeleine in Chevreuse. That was why he kept staring at me. He couldn't believe I was there, a threat to the success of his heist. My eyes turned to him in disgust and bitter disappointment. How could he be party to this crime? After all we had been through together, after all the convincing I had to do to get Luke to trust him following years of estrangement, and in one stupid act he had proved me wrong. I should never have trusted him. Once a thief, always a thief. His father, Luke's dad, had disowned Aras for that very reason. Aras had embezzled money from his own father. Granted he was very young at the time—a displaced and confused youth having recently been removed from his homeland—but that was no excuse.

So, what was she doing with it?

That was a dumb question to ask. I knew exactly what she was doing with the Mayan ceremonial shield. Or at least I was aware of how she had acquired it. I was witness to the theft.

But *why* did she want it? A gasp caught in my throat. Did she suspect that it had something to do with locating the lost island of Atlantis? Or did she want it simply for its assumed monetary value? On the black market it could bring in well over a million dollars, even with the piece broken off at the bottom.

Natasha stared hard at me, seeing through my thoughts even as I unraveled the truth. "Don't play coy with me, Lucy. I know you have the missing piece. Where is it?"

"I don't know what you're talking about," I said, feigning ignorance.

"The missing piece of the mosaic." She turned and jabbed a finger at the sharp edges where a section of the shield had broken off. In this empty space a critical piece of the puzzle fit. "I know you have it. My sister insists that you do."

Her sister? Now the pieces of my own puzzle were falling into place. Anastasie Kirsche was Natasha Borg's half-sister. They had the same father. Or so she claimed. But the age gap was suspect. They looked to be fifteen to twenty years different in age, with Natasha being the younger. Apparently, Natasha took her mother's name. That was what Anastasie had allowed me to believe, anyway. At this point I was hard pressed to believe anything anyone said. Everyone was hiding something. Including Aras. Why was he helping Natasha? She was bad news. And Anastasie—CIA gone bad—was currently in prison awaiting sentencing. For crimes that included murder.

"If you don't tell me, I will have the family of your friend Aras, here, executed."

I swung my head to sight Aras.

Was that why he had agreed to kidnap me?

The look on his face told me he believed her.

"She's lying, Aras," I said. "She doesn't have your family."

"She does. She had the extremist Cham Nassar's thugs abduct my mother and grandfather from their home. He's holding them somewhere in Idlib."

The current terrorist stronghold in northern Syria.

"I saw proof. Nassar let me speak to them. He had them tied up and his men were torturing them. It's my mother, Lucy…" His voice trailed away in despair.

This was getting way beyond what I had imagined. Terrorists and Nazis joining forces? Why? How did Natasha even have contacts in the Arab world? And then it hit me like a tsunami. What was the common denominator? They both dealt in black market antiquities. Sooner or later, they were bound to meet. Antiquities trafficking had arms reaching from the Americas to Europe, Asia and the Middle East.

Cham Nassar wanted in on the biggest discovery yet to be found. Atlantis and all the treasures associated with it. With that kind of wealth, he could dominate the

Middle East.

What an idiot. They were both idiots. Atlantis, if it existed at all, was supposedly drowned by a huge deluge. Even if it was found, what could possibly have survived?

"Lucy," Aras said. His eyes pleaded with me. "It's only an artifact."

I dragged my gaze from Aras and returned them to Natasha. "How do you know Nassar will keep his word and let Aras' mother and grandfather go free if I give you the mosaic?"

"I promised him one third of what I find."

I shook my head. "He'll take it all."

"No. I won't allow it."

"You don't know who you're dealing with."

She laughed. "And you do?"

Only too well.

"Where is the missing piece, Lucy?" Natasha demanded.

"You think I stowed it in my wedding dress?" I scoffed.

She scowled. "I know you don't have it *with* you. You've hidden it somewhere. I want to know the location. And then I want your boy toy to bring it to me."

He—Norman Depardieu—had more brains and more heart in that gorgeous body of his than she had in her entire gang of crooks, herself included.

"*Fiancé*," I snapped. He would have been my *husband* by now had she not interfered. "And then you'll let us all go? Including Aras' mother and grandfather?"

Her split-second hesitation told me to doubt her.

"Of course. What will I need them for if I have the

mosaic?"

I strolled over to her desk, cavalierly. Then walked around it to the table in the alcove. She was indignant at my audacity. *Who cares?* She wasn't going to harm me. I was the only one who knew where the missing piece of the shield was.

I gazed at the beautiful thing. This was a map. If only we knew how to read it.

Natasha turned to join me.

It was all there. The turquoise sea. The two-headed serpent… The golden— *The two-headed serpent!* All along I had thought the double-cranial snake was metaphorical. It was, and it wasn't. Sure, it represented renewal. But at face value it was exactly what I was seeing. The shape was almost identical to the serpentine geography of the Yucatán Peninsula and adjacent countries (Guatemala, Honduras, Nicaragua) that made up the slim stretch of land linking Mexico to South America.

The white conical teeth. I was certain that they represented mountain peaks. What mountain range existed in the Yucatán? The center of the shield was an irregularly shaped golden circle with concentric rings. An island for sure. I had no doubt it symbolized an island or a continent. Was it Atlantis? And the semi-crescents of mother-of-pearl were boats. From the top, bottom and sides of the shield, pyrite and gold shapes —bridges—radiated from the island. The missing piece had writing on it. So, the shield must too.

I moved closer. And Natasha shoved her forearm into my collarbone to prevent my approach. I was never allowed to study the shield very closely when I first found it. It had been taken away before our team could do a proper analysis.

Aha. There were glyphs. Several of them. Very small, almost invisible at a few paces back.

Natasha wanted the missing piece because it would tell her the general location of Atlantis.

Well, I already knew the general location. She had purchased her hacienda right on its doorstep. The real question was: where in the Caribbean Sea was its *exact* location? God knows numerous researchers, scholars, adventurers and quacks had gone in search of the mythical island since Plato first wrote about it. But no one had found it.

It made sense that it should be here. Somewhere in the mid-Atlantic.

I tried to remember what was inscribed on that broken piece. There had to be some kind of glyph, critical to identifying the precise spot where the island sank.

"How did you know about the Mayan connection?" I asked Natasha.

She gave me a blank stare. "Anastasie discovered the artifact that you now have in your possession. She recognized it to be Mayan."

Anastasie had given us a run for our money. We had tracked her to Cadíz in Spain, following red herrings that led from a pair of silver doves to Hitler's golden bookmark. It was not until near the end when she went chasing after the broken piece of mosaic that we realized her true motives. She had us all fooled. And some had died because of her. I refused to be fooled again.

"Did she always have this obsession for Atlantis?" I asked.

"Always."

I returned my gaze to the shield. Anastasie was a trained archaeologist before she joined the CIA. Her fixation with Atlantis had driven her mad. At least in my opinion. She had murdered her own partner, as well as colleagues, to find the clues that would lead her to the site of the mythical land. She almost got away with it. Until I stopped her. I discovered the shield and had her sent to prison. Was this my chance to find the lost land of Atlantis?

"The precursors of the Maya traded with the Atlanteans."

I looked up at the sound of Natasha's voice. So, Natasha was just as obsessed as her sister. And likely just as crazy.

"In fact, the Atlanteans traded with the Egyptians. They also traded with the indigenous peoples of Mesoamerica. They brought tobacco and cocaine from the Yucatán and exchanged them for coins and goods from the Arab world. The Atlanteans were seafarers. They were the means by which trade routes were possible between the Old World and the New."

My mouth had dropped open but she ignored my astonishment. "How do you know this?" I asked.

"We have proof."

"We?"

"My sister and I."

"What is the proof?"

"It is inside a trio of Egyptian mummies, and one Syrian frieze."

"What do you mean? What is inside three Egyptian mummies and a Syrian frieze?"

"You will have to ask my sister—" She smiled.

And if a smile could be said to be evil, this was it. "—*After* your buddies break her out of prison."

CHAPTER 11

Was she insane? Nothing on God's green earth would make Luke and Norman commit a felony.

"Let's just backtrack a moment," I said. Anything to get her off the idea of a prison breakout. "Atlantis is supposed to be 11,000 years old, about 9,000 years before Plato's time. How could there possibly be trade between the Yucatán, Atlantis, and Egypt and Syria. The first civilizations didn't exist until around 6,000 years ago."

"Yes, but there *were* people. And like people everywhere in every century and even millennia, *they* wanted tobacco and drugs." When I said nothing, she continued. "And there were seafaring peoples who were the intermediaries between these unlikely countries."

Did she mean the Phoenicians and the Carthaginians? I remembered someone had once brought a cache of coins to the museum (The Royal Ontario Museum where I worked in Toronto) that they had inherited from an old relative who claimed that the lot was excavated during a construction project in Panama. These coins had been identified by the museum's Classics specialists as Carthaginian. The owner was certain that the coins were proof that seafarers from Carthage (North Africa) had arrived in the New World long before Christopher Columbus. Did she mean that she believed the Phoenicians or Carthaginians had navigated the Atlantic and touched down on Central American soil via Atlantis? What was the evidence? Neither the Phoenicians nor the Carthaginians were around that far back. Although their precursors were.

I frowned. Then looked up, eyes widening as she nodded. Natasha's—or was it Anastasie's—theory was a whole new proposition.

"Either that or Plato made a mistake with the date. In fact, if you ask me, I'd say Plato missed by about 5,000 years." She paused to allow me to catch up with her thinking. "What is 9,000 turned upside down?"

"6,000."

"Likely a misprint."

Natasha was about as crazy as Anastasie. But then I already knew that.

"I want the missing piece," Natasha said. "Where is it?"

"Somewhere where you will never get your hands on it."

Natasha's face went three shades redder. She took a few deep breaths. Was she counting? She was undeniably making an effort to control her temper.

She dropped her attention to the computer and made a few clicks with her mouse. She spun the monitor to face me.

On the screen an ugly, familiar mug sneered at me. Thick, dark unkempt hair, bushy beard, sun-browned skin, dressed in olive drab. And black piercing eyes. Had he just been waiting around for her summons?

"I remember your face," the heavily bearded terrorist said to me. The image buffered slightly. His Arab accent was thick and it was hard to catch his words. Not the best connection.

I had once been unfortunate enough to suffer his hospitality. His men had kidnapped me, so no this was not my first experience as a hostage. He had assessed my physical traits as though I were a cut of lamb. And he was doing the same now.

Cham Nassar had terrorized me then, but I was not so terrified now. Experience had taught me one thing about men like him. They were all ego. And yes, getting a piece of Atlantis was more important to him than killing me. And he could only get his share if I was alive.

"I want to see Samar and Rafiq," I said calmly.

He signaled to someone and they dragged a struggling woman in front of the camera. It was Samar in traditional Syrian dress, her head covered by a plain scarf, wisps of tangled, graying hair escaping as a result of the altercation with her captor. The man holding her had a knife at her throat.

"Tell my friend where the missing mosaic is."

The kidnapper pressed the point of the knife against Samar's throat and a drop of blood appeared. "Stop it!" I shouted.

"You will do as you are told?" Nassar said. His voice was viscous and cold.

I nodded. I could see in the background, a man on his knees with his head covered with a black sack, as though he were about to be executed. Rafiq, Aras' grandfather. "Don't hurt them."

"Then do what the lady says."

The image vanished. He must have disconnected. I turned back to Natasha. "You won't be able to find it. I will have to return to Paris to get it myself."

Natasha sneered. "You must truly believe I am an imbecile."

Truly, I did not. I knew she was smart.

"You will phone that hunk of muscle you call your fiancé. And tell him to bring it."

"I don't have a phone."

She nodded at Aras. "Use his."

There was no hesitation on his part. Aras unlocked and tossed his cellphone to me. I scrolled through the contacts until I found Norman's number.

"Now call him."

I tapped.

What time was it in Paris? For that matter, what time was it here?

"Remember, no police. If your pals get the police involved, it's the end for all of you."

She was serious. Natasha Borg, as far as I knew, had not yet killed anyone. But I wasn't about to test that theory. I listened to the phone ring, and Norman picked up almost immediately.

"*Merde.* Lucy! Thank God. Are you alright? Where are you?"

His voice was sharp and clear, not like he had been sleeping so it must be late afternoon or early evening there. His French accent was thick. And I knew he had not slept since my abduction. "You'll never guess. I'm in a small town called Espita in Yucatán."

"What?"

"Mexico."

"I know where Yucatán is. How did you get there? Who kidnapped you?" By the strain in his voice, I knew he was bursting to take action. Every powerful muscle in his body was pumped. But I was thousands of miles away and he was in Paris. I know he wanted to reprimand me for my escapade to the Château yesterday morning. Had I not done that, probably none of this would have happened.

But he was wrong. It would have happened anyway. Aras was invited to our wedding. He knew where we were staying and where we would be at 11:00 am. It was only a matter of a call to the hotel to learn the new time of the ceremony.

My showing up at the castle in Chevreuse changed nothing. The plot was always to kidnap me.

"Lucy! Are you there?"

I snapped out of my musings, the humidity and heat from outdoors catching up with me.

"Natasha Borg."

Dead silence steamed for a moment before he realized I was answering his question.

"What?" His mind had to spin back several months to bring her into focus. Natasha had forbidden me to use video, so I couldn't see his face. No memory of my surroundings meant no cavalry after us. But I was certain, after Natasha's cold-blooded abduction of Norman's little daughter Gigi a few months back, his heart was ice when it came to Natasha Borg…

"Natasha Borg kidnapped you?" He cut into my thoughts. "Why? What does she want? We'll pay anything." By we, he meant Luke and himself. And hopefully my newly discovered father. "Moz has contacts. He can—"

"No, Norman. Leave him out of it. She specifically said no police." Before he could respond I hurriedly added, "She doesn't want money. She wants an artifact. Something that she learned was in my possession."

"*Quoi?*" He had switched to French, hoping that if we spoke in his mother tongue, Natasha would be unable to follow. He talked quickly demanding that I explain where I had acquired it and why I had kept him out of the loop. At my hesitation, he slowed down his breathing and took control of his emotions. His question, still in French, came out calmly. "*Qu'est-ce que c'est? Cet artefact?*"

My response began in French but Natasha slapped my arm with an open fist. "In English."

"I'll explain later. You'll know it when you see it." Was light beginning to dawn? There could only be one artifact that was so important. "It's in my carryall, in the safe, in my room at the hotel…" I recited the code. "Please, *please*, tell my family I'm alright."

"Don't worry, sweetheart. Luke has spun them a yarn. Just until we learned what we were dealing with. Shaun knows you've been kidnapped. And your… and Moz. No one saw what happened. You were plucked right out from under our noses while everyone's attention was drawn to the rear of the chapel where the theft was taking place. We told them we had gotten you out to safety."

"And they bought it?"

"For now. We told them we had to keep you hidden until the dust had settled. That it had to do with the incident in Chevreuse, the theft of the Mayan shield at the Château. That you being a witness had put you in danger. And until the thieves had been caught you had to remain incognito. It worked. Shaun will keep the ruse going for as long as he can. I'll let him know I heard from you… I'm leaving on the next flight out. As soon as the plane is ready."

Mom and Colleen would not sit tight while my whereabouts were unknown.

At this point Natasha broke in. Norman had been doing too much of the talking and I was talking too little. "End it! Tell your boyfriend you will text him where to deliver the mosaic when he lands."

"Did you hear that?"

"*Oui*." I knew he wanted to ask how it was that I still had the mosaic. It should have been surrendered to the authorities along with the Mayan shield.

He let it pass. All he said was, "*Je t'aime, ma coeur.*"

"*Moi aussi.*" I turned back to Natasha just as she snatched the phone away and disconnected the call. "He's on his way."

Natasha smiled. "Good. Now I want you to call your billionaire buddy, Luke Trevanian. I have a job for him to do."

The prison break? She was out of her mind.

"Luke will never consent to committing a felony," I warned before another word left her lips. "Not even to save his own life."

The expression that spread across her features gave me the willies. "How about to save yours?"

My eyes flickered to the door. Not that I was actually going to try to make a run for it. But the men who had brought me here flipped their guns on me.

"Your sister is a murderer," I yelled. "A serial murderer. There is not enough bail money on the planet —"

"Control yourself, Lucy. If you want this situation resolved and in such a way that we both get what we want…" Natasha paused for a breath. And I swung my arms down and squeezed my fists to my side. "That's better. That is why I need Trevanian's help. Anastasie's bail was through the roof. I'd have to sell my hacienda and everything I own to make her bail…"

Aras' phone was gripped in her fist. She went to his contacts and scrolled down under the Ts. She hit Luke Trevanian's listing and brought up his contact information.

"He won't do it," I said as she thrust the cellphone at me. "He will not break into a prison to help your sister escape."

"I am not asking him to break in. He has resources and connections. All I want is for him to get her out. How he does it is up to him. She has another hearing in two days. This is his chance."

"But it's impossible."

"Nothing is impossible if enough is at stake. How much is your life worth, Lucy Racine?"

Not that much, I thought.

I darted a glance at Aras. He looked like he wished he had shot himself instead of getting me entangled in this.

Natasha shook the phone at my face. "Call him."

"I won't," I said.

Natasha pulled a pretty, pearl-handled pistol out of her pocket with her other hand, and aimed it at Aras. "Call him."

I took the phone. He answered in three rings. Luke already knew about my conversation with Norman and was making arrangements to fly them both to the

Yucatán on one of his private jets.

"You can't come with him," I warned. "She has a different mission for you."

I explained the dilemma to him. The mention of Anastasie's name sent Luke into a fury. I reminded Luke of Samar and Rafiq, and what they meant to his half-brother. He went into a second rage and then was silent. I made no effort to appease him. At times Luke could be emotional, but he was always rational. I knew his quick mind was already working on a solution. What that solution would be was as yet an empty space in my own thoughts.

"Inform him that if he tries to cheat me—don't. I have eyes and ears everywhere. I will know exactly what he's up to. There's a lot at stake. And he will not like the consequences if he betrays me." Natasha glared.

There was no need to remind him. But I did so regardless. My voice came out as a whisper. "If you don't bring her here with you, she will kill me and Aras."

I was locked in an isolated room, a long-ways off from the remodeled part of the house. The room was shabby. There were no light fixtures—none I could find anyway—as I fumbled around in the dark, feeling the grubby texture of the walls, peeling paint and the plaster underneath, but no light switch. The window had been boarded up and I found myself going completely stir crazy. In the absence of light and with only muffled sounds audible, I convinced myself that this was what it felt like to suffer sensory deprivation.

Was that her intent? Was she trying to weaken me? What more could she possibly want that I had refused to do?

There was a chair to sit on and a musty bed, but nothing else.

About an hour later Aras came to let me out.

As long as Rafiq and Samar were captives of Cham Nassar, I realized Aras could be counted on to comply with Natasha's wishes. That was why he was allowed to remain free. He had gone to all of the trouble of kidnapping me. He wasn't about to help me escape because of a bout of conscience. In any other circumstances Aras would have leaped into danger, risking his own life to protect an innocent. But this was his family, and his family was his Achilles' heel.

I, on the other hand, was a wild card. Natasha mistrusted me. And until Norman brought the missing piece of the Mayan mosaic shield, and placed it in Natasha's claws, she was taking no chances.

Aras was quiet as he led me down some twists and turns along a corridor. Okay by me, since I was still trying to adapt to the sudden exposure to light. I had a hand up to shield the overhead brightness from my long-dilated pupils, and was blinking like mad to hasten the adjustment. When it finally stopped hurting to see, I was disappointed to learn that these corridors had no windows. Not a chance that I could bolt.

"I'm sorry, Lucy," he said.

I had no response. I understood why he had kidnapped me. I fully comprehended his reasons for aiding this slimy criminal. But surely there must have been some other way. And then I remembered who we were dealing with. I had experienced, first hand, the brutality of terrorism in the Middle East. The team had faced them in Syria, and I had singlehandedly followed them to Baghdad to save my man. They in turn had followed me to Cairo where I thought the final showdown over Cleopatra's tomb would end it. I was wrong. In extremist Islam, vendettas were never forgotten. Cham Nassar thought nothing of human life.

We arrived at the dining room. The room was partially finished. New floors had been installed but the walls were yet to be painted and the old light fixtures still hung from the ceiling.

The table was set for three, and spread with covered silver dishes. The smell to my surprise made my mouth water. I hadn't eaten for almost a day, and with all that had happened in the last twenty-four hours I was sure I had lost my appetite for good.

"Don't worry, Lucy," Natasha said, seated at the head of the table. "I wasn't about to let you starve. You may still have your uses."

The table was twice as long as was necessary for the three of us. There was seating for nine more. I suspected when the entire house was renovated it would rival the residence of the region's drug kingpin. Inside the door of the massive dining room several armed men stood guard. None of them were recognizable. I guess Diego and El Peludo had been given time off for good behavior.

"Sit," she said.

We sat.

A uniformed server came and lifted the lids from the dishes. So, she had servants. Just like her to hire the locals to do her bidding. Aromatic steam wafted toward the ceiling. Fans hanging from the rafters spun in a puny effort to cool the room.

The server attended Natasha first, then came to my side and placed some slices of juicy meat on my plate, and topped it with a luscious jalapeno, tomato, red onion and avocado salsa. He scooped roasted sweet potatoes and cheesy polenta and left a generous helping alongside the meat. There was a delicious-looking green salad with sliced orange segments and sweet yellow peppers.

"We can be quite civilized," Natasha said as the server loaded my long-stemmed, crystal glass with wine. She pushed her wineglass with her forefinger to be refilled.

The wine was exquisite.

The pork would have been as well had it not dawned on me that this was probably the wild boar shot on my arrival.

CHAPTER 12

When I woke up, I thought I was blind. Until my brain fully cleared. Then I realized where I was. In that tiny musty cell of a bedroom, which was formerly part of the original servants' quarters, at Natasha Borg's jungle hacienda.

My eyes refused to adjust to my surroundings. It was just too damned dark. What with the boarded-up windows and the locked door, I was deprived of any sources of light. What I did have, though, was my wedding song playing in my ears. *Love, love, love. All you need is love, love... Love is all you need...*

I did not love these people who had kidnapped me. *"It matters not who you love, why you love, when you love or how you love, it matters only that you love..."*

Thank you, John Lennon, for reminding me of that. Because right now my heart was filled with hate. How dare Aras kidnap me!

I was going to have to control my emotions. But did he have to do it right in the middle of my wedding ceremony? It wasn't entirely his fault, I know. What did I expect? For him to sacrifice his family? They had given him a deadline. Kidnap me or see his family dead. What would I have done in his place?

The problem was: I just wasn't sure if I could trust him. Norman once told me that a person's worst fear is to be betrayed by someone you trust. In the short time I had known Aras he had never let me down. But then the stakes had never been higher.

I turned over in the musty bed, cursing him for putting me in this horrible and ultimately impossible situation. Lucky for me I was so exhausted from my ordeal that I had fallen asleep as soon as I was returned to my jailcell. There was nothing for me to do but wait. Once Norman arrived, I would have an ally. We'd still be in a fix. But Norman always made me feel safe. And even when I wasn't safe, his very presence made me feel otherwise.

Right at this moment, I was certain that it was just me against this alien corrupt world.

Something moved in the corner of the room. A slight squeak or creak of a floorboard or a piece of furniture. My heart jerked. Esophageal spasm or cardiac arrest? Oh, crap. Were there bats in here? Bats creeped me out. I bolted upright and the thing did as well. It was sitting in the solitary chair in the corner, a substantial shadow.

Any visible light came from cracks in the window boards. And this was minimal. Eventually my eyes adapted and made out a familiar shape.

"Shit," I said. "Is that you, Aras?" In my frustration and anger, all of my filters were off.

He grunted. Then whispered, "Keep your voice down."

"How did you—" I stopped. Stupid question. He had a key to my room. Or else he knew where our benevolent hostess kept it. I was being sarcastic. Natasha wouldn't even know what the word 'benevolent' meant.

Was it his presence that had awakened me? Or my dead-end dream?

The shadow rose from the chair and came to sit at the foot of my bed. The bed had no footboard; it was simply a box spring beneath a thin mattress set into a basic metal bedframe. Why did this remind me of something? Oh yeah. That night in Baghdad when I first met him. He had come to my hotel room to tell me that Norman was safe and following the thieves who had heisted a pair of priceless statues, twin winged bulls. Aras had entered silently through the window, delivered his message with a brief visit, and then disappeared. Was he about to do a repeat?

No way was he going to leave me alone with that crazy bitch Natasha.

I rolled out of bed, suddenly aware that I was dressed in nothing but my underwear. It was warm and stuffy in this room when my head first hit the pillow—if you could call that shrunken lump of feathers a pillow. But now the night had cooled. And my clothes were at the end of the bed somewhere. Thankfully, it was dark. And even if it wasn't, I decided I could not care less what he saw.

"What are you doing here, Aras. Unless you came here to break me out, I don't feel like talking to you."

He inched forward on the mattress, making the springs squeak.

"The least you could have done is upgraded me to a better room."

He gave a soft chuckle. "Don't worry, Lucy. Mine is no nicer. The only advantage it has over yours is that it has no lock on the door."

"So, you're free to come and go?"

"Apparently." A pause. He was as cavalier as England's Robin Hood and as dashing as Mexico's Zorro. Did the Arab world have an equivalent? That was how I used to think of Aras. Like an Arabian vigilante.

"Unfortunately, I showed my hand when they made me aware of the identity of their hostages," he said, bursting into my thoughts.

"It's your mom and grandfather, Aras. Naturally, you care," I said, softening. "Anyone would feel the same way. Anyone with a heart that is." And a soul. Of which our gracious hostess had neither.

"I shouldn't have put you in danger, Lucy. I am sorry." He slammed his fist down on the mattress. I felt the vibrations ripple towards me. "I made a mistake. Now that they know how much my mother and grandfather mean to me, they've got me… But I am going to fix it."

I leaned forward and grabbed his knee. The fabric of his pants was coarse. "Don't do anything stupid. Norman will arrive tomorrow and Luke is already working on the problem."

Aras' exhalation was loud. "That's the other thing. I don't want my brother to have to always bail me out."

"He is never going to stop helping you, Aras. You're family."

"Then you understand." He was referring to his mom and grandpa.

"Of course, I understand. Doesn't mean I'm happy about it. But I know there was nothing else you could do. Natasha wants the missing piece to the Mayan shield. I have it in my possession. You had no choice but to bring me to her."

"I regret it, Lucy. You have no idea how much."

This conversation was making me bemoan my earlier thoughts. I got up and went to him and put my arms around his head. His hair was unruly, wiry, and his skin felt damp. I probably shouldn't have done that, but I was desperate for the feel of a warm body that I could trust. Honestly, in the emotional state I was in, I would have settled for a hug from that wild boar had it not been shot and served for dinner.

He moved away from me when he realized I was half-naked. He took off the loose shirt he was wearing overtop his tee and dropped it in my lap.

"Put that on. Tomorrow, I'll see about getting you some more clothes. Even if I have to steal them from Blondie."

It was strange having a conversation with him without actually being able to see him. I could sense his presence, feel his breath and see vague movements in the dark, but it was nothing like being able to read a person's body language. We took so much for granted when we could see.

"How did she know about you?" I asked.

"From her buddy, Cham Nassar. The moment she mentioned the name Luke Trevanian—and that he was her prime obstacle to finding Atlantis—the bastard was already hatching a plan. He never forgave you for getting his cousin killed."

"I thought terrorists didn't form family attachments."

"They don't. They form vendettas. The murder of a cousin is a good reason for revenge."

I had finished buttoning up the shirt and now

sat sidesaddle on the small bed opposite him. The shirt smelled like him. Dirty and greasy and pleasantly familiar at the same time.

"Norman is going to kill me, isn't he?" Aras said.

I knew he was half-joking but I believe he felt he deserved it.

"Not physically," I said. "But you are not exactly on his current favorites list."

"Nor Luke's either, I imagine."

My shrug was invisible in the darkness. "You know, I have no idea what Luke thinks. He is certainly not going to give you any awards for best brother." I sighed in frustration. "How on earth is he going to get Anastasie out of prison?"

"You forget who you're talking about. It's Luke Trevanian. If anyone can do it, he can. And will." Aras glanced across the darkness to where starlight entered between three cracks in the board over the window. "How is it you're acquainted with her?" he asked. "You talk about her like she plays a significant role—or *played* a significant role—in your lives."

"She did—up until the part where she tried to murder me."

Aras' soft chuckle gave me a sensation of release. The tension between us at dinner had been gaining unbearable traction.

"Do you see why I never thought twice about involving you, Lucy? I knew you could stand on your own."

While I was flattered, I was beginning to have my doubts. "Let's not make a habit of it, though. Okay?"

He grinned. His expression was concealed by the dark, but I knew Aras—and he was grinning.

"Deal," he said.

I returned the sentiment. "Now, spill. I want to hear everything you've learned about Natasha's plans."

First, he wanted to know how Anastasie Kirsche figured in the plot. So, I explained how we had met her on an archaeological site.

A pair of silver doves had been stolen from the dig near the Spanish city of Cádiz, an ancient ruin rumored to be the mythical City of Silver. Some theorists even believed it to be the legendary site of Atlantis.

Norman's sister, who had fallen for a scoundrel, had helped the crook steal the silver doves. When the scoundrel was murdered, we learned that he was CIA on the trail of a neo-Nazi cult operating in the area.

"Nazis?" He interrupted. "You were chasing down Nazis?"

"Not us. Him. The CIA agent. Turned out he was one of the good guys. Undercover. He was trying to figure out what they were up to. The Nazi resurgence is real. They believe the same things as the originals. They are searching not just for treasure but for proof."

"Proof?"

"Proof of a super race. Which they believe they are descended from."

Aras would have laughed, but this was serious. Nazis were nothing to scoff at. They were dangerous.

He had a number of questions for me. Why was the CIA so interested in the doves and the silver city? Did the Nazis want to loot it? And what did Atlantis have to do with the ancient sites near Cádiz? All of these questions I answered in short form or avoided for another time. I lingered a little on Cádiz. It was purported to be one of the possible sites of Atlantis but

Luke had pretty much dismissed that theory. And then I told him what he really wanted to know.

I could sense the truth dawning in his mind.

"They were hunting for a turquoise mosaic, an artifact found at the dig, that just might be the key to the location of Atlantis. Yes, that damned piece of turquoise and mother-of-pearl. The source of all our woes. It fits the broken space in the Mayan shield that Natasha now has in her possession."

Anastasie Kirsche—cult leader—had killed to own it. And I had gotten in her way…

Silence fell, then Aras said. "Wow. You guys have been busy."

CHAPTER 13

From the growing brightness visible in the cracked boards, I knew the outside world was on the cusp of daybreak. Aras and I had sat up talking all night. Not exactly scheming but getting each other up to speed. Anastasie was the only one who could read the Mayan glyphs. That was why Natasha wanted her released. If she contacted another expert at some university or museum, she would need some sort of convincing explanation. Someone she could trust was critical to keep her activities secret. Natasha was not about to share. Except I supposed with Cham Nassar. I hoped I would be long gone before that confrontation took place.

When Aras noticed the direction of my head, he sat up. He cursed in Arabic. It was only a matter of minutes before sunrise. "I didn't mean for us to have a slumber party..." He suddenly leaped off the bed. "I'm breaking you out."

I stood up. "Seriously?"

"Quick. Get the rest of your clothes on."

"You're sitting on them." He felt beneath his backside and removed my jeans and tank top. I was already extricating myself from Aras' shirt. The other clothes went on swiftly and then we were standing at the door, listening.

"They'll be up any minute," he whispered. "We need to go."

"But what about Norman? He'll be coming here."

"No, he won't. If we hurry, he'll be waiting for us at the airport."

My hand groped in the dark until I touched his arm. "Natasha won't stop. She *will* track us down. We can't leave."

"I have to make this right, Lucy."

I grabbed his forearm. My mind was whirling a mile a minute. I was certain I was right. "I don't think escape is the smart thing to do just now. We have to figure out where Atlantis is. Natasha is on the brink of that information. As soon as she is reunited with Anastasie they will decipher the map. I could make a guess right now, but all I really know is that it's somewhere in the Caribbean Sea, south of Florida and north of Caracas. And west of Yucatán. That takes in a lot of area and it's all underwater.

"Don't you see, Aras? If we don't stick around, we won't know what they know. We won't be in a position to find it before she does. And that means getting the whole team over here. Norman will land any minute. Luke is already working on getting Anastasie out of prison. If I know your brother, he's already sent the rest of the team aboard his yacht with its GPS set for Central America. Johnny, Alessandra and Arianna will all be here in a matter of days.

"If we run now, we'll have to keep on running. I won't do that. And what about your family? Aras, I'm here because of them. They're safe as long as I remain where Natasha can see me."

"You're right." He banged himself on the forehead with the heel of his hand. "What was I thinking? Nassar will execute Samar and Rafiq if I help you escape."

"Be patient, Aras. We're a team. We'll figure it out."

He seized my wrist in turn. His voice was urgent. "Natasha can't know that the team will be here."

"Natasha said no police, correct?"

"Yeah."

"Did she say anything about the rest of the team?"

"Not in so many words."

"They'll be discreet." Then, it occurred to me. Why hadn't he enlisted the ISORE team in the first place? We would have done everything in our power... But then I realized who we were dealing with. Natasha we could predict, but Cham Nassar? He was not only heartless, he was soulless. Just like her. Only worse. If she was a demon, he was the devil incarnate.

"Don't worry. Luke has a plan."

I hoped.

Aras abandoned me then to report to Natasha. He had left his cellphone with me and then locked me back inside the tiny bedroom.

I used the light from his phone to find Norman's number and tapped to make contact.

It rang twice before he answered it. "I'm here, Lucy."

"How did you know it was me? This is Aras' phone."

"I know. I'm bringing you a new one."

"You're on the ground?"

"Debarking as we speak... I have a rental waiting for me." Money spoke. Luke had arranged to have a car at the landing strip. "How long to the hacienda?"

"Thirty minutes tops," I said. "If you drive fast."

A key turned in the latch and the door sprang open. Aras stood in the doorway while I dropped to the bed to collect my balance. The sudden exposure to light had knocked me for a loop.

"Come on. Breakfast is waiting. And so is Natasha," he said.

"Norman has landed," I answered, mid-talk on the phone.

"Give him directions to the hacienda. She's expecting him."

I did and we disconnected.

"Natasha has a proposition for you," Aras informed me as we walked.

"Oh? Is it a good one?"

"It might save your life."

"She isn't going to kill me, Aras, or she would have done it by now."

"She doesn't have the missing mosaic yet, but when she does…"

I went quiet. I saw his point.

Breakfast was not in the dining room, but in a breakfast nook, partitioned off of the kitchen by a demi-glass brick wall. The table was surrounded on three sides by enormous latticed windows with a glass-domed ceiling, and double glass doors at the rear opened out onto a flagstone patio and enormous garden. It was more of an atrium than a breakfast nook, but hey, who was I to debate architectural terms?

The kitchen had been recently renovated. The most updated appliances, floors, subway tiles and fixtures spread out before us. The kitchen staff, consisting of a Hispanic cook and server were busy making omelets, fruit salad and corn bread. Natasha had been busy since we saw her last. Just how much money had she managed to accumulate for selling illicit artifacts? A lot I'd bet.

The server, a young woman this time, came around and poured coffee into heavy orange mugs as soon as Aras and I sat down opposite our hostess. The fragrance was exhilarating and awakened my appetite.

"I trust you slept well," Natasha said with a smirk.

She knew very well that I had not. That room was a jailcell and smelled like one. "Is this how you treat all of your guests," I asked sarcastically.

"Just a reminder of who is in charge."

"So, if I'm on my best behavior I get to sleep in one of the renovated bedrooms?"

She sneered. "We'll see. I have a proposition for you. But I'll wait to explain it after Depardieu gets here. When is he expected?"

I shrugged. "Any minute now."

I squinted out the window. The view was to the back garden. At first glance it appeared to be a riotous mess, but on closer inspection I could see that there used to be some order to the design of the plantings and the native vegetation. I recognized prickly pear cactus, blue agave, magnolias, poinsettias, ferns and bromeliads and various succulents in what used to probably be a very beautiful rock garden. Flowers sprang up haphazardly in groups and in isolation: marigolds, orchids, sunflowers and the ubiquitous dahlia in every hue of the red spectrum. This place was costing Natasha a fortune to restore.

The screeching of car tires outside told us that Norman had arrived. I looked behind me to the glass doors and saw that instead of pulling up to the front of the house he had come around to the side, veering off the driveway and over the unkempt grass. He exited the silver Range Rover like a cowboy leaping from a fast horse, and slammed the door shut. I rose to my feet.

I don't believe I have ever seen a more welcome sight in my life.

"Sit down, Lucy," Natasha said.

Outside, a greeting party was swarming Norman with AK-47s but it was apparent they had orders to withhold fire. Two of them escorted him to the glass doors and at a nod from Natasha, Diego (who stood just outside the kitchen), went to let him in. Norman towered over the Mexican just as he towered over most people.

Patted down and his guns removed, they directed him inside. He had a Kevlar satchel with him, which I assumed held the missing mosaic.

He glared at Natasha as he stepped onto her sunlight-yellow, Italian-tiled floors. That's right. Mexican tiles weren't good enough for the lady of the manor.

Natasha rose from her place at the table, which had been set for four. So, she was expecting him for breakfast.

"Have you eaten yet, handsome?" she asked.

He ignored her and his eyes landed on me. Screw Natasha, I thought, and leaped up and ran to him. He cupped me in his arms while Natasha glared at the obvious slight.

"Ça va, chérie?"

"I'm fine," I whispered into his ear and bit it.

He grinned and gave me an enthusiastic kiss on the

mouth.

"Enough!" Natasha said. "This is getting pornographic."

"Maybe if you would give us a decent room," I said smartly.

Aras was seated by the window snickering and loving every minute of our public display.

"Do you have it?" she demanded.

Norman gently nudged me off him while he unslung the Kevlar satchel from across his chest. By the tension in his massive muscles, I knew he wanted to wipe the room clean with the goods, knocking Natasha and her henchmen off their feet in the same swoop. But he refrained from any inappropriate action and gently laid the satchel onto the table between the place settings of traditional, hand-painted breakfast crockery.

Natasha's eyes gleamed maniacally. She looked like a classic villain. If she wasn't so concerned about appearing sophisticated, she would have been salivating.

She unclipped the fasteners and removed the bubble-wrapped oblong from among the rest of the stuffing that Norman had managed to dig up on short notice. Most of this was tissue paper from wedding gifts.

As she unrolled the artifact from its cushion of air-filled plastic, we all stood tense and alert, as though any moment a bomb would explode.

For an instant I worried that Norman might have tried a decoy or hidden it, in order to bargain with her, but I guess he knew her as well as I did. Had he tried to pull a fast one she might have shot me. Or Aras.

Sunlight broke through a cloud, arrowed through the window glass, and struck the object fully as it sat in her hands.

"Finally," she said. "I have the missing piece."

Norman took my hand and sat down at the table. I settled next to him, with Aras on my other side. Natasha was still standing with the artifact in her hands.

"Well?" Norman said. "Where's breakfast. I'm starving."

Natasha peered at him through her eyelashes, and laughed. She was in a great mood. Guess she wasn't going to kill us today.

She signaled to the two henchmen standing guard at the glass doors and spoke something in Spanish to Diego who waited at the kitchen entrance. Outside the window four more men stood guard. All were armed with assault rifles. If we planned to make a break for it, we'd be riddled with holes in seconds.

The girl that had served us coffee was summoned by a single gesture and Natasha ordered her to bring us breakfast.

"Enjoy," she said. "I'll be back momentarily."

She gathered up the mosaic and quickly exited, and the last thing we saw was her swinging blonde hair and the back of her white silk blouse.

"What happened with my father?" I asked Norman.

He stopped halfway from shoveling eggs into his mouth, and lowered the fork and picked up his napkin to dab at the corner of his lips. Now that he knew I was safe, his appetite had returned. "I'm not completely convinced he *is* your father," Norman said. "I mean, really, what do we know about him?"

"My mother vouched for him. She recognized him. And so did Colleen."

He frowned. "Okay. Fine. I won't argue with that."

"Does he know what happened to me?"

Norman nodded. "When Luke spun him the story of us having whisked you off to safety, he said he saw what happened. He wants to help."

"Does Moz know I'm here. Did you tell him you were coming to me?"

"Yes. He wanted to join me. But I wouldn't let him."

"Was he upset?"

"What do *you* think?"

"They would have killed him or held him hostage too. You were right to deter him."

"God, I hope so. All we need is to have to worry about your father as well."

"Moz is with Interpol," I reminded him. "Antiquities International Division. He's a cop."

Norman frowned. "Doesn't mean he's equipped to deal with Nazis and terrorists."

CHAPTER 14

We were almost finished eating when Natasha returned. She ordered another round of coffee and along with it the girl brought some sweet Mexican breads called conchas concha and campechanas.

"I kept my bargain," Norman said. "Now it's your turn."

"Not yet. Trevanian has to bring me my sister. After that, we'll talk some more. Meanwhile I have a proposition for you. If you agree to it, you can't leave to fulfill your end until after Anastasie and Trevanian have arrived."

"And if we don't agree?" Norman said.

"Then you stay here as my guests."

"You mean your *prisoners*," I corrected.

"Semantics," she countered.

"Just say what you mean, Natasha," Norman growled.

She sat back with a self-satisfied smile. Everything was going according to her plan. She could afford to smile, *and* to relax.

"Did you know that tobacco smoking and cocaine

use were not limited to the New World aboriginals?" This question seemed so out of the blue that none of us responded. "There is evidence of tobacco use in ancient Egypt and Syria. As far back as the first pharaohs."

We gawped. Okay maybe that isn't the right description. What is the word for having your eyeballs pop out of your head?

Both Norman and I who had taken archaeology in school knew this was wrong. Aras did not contradict her, although I suspected he was in agreement with us. Tobacco was native to the Americas, and coca from which cocaine was extracted, was indigenous to South America. Before Christopher Columbus landed in the West Indies in 1492 ancient Egypt and Syria had yet to be introduced to the drugs. I scoffed and pressed home these facts.

The arrogant Natasha shook her head reprovingly. "But you are wrong, my dear. And *I* have proof. My sister spent a year in Cairo while doing her Ph.D. She discovered an interesting fact, the significance of which never struck her until she saw the Mayan shield.

"There are mummies in Egypt where tobacco has been found in their wrappings and preserved body parts. In fact, while at the institute of Anthropology and Human Genetics at Munich University, Anastasie tested bone, skin and muscle tissues which confirmed the presence of large quantities of the drugs in various mummies… The pharaoh and his buddies were getting high."

Where was this going? Aras and Norman's expressions were an exact reflection of mine. When I looked at Aras, he quickly turned to the view outside the window. Did he think this dialogue was as preposterous as I? Norman stared at Natasha in total silence.

"Did you hear me?" she asked. "Mummies with drugs in their systems."

"So what?" I answered. "What does that prove?"

"It proves that there was trans-Atlantic trade between the Americas and the Middle East. Long, long, *long* before the Europeans arrived."

"Even so," Norman cut in. "The time period is all wrong. There is a big difference between 6,000 years when the first civilizations arose in the Middle East and when Atlantis supposedly existed."

Norman was well acquainted with Natasha and Anastasie's obsession over Plato's mythical land. What else had he to think about during that lengthy transport of the Mayan mosaic on the flight from Paris to the Yucatán?

"Screw the time difference," she snapped. "For all we know Plato got the dates mixed up. History is like that. Depends on who is telling the story and what information is skipped or embellished. We'll figure that out later. The fact is, people were sailing ships across the Atlantic long before Columbus. Thousands of years before Columbus. And when I find evidence of those ships or the remains of at least one of those ships, I will find the gateway to Atlantis."

The three of us were dumbstruck.

"I want the two of you to find that shipwreck."

I attempted to squash my skepticism. "How?"

"Your buddy Trevanian has international connections. Researchers were on the verge of huge undersea discoveries to prove that the Spanish and Portuguese were late colonizers of Latin America. They did not discover it. Ancient seafarers, the precursors to the Phoenicians, did. Unfortunately, the current governments of most countries in Central and South America have colluded to ban all research that might prove a pre-Columbian link between the Old World and the New. They don't want any proof to change their version of history. They are the conquerors; they believe they won the land fair and square… and will do whatever it takes to keep the history books unchanged. Not that I give a damn about their politics. But I don't want their interference with my search. I don't give a shit what happens to anybody in this second-rate hellhole. All I want is to find Atlantis."

Silence dropped like a curtain.

"How do you know there's a shipwreck?" I demanded.

"There is not just one shipwreck. There are four."

Four? "How do you know?"

"Come with me."

She led us down a corridor with paint tarps edging the floors. It opened out to the lobby with the lovely floral tiling. Off to the side were the pillars leading to her study. She unlocked the latticed, bulletproof glass doors and we followed her inside.

Her guards were told to wait by the door. Only Diego joined us. At her desk by the enormous bay window, she stopped and looked down. The ceremonial shield was still there. It was so heavy it took two men to lift it.

"See those crescents?" she asked as Norman, Aras, and I gathered around. "Four of them. They represent ships. Sunken ships."

"How do you know?" Norman repeated the burning question.

"Anastasie told me they were shipwrecks."

And you believe everything she says? There was no point in arguing. If she wanted to believe those symbols represented shipwrecks, then so be it.

"And the four rectangular shapes at the top, bottom, left and right leading to the circle—the island—they are piers or bridges." Made of gold or pyrite.

"Or maybe roads," I muttered.

"We need coordinates," Natasha said. "Those coordinates are on that missing piece." She unlocked a drawer in the desk and removed the rhomboid shaped piece that she had stolen from me. It was only about eight inches long but it was the missing piece of the shield. She locked it into place and the squiggles matched.

None of us could read Mayan hieroglyphics. What did it say? Obviously, Natasha was hopeless in epigraphy or her sister would be extraneous. But did Anastasie actually have the ability to decipher this script? CIA, professional con artist, PhD in Archaeology, *and* an epigrapher? Must be hard being Superwoman.

Too bad she had not used her powers for good instead of evil.

"The ancient Maya knew the location of Atlantis," she insisted. "The ceremonial shield proves it. The stories were told and retold through the ages and passed on by seafarers who eventually returned home with tales of a fabulous uncharted land." She tapped the table dramatically. "This mysterious mosaic is only one artifact depicting the story of Atlantis. There are others."

"Where?" Norman demanded.

"I don't know. That's what I want you and your team to find out."

"We are *not* going to work for you."

She shrugged. "Oh, I think you will, Depardieu. Trevanian, doubtless, will want to know the true location of Atlantis. And where he goes... Don't you?" Her smug eyes landed on him, then took in the rest of us, me and Aras.

God, I hated it when the villain was right. Especially, since she was a Nazi. It was hard to decide what I detested more, terrorists or Nazis.

"Each of these ships, and each of these piers or bridges, points to a shipping lane. The Atlanteans were expert seafarers. Professional navigators. They knew the tides, the currents, and the weather patterns. But every now and then, they misjudged. There are ships blown off course and they very likely point to one of the four gates that enter Atlantis. We know where one of those piers is. We just don't know which one of the four it represents."

This pier or what some people called the steps to Bimini was long disputed as a stairway to Atlantis. It was discovered in the 1960s, an underwater structure, 638 meters in length composed of a double row of large, seemingly hand-hewn blocks, set in a straight line and mostly buried in the seabed, off the coast of Florida near the westernmost chain of islands known as Bimini. Some of the stones are as much as four square meters with smooth surfaces. Beyond this section is a mosaic of smaller stones, half the size, gracefully curving the road towards the modern-day beach.

Geologists debunked it as a natural formation, an ancient shoreline formed before the landscape was submerged. It was forgotten until Natasha and Anastasie got hold of the Mayan shield. I could see why she thought this stone road might be a pathway to Atlantis. No one had actually gone into the deepest, darkest depths to see if this road reemerged elsewhere.

And it had never occurred to anyone that this 'road' might actually be a pier connected to the island of Atlantis. Natasha believed that, once upon a time, merchant vessels arrived and departed from here. Their destinations? Mexico and the Eurasian continent.

Nothing she was saying was indisputable. Or it could all be a lark. But one thing she had right. I had caught the virus. I wanted to see with my own eyes, Plato's mythical land.

CHAPTER 15

Luke's yacht, the Madonna II was enroute to the Yucatán. It was a brand-new boat that he had only had for a month. He thought it best to keep it out of the sight of the greedy sisters, so he had diverted the ship via cellphone to Florida. There was no need for Natasha to meet the rest of the team. And no reason for her to inspect our state-of-the-art remote sensing and imaging equipment or see the massive luxury of the billion-dollar vessel.

Luke arrived in three days with Anastasie in tow.

"I told you he could do it," Natasha said as we stood outside on the grounds watching the car—a gold Mercedes G-550 off-road SUV—careen into the driveway.

I shook my head in bewilderment. Anastasie was a murderer. Not *just* a murderer, but a serial murderer. As far as I knew she had killed up to three people. Sadly, there was no real proof. I was the only witness to the murder of her CIA partner. The other people involved were accessories. That was why 'innocent until proven guilty' was such a stanchly upheld principle in all civilized societies. But as an alleged murderer, bail was posted at beyond what most accused could pay. Had Luke paid it?

Natasha read my mind. "Trevanian took care of Anastasie's bail. Because—*there* she is."

She pointed to the car where her sister was seated beside Luke who was in the driver's seat. They almost looked like a normal couple out on a leisurely road trip, except that Luke in his designer shades and windswept honey blond hair was Hollywood handsome and Anastasie reminded me of a scarecrow in sunglasses.

Under the presumption of innocence, the burden of proof was on the prosecution to present compelling evidence. Anastasie's trial date was nowhere near being set. These things took years, and paying her bail was the easiest way to get her released until her trial. I could laugh at myself for thinking that Luke would devise a plan to break her out of jail. Not that we hadn't performed quasi-illegal antics before. If—breaking into a museum to rescue an object stolen by a crooked museum director, or stealing endangered artifacts from thieves was considered illegal.

Natasha stood by the side of the hedge, hands on hips full of confidence. "My gamble paid off."

I turned to face my host and wished I hadn't. Natasha's smirk disgusted me.

"I knew he'd cave if I had his brother *and* you," she crowed. "You're lucky to have Luke Trevanian for a friend."

Yes, I was. But I also understood that Luke himself was betting on his own theory paying off. The satisfaction he would get from proving the existence or non-existence of Atlantis far outweighed any treasure he might find.

"He's one of us now," Natasha said smugly.

Typical. She was misreading Luke's motives.

"No, he isn't," I strongly objected. Luke would never be an accessory to a criminal. Sure, he had his reasons for bailing Anastasie out of prison. And most of it did have to do with me, Aras, and his family. But this was about loyalty, devotion and love. Not greed. The discovery of Atlantis came second. It always would.

"Luke!" I shouted as he climbed out of the mud-spattered car and drew near. The rural road from the outlying private airstrip was in a clearing in the jungle and was more of a muddy, potholed, dirt track than a road. Instinct told me that it belonged to one of the drug cartels, and that somehow Natasha had made a pact with them. In fact, prior to being recruited by her, this militia guarding her property likely worked for the cartels.

If Luke was smart (and he was), he would have sent his private plane back to wherever it came from before the cartel claimed it for their own.

The grass flattened as I ran, and I even decapitated a few flowers in my path as I threw myself into the billionaire's arms. He gave me a bear hug. "Lucy. Thank God, you're okay."

His height forced me to stand on tiptoes. His strong, athletic build engulfed me. Dressed in clean casual slacks and a crisp, short-sleeved linen shirt, he appeared alert and refreshed, not deadened with jet lag and wrinkled. The comforts of his luxury jet had saved him much discomfort.

Aras stood off to the side, miserable. Seeing him thus, you would not guess that he had spent most of his life in the desert, a knife strapped to his boot and a semi-automatic rifle slung over his shoulder defending his village from the rogues that wished to enslave it. This tough dude, when in the company of his brother, shrank. He was going to have to get over it. Courage could not be measured by comparing yourself to others. Courage could only be measured by comparing yourself to yourself. *Only when you face what you most fear do you show true courage.* And for Aras, that wasn't terrorists or thugs of any sort, but confronting his brother's disapproval.

Aras had been my defender and my protector in Baghdad when I thought I was alone in my search for Norman. He was a resistance leader and a freedom fighter and among his colleagues he had no peer; there was no question of his courage. But when it came to his brother? I could relate. All of my life I had lived in the shadow of my older sister. Sure, I loved her. But that didn't mean at times I wasn't jealous or resentful. Like me, all Aras wanted was respect from the one person who meant the most to him.

I knew what Aras was worth. And I would give up a dozen friends for just one friend like Aras.

At a nod from Luke, Aras returned the subtle gesture.

Norman and Luke gave each other man hugs. *Dammit, please go and hug your brother. Can't you see he needs it?*

Luke went over to Aras. Finally. But not for an embrace. How long ago was it since they had last seen each other? Must be a year.

Before the half-brothers could have words, Anastasie cut in, "Okay. That is enough. One big happy family. We didn't bring you all the way over to Mexico for a family reunion. Let's end this Hallmark moment and get to work." She resisted displaying any affection for her sister; they merely gave each other self-satisfied smiles.

The former CIA agent seemed thinner and older than I remembered her. Her short, rust-colored hair had grown out from its boy cut and hung halfway to her shoulders. She was never pretty but now she looked downright dowdy in juxtaposition to her poised, composed, and definitely attractive sister. The resemblance was there in expression but in nothing else. It was the thinness without the feminine curves of her sister, that made Anastasie remind me of a scarecrow. That and the hair. She had traded her orange prison garb for khaki pants and an off-white shirt, a uniform she'd worn the day I met her.

Luke turned to Anastasie with loathing. Natasha signaled her militia to usher us all back inside the house. We had no intention of fighting her. Or her small army. She had Aras' family as hostage. We were going to cooperate, at least as far as searching for Atlantis was concerned.

Inside her study, Luke whistled at the opulence of the room. *I know*, I wanted to say. If this was how she had renovated her study, exactly how fancy were the design plans for the rest of the house? No wonder she was unwilling to foot her own sister's bail.

Natasha led the way to the Mayan shield and when Anastasie caught sight of it on the desk, her mouth opened. She had only seen the artifact for a short time after I first discovered it in the subbasement of that Spanish cathedral. At the time she never even noticed the glyphs. For that matter, neither had I.

I paused to absorb her reaction; I swear Anastasie's eyes lit up, like a fire burned behind the irises.

"At last," she said. "It is complete."

Luke studied the restored shield. The turquoise tesserae shone like gemstones in a shining sea. The gold glinted in the sun. The white mother-of-pearl gleamed like silver. It was definitely some sort of map, but how to interpret it?

"How long will it take to translate this thing?" Natasha asked.

"A few days, at minimum," Anastasie answered. "I'm rusty. The last time I deciphered Mayan glyphs I was in grad school.

The former CIA agent had originally been searching for clues to Atlantis in Spain. All of Plato's writings seemed to point in that direction until she found the broken piece of mosaic which told her otherwise. I had interfered in her scheme then; I had no plans to do so now. Too much was at stake.

Luke backed away from the unlikely sisters. I crept up to him and whispered, "Could you make anything of those glyphs?"

He shrugged. "When you get the chance, take a picture."

My smile was smug. "I already have."

I had taken the picture with the new phone that Norman had slipped to me—when Natasha had hurried out to meet the new arrivals—joining them minutes later.

The glyphs and the image on the Mayan shield remained a mystery, despite the fact that it was now complete. It all came tumbling back to me. Plato's descriptions. I tried to match it to my vision of Plato's narrative.

Surrounded by mountains and pyramids, the central city of Atlantis had temples, a royal residence, harbors, docks and roads. The citadel perched on a central islet enclosed by three, waterfilled, circular canals, crossed by a single transecting road. In between the waterways were buildings and gardens. A roofed channel that began at the sea cut through each of the rings of land until it reached the inner islet. Nothing on the shield's mosaic showed this depth of detail. Could this image on the shield be of the citadel, rather than of the island?

Towers and gated bridges appeared at either end of the great channel to monitor the large sea-going vessels that brought goods from the outer lands. The buildings on each of the rings of land were coated in different metals: copper, tin and orichalcum, which gleamed like fire. The gold and pyrite in the mosaic certainly 'gleamed like fire' but there was nothing as distinct as buildings.

And then there were the temples. None of which appeared in the mosaic on the shield in our possession. With roofs of ivory and ornamented in gold and silver, they sheltered beautiful gold statues encrusted with jewels. Diamonds, rubies, sapphires, emeralds and other lesser gemstones. And yes! A statue of the Sea god in his chariot drawn by six winged horses and accompanied by a hundred Nereids riding dolphins! That was also purported to exist in the grandest of Plato's temples. These statues were so large that their heads were said to touch the ceiling.

I silently gasped. Could such splendid treasures survive the wear of time? Being submerged as I assumed they would be, could the saltwater of the sea have any destructive effect?

If any of this detailed description was based on truth, it was understandable why the Nazi sisters and their terrorist compatriot Cham Nassar yearned so desperately to find Atlantis.

"So, what's the plan?" Luke asked, while Anastasie admired the mosaic shield, her eyeballs glued to it as though it were a magic mirror. Was her imagining of the lost city as spectacular as mine?

"You three go find my shipwreck," Natasha said before Anastasie could tug herself away from the compelling mosaic shield. Natasha's words were aimed at me and the ISORE members. We worked best as a team, and the faster we got this expedition underway, the closer we would get to her goal. "Aras. You stay here."

Aras glared. "And do what? I'd be more use helping with the search."

"Then you will do it here."

So, Aras was further insurance in case we got any ideas about shipping out.

"Do as she says," Luke ordered.

Aras glared. He hated having his brother tell him what to do. And he wasn't the only one. The same feelings of resentment emanated from Anastasie. Her younger sister had taken charge in her absence. The militia that protected the hacienda jumped when she barked. To top it off, Natasha had objected to using her own money to pay her sister's bail. She had forced Luke to do it instead.

CHAPTER 16

We meant to spend the night at the Casa Los Cedros a lovely boutique hotel in the small town of Espita. The Nazi sisters had agreed to release us on our own recognizance. The abandonment of Aras and the sacrifice of his family was not an option for any of us. We would do everything in our power to find Atlantis.

It never occurred to me that Atlantis might not exist. By this time, my personal beliefs were inconsequential. Atlantis *had* to exist. We would make it exist. Aras' life and his mom and grandpa's lives depended on it.

Compared to what Luke was used to the hotel was modest, but in juxtaposition to what I had been forced to endure under Natasha Borg's hospitality, it was luxury. There was a restaurant and bar, and a floodlit pool. The rooms were spacious and air-conditioned with luxurious, attached bathrooms. And all around us were the enticing sounds of the rainforest.

Open-leafed trees and climbing vines, spackled with wild local color, bordered the property and we were informed by the hotel staff that virgin cenotes existed nearby. Deep blue sinkholes, some fifty or more meters deep appeared when the extant porous limestone—which allowed the seepage of freshwater creating underground caves—collapsed, exposing the azure pools to the surface. Used by the ancient Maya as places of worship, cenotes were also what the ancient civilizations depended upon for freshwater, as the karst landscape (limestone bedrock), prevented the formation of lakes and rivers.

After what we had just endured it was heavenly. We lounged in deck chairs around the pool and traded news.

Luke was somewhat preoccupied, but naturally, he would be. The cost of this whole fiasco was on him. What was on his mind? What else? Aras.

"It's okay, Luke," I said.

He shook his head. Initially, Luke may have thought exactly what I had. How could Aras have kidnapped me at my own wedding? And surely, he had asked himself the question: what would *he* have done in his brother's place? At the same time, I believed Luke Trevanian truly thought he would have devised a different plan. Would he have? No one will ever know because he was not in that situation.

I chided him gently. "It was the only thing Aras could do."

Luke was doing his best to contain his anger at his brother's choices. "It couldn't be. There is always another way."

Maybe in business, but in life? When it had to do with hostages?

"It's Cham Nassar, Luke," I pressed. "He's a terrorist. Remember? To him, Samar and Rafiq's lives are worth less than that beer you're drinking."

Luke scowled and set the beer glass down on the table between our chairs. Sometimes Luke could be irrational in his expectations of others.

"*Hola*," someone said.

At first, I thought it was one of the Mexican hotel staff come to collect our glasses and bottles, and to ask if we desired a second round. Speak of the devil. When I turned, I saw that it was Aras.

His sojourn with Natasha in this Spanish-speaking country was transforming him into a local. That was one of his talents, he could fit into any environment.

"Aras!" I exclaimed. I was the first to jump up to greet him. "Did Natasha give you time off for good behavior?" I grabbed his arm to drag him over to where we were seated by the pool.

"She doesn't know I'm here. Can't stay long. Just wanted to tell you about something I found."

"What is it?"

His eyes fell on Luke who had twisted to check out the new arrival, but then swung to his original position. Luke was silent with his back to Aras, even when Norman rose and approached to offer a friendly handshake.

"*Salut. Hola*, Aras. Good to see you." Norman was always slipping in and out of the multiple languages he was fluent in. French and Spanish being two of them. Not to mention English.

"You too."

His eyes returned to Luke, who remained facing away. While at the hacienda we had no opportunity to catch up or exchange notes. That was why Aras had risked life and limb to locate us to give us his information.

"What did you find, Aras?" I asked. I was surprised he hadn't mentioned his discovery to me earlier during our sleepover in that dingy, oversized dog crate Natasha called a guestroom.

He hesitated for a second, and then said, "I believe it to be some sort of petroglyph. I found it behind some vegetation in the west wall of a cenote, not too far from this hotel. It might help in your search."

"Did you hear that, Luke? Aras found a petroglyph that he thinks might be related to our search." I felt like a parrot repeating word for word Aras' speech. I was certain Luke had heard the first time around but he showed no sign of it. He grunted and refused to rise or turn around to greet his brother.

I readjusted my attention to Aras. "When did you find it?"

"Days ago."

"You never mentioned it to me."

"Slipped my mind."

Of course. He had other things to worry about. Namely his mother and grandfather.

"Anything else you haven't told us about?" Luke demanded from where he remained seated, his voice projecting louder than necessary, while his back remained to us.

Tone sharp, and sounding like the reprimand of a wayward child, Luke was being rude by avoiding his brother. No call for that. I was about to say something, when Aras spoke.

"Look. I'm doing what I can to make up for kidnapping Lucy. I'm sorry I did that. At the time, I couldn't think of anything else to do." He had raised his voice as well.

"So, you just obeyed the commandant," Luke snapped.

Aras growled. "What did you want me to do, big brother. Feed my mother to the lions? It's easy for you Trevanian. You are the golden boy. Your father—*our* father—adores you. The son who can do no wrong."

He was way offtrack there. But I made no attempt to correct him. Maybe he didn't know about the escapade in Luke's youth when he was actually trafficking antiquities instead of saving them. Not my place to say, and not the moment to say it.

"Your mother is a rich girl. She's safe behind her marble pillars and iron gates with security running willy-nilly all over her estate. You come from money," he accused. "All you have to do is throw it at someone and they'll do what you want. You—"

Luke bit off his half-brother's tirade. "You could have come to me. I would have helped you."

Aras went silent.

Luke twisted in his seat, tone still sharp. "We would have come up with a plan to free your family."

"How? You don't live in a terrorist-ridden country where the beast rears its ugly head without warning. You don't live in terror where any moment armed men commandeer your home, boot out children and babies and leave them destitute while they kill the father and rape the mother. Kidnappings and murders are par for the course where I come from."

Luke slammed his hand down on the table beside him, rattling the beer bottle and glasses on it, and spun in his seat. "Kidnapping Lucy, and throwing her into the jaws of that female Nazi snake would not have been my first choice."

"You don't know what you're talking about!" They were shouting now and I swiveled toward the hotel windows to see if the commotion had disturbed guests. I half expected to see the hotel staff racing out to chase off bandits, or at the very least, the glare of annoyed faces. But there were none.

Luke leaped out of his chair and stormed over to his half-brother. "Impulsiveness will only create more problems."

"It bought my family more time. Your mother is not being held in a cave somewhere in the middle of the Syrian desert with a knife at her throat. So don't tell me what creates problems. You know fucking nothing about real life. And nothing about mine! You're a pretty boy, a prima donna, with soft hands and a bodyguard to take your bullets for you!"

That wasn't exactly true. Well, maybe the bullet part. Norman had originally been hired by Luke to serve as his bodyguard, and he did once take a bullet for him. But the rest of it. A prima donna, a pretty boy. Sure, he was handsome if you liked the type, but soft hands? I dated Luke before Norman and I got together. I knew what his hands were like. They were strong and I had seen him take down a terrorist with them. And Aras should talk. At six feet plus, he was a freedom fighter's dream—with a face to match. Talk about a pretty boy.

Luke went to grab Aras' collar. That was so unlike him.

"Stop it," I said before either of them could get creative with their fists. "This is getting us nowhere." I planted my body between them. "I am fine. They did not hurt me. And I forgive you, Aras." My eyes turned to Luke. "Did you hear me, Luke. I forgive your brother. You have no reason to be so upset with him. I believe he had no other choice. He could hardly call us up and ask me to call off the wedding on the day so that we could form a posse and go and storm a terrorist's lair. We would have been killed and so would Samar and Rafiq."

Luke scowled. Sometimes I think he really believed he had superpowers.

"You know I'm right, Luke. You've seen Nassar's militia. We wouldn't have stood a chance even if we could have gotten inside his hideout. How would we get a middle-aged woman and an old man past those machine guns and across the desert?"

"I would have thought of something." He glanced at Norman. "Or *he* would have." He relied on Norman for his brute strength and his tactical intelligence. But sometimes all that got you was dead. Even Norman would agree. Although he was not taking sides. Or if he was, I'm sure his loyalty was with Luke.

"Now kiss and makeup," I ordered.

They didn't of course. What they did do was stop snapping and snarling at each other.

Silence. While they tried to figure out what to say.

"I have to go. Before Blondie misses me." Aras turned to march away.

Luke was about to make some biting remark when I dug my nails into his wrist.

"Before you go, Aras," I said. "Tell us how to find the petroglyph."

CHAPTER 17

I studied the beauty of the water in the aquamarine pool, after having my mind flit back and forth over too many unrelated things. Water and elegant architecture had a way of soothing the savage beast. And I felt myself relaxing in the warmth and pleasure of our remote but fully equipped boutique hotel.

The architect of the complex had replicated the idea of a sandy beach in the stone patio, and the elevated pool matched the blueness of the sea, creating a serene imitation of nature's waterfront. The buildings housing the guestrooms were single story, and sprawled like a massive hacienda, surrounded by rainforest.

"He didn't mean it," Luke I cajoled after Aras had vanished into the jungle. "He was angry, and stressed. Try to put yourself in his shoes."

"Oh, he meant it. I know what he thinks of me."

"But still. Deep down inside, he admires and respects you. That's all he wants from you. Some patience, understanding—and respect."

"Well, he'll have to start making some different choices then, won't he?"

I shook my head and leaned lazily back in my

deckchair. Luke was in the seat next to me and Norman reclined in the one on my other side.

Luke was in no mood to be generous with his brother. He needed time. Sure, Aras had cost him a fortune, forcing him to pay millions to get Anastasie released. I could only imagine what he had to engineer to sneak her out of the country. Paying her bail was one thing, but I am certain the conditions of her release required her to stay inside the borders. She would have had her passport confiscated. And that would mean her presence in any other country would be precarious. At some point in this scheme, he would have to bend the rules. Because if I knew Luke, he fully intended to get his money back.

American law in most states forbade alleged murderers to leave the country. In fact, only in special circumstances were they even allowed out on bail. So, yeah, it must have been a headache to free Anastasie. And a huge risk. But millions squandered over a criminal wasn't the reason Luke was frustrated and (or) angry. The only reason he was so upset was because Aras meant a lot to him.

After a long silence, Norman leaned over me to catch Luke's attention. I recognized what he was up to. And was grateful he meant to break the awkwardness by raising a new subject.

"You're not really serious about searching for Atlantis, are you, Trevanian?" Norman slumped back to await his buddy's comment, and meanwhile stared at the aquamarine water of the hotel's raised pool. It reminded me of the cenotes that dotted the Yucatán landscape.

"You aren't going to partner with her, are you?" He

was making a concerted effort to distract Luke from his blowout with his brother.

Luke nodded and thanked the server who brought us our second round of drinks. Beer for Luke, water for Norman, and a glass of white wine for me.

Luke was not in the mood for reliving that spat with Aras. He was starting to cool down, and that was the goal. Boys will be boys, I wanted to think. But did I really believe it? Colleen and I had had our share of catfights while growing up. It didn't help that she was five years older than me, and that our mother had to work fulltime after our father disappeared. Yep, we thought he was dead. Turns out he wasn't. What was he doing right now? Was he concerned about me? I had this repeating daydream that Mom and Dad would get back together, but how could they? My mom had remarried. And Ted was a good man. It would be wrong.

None of that mattered at the moment. We were spending one last night in Espita before flying to Miami. Aras had promised to stay with Natasha and Anastasie while they deciphered the Mayan shield. Hopefully his little excursion to see us had skipped their notice. And no repercussions would result.

I had spent days in Natasha's company and was well versed in her thinking. And could see how it reflected Luke's line of thought. Which now appeared to be changing tack thanks to her sister.

"Natasha believes that Atlantis is somewhere in the Caribbean," I chimed in. "She has evidence that a sophisticated maritime culture existed there during the last Ice Age. That's why she wants us to find the shipwreck."

"The Nazi sisters might be on to something," Luke

said tipping his beer up and handing a second bottle of Evian to Norman. "Anastasie regaled me with some of her theories on our flight out."

I gave Luke a nervous sideways frown. It was not that I believed Natasha when she said 'he's one of us now'. And since when did he listen to the theories of a Nazi and a criminal? But this was a more comfortable topic than rehashing who was right or wrong when it came to Aras' behavior.

"At the end of the last Ice Age, a comet crashed into Earth's atmosphere, exploding into fragments that struck the landmasses of Cuba and the Bahamas," he explained. "It left a devastating impact resulting in splintering the land into islands and submerging the rest."

"But that would have destroyed all evidence of the civilization," Norman argued.

"Not necessarily."

Really? He was going to accept Anastasie's speculations?

Luke nodded. "There is some geologic evidence to suggest it was a possibility. Meteorites and comets have wide-ranging effects. They cause earthquakes and tsunamis, and large-scale flooding. The island could have sunk."

"Well, Natasha confessed to believing that ancient seagoing merchants reached these parts around the time of the Phoenicians and Carthaginians," I elucidated. "And it was these people who carried back the tales of an Atlantic continent to the Old World, stories about a land of great wealth and sophistication that eventually reached Plato's ears. At least that's the theory."

"But why was Plato the only person who wrote about it?" Norman demanded.

Luke sucked back his beer, and set it on the end table. "He wasn't. From what I could gather from Anastasie, she and her sister believe that there have been many references to the lost land. They just didn't call it Atlantis."

Norman snorted. I smiled. Luke smiled too.

"I have to admit," Luke said. "Her theory has sparked some of my own. There are compelling local myths and legends in the Yucatán, Peru, Brazil, and the Caribbean islands that have striking similarities. It doesn't always mean anything. But sometimes it does. Oral histories have their uses. Worth checking out when we're done searching for the shipwreck."

"Do you think we'll find anything?" I asked.

"We won't find a ship. The timbers will have long since rotted away. But anything on board that wasn't perishable like pottery, jewelry, coins, metal tools and weapons or stone anchors would qualify. And hopefully satisfy her."

"If we can date these things."

He agreed. "If—we can date them."

I leaned back in my deckchair and tasted my drink. "You don't think we'll find anything?"

"Nothing like a ship of that vintage. No, we're better off searching for underwater roads, buildings or other features."

All of this cloak and dagger stuff was getting to me, and to top it off my confinement in that dingy black cell of a bedroom had made me antsy and eager to stretch my legs and test my newfound freedom. I still hadn't forgiven Natasha for having me abducted or confined, but for a few hours, I was determined to enjoy the natural beauty of the Yucatán.

I tipped my glass back to collect the last drops on my tongue. "So, what do you think of Aras' report about the petroglyph?"

"I'm not sure he would know a petroglyph from a rock sticking out of a wall."

"Luke!"

"He's not an archaeologist."

"Doesn't mean he doesn't know what he saw."

"I say we check it out," Norman offered.

Luke shrugged. "Don't say I didn't warn you."

The day was waning. The three of us finished our drinks and escaped into the nearby jungle in search of one of the Yucatán's natural wonders. We found it by following our instincts and by reinterpreting Aras' inconclusive directions. He had not waited around long enough to instruct us adequately. It was a virgin cenote he said, unopen to the public. Almost no one knew of its existence, but some rough form of steps had been temporarily rigged. It was so well buried in the jungle, though, it would be a miracle if he could find it again. Thanks to Luke's hostile reception, he decided his brother didn't deserve his help.

A footpath through the jungle, ungroomed and seldom trodden, was enough for us to make out the route it led. Someone had come through here recently and we were betting on it being Aras.

The weather had remained fair, with no rain, so, except for some muddy patches, the ground was relatively dry. Through the lush vegetation, I recognized the pale pink of wild ginger and the purple veined wild white orchids; and did my best not to tread on the beautiful flowers. My Sketchers would survive the excursion, even if my skin didn't.

There were an awful lot of bugs. And I stopped to spray repellant on my exposed parts before continuing into the forest. The local wildlife—numerous colorful, long-plumed birds, reptiles and howler monkeys—were making their early evening sounds and once again I felt like an actor in a Tarzan movie. Hopefully we would not cross paths with a jaguar.

I scrambled to catch up. We hiked single file, Norman in the lead, me in the middle and Luke taking up the rear. It would be another hour before dusk and we foraged through the rough terrain until we came within three meters of a sunken hole filled with shade, stretching across startling blue water. At this point Luke took the lead as we fell in side by side.

It was not large as far as cenotes went. Despite its size we knew it was just one exposed cave of a system of caverns, carved by underground rivers, formed by percolating rainwater over millennia. Subsurface drainage eroded away the rock, creating waterfilled tributaries. When the surrounding bedrock became fragile, it collapsed exposing the cave below. And wow, what a cave! Stalactites, long and tapering, formed from calcium salts in dripping water, hung from the remaining overhangs of the former cave ceiling arrowing towards the pool below.

"Did you know cenotes are linked to the dinosaurs' extinction?" Luke asked.

I did not know that.

"There is a circular pattern throughout the Yucatán jungle, a high-density ring of cenotes that marks the rim of a gigantic crater when a comet struck Earth

66 million years ago. It had a devastating impact on the environment, completely exterminating dinosaurs during the Cretaceous period."

"No kidding." I slapped at a particularly stubborn mosquito. "That concurs with Anastasie's theory of a comet exploding sending fragments onto the earth, one of which wiped out most of Atlantis millions of years later."

"Exactly."

"You seriously think she's on to something?"

Luke shrugged. "That's why I'm here."

"Hey," I objected. "I thought you came to save *me* and Aras' mom and grandpa from being killed."

He grinned. "Yeah, that too."

I was happy that my mention of Aras had brought a smile rather than a scowl as we continued to walk the last few paces to the edge.

Before us was a steep set of narrow, very shallow wooden steps (more like a zigzagging ladder than a staircase) leading down to a platform at the bottom of the cenote, atop a tumble of limestone boulders on the water's edge. It was a precarious descent in the gloom but we made it.

Almost everything was in shadow at the very bottom. It would be a wonderful and secluded spot to go swimming. But at this very instant? No. When the sun set the interior of this cenote would be black. And I had had enough of being kept in the dark both literally and figuratively.

"We should return in the morning…"—Norman fiddled in his pocket and retrieved his phone—"…when we can see. My cell is dead. And I didn't bring a flashlight."

None of us had. Because it was still daylight when we left. And, due to all the adrenalin in our systems caused by Aras' visit, we weren't actually thinking. We were desperate to get away to escape Luke's gripe with Aras and forget the situation I had inadvertently dumped us into.

Luke agreed. "My cell is almost dead too. No point in wasting the charge. We'll need the light to make our way back through the jungle." He shoved the device back into his pocket. "How's yours, Lucy? Much juice?"

Probably not. None of us had had time to charge our phones with all the excitement.

"Tomorrow is soon enough," Luke said. "If I know Aras, it's probably nothing anyways."

I was tired of hearing Luke badmouth Aras. Why couldn't those two get along? "They should put floodlights in here so people can swim at night," I suggested.

Norman chuckled. "But then, everyone and his donkey would be here."

True, true.

Luke turned towards the stairs. "Until morning then."

I planned to bring Norman out here at dawn to go skinny-dipping. Among other things.

Norman stretched out a hand. "Come on, Lucy. What are you waiting for? Anything worth seeing can't be seen unless you have infrared vision. Do you?"

It was a joke—and typically Norman—but I was no longer paying attention. Something had caught my eye. Among the vines and other hanging foliage racing towards the water, a strange red thing stood out.

Was it a rare flower?

No. I moved away from the boys who had headed towards the steps.

"Lucy. What are you doing?" Norman's voice boomed out of the near darkness.

"Wait, I have to check this out before we lose all the light." My hands fumbled in the growing murk ripping away strings of vine. "I think I might have found it."

"Be careful. The light is almost gone. You won't be able to see where the water is. That cenote is deep. Maybe 60 meters."

Yikes. That was deep. And we had no rope if one of us fell in. I hurried to complete the task of tearing away some hanging vegetation, and lo and behold, I was right. There was something hidden there. It looked to be an ancient carving, smeared with red pigment. Half of it was on the rock wall and the other part was submerged in the water. It seemed Aras was telling the truth.

"How old is this cenote?" I turned my head to look up. The boys were coming towards me, their silhouettes large and black.

"I don't know," Luke said. "Why?"

"Doesn't this look like a petroglyph?"

None of us had a flashlight, but Norman had a cigarette lighter. He flicked on the flame and leaned in.

CHAPTER 18

An ancient Sea god in his chariot drawn by winged horses and accompanied by Nereids riding dolphins. A Classical Greek or Roman image or—up until now—what I had thought to be a Classical Greek or Roman image. There was nothing Mayan about it.

I had seen this image once before. And it was with Moz at the castle in Chevreuse. Norman handed the lighter to Luke who wanted a better look. I removed my carryall from my shoulders and dug out my phone and took some pictures. In my excitement and hurry, my hands were shaking. The photos weren't very clear, but better than nothing. I returned the phone (to save what was left of the charge) to my bag and rejoined the boys. But none of us had time to speculate on what we were seeing. A rifle report deafened the skies and a bullet whizzed past my head. And smashed into the side of the cenote.

Norman grabbed me instinctively and covered me with his body throwing us both off balance, while chips of stone sprayed over us. Luke who was closest to the petroglyph, dropped to the ground just as Norman and I grappled to get purchase on something to keep us from falling. Unfortunately, that was Luke. And we all went tumbling into the cenote. With a definitive splash we plowed into the cool depths.

Being the lightest, and therefore not plunging through the water as deeply as the men, I came flailing up first.

I dared not scream out Norman or Luke's names, but managed a whisper. Instinct told me that whoever had just shot at us was not by accident. Nobody went hunting in the dark. "Norman? Luke?"

A gunshot. Yeah, definitely a gunshot. But who would shoot at us? Were we anywhere near a drug plantation? Not likely. Too near the hotel. What was that, an hour's hike through the bush? No more than that. So, definitely not intruding on drug cartel territory. And if that were so, then why would anyone be shooting at us?

I was beginning to sound like a parrot again in my own head. Or maybe it was panic. The brain did strange things when you were panicking.

"Norman?" I whispered harshly. Tried again. "Luke!"

Someone had surfaced, and then another sound of breaking water. Then shots. And we all three dived under, pitching as deep as we could and aiming for the far wall. At least we wouldn't be an open target at the wall, and maybe there would be a cavern to duck into. There was. I could feel my companions' powerful bodies twisting beside me, groping for a handhold and a chance to breathe as we slid into the rock overhang. We tried to keep our splashing to a minimum. But in all the chaos how could it matter? The gunshots kept coming, slamming into the water, gunning for blood, until the bullets were depleted.

Then quiet. Deep, frightening quiet.

The creaking of wood and footsteps on stone came from outside the cave.

Whoever had shot at us, they were unsure if we were dead.

They waited ten minutes. When we failed to surface, they assumed they had succeeded. A light flashed on and skimmed the surface of the cenote pool, sweeping back and forth like helicopter searchlights.

It was hard to tell if there was more than one person. No one spoke. But it was clear he or she was trying to determine if we were dead. How could we possibly escape without them seeing us? Those walls were a twelve-meter climb from the rocks to the surface.

More twigs cracking, a kicked stone. Then, silence once more. And then the creaking of the stairs.

After another ten minutes Norman touched my arm. By this time, I was shivering from being wet and over-stimulated. "Everyone okay?" he asked.

"I'm good," Luke said hoarsely.

"Me too." My echo soft. "Who was that?"

"I don't know. But it's clear he was up to no good," Luke said. "I think he meant to kill us; and failing that, he was bent on scaring us off."

But were we? Scared off? Not on your life. If anything, the shooter's actions had made us more curious. Something huge was at stake here, and we were damned if we were going to just let it go.

The shower of rock shards had missed us, as had the bullets, and we had escaped with only a few scratches and bruises. That was the price one paid for chasing after other people's secrets.

"Do you think it was just one person?"

"I believe so," Norman answered.

My teeth began to chatter, and I gritted them as I spoke. "What do you suppose they're up to?"

"Something they don't want anyone else to know about," Luke answered.

When we reported no serious injuries, Norman said, "Stay put, I'm going to see if the coast is clear."

Luke and I remained treading water beneath the stone ceiling of the cave. No more than one pair of eyes was needed to detect a sniper, and so much the better if that person had good ears because by now it was full dark. Having once been in the military, Norman was the perfect choice.

I stretched out a hand and found a rocky shelf, and dragged myself towards it. I kept my voice low as I beckoned the billionaire over. "Back here, Luke. There's a ledge. It might even be big enough for us to crawl onto."

He followed my hushed voice and joined me. It was so dark inside the cave that the faint starlight descending into the cenote gave us a landmark by which to measure our position.

"Why would someone shoot at us?" I wondered aloud. I immediately shut my mouth as my voice reverberated back at me. No matter how quietly I spoke, the acoustics in here were phenomenal. And echoed softly like the drone of a horn against the rock.

"Maybe it has something to do with the petroglyph. Maybe someone didn't want us to see it," Luke answered in barely audible whispers. "Did you get a good look at it, Lucy?"

I did. Not only that, I had snapped a photo of it on

my phone, but the phone was in my crossbody carryall which fortunately or unfortunately was on the stone platform near the petroglyph where I had dropped it.

"Where's the lighter?" I asked.

Luke's body squirmed beside me. "It's here. Can't believe I didn't lose it. Don't know if it will still work though after that dunking. Claims to be waterproof but —" He flashed it on. It spat blue sparks, and rushed into flame. He quickly switched it off. "Hope nobody saw that."

"You know what? I'll bet there are other petroglyphs in here. Either that or something else that that sniper didn't want us to find. Should we wait for Norman before checking it out?"

Luke paused for a moment. "No. We can at least determine if there is anything inside this cave. No question something is in the cenote that our shooter wants to keep hidden. Let's go deeper into the grotto where the light won't show outside."

We followed the ledge to the far end of the cave. When Luke flashed the lighter on, it sputtered to life, and we could make out the cave ceiling three feet above the water. And yes, there were pictures on the walls.

What little we could detect in the tiny dancing flame astonished us. *This* was what the gunman was trying to hide.

Luke and I exchanged glances.

Above us on the rock ceiling was the carving of a man in a boat, executed in the spare and angular Mayan style—with a large burning ball over his head. I would have thought the ball represented the sun except that it seemed to have a tail.

The light spread as far as it could, which was not

particularly wide. The next scene choked my breath away. "Do you see what I see?" Luke asked.

Before I could answer, the lighter sputtered and the flame extinguished.

"Shit," Luke said. "Just as it was getting interesting. Guess the water killed the lighter after all. I'll try my iPhone. They say it's water resistant but they don't advise swimming with it."

The blackness had been sudden and all encompassing. My heartbeats had jacked up. I tried to focus on Luke's breathing and his last words in order to orient myself. I was dizzy from not knowing up from down or left from right.

"No good. It's dead. Will have to replace it when we get back to the hotel…Where are you, Lucy?"

I stuck out an arm and felt his knuckles bump into my shoulder. He groped past my elbow until he held my hand. "You okay?"

My eyes were beginning to adjust to the near total darkness, but now I could just make out the gray glow that was the cave mouth. It led out to the cenote and freedom. My breathing was irregular; the urgency to get outside overwhelming.

"Lucy? Are you okay?"

I gulped in a deep breath, exhaled. "I am now."

Without a light, this was not the time to explore. We returned to the cenote's entrance to see if Norman was there. On discovering our disappearance, he would conclude that we were hiding from the gunman whose idea of target practice was to aim at hapless tourists.

I desperately wanted to see the original petroglyph once more, the one by the wooden steps. But if the bullet had hit the brittle limestone wall in the exact spot where the petroglyph had been carved it would have shattered. The part below the water was possibly still intact, but it was too dark to see without even our tiny flame.

We heard splashing and a figure loomed at the cave opening to the cenote.

"It's me," Norman said. "All's clear. Whoever that was, he's gone."

CHAPTER 19

What if the Caribbean Basin where the sea is now was once isolated from the Atlantic Ocean by a contiguous landmass which is the current West Indies archipelago? What if shifts in the Earth's crust and climate change caused changes in solar energy that increased evaporation rates. The basin would have dried up and cities could have been built in it, lasting for a thousand years, before it sank via some tectonic event.

And what if this tectonic event came in the form of a meteor or comet exploding before making impact with the Earth and creating all sorts of havoc as the huge chunks fell? And this all took place during the last Ice Age which killed the remaining megafauna and transformed hunter-gathers into agriculturalists—because of the comet fragments? It had a name, the Younger Dryas Impact event, causing climate change and erosion, and weak spots in the West Indies ridge—at that time a ring of mountains—that eventually gave way to the flow of the ocean.

Hypothetical, sure. But if something like that had occurred, it would sink *any* city. Especially one that had existed prior to any others.

And here it was. An etching of the amazing city of innumerable theorists' dreams. In this cave—inside the cenote. I had seen it with my own eyes.

It was all there, carved in pictorial detail, in solid rock. The mountains and pyramids surrounding the central city's temples, a palace, harbors, docks and roads. Perched on a central islet the citadel was surrounded by three circular canals crossed by a single transecting road. In between the waterways were buildings and gardens. A roofed, manmade channel that began at the sea cut through each of the rings of land until it reached the inner islet. Towers and gated bridges stood at opposing ends of the great channel. And buildings flanked each of the rings of land. All of this I had witnessed with Luke in the flicking light of the cigarette lighter on the ceiling of the cenote cave just before it winked out.

And the temples. Let's not forget the temples. These were purported to be roofed with ivory and ornamented in gold and silver, sheltering golden statues so large their heads touched the ceiling, encrusted with jewels. Could there actually be a horde such as this with diamonds, rubies, sapphires, emeralds and other precious gems?

The Sea god in his chariot drawn by six winged horses and accompanied by a hundred Nereids riding dolphins. It must exist.

Because that was what we had seen on the wall of the cenote and inside the cavern. Petroglyphs of the citadel on what *had* to be Atlantis. It fit Plato's description perfectly. Had the ancient Maya carved these petroglyphs? Or were they left by another civilization?

Neither Luke nor I had brought up our findings vocally. We didn't even mention them to Norman. We were nervous to speak out loud. If anyone was still around, they must remain ignorant of our discovery.

"We'll return in the morning," Luke whispered. "In the daylight. No one would dare shoot at us then."

The lighter had died. Either the water had finally seeped through and destroyed it (despite the manufacturer's claims of waterproofness) or the fuel had run out. It was time to find our way back, to the platform and the stairs.

We made it across the pool without incident and reached the tumble of boulders on the opposite side. Climbing onto the platform, dripping wet, I groped about until I located my handbag which had been kicked, during the gunfire, just under the stairs. Thank goodness the shooter had failed to spot it. I retrieved the bag while Luke and Norman inspected the condition of the petroglyph. It was too dark to see, but running his hands over it, Luke remarked that it must be damaged because the stone had shattered. Only daylight would reveal just how serious the impact was.

I wrang the ends of my hair to squeeze out the excess water, and slung my bag over my shoulder across my chest, and started up the stairs.

When we reached the top, I fumbled in my bag to find my phone. After a good look around, Norman declared the intruder was gone. And it was only then that Luke dared mention what he and I had seen in his absence.

I had to see that image again—the one of the Sea god. Like the ones inside the cave, it was unlike any

Mayan petroglyph any of us had ever experienced.

"And you say there are others?" Norman asked.

"Roger that," Luke replied. "Inside the cavern on the west side of the cenote. The rock art is amazing. One of them, I'm sure, is the depiction of a non-Mayan city. And the other... well, I can only guess."

"It looked like a man escaping in a boat," I said. "And something dangerous in the sky, crashing down on him."

"Like a comet?" This from Norman.

"Exactly," Luke confirmed.

"*Mon Dieu.*"

Indeed.

"Let's get out of here," Norman said. "Before our sniper decides to return."

As we crossed the hotel's stone courtyard, and approached the terraces to our hotel rooms, someone called out my name. "Lucy?"

I turned, shocked at the familiarity of the voice. I knew I must be a sight, hair hanging in damp strings; my borrowed, white tank top now a muddy gray. The skinny jeans clinging to my legs like ballet tights, and every step I took producing squelching sounds, like a mouse with a serious case of catarrh.

"Moz! How did you know where to find me?"

He came to me and took my hands. I was self-conscious of my grubbiness and retracted my fingers after a quick moment. We were still relative strangers, so I imagine he found it awkward to give me a hug.

"I stowed away on your friend's yacht," he joked.

Only now did I notice two other figures standing

in the shadows. Johnny Sayid and Alessandra Piero. Johnny was our Arab helicopter pilot and the Italian, Alessandra, was ex Interpol and a veteran member of ISORE. Both had accompanied us on previous missions and gotten me in and out of more scrapes than I cared to count.

"Big yacht," Sayid said. "We didn't find him until it was too late to turn back."

Moz wasn't joking when he claimed to be a stowaway. I grinned. John Mozely Racine was an Interpol cop. He had run secret operations before so he knew how to hide. His sudden appearance was not unexpected. Why wouldn't he come to find me? He was my dad.

"Are you alright, Lucy? Did those thugs hurt you?"

"No. Their intention was never to hurt me. They just wanted something I had."

He nodded. "That's right... Depardieu here, let me in on it. Where is it? The mosaic, the missing piece."

He seemed a little overanxious as to the location of the missing piece. Even more so than his concern for my wellbeing. But I chalked it up to nerves in general.

"Natasha Borg has it," I answered.

His pause was unusually long. What was he thinking? It made sense that his branch of Interpol, the Antiquities International Division, was anxious for the return of the Mayan shield—plus the chunk that had broken off and was lost for so long. How did he propose to reclaim it from Natasha and Anastasie? No way, after all they had risked, would they meekly hand it back to the superintendent of AID.

"Ah. So, this is where she has been hiding out. She has been on Interpol's most wanted list for a year." Moz's voice was grim.

"So, you know about her."

"I do. She is dangerous, clever, and ruthless. And she is searching for Atlantis."

So, he knew about that too. I was tempted to ask him about the artifact inside the display case at the Château de la Madeleine. It had sat there, side by side, with the Mayan shield.

A lightbulb exploded inside my head. Did that mean Natasha knew nothing about the petroglyph? Because it was the same image as on the ancient manuscript. The scroll illustrated with what appeared to be a Sea god on a chariot drawn by six winged horses, and accompanied by dolphin-riding nymphs. It was the identical image. I was sure of it.

Natasha would have had her thieves steal the scroll as well, had she thought it pertained to Atlantis rather than the ancient Greeks. Was she oblivious of its existence? Were we privy to something she wasn't?

I must brief the team as soon as we were alone. But what to do about Moz. Would ISORE accept him as a temporary member of the team?

"I hope you came alone," Norman said. "I told you what was at stake. You should have listened to me."

Moz was obviously struggling to contain his emotions. How dare Norman tell him what to do? He was the superintendent of the Antiquities International Division of Interpol and twenty years Norman's senior. Norman was a bodyguard with an adjunct position in tactical with our secret organization, the International Save Our Ruins Effort. No one knew about us. We worked undercover on antiquities rescues decided upon by Arianna Chase, our boss (Luke Trevanian's ex-wife), museum director of the Royal Ontario Museum. I had sworn Colleen to secrecy. Was it possible my sister had spilled the beans regardless?

She had recognized Moz as our father. She must trust him. But I had made an oath to keep all of ISORE's activities hidden. And even though he was my long-lost dad, it was a given that none of us would breach that trust.

"Alessa," I said to distract him from asking me any more questions. "So glad to see you!" I rushed over to give her a hug which she only minimally returned, while Johnny gave me a double kiss on the cheeks.

I glanced at Norman who was unhappy at this turn of events. Luke seemed to pick up on Norman's misgivings. And although he turned on the Trevanian charm—because the man after all was my father—his manner was slightly less warm than normal.

I could hardly blame Norman for being perturbed by the sudden appearance of Moz. He had been warned against interfering. And although I was his daughter, he had never been a part of my life. What gave him the right to meddle except an alleged biological connection?

"Norman," I said, and glanced back at Luke. "Moz is here *now*. He might be able to help."

"Besides," Moz said, his voice authoritative but not combative. "I came to retrieve the Mayan shield."

"Alone?" Luke asked.

"I didn't want to jeopardize my daughter's life. So, yes. I came alone. But I can call backup any time."

"No," Luke said. "That would be ill-advised. My half-brother's family is being held hostage by Natasha Borg's terrorist cronies in Syria. That shield is the only thing that is keeping them alive—until we find Atlantis. So, you can understand that we cannot risk you retrieving the artifact until his family is safe."

"Then let me help you," Moz said.

The moment of truth. I was ready to make that exact suggestion. But now it seemed unnecessary. The best solution in my opinion was to benefit from Moz's experience and expertise.

Indecision plunged us all into inertia.

"Do you believe in Atlantis?" Norman asked, staring the superintendent down with his piercing gaze.

Why was he asking that? What difference did it make? Moz could help us whether he believed in the legend or not.

Moz hesitated.

"If you *don't* believe in the legend, then you are of no use to us."

Wait a minute—my thoughts were buzzing a mile a minute.

"Do *you* believe it?" Moz asked the belligerent bodyguard.

"I have made myself believe—if it will save Aras' family. And because I wish to save Aras' family, I believe."

Good answer, I thought.

Luke slapped a hand on Norman's shoulder. "We shouldn't stand around in public discussing sensitive issues."

True. The Nazi sisters could have spies everywhere. Aras had found out where we were staying and now Sayid, Piero and Moz had too. We were leaving a trail like Hansel and Gretel with their breadcrumbs.

"I say we table this all until tomorrow." Luke turned

his eyes to me and Norman, unfortunately drawing attention to our disheveled state. "We need to get cleaned up, have something to eat, and then sleep."

The superintendent of AID wasn't to be sidetracked so easily. Our appearance belied our calm composure, and Luke who was normally impeccably dressed looked wrinkled and disheveled from his dip in the cenote. And Norman—well, his clothes were clinging to him like Saran Wrap, emphasizing his bold physique. And not to forget myself—I could give a ragdoll a run for its money. If they still made those.

"What happened to you three?" Moz demanded.

That provocative question was on Sayid and Piero's minds as well, but they made no effort to get the answer. They knew better. Information that was not openly offered was meant to remain secret.

I was about to mention the gunshot when Norman cut me off. "We went for a hike in the jungle. Got caught in a brief rain shower and Lucy slipped."

That would account for the ragdoll condition of my clothes.

"When did it rain?" Moz asked. "We didn't see any rain." His eyes flitted from Sayid to Piero.

Clearly not, as they were dry as bones and fresh.

I desperately wished to tell my father that someone had shot at us. I desperately needed him to be on our side. But I wasn't getting the green light from any of the team. And when I went to open my mouth to elaborate, Piero swiftly cuff me off.

"You three look like drowned rats." It was a lame effort to lighten the mood.

"I *feel* like a drowned rat," I said.

"Hope they'll still let us inside the hotel," Norman

chimed in before I could speak further.

Luke smiled. "That's the beauty of having the room entrances facing the outdoors." He shot a glance at his low-walled terrace, and turned back. "Were you able to find rooms, Piero? And by the way." He addressed Sayid and Alessa. "Weren't you supposed to dock in Florida?"

Our nimble-witted helicopter pilot answered, "The boss had a change of plans. We're in the bay. Took the helo to Espita." He nudged an elbow in Moz's direction. "We couldn't let him stay on the yacht."

No, they could not. Not without Luke's knowledge and permission. But surely, they were making a fuss over nothing. Moz was just doing his job and he was worried about me. Hitchhiking a ride on the yacht was the fastest way to find us.

I went to Moz. "Do you have a room in this hotel?"

He shook his head. "They're full up."

"We couldn't get rooms here either," Alessandra said. She kept looking at me like she wanted to say something off-topic but refrained. "No vacancies. Johnny and I will head into town and see what's available. Give you a lift, Moz?" She made the offer quickly before I could suggest anything else, the generosity and politeness atypical, almost forced.

"That would be much appreciated." He turned back to me. "Lucy, I would love it if you and your fiancé would join me for dinner."

Piero flinched. I glared at her, warning her off any objections to my dining with my father, and she collected herself and was quiet.

"Delighted," I said, and meant it.

Norman grunted. That was hardly a gracious answer. Luke darted him a questioning look and

Moz observed us thoughtfully. He didn't seem to be particularly concerned. After all he had stowed away on Luke's yacht after being asked to remain in Paris to look after my mom and sister. However, they were embarrassing me. I understood their concern but they were treating my father with undeserved suspicion. What exactly was it that they thought he had done?

"What about you three?" Norman asked, pointedly staring at the remaining team members.

"Oh, I'll join Sayid and Piero in town in thirty minutes," Luke said. "Sample the local grub."

Johnny and Alessandra nodded. They had a lot to catch up on and would get us up to speed at breakfast.

"Goodnight then," Luke said to us, and continued on towards his terrace.

Moz nodded, and called out, "Goodnight, Dr. Trevanian." He returned his attention to Norman and myself. We were both obviously in need of a shower and clean clothes, and he seemed to register the fact. "Meet you two back in town in say, an hour?"

CHAPTER 20

When I left the bathroom, Norman was outside on the terrace smoking a cigarette. He only smoked now when he was particularly stressed. Why would he be stressed? He had found me unharmed.

I opened the glass door and stepped out in a new sundress that Aras had bought for me. One thing I had to say for the man, he kept his promises. It was peacock green with double spaghetti straps over each shoulder, a tapered waist and a short flouncy skirt. The sandals that came with it were delectable. Who would have thought a freedom fighter had such exquisite taste? Must be in the Trevanian genes, because, casual or formal, Luke was always immaculately and stylishly dressed.

"Your turn," I said as I drew near.

Norman snuffed out the butt in an ashtray and set it on the low wall, smiled, reached out and engulfed me in his arms. "Missed you so much, sweetheart," he said.

"Me too," I murmured into his chest. I raised my head and swallowed his lips in a deep rewarding kiss. His reaction was almost instant.

"You need to shower," I warned, a note of teasing in my command. "Moz is waiting for us."

"I'd rather have room service, in bed, with you."

"Not tonight, honey. My dad is here. We have to hurry. You have half an hour."

He was about to say something. And it made me wonder what had happened in Paris after I was kidnapped. I knew it had to do with Moz. Had they blamed each other? But when Norman saw me tense up, he withheld any comment.

"Fine," he said. "I'll be in the shower."

I hated the fact that my loyalties were being tugged in opposite directions. It shouldn't be like this. We should all love each other because we were going to be family. I looked at him imploringly and desperately tried to hide any sign of reproach or annoyance. His eyes softened and he gave me a small smile. And I interpreted that to be an invitation to hug him around the waist before I let go.

The view of the floodlit, cerulean pool, bordered by lush green plants had a surreal appearance in the night, and I admired it before I turned. I was about to follow Norman. And opened the glass door wide, when I heard footsteps racing up the stone path. I swung back to face the pool and saw Alessandra pop out from between two potted fig trees. "Hey, I need to talk to you for a minute," she said.

"Sure." I gestured her onto our private stone terrace, and she hopped over the low wall, not bothering to detour to locate the actual entrance.

"I only have a minute. Don't want Moz to get suspicious."

Oh no. Not Alessa too.

"Suspicious of what?" I asked, struggling to contain my impatience.

A split second of hesitation. Which disconcerted me. And then she said, "He says he's your father."

"He is."

Her eyebrows cocked. "I thought your father died when you were a baby."

"That's what we were told. What my mom and sister were told. I wasn't old enough to speak let alone listen. Anyways, it was all hush-hush. We didn't know he worked for a covert organization and that he was on a secret mission that was going to last the rest of his life." I smiled sheepishly, although the effort was exhausting me. "Like father like daughter?"

The expression on Piero's face was grim. She did not smile, but then she rarely smiled. It was clear she found it hard to wrap her brain around the idea of a family being told such lies. And worse. Buying it.

"Lucy. Did you actually check out his story?"

"You've been talking to Norman, haven't you?" I accused.

She nodded. "Well, to put it bluntly. He's got a point. The guy just shows up at a crime scene and tells you he's your daddy."

"My mother recognized him."

"After thirty-odd years, she was able to identify him?" Her face expressed incredulity and her voice emphasized the sentiment. "Did she check out his history? His credentials?"

"Luke did an identity check. He's registered with Interpol as superintendent of the Antiquities International Division. His history is classified, but Luke knows people in high places. They gave him enough to prove that Moz is legitimate… Why? What dirt have you got on him?" My color was rising and I was getting a tight, fist-like knot in my stomach. Why were she and Norman so suspicious?

"It's just that, while I never met him during my stint on the force, I heard about him. And for the life of me it never occurred to me that you and he were related. No one ever called him by his real name. He was known only as Moz. And he's one of those people whose activities have made him famous." She stopped for breath. "He's taken down some pretty big, black-market organizations."

The glass door behind swung wide from the breeze. It never even occurred to me to shut it.

"Isn't that a good thing?"

A pause. "It's not… it is not so much his accomplishments that are questionable. It's his methods."

"What do you mean?" I crossed my arms in a gesture of defiance.

"I don't know how to say this, Lucy. But do you know anything about the Nazi atrocities that transpired during the second world war?"

Where was this going? I shrugged. "I know a little. The Nazis weren't above using torture to get information or just because they were so hateful, they got pleasure in the suffering of others."

She nodded.

What? She was comparing my dad's methods to that of a Nazi?

"No," I said, shaking my head violently. "I don't believe it. My dad would never do anything immoral or illegal. Or unethical." I was adamant about that, but…

what did I really know?

"I am not saying he made lamps out of people's skins while they were still alive, but I heard from trustworthy sources that he is not a man you'd want for an enemy."

"Are you finished?" I was getting upset now.

Norman had heard us arguing and came out with a towel wrapped around his waist, hair dripping with water. He barged through the door, bringing with him a puff of steam. "What's going on here?" he demanded.

"It's nothing," I said, getting defensive. If they planned on making this two against one, they were going to have a fight on their hands.

"I was just arming Lucy with some intel concerning Moz," Alessandra said.

"It's okay, Piero. She knows."

"And you're okay with…" Her voice trailed off. Their eyes were locked together in a silent wrestling match. What was she about to say? That my dear old dad was no better than—

That did not bear repeating. Or even thinking about.

"You're wrong. You are both wrong. Moz came here —to the Yucatán—to rescue me. He came here because he loves me and he wants to see me safe!" My voice had risen. This was so unlike me. I had to get it together, had to fix my makeup before the tears and sweat of my agitation made a mess of my face. We were meeting him in twenty minutes. "I have to go," I snapped.

"Lucy. I'm only—"

"I know. You're only trying to protect me." I swung on her. "I didn't ask you to."

She nodded. "I agree. You did not ask for my help or my opinion. From now on, I will keep it to myself."

My heart was battering against my ribs, I was so

upset. Both of them could see it and Piero nodded quietly. "My apologies. I won't mention it again. I just wanted you to know."

I said nothing and she spun and left.

I ran into the hotel room, tears threatening to break. Of all people to accuse my estranged father of such hideous criminal acts! Alessa was like a sister to me, even more so than my real sister because I had hidden nothing from Alessa while I had kept a dangerous secret from Colleen.

But now Colleen knew everything and *she* would never betray me like this. *Which just goes to show, blood is thicker than water.* Colleen was my true sister. Alessa was just a stand-in who had adopted me because she felt sorry for me, and thought I needed her guidance and training.

Well, no more!

"Lucy." Norman followed. He shut the glass door, making it rattle in its newly varnished, honey wood frame.

I collapsed onto the king-sized bed. Steam was still floating out of the bathroom, making the air thick. "Why did she have to do that?" I demanded, thumping my fist onto the mattress.

"She's your friend. She doesn't want you to get hurt."

I scowled at him. She was more than a friend and he knew it.

"What she said." I slammed a hand against my chest. "*That* hurt."

He sat down beside me and placed his broad, sun-browned hand on my naked thigh. He ran his palm gently over the moist skin, the results of humidity and a recent hot shower. There was nothing sexual about it.

Surprisingly. He was trying to soothe me, like he would pet an anxious puppy or a hyperactive kitten.

"Let me tell you something, *ange*." His voice softened, deepened and became a mesmerizing drug. "Whenever a new person comes into an already established group, the members of that group get suspicious. *C'est naturel…*"

I huffed. He was not going to seduce me with his sexy French.

"*Alors*. Be that way. I am still going to tell you a story." His hand found my knee and cupped it. His eyes lowered, then lifted and caught mine. "Once upon a time, there were two best friends and the best friend's ex-wife. We were like The Three Musketeers. We didn't need anybody else. The three of us were saving the world and protecting the innocent. But then one day, a feisty, cute museum illustrator in a janitor's getup fell backwards while sweeping up some packing peanuts. And collapsed right into the best friend's arms. He just happened to be a billionaire and a renowned archaeologist—"

He was referring to Luke, but all I could picture were the comical, armor-clad swordsmen of some archaic French author's imagination.

I laughed in spite of myself. "I remind you of D'Artagnan?" A hot-headed youth ready to fight the Musketeers and the Cardinal Richelieu all by himself? I poked him in the ribs. "You think I'm like D'Artagnan?" I grinned despite my annoyance. Impulsive, eager and heroic. And sadly inexperienced. Yep, that was me.

"You miss the point, my sweet. What I'm trying to get at is this. That day changed everything."

"You remember that?" I asked.

"I sure do. I even remember the exact moment I met you. And it wasn't when you fell into Trevanian's arms."

He paused to gather his thoughts. And his emotions. I often wondered if he harbored any resentment against Luke. I had fallen for Luke's charms first. It wasn't love. I never thought I was in love with Luke but I liked him immensely and enjoyed spending time with him. But most of all I loved how he pampered me. When all was said and done however, when the chips were down, it was Norman who came to the rescue.

"You were in Arianna's office." His words broke into my thoughts. "Waiting to get her signature on something, and you dropped the papers and banged your head on the admin's desk trying to retrieve them. I was there; and just before that incident, you told me there was no smoking in the building." His eyes sparkled with the memory. "Poor Lucy. Such an adorable klutz. I think I fell in love with you the moment you opened your adorable mouth."

I tried to suppress the smile. He had had to wait another few months of watching me date Luke before I realized I was dating the wrong man. "And the moral of the story is?" I nudged.

"Things change. New people come into our lives. Sometimes—if it is someone who is going to have a large impact on someone we care about—it takes an extra effort to be openminded and welcoming."

I suppose my getting in between him and Luke would have done that. "Do you think that's all it is with Alessa?"

"I'm sure it is. She heard tales. Rumors. Maybe real, maybe not. Only by giving Moz a chance will we learn what is real and what is not."

"You're so smart, Norman. That's why I want to marry you." I nuzzled his throat.

He snorted. "I thought you wanted me for my body."

He stripped off the towel and started singing me a French love song. "*Ma Cherie amour, pretty little thing…*"

"Okay, stop it," I said. "I don't have time to jump your bones. We have to get ready to meet my father for dinner. And you—you need to cover your junk." How did he do that? Two minutes ago, I was furious. Now I was making lewd jokes. "And look respectable."

CHAPTER 21

"My father means well," I told Norman on the way over.

Norman said nothing. I intended to ask Moz what he knew about the petroglyph. I was certain Moz knew something because he was here in the Yucatán, and he had seen the scroll at the Château de la Madeleine when he and his men raided the medieval French castle after the robbery. I was sure that once Moz understood I was acquainted with it, he would explain. And then—everything would fall into place.

We were to meet Moz at a local restaurant. He had texted me a description of it and said we couldn't miss it. I saw what he meant.

Norman parked the SUV on the street. We walked to an ornate plaster building painted with giant dahlias, sporting traditional arches and a stone patio, with small round wooden tables shaded in daytime by hat-like thatched roofs rather than umbrellas.

The humidity was dense and the mosquitoes matched. The piquant sting of chilies was in the air and the toasty smell of tacos. Moz was not among the outdoor tables; they were all in use by locals. I was nervous, not because he was my father and I wouldn't know what to say to him, but because I knew *exactly* what I wanted to say. Norman had counselled me otherwise, citing the less said, the better. I disagreed. The click of our heels on the stone path only emphasized my resolve.

The interior of the restaurant was small and intimate. And not only painted in traditional tones— bright reds, oranges and yellows—but filled with local color. There were few if any fancy eateries in Espita and this was a favorite of the neighborhood. Besides, Espita was not a tourist haunt, unlike some of the surrounding villages and towns. If you wanted an authentic experience, this was it.

Moz sat just inside by the open windows, with Mariachi music playing in the background.

Before we left the hotel, I had decided against being hesitant and shy with my newly found father. First of all, it just wasn't me. Secondly, I was wired so tight from my experiences of the last few days that I was ready to explode.

I was being railroaded. Free will had been stolen from me. And I was taking back control. So, the first thing I did after giving my order for a margarita was to fish out my phone and show Moz the photograph that I had managed to snap at the cenote before we were so rudely interrupted by gunfire. I also mentioned that the shooting was directed at us. Moz's reaction was to arch his eyebrows while his body language indicated he was waiting for more. Although Norman looked to object, I ignored him and shoved my phone across the table. "You've seen this before," I accused my father.

There was no point in denying it. I was standing

right next to him when we saw the image on the scroll at the Château. "It's been destroyed now," I said. "I doubt that anything is left except maybe a small section below the waterline. Do you recognize it?"

"Back up," he said. "You were shot at?"

It never occurred to me that the idea of my being shot at might disturb him. But of course, it would. Anyone being shot at would be troubling. "No one was hurt."

"Did you see who they were? The gunmen?"

"No. And we think there was only one."

Norman remained silent.

I could see the question in Moz's face. Why would anyone be shooting at us. Was it one of Natasha's men?

Could be, I supposed.

As he waited for more information, he took note of Norman's indifference to our discussion, and lowered his face to my phone. Whatever was going on in Moz's brain, he was not about to share it with us.

"Yes and no," he finally said, responding to my accusation. "I don't recognize the petroglyph. But…Yes. I recognize the image. Its significance was not obvious to me when I first saw it at the castle museum, the Château de la Madeleine in Chevreuse."

"Where is it?" I asked. "The scroll I mean."

"Safely in the custody of the International Police."

"What is its significance?"

"I think you would know better than I." He glanced at Norman who was sipping at a glass of sparkling water, watching and listening intently. He was confused by our conversation but thought it best to allow things to unfold in their own time.

When I failed to react, Moz asked, "What about

Trevanian? He's a well-known archaeologist. What did he make of it?"

"We don't know," Norman answered for me. Clearly, he did not wish me to give anything away. "He didn't say."

Moz's eyes penetrated Norman's. What was going on here? Like a challenge, Norman returned the look. When Norman appeared to resist and not back down, Moz reexamined the photo on my phone. He studied it for a while before he spoke. His voice was calm and even, and showed no evidence of the animosity that had flared just moments ago between a father and what should have been his son-in-law.

It was probably normal. What father ever liked the man his daughter was about to marry on first meeting?

"Obviously, both the scroll and the petroglyph are depicting the god of the sea. Poseidon maybe. It looks more Greek than it does Mayan. As a matter of fact, there is nothing Mayan about the petroglyph... Or the scroll," he concluded.

And Moz would know. His department at Interpol dealt with nothing but missing and stolen artifacts.

"You keep referring to a scroll," Norman said, eyes switching from me to Moz. "What scroll? Why haven't I seen it?"

I tipped my Margarita to my lips. The salt stung and the lime made me pucker. The scroll was something I had kept from Norman, not deliberately, but because I had failed to recognize its importance. "It was at the Château de la Madeleine. It was in one of the display cases, next to the shield. Oddly, the thieves left it alone."

"You saw the exact same depiction in two such incongruous places?" Norman's expression was incredulous.

I nodded. Moz sucked at his beer and shrugged. "I never saw the petroglyph. I just got here, remember?"

"Any theories?" Norman asked.

"The only thing I can think of," Moz offered, "is that this Sea god is not indigenous to the area. It is not Mayan or Olmec or Toltec and was not created by any of their ancestors."

Norman's incredulity grew as he realized where this was heading. But he needed confirmation. "What are you saying?"

Another shrug. "We have to talk to Dr. Kirsche and her sister Natasha. They have the Mayan shield, don't they? Isn't that what you said?" Moz's question was directed at both of us as his gaze moved back and forth. "There were glyphs on that shield. I saw them myself when it was surrendered to my department."

I slid my phone back and swiped right several times until I reached a photo of the shield, the one I had taken just before Luke and Anastasie arrived in the rental this afternoon. It was clear as day. The missing piece had fit. And all of the glyphs lined up and were in focus. I shoved the phone at Moz. "Can you read that?"

He shook his head. "Wish I could. But no. To me it might as well be alphabet soup." His chin rose. "Do either of you read hieroglyphics? Does Trevanian? Otherwise, Anastasie Kirsche is our only option."

Luke was not an epigrapher. Even with all of his talents, he didn't know a Mayan glyph from a Cyrillic letter in the Russian alphabet. He might be a superman in some things, but hieroglyphics was one of his deficiencies. And Norman and I… we had even less experience than Luke.

"Do you suppose, the petroglyphs—" I began. Norman shook his head ever so slightly. He was willing me to conceal the existence of the other rock art in the cenote cave. I almost ignored his subtle warning but then thought better of it. "Do you suppose," I started again, "That the—the petroglyph—had something to do with the Underworld, maybe? After all, it was carved in the wall of a cenote. And aren't those symbolic of the Mayan Underworld?"

"Except that the petroglyph *isn't* Mayan," Moz reminded me.

But other cultures believed in the Underworld. The Greeks for sure. Plato no doubt believed. Why not the Atlanteans?

My mind was running on overdrive. Would it be outrageous to suggest—

"How do we even know that the petroglyph is ancient and not modern?" Norman asked, always the pragmatist. "Maybe some practical joker decided to play the ultimate hoax."

"Luke believes it's genuine," I said. "And there is nobody more cynical than Luke when it comes to archaeological discoveries. And why would someone shoot at us if it wasn't real? Obviously, they didn't want us to see it. They wanted to hide it so badly that they were willing to destroy it."

Norman's phone suddenly rang. He withdrew it from his pocket and glanced at the caller ID. "Sorry, I have to take this," he said and excused himself.

Was it Luke? He would only take the call in the middle of dinner in a restaurant if it was Luke. He stepped outside and I was alone with my father.

I was glad Moz was here, and was genuinely pleased

to have these few moments alone with him. I needed to know where he had spent his time over the last thirty plus years. What could have been so important that he had abandoned his family and allowed us to think he was dead?

Multiple emotions wrestled in my heart. Mom was right to be angry. Colleen was justified in playing it indifferent. And me? I wasn't sure how I felt. I never knew him. But one thing was certain. I wasn't ready to hear the answer.

Instead, I asked, "Is everything alright with Mom and Colleen?"

He nodded. "They don't know where you are, but we've reassured them that you're quite safe. I explained about the robbery at the Château and how the authorities had to keep you under protective custody until we caught the thieves. I also informed them that their knowing of your whereabouts would put them both in danger—because of the Middle Eastern connection. The mention of terrorists always puts fear into peoples' hearts."

He had no objection to putting fear into their hearts?

I shrugged and asked, "They didn't insist on knowing where I was?"

"Well, your mother was a bit stubborn at first, but I finally convinced her. I told her your fiancé was with you, as well as his best man. They seemed to find that comforting."

"Oh, Moz." I couldn't quite bring myself to call him Dad yet. That label was so foreign to me. "I hope we find what Anastasie and Natasha are looking for so that we can free Luke's brother's family and get them to safety."

"Don't worry, darling," he said. "I know a thing or two about dealing with criminals. We'll find what they're looking for."

"Then you really believe Atlantis exists?"

He shrugged. "Why not?" He smiled and the sincerity of it touched me. "There was a time when no one believed that Troy was a real place. Scholars thought it was just some contrivance conjured up by some poet name Homer, and not a place that anyone should be digging for. But turns out, it is real after all. There *was* a Troy and perhaps there was also a Trojan War."

The urge to reveal the other two petroglyphs in the cave at the cenote was too great. I had to spill. He was my father. And he was also the superintendent of the Antiquities International Division.

"We found something last night," I blurted. "Inside a cave, inside the cenote."

"So, that's how you got so wet. Your story sounded a little fishy."

My dad had a sense of humor? I ignored it. "There was more than one petroglyph. The one outside on the cenote wall that was destroyed—and two others. Maybe more."

I described them to him, the one with the man in the boat with the threatening comet overhead and the marvelous island city.

He said nothing throughout my monologue and then he interrupted me. "Does anyone else know about these petroglyphs inside the cave?"

"I don't think so. Only Norman, Luke and I. We didn't disclose the find to anyone else. Especially not Natasha or Anastasie."

"Good," he said. "Let's keep it that way. What does Dr. Kirsche and her sister want you to do for them, specifically?"

"Find evidence of a shipwreck that she thinks will help pinpoint the gateway to the underwater city."

"While *they* decipher the glyphs." His tone was matter-of-fact.

At that moment Norman returned to the table. "We have to go," he said. "That was Luke. Aras just called him. Natasha is having a fit. Anastasie has made off with the Mayan shield. She's gone!"

CHAPTER 22

It took us less than ten minutes to return to the hacienda by car. The three of them—Luke, Aras and Natasha were waiting in the study. Johnny Sayid and Alessandra were in their hotel room asleep. Luke hadn't troubled to wake them as there was nothing they could do yet.

"Where the hell did Anastasie go?" Luke demanded.

"How should I know?" Natasha's reply was as enflamed as her face was red. "She asked me to leave her alone to work on the translation. I did. That was three hours ago." It was almost midnight.

The six of us crowded together in a circle, staring in astonishment at the empty space on her desk. Aras was particularly agitated, and went to the French doors in the bay window which were wide open with a hot wind blowing through. He shoved his head outside for the umpteenth time, but no one but Natasha's guards, who were now performing double duty for their blunder, were in the garden. They fanned out across the property; some had been sent into the jungle to search, but it was certain the culprits were long gone.

"They obviously left that way," Natasha said, a hand

flying towards Aras and the open windows. I never should have trusted her. I can't believe she backstabbed me like that!"

"They? You said 'they'," Luke reiterated. He crossed his arms as he stood in front of Natasha vying for attention. "Who are *they*?"

"That traitorous pig, Diego and his buddy."

El Peludo. Whose real name I soon discovered was Miguel. The two men had helped Anastasie abscond with the heavy mosaic. The Mayan ceremonial shield. How else could she have escaped with it so quickly and easily. By herself she could never have lifted it.

"After everything I've done for Diego and his mother, he just switched sides and ran off with Anastasie. She must have paid him off big time."

"With what money?" Luke asked. "She had none with her when we left for the Yucatán. I made certain of that."

"Your guess is as good as mine. But she must have promised them a fortune. I trusted those dicks; I put the fear of God into them and they double-crossed me."

Luke's lips flattened. "Maybe *that* was your mistake."

"You're damn right I made a mistake." But I could see a chip in her armor. If her henchman could betray her, then might Cham Nassar do the same? The only hold she had on us was the fact that Aras' mother and grandfather were in the hands of that terrorist. Would he remain loyal? Or would he turn on her too? Nassar needed a pile of money to refinance and rekindle the war in Syria and Iraq. If Natasha found Atlantis, he was promised one third of the riches.

The laptop on the desk chimed. Natasha was getting a video call. Who would call in the middle of the night?

She lifted the lid and, to her horror, Cham Nassar's name appeared on the screen as the caller. In Syria it was daytime; he was calling to check on her progress.

Admitting she had lost the Mayan shield—the map with the code to the location of Atlantis—would incur his wrath. If she let that bit of info leak, Samar and Rafiq were dead.

Aras was about to speak up, but Luke's voice drowned his attempt. "Not a word about the stolen shield. We will find the lost continent, island or city—whatever it is—without it." Luke's hand landed on Aras' shoulder; his eyes gripped his. "That's a promise."

Luke turned to Natasha. "Did you hear me? What I said to my brother. I meant it. We *will* find Atlantis."

Natasha took the call, while the rest of us moved behind the laptop so that we were hidden from view. The volume was loud enough that we could hear every word that transpired. Nassar was getting impatient. Natasha reassured him that everything was on schedule. We had nearly translated the glyphs of the shield, and it would only be a matter of days before we pinpointed the location.

"Make it fast." Nassar's thick, Arab-accented words sent shivers up my neck. "Or I won't be responsible for what happens to the hostages."

Aras made to leap at the computer. Norman grabbed his arm. "Don't give him the satisfaction," he whispered. "Knowing he's gotten under your skin will only encourage him to hurt your family."

Aras scowled, nodded and returned to his spot.

Natasha ended the call and slammed down the lid of the laptop. "You heard him. Their lives are in your hands."

Aras was ready to strangle Natasha, but he forced himself to stay calm. Like it or not, we were partners with Natasha now.

"How much do we know?" Luke asked the circle of faces.

"Not enough," Natasha said.

"Did your sister divulge any of the translation?"

"After she explained some of the symbols, she told me to leave her alone to work. She did point out that the writing had something to do with *Xilbalba* and that there was a four-lobed shape in one of the glyphs that she deciphered as the symbol for a cave."

Luke, Norman and I traded glances. Did Natasha just say a *cave*?

Moz suddenly caught Natasha's eye. He stood out, mostly because he was twenty to thirty years older than the rest of us. For the most part, he had kept himself in the background, but now Natasha was taking a headcount of her visitors. Her glare fell on Moz. "Who are you?"

"I'm Lucy's father," he answered quite simply. "Did you think I was going to sit cool as a cucumber back in Paris while you kidnapped my daughter?"

I stared at Natasha. I had to divert her attention away from Moz. She mustn't know he was with Interpol —or she would have him killed. "What happened with your militia?" I asked. "How did those two henchmen and your sister escape their notice?"

We hadn't escaped it. On our return to the hacienda, we were frisked. Fortunately, we weren't packing heat. All of our handguns had been locked in the safes in our rooms.

Natasha paced the floor. Her hair was falling over

her shoulders and she looked like she had been getting ready for bed when she decided to go and check on her sister's progress. Her muscles were twitchy and her jaw set in a tight line. She was feeling smothered by the number of people in her study and shoved me and Aras out of her way.

"My guards had no reason to think Diego and Miguel were sellouts," she said. "Hell, *I* had no reason to think that. They were my number one and my number two. I trusted them. And Anastasie. She was my sister! They had free reign of the property. The three of them probably just casually walked out of here with the artifact inside a sack, and took off in one of my vehicles."

"Never mind that now," Luke said. "We have to beat them to the spot before they find it. Now reiterate everything that Anastasie reported to you before she bolted. What exactly did she say before she decided to go solo."

Natasha paused to recall. The betrayal had her so incensed that she wasn't thinking straight. Finally, she looked back at Luke. "She mentioned something about a mountain god. I think she called him Witz. And the Mayan word *Ak'bal*. That one I know. It means darkness. But it wasn't until she came to a set of glyphs—which she deciphered as a man in a boat—that she went weird. I should have suspected something then. When I asked her what was wrong, she got very squirmy. That was the reason I went back to check on her before hitting the sack. Her strange behavior was preying on me."

Luke went to Natasha's desk and tugged at a drawer. The look on the boss lady's face could have melted steel, but she kept her cool. If anyone was going to figure this out, it was Luke. He sat down, pulled out some sheets of paper and took a pen from a holder. And then spent a moment scribbling before he glanced up.

"*Xilbalba* is the Mayan word for the Underworld."

"And Witz, is the mountain god, whose gaping mouth in Mayan art represents a cave," Norman offered.

Luke added this to his scribbles.

I pulled out my phone and located the photo I had taken of the shield minutes before Luke's arrival on the estate.

Natasha made to grab it from me, but I snatched it back. "Where did you get that?" Her accusation biting. "How did you get that picture?"

"Doesn't matter." Luke came to my defense. "You can thank her later. If it wasn't for this picture of the Mayan shield, we would have nothing."

He uploaded it onto her laptop so that we could get a larger view of it. The greater image of the serpent with the white teeth and the circle with the four long rectangular mosaic strips leading inward filled most of the screen. Luke targeted the lower portion of the shield where the missing piece matched and enlarged the image. The symbols of the Mayan glyphs came into sharp focus.

"Look there," I said, "those symbols are of a jaguar, a bird, a snake, a flower and a leaf around the mouth of the mountain god… It must mean something."

"It does," Luke cut in. "It suggests that a cave is the opening into a supernatural paradise."

"*That's* what you get from this?" Natasha scoffed. "I thought you couldn't read hieroglyphics."

"I can't. But it makes sense."

Especially after what we had found inside that cave

with the petroglyphs.

"What's that there?" Aras asked, pointing to a triangular shaped symbol.

"A tree?" I suggested. "A pine tree."

"Is that significant?" Norman swung the laptop in his direction to get a better look. "There are not a lot of different species of pine in the Yucatán. It might mean something... Flag it."

Luke nodded, scribbled some more, and turned back to Natasha. "Did Anastasie mention any details about the man in the boat?"

"I'm not sure. Like what?"

Luke had a fair knowledge of Mayan art. He was looking for something specific.

"Was he carrying offerings?"

I wedged myself in between the tall men and tilted the laptop to face me. In the photo of the shield there was no picture of a man in a boat. There were crescent shapes that might represent boats, but no symbol of what might be a man inside any of them.

Natasha answered Luke's question. "She may have said so."

"Did he have stars on his legs?"

"How should I know? I don't even know if she mentioned a god or gods, and I can't read hieroglyphics. That's why I had you get her out of jail..." She scowled, and her normally attractive face turned ugly. "Fat lot of good that did me."

Luke refrained from reacting to Natasha's growing impatience. "The description of a man in a boat—carrying offerings to a god with stars on his legs—connects him to the night."

"Big deal." Natasha's scowl had not eased off. "That

is supposed to mean something to me?"

"Maybe not to you. But it means something to me." Luke was doing his best to keep from blowing his top.

Natasha shrugged. "Okay, so let's just go with that. What does it mean? To you."

"Yeah," Aras interrupted. "How does any of this have to do with the location of Atlantis? If you ask me, we're wasting time. Every minute we piss around is one less minute my family has to live."

Luke ignored both of them and continued scribbling.

In the silence, the carving in the cenote cave came to my mind. There too was a man in a boat, but whether he had offerings for a god, or not, I wasn't sure. We hadn't had time to study the petroglyphs too closely. We were too concerned about being turned into chopped liver by the men with the guns. The only thing I remembered well was the carving of the tailed fireball (or what appeared to be a tailed fireball) over the boatman's head… But there must be a connection.

"The Underworld," Luke said just as it occurred to me as well. "The night, darkness and caves. These are the key." He circled the words on the sheet of paper.

"And mountains," Norman reminded him. "Don't forget the mountains. Either the cave is in the mountains leading to paradise—or paradise is surrounded by mountains."

Paradise?

Or Atlantis?

We all exchanged glances.

"I think you're on to something, Luke," I said.

He exhaled, shut his eyes, then opened them. "But we are too tired to figure it out tonight. Let's say we go back to our hotel and sleep on it."

"All right," Natasha said, as though she were still in charge. "But don't even think about leaving me out of your plot. All I have to do is make one call to Syria and the mama and grandpappy are dead."

She skirted the desk and stalked past us. She made it to the exit and stood with her hand on the lever of one of the latticed double-glass doors—our cue to vacate.

We were about to leave when I happened to glance down. Just under the desk was a rhomboidal shaped object.

I leaped forward and dropped to my knees.

It was the broken piece from the shield. When Anastasie had the traitors heist the heavy mosaic shield, the piece must have fallen out and onto the floor. In their hurry, they must have missed it and accidentally kicked it under the desk. If it wasn't for the fact that the desk was placed on top of a no-skid office carpet, the piece would have smashed on the hard tiles.

I lifted it and all eyes turned to me. For the first time I noticed something about it I hadn't noticed before. What had originally just appeared to be squiggles now had a recognizable shape. These were glyphs of gourds.

I looked up at Luke and Norman and they both noticed it too.

"The meaning of gourds…" Luke said.

"Is that they 'hold the blood of humanity'," Norman quoted.

"What are you two jabbering about," Natasha demanded from the doorway. She started towards us. "What have you got there?"

I was about to answer when an explosion in the lobby blew the glass doors in. And the pillars framing the doorway crashed down over Natasha and her gorgeous, newly tiled floors.

CHAPTER 23

The hacienda was on fire. The blast had thrown us to the ground. Luckily for us we were all still gathered at the desk at the far end of the room. Except for Natasha.

"Is everyone okay?" Norman shouted. He rose and hunched his way to me and helped me to my feet. Luke was aiding Moz, and Aras was already upright.

"Oh my god," Aras said.

We turned to look. Natasha's beautiful white silk blouse and pants were charred and soaked with blood as she laid sprawled, facedown, with a collapsed pillar and spilled glass across her back.

Norman was the first to react and started forward. Flames lashed through the damaged entrance on the other side of the body.

Moz seized his arm. "Don't risk your life, son. She's gone."

"We have to be sure," Norman said.

But Moz was insistent. "It's more important we get out of here. The whole place could come down. Whoever did this isn't finished yet."

In the distance, came another explosion. It

originated from deep inside the house. Haciendas, being ranch style, often had multiple corridors and a maze-like organization for the rooms. The bombs could be anywhere and the next one could be coming right through that window.

Moz reached a hand out to me but I hesitated. Norman had a point; Natasha could still be alive. We couldn't just leave her there, injured and bleeding.

"Come on, Lucy. There is nothing we can do. If we don't leave now—out through that window, in the next few minutes—we may not be able to."

"Don't tell her what to do," Norman said.

His deep French tone was threatening. It wasn't the loudness of the command but the softness of it that was frightening.

Despite the heat, the room went cold. No one spoke. I placed a hand on Norman's arm. The smoke was thickening and choking. Flames were flashing beyond the destroyed entryway and it was clear that that manner of egress was blocked. I waved the stifling fumes out of my face, blinking at the stinging fog and looked at Moz.

The moment passed.

Aras approached. He had no love for the woman who had put his family in danger. "Natasha is gone. Let's go." He started for the window and Moz did likewise, urging me to follow.

"*Mon Dieu.* She could be alive," Norman growled.

Natasha had caused us more trouble than she was worth, but nobody deserved to be left, trapped, and burned alive.

"Be quick," Luke said. "And don't take any unnecessary risks. The rest of us will wait outside. Lucy, you still got the mosaic piece?" I nodded, clutching it to my chest, and he reached for Natasha's laptop; it had information we needed. Sweeping it off the desktop, he tucked it under his arm, then grappled my wrist and pulled me towards the open window. I tried to resist but Norman gave me a pleading look and I complied. The wind outside was fanning the fire in the lobby. If we stayed here any longer, if I delayed Norman further, we would all fry. And he especially.

Norman tore a piece of fabric from the flapping sheers, triple-folded it, and covered his nose and mouth, then scooted between the furniture to the burning entrance. My last sight of him, before Luke yanked me through the window, was Norman squatting, reaching for Natasha's wrist as the flames encroached through the ravaged doorway.

"Hurry!" I shouted. The fire could shoot into this room at any minute and I hated the idea of leaving my man in the midst of the inferno. But he could be as stubborn as I. And until he knew Natasha was beyond help, villain or not, he wasn't about to leave a live person helpless to be consumed by the fire.

He was back with us in the courtyard within a matter of minutes.

"*Morte…* She's gone," he said, tossing the makeshift fabric mask to the ground and wiping the sweat from his brow with his forearm. His face was streaked with soot, his skin shiny with perspiration. He coughed and cleared his throat. "Don't think she even knew what hit her."

"What are we going to do?" I demanded and clung to his arm.

In the garden, men were rushing around. Most had

disappeared to the other side of the house to see where the breach had originated, or else they had fled to save themselves. Jeep engines started up and the roar of them drowned out the thunder of the fire. So much for loyalty. None of them had even tried to get inside the house to see if their boss was okay. Whoever had set off that blast wasn't finished yet. There were further explosions coming from all sides of the hacienda. Someone was very unhappy with Natasha Borg.

"The house is gone," Moz said. "The fire will eat it up before any help arrives. We should get out of here if we don't want to be implicated."

"What about the police?" My nerves were jangled and I was trying not to stamp my feet. "Shouldn't we call the police and the fire department just to make sure someone is coming?"

"I'm not certain they even have a police force or a firehouse in Espita," Luke said. "Moz is right. Nothing we can do. Not a good idea to be found in the lair of a wanted criminal. And this militia of hers is not legal. Most of these individuals worked for drug lords before she recruited them." The remaining, scruffy, mixed uniformed men scattered towards the remaining vehicles and didn't even take any notice of us.

The hacienda was lost. How much had Natasha paid for it? All of her efforts, all of her conniving with hardened criminals and terrorists had gotten her nowhere. She was dead.

Was her sister the guilty party?

Or was there someone else.

Heavy smoke clouded the air, it was becoming impossible to see clearly. Explosion after explosion boomed from various points of the house. Who was responsible for this?

Norman wiped sweat from his eyes. The heat from the fire was reaching us. "The bomber is still here somewhere. I'm going to take a look."

Luke handed me the laptop, and I clutched it with my already full arms that held the broken piece of mosaic. "You go east, I'll go west." He pivoted to seek his brother. "Aras, you take the north entrance…Moz?"

"There's no point." Moz, clearly agitated by our insistence on doing the right thing, was adamant. "We *have* to leave before anyone sees us here!"

"We've already been seen," I said. "Natasha's men frisked us before we were allowed inside the house. Fortunately, we had no firearms for them to confiscate."

But Moz was not to be deterred and I realized that wasn't what he meant. Why was he so anxious to leave? Surely, the police wouldn't blame us for the fire. We were the victims here.

He scowled at me. This was the first time his manner towards me was rough. "They are *not* going to say anything. Trust me. Otherwise, they will have to admit to working for a criminal. I told you. Natasha Borg is on Interpol's most wanted list." He paused. "Besides. Look around you. All of her men have run off. One of them must have looked into the window and saw that she was dead. Or one of them has turned on her and is responsible for this. The rats have abandoned the sinking ship—or should I say the burning house. There is *no* loyalty among crooks."

He was talking to me. All the others had left to check out their designated points. I was glad Norman was gone. The look on his face was one I had seen before. He was ready to slug my dad in the face for his arrogance and condescension.

I ignored Moz's objections and handed him the laptop. "I'll go south."

He took the computer eagerly. I thought he was about to desert me when he said, "Lucy, please come with me."

I shook my head. Whoever had set the fires could still be around. He had to be caught.

I searched my end and Moz accompanied me. Sure enough, the militia were gone, and there was no sign of the culprit who had murdered Natasha and almost killed the rest of us.

After a while, I was satisfied with my efforts, and I saw Norman and Luke returning to the courtyard. Aras' masculine form reappeared as well, and we rendezvoused back in the garden where we had started. Our search had taken all of twenty minutes. We agreed it was no use. The bomber was gone.

"Do you think this was the work of Anastasie?" Aras asked. "She didn't seem to be too pleased with her sister."

Luke shrugged. "She had the shield with the map. Why would Anastasie kill her?"

"So that she could have the treasure all to herself?"

"Maybe." Luke coughed. "Doesn't make sense if you ask me."

No, it did not. But there was no point in hashing it out with a blazing inferno in our faces. The house was lost and the last thing we needed was to be found in the midst of it.

Moz gestured at the parked cars, reading my mind. "We have Natasha's laptop and the broken piece of mosaic. Let's go."

"Give the laptop to me," Luke said.

Moz hedged. Then passed the computer to Luke.

I didn't wait for Luke to ask me for the mosaic. I didn't want to be responsible for it. I handed it over and he graciously accepted it.

We split into two groups and headed for the cars. Me, Norman and Moz for the silver Range Rover, and Luke and Aras for the Mercedes SUV.

The comfort of the hotel and a hot bath awaited us.

We piled into the vehicles and raced out of the driveway.

Already I could hear sirens.

The smoke had been seen outside the town.

CHAPTER 24

It was the voices that woke me up. I recognized them. Norman and Moz. They were arguing about something. Please, not about me.

"How can I trust you?" Norman was saying, his French accent thick and his cursing thicker. "*Putain.* You abandoned your family. Where have you been for the past thirty-two years?"

Was it because men have deeper voices? Their argument was coming through the closed glass door, clear as day. I rolled out of bed, patting the right side just to be sure that I was correct about the second voice belonging to Norman. His spot was empty. Groggy, groggy brain. I stood up, dizzy. Should not have had that second margarita. I was suffering from its consequences, over stimulation, and from smoke inhalation. The reek in my hair, even after a serious session with shampoo and hot water, was still there. Oh my god. Look what happened tonight! Natasha Borg died, and Norman and Moz were arguing about me?

I lifted my silk robe, a gift when Norman arrived a few days ago. He had brought me my things. Thank goodness. Now I no longer had to wear the borrowed duds, which were also in need of a good soapy bath. Please, I hadn't fouled the silk with the smell.

My smoky hair fell over my eyes and I tucked the front locks behind my ears, wrapped the robe snuggly around my torso and tied the sash at my waist.

Norman and Moz's discussion had gone from spirited, liberally laced with F-bombs, to sudden quiet. Did they realize they were speaking loud enough to wake the guests?

On the terrace, past the window sheers, Norman was smoking, facing the pool. It glowed azure blue in the dark of night. The live fronds of green, broad-leafed plants filtered the floodlights, creating stark shadows.

"*Putain.*" Norman repeated the F-bomb in French. "You haven't answered my question."

"When you have asked a reasonable one, I will answer it."

Norman's bulky muscles flexed. "None of what concerns Lucy concerns you—until you tell me where you have been over the last thirty years."

Because they faced the pool, they did not see me through the glass with my hand on the door lever. I gently pressed down, hoping to minimize its squeak.

Moz must have hit the hotel's bar. Which would explain him standing outside my hotel room with a bottle of beer in his hand. He set this down on the low wall of the terrace. And with Norman taller than him was forced to look up. "I do not owe you an explanation, Monsieur Depardieu."

I swung the door wide. Both men turned.

My sight set on Moz. "No, but you owe *me* one."

I stepped out onto the terrace. I may not be ready to hear what my father had to say, but Norman would not rest until he knew why John Mozely Racine had abandoned his baby.

"Sit down, Norman." I nudged one of the deck chairs with my hip. He ignored my offer of the chair. Instead, he went to the terrace wall and perched on the edge of it.

I planted a hand on the top of the deckchair that Norman had refused. "You too, Moz."

Moz obliged me and sat. I turned the other chair to face him, with Norman towering behind me. The smoke from Norman's cigarette blossomed up and over my head. I waved it away, a signal for him to put it out, and he did.

"Now is not the time, Lucy," Moz said. "A woman has been murdered. And we still need to retrieve the Mayan shield."

I leaned forward. "Not before you answer the question. Why?"

Moz frowned. "*Why?*" He stared at me like the answer was self-explanatory. "Because that valuable artifact doesn't belong to that female felon. She is probably the one who set her sister's house on fire."

I shook my head. "Not that. That is not what I am referring to. The Mayan shield isn't important. I have a picture of it. We will find Atlantis without the artifact. But I don't want to talk about that now."

He nodded, said nothing.

"You know what I am asking, Moz. It's the same thing my mother asked, your wife Eleanor, and your oldest daughter Colleen. Why? They were sent a report by the authorities that you were incinerated in a car crash when it exploded due to a collision with a fuel truck. So, why? Why did you desert us and let us believe you were dead?"

He sighed. Of course, he sighed. What else was there to do? A sigh was always the answer when you were about to unleash a lie.

It mattered little to me, but it mattered a great deal to my mom, and it mattered to my sister. It also mattered to my fiancé. And for those people, I needed to know.

"I have no good excuse, Lucy. Nothing honorable… Maybe only selfish."

Well, that hardly surprised me. Like I said, when you've never had a father, it's kind of hard to miss him. It's also easier to forgive.

"Tell me anyways," I urged. "For your future son-in-law's sake. He needs to know if he can trust you."

"I would never hurt you, Lucy. Now that I know you're my daughter."

"You're getting off track, Moz." I crossed my legs and settled back. "You have over three decades to account for. Where did you go?"

Silence.

"*Where?*"

"Antarctica."

"*Antarctica?*" That was not on my list of possibilities. Somewhere in the back of my mind I had imagined him like an Aras or a Luke or a Norman. Fighting the good fight. Saving antiquities from dangerous terrorists and criminals and rescuing people from lawless war-torn countries. Antarctica not only had no permanent residents it had no antiquities. And it certainly had no war. "What were you doing in Antarctica?"

"I was working for Interpol's Mysterious Artifacts Department."

A lengthy silence from me. M.A.D. Was that meant to be funny?

"There's such a thing?"

"Not anymore. They disbanded it a few years ago when it became clear that it was encouraging people to believe in ancient aliens and such." He noted my undisguised smirk and Norman's out and out guffaw.

"So—you were working for them." I made a mental note and tried to disregard the hilarity of this discussion. "You were there before I was born?"

"No. *After* you were born. Your mother thought we needed another child to get us talking again."

"Ah, your marriage was already on the rocks."

"To put it bluntly. But you have to understand, Lucy. We were married very young. We were in our early twenties. We hadn't grown up enough to know what we really wanted out of life."

You had children!

"But that wasn't why I left." He paused and then dug into his pocket and removed a stone pendant. It was about two inches long and half that wide with a hole drilled at the top, where a leather thong might have once been. On the pendant was engraved the stylized image of a man in a boat with what looked like a fireball over his head. The picture of the man was stained with red ochre.

The sight of it made me gasp. Involuntarily my hand reached out. "Where did you get this?"

"It came in a collection of stolen artifacts that was recovered in a police raid. This one struck me as unusual… At the same time, scientists stationed in Antarctica reported the theft of a small artifact collection, and this piece was included in the manifest."

"Wait a minute," I said. "You came across ancient... *human* crafted artifacts from Antarctica?"

He nodded. "Among the collection were pieces of stone building blocks that belonged to what must have been a large and very ancient building. Along with these were coins minted from orichalcum—"

I stopped him there. "*Orichalcum?* That's a real thing?"

He shrugged. "It's debatable. But it's been mentioned in many ancient writings and is thought to be an alloy of copper and zinc."

Plato mentioned it in his description of Atlantis.

"These coins were tested, and definitely had some copper in them. They were stamped with animal images, the most frequent of which was a mysterious feathered reptile. They were dated to circa 4,000 BCE. But it was this—this pendant that struck me. I had seen something like it before."

So had I. But I was still struggling with the discovery of metal coins in Antarctica. Why had I never heard of this?

"That was when my obsession to find Atlantis began. Don't you see, Lucy? I was getting so close. I couldn't stop." He paused and then continued. "I went to Antarctica, spent the better part of six months searching for more evidence. I was sent to follow up on a lead, a discovery from an aerial photo of three pyramids, smooth and flat-sided, not unlike those of Giza in Egypt."

I did my best not to snort, and so did Norman. Pyramids. In Antarctica. *I mean really.* "What happened."

"They were there. But the conditions were too

dangerous to take samples. They were half covered in ice and snow. Only the peaks showed. Climbing them was out of the question. My team was unable to determine their authenticity or date them. Some geologists did studies with aerial photographs and decided they were a natural phenomenon. Peaks of mountains transformed by weathering to look like pyramids."

"And the coins?"

"Turned out the whole thing was a hoax."

Of course, it was.

"Except the pyramids looked real… Anyways, my next missions were to Cyprus, Santorini, Malta, the Azores, Mauritania, the Sahara and then Morocco. I spent years in those places hunting down clues to Atlantis."

Atlantis in Africa? I wasn't even going to ask.

I had a better line of inquiry to pursue.

"Why? Why would an official organization like Interpol care about Atlantis?"

"Because of the possible artifacts that might be found. You've read the descriptions, haven't you? Gold and silver statues, jewels and coins. A whole city waiting to be plundered. All of that had to be protected from—" Here he stopped.

"Protected from what?"

"Lucy, you are probably too young to know about any of this, but do you know what happened in the second world war? The Nazi doctrine found a home in the fictional continent. They were searching for evidence of a superior race. Well, it might not be all that fictional. The Nazis encouraged archaeologists and other scientists to find proof of its existence. The search never ended even with the defeat of the Nazis in World War Two. The resurgence is real. It never really went away. And has been gaining traction over the last forty years. Our job was to get there before they did. Only it backfired. It seemed our efforts were encouraging even more people to join their ranks. So, the organization disbanded."

"But—but *you* are still searching for it?"

He nodded. "Because I believe it exists."

"So, for some thirty odd years, you've been traipsing all over the world in search of a lost continent?"

He nodded. "My last investigation was in Spain."

Spain? We recently came from Spain. That was where we linked up with Anastasie Kirsche in the first place. She was hunting for Atlantis and she thought it was in Spain.

Until she found the Mayan mosaic, the missing piece from the shield.

"When were you in Spain?" I asked, barely able to quell my disbelief.

He looked like he wanted to lie to me.

"When...?" I demanded. "A month ago?"

He nodded.

"Where...? In Cadíz?"

Again, he nodded.

"We were in Cadíz four or five weeks ago." I will never forget sunrise on Cadíz. I sent a backward glance at Norman who sat up and lighted another cigarette. I grabbed it from him and ground it out.

Moz watched our interaction, mulling over the options. Then gave up all pretense of lying and admitted that he knew of our involvement. "I left just before you arrived at Anastasie's camp. I was there undercover. I had hooked up with a CIA agent who discovered a Nazi revivalist cult called the GGG."

Gold, God, Glory.

Oh my god, I knew exactly who and what he was talking about. Ryker, Anastasie's CIA partner who died saving me. Anastasie shot him.

"When I heard you were one of Luke Trevanian's team, I had to vanish. I wasn't ready to face you. Turns out it didn't matter. Atlantis is not in Spain."

"So, you knew about Anastasie. Before ever coming here."

He nodded. "But I had never met her in person. Ryker and I met in secret. When you arrived on the scene I bowed out. And set my sights on the Caribbean."

My head was spinning with all of my newfound knowledge. I had so many questions, but no way to articulate them. My father had abandoned his family to search for Atlantis. It was so ludicrous that I almost laughed.

And yet, some part of me understood. He was obsessed and no longer afraid to admit it.

"It was the best solution, Lucy. Your mother, and you, and your sister were better off without me."

That was what all deadbeat dads said.

I was beginning to think he was right. My dad was more than a little crazy. Still, he had a point. If he was going to go off chasing rainbows or—in this case—clues to a mythical island, it was probably best if his family thought he was dead.

"Try to understand, Lucy. Your mother never could."

I took in a solid breath. His personal reasons? For doing what he had done? They weren't important at the moment. We still had to find Atlantis, whether it was a real place or not. Aras' family remained under threat. Only now, things were even more complicated.

With Natasha dead who would be the mediator with Nassar?

We had a history with him. I was responsible for the death of one of his most valued generals—his cousin. We had defeated his war plans and kept him from claiming Cleopatra's treasure tomb. He wanted revenge. He wanted the whole ISORE team dead. If he knew we were involved he would kill us. But not quickly. He would want our deaths to be slow and painful. For the sheer joy of watching us suffer.

After my father left, Norman and I returned to our bed. It would be morning in a matter of hours and I knew after everything that had happened tonight, sleep was gone for good. The sheers were wide open; we had a perfect view of the moon.

Norman lay on his back beside me. I rolled over and draped my arm over his chest and started to feel my way down. He never wore pajamas. Not even a pair of shorts.

I started to kiss the skin on the side of his chest and he grunted.

"Seriously, you want to do it now?"

"Don't you?" I asked.

He turned to face me, eyes gleaming in the starlight that silvered the room. "I am conflicted, *Cherie*. *Je t'adore*, and your body does things to me I can't even begin to describe. But your so-called father, he pisses me off."

"Forget about him." I reached for his face and drew

his lips down to mine. Usually, it was he who was the aggressive one but tonight he seemed defeated.

His response was gentle and unenthusiastic.

"What's wrong, Norman?" I asked. "Specifically."

"Natasha. She is dead."

"I thought you didn't like her."

"I don't. But no one deserves to die that way. Not even a criminal."

True, she had never actually harmed me. Just had me kidnapped and locked in that unbearably small room.

"It's not Natasha, is it?" I asked, and sat up.

He pulled himself up against the headboard, shoulders buried in the thick pillows. "No."

So, it was Moz. The man had gotten under his skin. Why? I looked over at him and said, "He agreed to get a DNA test."

"I doubt he had time to do that."

"He *did* do it. He told me he did while still in Paris. He fast-tracked the test before the wedding. He just hasn't got the results back yet."

"He will lie when he gets them back."

I glared at him, though I doubted that he could see it in the near darkness. "Why would he do that?"

"Because for some reason he wants you to believe he is your father. That's what worries me."

"Why on earth would he want to do that if it isn't true?"

He raised his shoulders and the pillows shivered with the movement. "So that he would have an in with our organization? Don't forget ISORE is secret."

I knew that. But how could Moz benefit from being connected with it or even just knowing about it?

We rescued endangered antiquities. The same thing that he did. Only we would go into places where we had no business being. Like a warzone. And where organizations like Interpol dared not go and had no authority.

"I don't know, Lucy. I just don't trust him." The dark expression on his face was hidden but I knew it contorted his handsome features because of the emotion in his voice. "*Zut.* What kind of a man abandons his family? That's what I want to know."

The sting of the accusation was startling, and I refused to answer. My feelings could best be described as mixed and I wasn't about to give in to any of them.

"But you believe his story." I kept my voice soft and calm. "I mean the part about Antarctica. And the other countries he's visited to search for Atlantis?"

"That part—strangely—I believe." He grabbed me by the chin and kissed me fiercely. "I just don't believe that you are his daughter."

Or maybe he didn't want to believe it.

"But I have to be," I insisted. "My mother recognized him. And so did Colleen."

"Your sister was a little girl. Her memory can't be trusted. As for your mother... *Eh bien*, how can she recognize a man she last saw in his twenties?"

Truth be told, I had no memory whatsoever of him. That came as no surprise. Babies remembered nothing of their infanthood. Psychologists believed that children had no real memories until age three or four. Certainly not in their first year.

"I'm sorry, Norman. But *I* believe him."

He slumped back and reached over to the nightstand for a cigarette.

"Uh-uh," I said, snatching the pack out of his hand. "You promised me you would quit when we were married."

He thrust his hand out, palm-up. "Yeah. But we aren't married yet, are we?"

CHAPTER 25

"So far, we're in the clear," Luke said as we sat down to breakfast on the outdoor patio. "Nothing to link us to the hacienda."

It was morning, the day was fine, bright and sunny and the horror of last night seemed like it never happened. We had reconvened outside, on the hotel patio. The bustle of waitstaff serving the morning repast mingled with the splashing of early risers in the pool.

None of the locals had ever seen us in Natasha's company, so no one would connect us with her. Luke shoved the morning newspapers across the table at Sayid and Piero who had joined us. They were in Spanish but there was one English paper.

The headline was jarring.

Glamorous Estate Owner Killed in Fire Blast.

Two photos of the property, a before and after, glared accusingly. The devastation from the fire was pervasive and nothing was left but collapsed walls and the stone foundation. Anything combustible was consumed by flame and damaged by smoke. The authorities suspected a criminal connection. Exactly what kind of crime, they hesitated to say. Did they know of Natasha's black-market activities, her laundering of antiquities and dirty money, and ultimately her partnership with a known terrorist?

"You let us sleep through all this excitement?" Johnny bemoaned.

Alessa was less dramatic. "Why didn't you call us."

Luke tried to appease them with a smile. "There was nothing for you to do. Might as well get your beauty rest."

I skimmed the article briefly and then let the newcomers have a gander. News spread fast. The police, firefighters and reporters must have arrived shortly after we fled the scene. There was no mention of any intruders or visitors, only mention of a body and a horrendous fire, caused by multiple incendiaries that had burned the hacienda to the ground.

Aras grabbed the frontpage and crumpled it in his manly fists. Last night's events had no effect on his singlemindedness. "Not our problem. Our problem is to find the location of Atlantis."

I saw out of my side vision Moz nod. I avoided his eye, not for any specific reason but because I was still processing his confession of the previous evening. No question his search for Atlantis had become an obsession. Norman's warnings, after we had gone to bed, still troubled me. I wanted to believe that my father's actions were benign. Maybe a little crazy, but harmless. Although Moz gave me no reason to support his excuses, everyone deserved a chance at redemption.

At the moment he seemed to have gone offtrack. He

was reading an article about an impending solar eclipse, nothing to do with the horrific events of last night. Solar eclipses in this part of the world were rare, but meaningful. To the ancient Maya an eclipse represented a jaguar eating the sun. A bad omen. Was this what had Moz concerned?

Was he superstitious and thought an eclipse would bend our chances of finding Atlantis?

Luke said, "First things first. We have to find Atlantis and free Aras's family."

And what if Atlantis doesn't exist? I wanted to say but dared not. Atlantis had to exist. Nassar would settle for nothing less.

"What happens if Nassar tries to get in touch with Natasha?" I asked.

Luke glanced up from examining some of the other newspapers.

"I believe that question is moot." Norman waved his broad, sun-browned hands over the various headlines before them. "Natasha's accident is in all of the international newspapers and on the internet by now. Cham Nassar will know about her death—if he doesn't know already."

Aras scowled. "That doesn't change a thing. He continues to hold my family hostage."

Luke glanced at his brother. Then gathered the remaining newspapers and stacked them on the floor beside him to make room on the table for the approaching waiter wheeling a beverage cart. "We will negotiate with him. Fortunately, we haven't heard from him yet."

"We had better hope that we don't," Sayid said. "Nassar is an animal. Worse than his cousin Tarek and we know what a serpent he was. We are on the top of his list for termination."

No one knew that better than I did. Despite the fact that I had never met Nassar in the flesh—and believe me I had no desire to—my experience with his cousin Tarek was enough to send my heart into hiccups. The less we had to do with Nassar the better. But there was still an issue of who was going to be the hostage negotiator now that Natasha was gone.

The waiter, a young Mexican, took our order after setting down several glasses of guava juice and filling our water tumblers and coffee cups. When he left, Luke removed Natasha's laptop from a Kevlar satchel and placed it in front of him. His gaze travelled from face to face around the large table.

"Any ideas on Natasha Borg's passcode?"

Aras who was seated kitty-corner, reached across my chest and swung the laptop to face him, and tapped the keypad. His fingers flew over the keys fast and I struggled to follow.

The…(something)… to Bim…

A *snick* and the computer allowed him access.

"How did you know her passcode?" Luke demanded.

"I've spent days with her." Aras smirked. "An opportunity presented itself. She has been obsessing over the idea of a shipwreck being the clue to finding the entrance to Atlantis. She was particularly focused on the area around Bimini. It was just a matter of logic. So, I tried the obvious. *The. Road. To. Bimini.*"

Almost too easy. But sometimes smart people were stupid.

Luke spun the laptop back and brought up the enlarged photo of the Mayan shield. We studied the mosaic image before us. No matter how many times we stared at this thing we had yet to break the code.

"I've been trying to get hold of an epigrapher at Cambridge University. But he hasn't returned my call yet," Luke said.

Yes, we could call in another expert, but that would take time. Luke knew someone who could help... But how many scholars could leave everything at the drop of a hat and on a whim? They had teaching and research obligations and... A thought suddenly occurred to me.

"Those are not piers." I passed my finger over the laptop's screen. "Or even roads or bridges. Those four long shapes leading to the central circle—or island—are tunnels."

"Tunnels?" Aras echoed, staring at the picture of the shield. "What do you mean tunnels?"

I captured his eyes and willed him to follow my reasoning. "It makes sense. The underground rivers around here, punctuated at the surface by open-air cenotes, all run towards the sea. Is there a cave system in Florida? In islands off the northern coast of South America? The Straits of Gibraltar? These subterranean networks all point inward—towards the Caribbean Sea."

Norman and Moz nodded simultaneously. Luke especially understood where I was going with this. Those petroglyphs in the cenote and the cenote cave was telling us something. Cenotes were sacred to the ancient Maya, not just because they were sources of fresh water, but because they represented the gateway to the Underworld.

My head bobbed up and down with understanding. "We have to go back to the cenote. If those long rectangular shapes really do represent tunnels, then that means the route to Atlantis is through the cenote and its system of caves and tunnels to the open sea. Wherever the cave system ends will be the exact location of the sunken city."

Everyone stared at me. Whether in amazement or disbelief was hard to say. But it made sense. Didn't it?

"What I'm thinking is that, from the ancient Mayan worldview, the cenotes go beyond the World of the Dead into Paradise."

AKA Atlantis.

Luke and Norman's eyes widened simultaneously.

"Of course. And if not this cenote," Moz said, voice escalating with excitement, "then, another one. It's worth a look... The Yucatán is directly west from this island." He pointed at the screen, and chuckled with pleasure. "Sometimes brilliance comes from the most unexpected places." He turned to glance at me. "But then the nut doesn't fall far from the tree."

Norman scowled. His thoughts were obvious.

I tried to ignore his blatant disapproval and muffled a grin despite myself. Did Moz mean to say 'nut'?

Because I was caught up in Atlantis fever. And even if my theory sounded nuts, we had to form some kind of plan. What would it take to find out?

Apparently, I wasn't the only nut.

Luke sent Aras, Johnny Sayid and Alessandra Piero back to the yacht to do some research on Luke's high-tech computers and to collect our underwater diving and imaging equipment. At Norman's urging, he tried to send Moz back to the yacht with the others, but the man refused and insisted on accompanying us to the cenote.

With Natasha deceased we no longer had to search

for a shipwreck. We were pretty certain the shipwreck was a dead end. Natasha's reading of those boat-shaped crescents had nothing to do with shipwrecks and everything to do with the Underworld.

The remaining four of us decided to do a preliminary assessment of the local cenote, and followed the footpath through the jungle. It was not quite as damp or mosquito-riddled as last time. The morning sun evaporated some of the moisture and lit the way through the shadowy growth.

During the hike we paired off. Luke and I walked behind my father and Norman. I don't know if Norman had planned it that way, but I do know that the conversation of last night was hardly finished.

"How can you be sure we're on the right track," Norman snapped.

"I'm as sure about that as I am that Lucy is my daughter."

Silence dropped.

That was the issue, wasn't it? Now that I thought about it, I realized Norman was still uncertain if Moz was telling the truth.

Norman was in the lead and Moz was beside and slightly behind him. I was behind Moz. And Luke was bringing up the rear. I had a good mind to race up to the front and give Norman a piece of my mind. He wanted Moz to do a DNA test, and he had agreed. But then I was kidnapped and that was slapped onto the back burner. I didn't need a DNA test to know that Moz was legitimate.

After the deathly silence they returned to low monotones. I could just make out their conversation. It was Moz's turn to respond. And he spoke with vigor.

"I know you think I'm a quack rogue agent. But I can

assure you every lead I have followed is legitimate. You asked me if I believed, Depardieu. You told me that if I didn't, I was useless to this mission… Now, you know *just* how committed I am."

The bit of Norman's profile that I could glimpse told me he was scowling. I understood the mixed emotions. We were all sceptics when it came to Atlantis. Our academic training had established our attitudes. But in this case, we had to forget everything we had ever learned about the vacuity of legends. And *believe*.

What made Norman so frustrated was the fact that he had to take the side of someone he thought was crazy.

Luke tugged at my wrist, indicating the two men ahead, yanking me out of my thoughts. The tension between them was electric. Even Luke could feel it.

"What's going on between those two?"

"Personality clash," I said.

Luke drew up parallel to me. "Oh?"

"A difference of opinion."

"About what?"

I sighed, and took the opportunity to explain Moz's recent confession. My dad was infected with Atlantis fever. As far as Norman was concerned, Moz had squandered almost his entire adult life hunting for evidence. So infatuated was he that he had even gone so far as to fake his own death and abandon his family. At the four corners of the globe, he had investigated clues and attempted to retrieve proof, only to be disappointed. So far, nothing was definitive. But now he was certain that he was on the right track.

To be honest, I wanted Luke's thoughts. I knew what Norman's were. And with each encounter with my dad

Norman was growing more hostile.

"Moz really believes Atlantis exists," I explained.

"And you don't?"

"Do you?"

He hummed and hawed. "I have decided to reserve judgement."

I smiled. "Me too."

Because the truth was, I was beginning to believe it. I really was. I was just conflicted. All of my professional training insisted that Plato's story was a lark, a fantasy, a metaphor, a fictional cautionary tale. But when Moz mentioned Troy, I realized he was right. Once upon a time, Troy was also a fiction—until it was proven to be fact.

Luke had no comment on my dad's peculiar backstory, especially the part concerning the abandonment of my mom. He and Arianna were exes, and although I still had hopes of their reconciliation, I saw that he empathized with Moz.

"I know it doesn't seem like it," Luke said, "but your father thought he was saving you all from a lot of heartache. When a man like that is possessed with an idea, he can't think about anything else."

I guess he would know.

Even though Norman deemed Moz certifiable, Luke appreciated my father's obsession. And why not? Luke was an archaeologist. He had travelled the world, risking life and limb to hunt down treasures that needed saving. The priceless objects recovered were returned to their rightful owners and placed in museums for all humanity to enjoy. The difference between him and Moz was that Moz was fanatical. Luke knew when a thing was over. And Moz?

That was the million-dollar question.

This time the cenote was filled with sunshine instead of shadows. If I had thought to take the time to live in the moment, I would have wallowed in just how tranquil and blue the water appeared and how golden the sun made the rocks, transforming the surrounding plants into luminous greenery, like emeralds. But time was racing, and the first thing I saw when we arrived at the bottom of the stairs was the smashed petroglyph of the charioteer. Most of it was destroyed, especially the representation of the wheeled Sea god and his winged horses, and some of the dolphin-riding nymphs. Below the waterline however, portions of the sea nymphs and dolphins had survived.

Luke squatted at the edge of the stone platform and indicated the formerly decorated wall to Moz. "What do you make of this?"

Moz was very quiet as he examined the splintered remains of the petroglyph.

Why did he not mention the scroll at the castle in Chevreuse? It depicted the same image, and doubtless had some connection to this place. Whatever his reasons for staying mum I chose to respect. This was no time for a spirited debate.

We were prepared with swim suits underneath our street clothes. We stripped, leaving our clothing piled on the limestone blocks. I hoped they would be safe there. Someone had shot at us the other evening. And although it was unlikely to happen in broad daylight, one couldn't be too careful in a country overrun by drug cartels and illegal militias.

Norman, still recovering from his heated dialogue with my dad, took the lead. It was clear Moz pushed his buttons. And I so wished it were otherwise. I loved this man more than life itself. He was the Romeo to my Juliet, the Rhett Butler to my Scarlett O'Hara. The Tarzan to my Jane. If he and Moz were destined to be enemies, I would be forever miserable.

Norman dived into the deep pool in the direction of the cave. The rest of us followed. The water felt glorious, the sun sparkling on its surface. Before following the others, I surfaced and took a strong look around.

On the opposite side below the waterline, it appeared that there might be another cave or alcove. One there as well to the north. Or were my eyes, and the sunlight and shadows playing tricks on me? At the bank with the stone platform and the stairs there might also be a cavern just behind the steps. Or against just a very dark shadow.

It wouldn't be unusual, I realized, considering most of the Yucatán was connected underground by waterways and sinkholes. I turned to point out my observation to the others. But they were already halfway to the cave.

Less loitering and more action I admonished myself. And took long, deep strokes across the tranquil pool. By the time I made it under the overhang I had completely forgotten what I had observed. My only thought now was what lay before me.

From where did this underground waterway derive and to what spot on the coast did it drain? If it did in fact empty at all. It could be a dead end. And if it wasn't? Did we have to worry about tides and currents? If we found ourselves here at the wrong time, could we be trapped by the tide and swept downriver if we swam too deep inside the caverns? It was well known that the caves and caverns were connected by tunnels, and ran deep under the towns and cities of the Yucatán.

Once inside the dark opening, Norman asked me to point out where Luke and I had located the other petroglyphs. We had diving lights attached to headbands and switched them on.

At the far side, I pointed up. We had also brought handheld waterproof flashlights. Luminescence bloomed over the rock ceiling. And Moz's jaw dropped at the sight of the carved man in the boat. My eyes swelled when I realized the pigment coloring the man's skin had survived the ravages of time, red ochre like the image on Moz's pendant.

Other than this one and that of the island city, there was one other petroglyph that Luke and I had missed the night we took refuge here. It was a carving of a feathered serpent, a recognizable deity, even to me.

Moz's eyes glittered in the light of my headlamp. "We need to go to Chichén Itzá," he whispered.

I suppose it was as good a place as any to start searching for clues to the Gateway. And we were all in agreement that a tunnel was the gateway. However, Chichén Itzá was a stab in the dark.

"Why there?" I asked.

Luke's brow suddenly rose like a lightbulb flashed in his head. "*Chichén Itzá* means 'at the mouth of the well of *Itzá*'."

Moz nodded vigorously. "'*Chi* means mouth. The Mayan word *Che'en* or *Chén* means well. And *Itzá* is translated as 'Enchanter of the water'."

CHAPTER 26

There is a temple in Chichén Itzá called Kukulcán. It was built for the Yucatec Maya Feathered Serpent god. The temple is at the top of a stone pyramid with square terraces and stairways up the four sides. Sculptures of plumed snakes run along the plane of the northern balustrade. And during spring equinox, the late afternoon sun casts a number of triangular shadows creating the illusion of a feathered serpent crawling down the temple. Every year, thousands of tourists gather at the site to see it.

It was Monday and the prehistoric city was closed to tourists. We were alone at the site after Luke had fast-tracked VIP permits from the National Institute of Anthropology and History. These permits allowed us to visit the monuments unimpeded as a scientific team, and even climb them. Which was prohibited ever since a woman had fallen to her death from the top of the pyramid years ago. We had permission to explore the temple at the peak, but were restricted from doing anything invasive—like excavating under the pyramid. Which was exactly what Luke wished to do.

Cenotes aligned to the ancient city—at the four

directions radiating from the pyramid. These below ground lakes had breached surfaces, and were not developed for access to swimmers. Many tourists swarmed the natural sinkholes for a look at the beauty of the geological phenomena, and their depths were relatively unexplored. Luke decided it was unlikely that any of them would hold significant clues to the direction of Atlantis. Only the Sacred Cenote might hide a clue. That particular sinkhole lay north of the temple and was filled with blue water and was thick with aquatic vegetation, making it difficult for exploratory diving. When we had our gear, we would test that option but for now, it was Kukulcán that held our interest.

Apparently, another cenote, a hidden sinkhole, lay directly beneath the pyramid, upon which we now climbed. Scientists had discovered its existence through a sophisticated imaging technique called Electrical Resistivity Tomography. They had determined that the pyramid had been built right on top of an underground lake and that it was large, 25 by 35 meters wide and 20 meters deep, with the water filling the cavern running north south. This mysterious sinkhole could very well represent the entrance to Hell. The Yucatec Maya believed in a double concept of the Afterlife—Paradise and Hell. Paradise was somewhere in the sea. And Hell...?

That was what we were here to discover.

All four sides of the temple had a 91-step staircase and—with the final one being the temple platform at the peak—added up to 365 steps, which equaled the days of the year.

I raised my sight in awe at the 24-meter-high

pyramid. It was a steep and dangerous ascent. There were no handrails and I was surprised that there were not more documented accidents in the days when the public still had access to the stairs.

There was no entry to the cenote through the summit temple. But that wasn't why Luke wanted to climb to the top. He wanted an aerial view, to see if he could trace the mapped course of the underground rivers against the topography of the surface landscape. He had maps of the subterranean aquifers. He had borrowed them from a buddy of his who had headed a mapping project of underground lakes and rivers throughout the Yucatán. This was one of the perks of being a billionaire archaeologist. If you helped to sponsor a project, they owed you one. And email made the acquisition of the results almost instant.

The view from up here was breathtaking. As expected, I saw no bridges, rivers, lakes or streams, and could only imagine the vast underground river that coursed beneath our feet. The thin layer of soil that supported the Northern Yucatán's dense, scrubby jungle met the southern horizon in low blue hills. The sun was steep, creating a landscape painting of pinks, rust and dark mauve in natural and manmade structures.

While the men sent a small drone flying across the site, receiving readouts even as we stood there gasping in the view, I decided to do some exploring of my own. The temple lacked doors and was open to the outside, so the temptation was irresistible.

Past excavations had revealed multiple temples. Or chambers. Inside the one called the Hall of Offerings was a Chacmool, a statue of a reclining man with a bowl in his lap meant to hold offerings to the gods. Its nails, teeth, and eyes were inlaid with frosty mother-of-pearl.

The next room labeled the Chamber of Sacrifices was empty except for two parallel rows of human bones, their yellowed skulls and femurs distinctive and easily identifiable, embedded in the back wall.

Deeper in the interior was the Throne Room where stood a stone seat carved like a jaguar. It was painted in red cinnabar and decorated with black flint and green stone discs. As the epicenter, Kukulcán was flanked on the north, south, east, and west by cenotes, placing the temple in the middle of the configuration. It was said that whoever occupied this throne sat at the center of the world.

If this room was the Mayan *axis mundi*, then how would one travel from the center of the world to Paradise or to Hell?

The bone room was oriented north-northeast. There was an ancient ossuary on the grounds, oriented in the opposite direction. Were they connected? An ossuary is any container or chamber meant to house human remains. I remembered Luke pointing it out when we arrived on the site. Sometimes caves and tunnels were used for ossuaries…

I ran outside to see if the boys were finished with the drone. They were excitedly discussing a find on Luke's tablet where the Ground Penetrating Radar readings were displayed in peaks and valleys.

Moz was speaking. "Trevanian." He was pointing to something on the screen. "I think we can gain access to the cenote under this pyramid through—"

"The Ossuary," I said.

Moz's eyes widened in astonishment. Luke nodded,

and Norman simply smiled. I no longer surprised my colleagues—who were also my friend and my fiancé—with my deductions.

"How did you know?" Moz asked. Because the readings on the GPR agreed.

"Something I saw inside." And I proceeded to explain my line of reasoning.

They followed me inside the temple and examined the multiple levels.

After a while, Luke opened his tablet. "It does make sense... And the readings from the drone verify it... Let's go down. And be careful. The sun will set soon and we'll be working in the dark."

It was the only time we could do what we planned. The authorities would never give us permission to excavate on such short notice. And we did not have the time to wait. Who knows how long Nassar would give us before he got fed up and killed the hostages?

By the time we descended the pyramid the sun was low in the sky. We moved our vehicles down the road to a place where they were less conspicuous. Then we retrieved the equipment we had managed to purchase at local stores in the nearest town. We had one chance to do this. And it was tonight. Monday was the only day the popular tourist site was closed. By tomorrow, the area would be teaming with visitors, and continue well into the night when the lightshow began.

The Ossuary was between Kukulcán and the Caracol Observatory, not too far away. The site map Luke had in his possession showed that the Ossuary had a subterranean cavern beneath it, where human remains were discovered in the 19th century. Originally these were thought to be the skeletons of high priests. But further research had left investigators in doubt. No difference to us. They were bones of the dead. And the dead, no matter who they were, must be treated with respect.

The walk back to the grounds took fifteen minutes. By the time we reached the Ossuary it was near nightfall. We lowered shovels, picks, and backpacks loaded with headlamps, water bottles and small digging tools to the dead grass at our feet.

Luke switched on his flashlight. "It says here in the tourist pamphlet that the cave leads to a tunnel, but the tunnel was blocked off by the ancient Maya, who never meant for people to enter."

"Where is the entrance?" Moz asked.

"Somewhere at the top."

We collected our things and looked up. Deep shadow fell over us and to the east the sun was sinking. The loss of daylight would have no bearing on our adventure as we would be inside the pyramid and then, hopefully, underground.

The Ossuary appeared to be a mini replica of Kukulcán. Only ten meters high, it was built from nine stacked blocks with stairs on all four sides and carved balustrades with interlocking snakes at the top, accented with turquoise discs. As we climbed over the bust, I noticed bas-reliefs serpents, birdmen, human figures with godlike masks and Mayan inscriptions.

The remnants of a temple appeared at the summit. When we reached it and looked down, a jagged opening yawned with a set of steep, uncertain stairs leading to the bottom.

At the base of the worn stone steps, we found ourselves inside a large, roughly-hewn cave. Years back, some locals and then archaeologists had ventured through this space. They had located a tunnel, which the authorities later sealed to prevent tourists from exploring and injuring themselves or getting lost.

"The tunnel is supposed to be twenty kilometers long ending at the ancient Mayan city of Yaxuná," Luke said.

But this wasn't the tunnel he was hunting for. There was another one. On the north wall. I was sure of it. And that one led to the cenote beneath the pyramid of Kukulcán.

We looked around in awe. The space had been deliberately created, and the bodies originally discovered in here indicated that it was a crypt for the deceased. All artifacts found in this cavern had been removed.

We were, in fact, right under the pyramid of the Ossuary, and this cave was supposed to represent the threshold between the world of the dead and paradise.

It was here that seven tombs were found along with crystals, jade objects, copper bells and shell beads.

Luke got down on his knees to examine the walls.

"Ah, look at this." He was inspecting a section of the bulkhead with loose stones, the light from his headlamp washing back and forth as he moved. "Someone has already been here. This is either the work of the archaeologists, the ancient Maya, modern looters, or someone else. These stones wobble... Hand me a trowel."

I dug into my backpack and fetched him the tool. He used it to scrape around the stones until they loosened further.

Norman, also outfitted with a headlamp,

approached with a crowbar. "*Alors.* Let me try it with this."

Luke stepped aside and Norman wedged the tool between two rocks and jerked them free. They tumbled onto the floor. He repeated the procedure until he had a hole widened large enough for a man to pass through. He thrust his flashlight in, followed by his head. "Definitely a passageway," he said.

"Who wants to do the honors?" Luke asked. "Lucy? Moz? Since the two of you thought of it—"

We heard a faint sound like that of falling rocks. Had it come from inside or outside the tunnel?

"Maybe I better go first," Norman said. "This passageway might not be stable."

CHAPTER 27

Norman listened for the sound of anymore falling rubble. He pocketed the trowel in his rear pants pocket, adjusted his headlamp, and disappeared inside the tunnel. It was only spacious enough for us to crawl on hands and knees in single file, and only I was low enough to carry a backpack. So, I was delegated with the job of carrying what little gear we could stuff inside it, and that included water and protein bars.

Norman led while Luke followed, then I came next and Moz brought up the rear. Norman stopped and weird noises pricked my ears as he brushed away some fallen dirt and rubble. That must have been what we heard earlier.

It was stuffy and dusty inside the tunnel. The air was so dry and stale I could barely breathe. Maybe we should have sent in a scout before we all jumped in on this venture. What if there was nothing at the end of the passage. How would we get out? And would there be enough air to sustain us? I did not relish crawling backwards for even a short distance.

Just as I thought it couldn't get any more stifling

or claustrophobic, Norman broke through into a wider cavern. It was large enough for us all to gather together and catch our breath.

"Odd," Luke remarked. "The air smells fresher here."

"How much further do you think?" I asked.

"No more than a few meters. We must be near the pyramid," Norman said.

Good thing, because I was ready to turn back. There was no guarantee that there was anything beyond this cave.

Norman had a look around while we rested. He returned and said he had found the opening where the tunnel continued.

"Then this is a good time to take a break," Luke said. He instructed me to dig out the refreshments. I passed around some small bottles of water and snack bars before I peeled back the wrapper on one for myself.

Moz declined on the food. He squatted at one side of the wall with the flashlight from his distinctive, aquamarine-covered cellphone roving across the rough surface and down across the floor. I finished my snack, took a swig of water and handed the remainder to Norman. As he took the water, I started to crawl towards Moz to see what had him so preoccupied. My hand landed on something sharp. I cried out.

Norman scrambled over to me like a great ape in the low-ceilinged cavern. "What's the matter, Lucy?"

I almost shrieked as my flashlight beam illuminated a human hand. The bones were still articulated. And the hand lay on the surface of the ground. A dead body, splayed on its back, joined the rest of the hand. And must have been there for centuries. No attempt had been made to bury it. The corpse lay entirely exposed on the surface. Was it recent or old? Had someone interred the body deliberately or was this an escape route. Or had somebody stumbled across the cave just as we had, and got lost? Either way, they would have died here, disoriented, and starved or thirsted to death.

"A mummy," Norman said to Luke's look of inquiry. "It's pretty well preserved considering how old it must be. These cave conditions—the lack of moisture—conserved it..."

Luke hunched beside me inspecting the find, and Moz joined us.

"A mummy indeed," Moz said. "Some of the clothing is still intact, although ready to disintegrate. And the flesh is entirely desiccated, leaving nothing but dried skin and bone."

I could see now that the clothing was definitely not contemporary. The dead figure wore some kind of loincloth with a fallen cloak woven from cotton and sisal on its back.

Luke nodded and the light from his headlamp waved, creating bobbing shadows. "And look what it has in its other arm."

The wooden box I stared at was small. And easily overlooked. Except for the fact that it was engraved with familiar motifs. And in the same strange style as I had seen earlier. Here once more were the Sea god, winged horses, and nymphs riding dolphins.

"Definitely not Mayan," Luke said, squatting for a better look.

"I agree." This from Norman who hunched down bedside him.

"Who then?" I asked.

"The Atlanteans," Moz answered.

Our heads jerked upward, although no one said a word.

I unslung the backpack from my tingling spine and removed a pair of cotton gloves. I dropped to my haunches and gently nudged the wooden box out from under the mummy's arm. When free, I slid it across the smooth stone floor towards Luke.

"Shall we see what's inside this?"

"You do the honors," Luke said. "You've got the gloves."

I gently tried to lift the lid but it refused to budge. Centuries of sitting here immobile had stiffened the joins. I pried it off by gouging my fingernails into the edge and pulled. The lid popped free and revealed its treasure of coral, obsidian and turquoise objects. Tiny figurines of sea creatures, some of which were dolphin effigies.

"Wow," I whispered.

"These are exquisite." Moz gently prodded at the discovery with the tip of his finger.

Norman leaned forward and shined his flashlight on the largest figurine. A likeness of the Sea god made of turquoise. There were also a pair of winged horses carved from coral, their craftmanship so fine, I doubted whether an artist could have matched them today. The dolphin figures, sculpted from black obsidian, were glassy as crystal and gleamed under the artificial light of our flashlights. Each miniature sculpture was perfect and glossy as though they were crafted only yesterday.

We were afraid to touch them because of their fragility. They would shatter if dropped. I could see that one of the obsidian dolphins had chipped, revealing a razor-sharp edge. This was the only one I dared pick up.

It was already broken. And these bulky gloves ruined my dexterity. So, if I wanted to be certain of the objects staying intact, I would have to remove them. I did and lifted the damaged dolphin with bare fingers.

"They look like game pieces," Norman said.

Luke agreed. "But what kind of game would they have played? These pieces are so elaborate. Almost Greek in style but not quite. More stylized and yet they bear no resemblance to any known pre-Columbian board game pieces."

However, that didn't necessarily mean anything. Game pieces of unknown origin or provenance were constantly discovered in archaeological sites. There really was no way to know if they truly were game pieces or how the game was played.

"They certainly are unusual," Moz added.

Norman leaned over to study the tiny sculptures more closely without touching them. He repeated the question that was in all of our minds. "I wonder who these belonged to?"

Silence reigned as we reexamined the question.

"They belong to me," someone said, breaking the silence.

We all turned in the direction of the familiar voice.

Anastasie Kirsche climbed out from the opposite tunnel holding a Sig Sauer pistol.

CHAPTER 28

Three men followed. The turncoats Diego and Miguel aka El Peludo and one other unknown to me. They all had handguns and they were aimed at us.

Four against four. We could have taken them except that they had firearms and we had none. The last thing we had thought to pack were guns. Why would we need them on a caving adventure?

Anastasie smiled. "Put the lid back on and stand up. Then slide the box over to me."

"Where did you come from," Luke demanded to distract her. Although he did slowly rise to his feet after covering the box, and the rest of us did as well. The box remained on the ground.

"You saw where I came from." Her head twitched towards the opposite tunnel, while her gun remained fixed on him.

"What's through there?"

"Wouldn't you like to know," she taunted.

"Well, if you're going to kill us anyway, why shouldn't you tell us? I would like to know before I die."

What was all this talk about dying? He wasn't just

going to give up?

Then I saw what Luke was doing. Keep her talking and eventually an opportunity would arise where we could turn the tables without casualties.

"The box," she said. "*Now*."

Luke looked down and nudged it gently with his foot. Diego went over and picked it up.

"Is it the secret cenote?" I asked innocently, gesturing at the tunnel. "Is that what you saw in there?"

Anastasie looked up at me in surprise. She must have known we had figured out as much as she had. Otherwise, why would we be here in the same place?

It seemed she was going to ignore my question, then changed her mind. She always did love playing games. "There's an underground lake there, yes, but nothing else."

From the looks of her and her cronies she had come totally unprepared to explore the cenote. She would need diving gear for that.

Just how much did she know? What had the shield revealed to her?

"Tell us what the glyphs on the mosaic shield said," I begged. I was not beneath begging when my life was at stake. "Please. At least we will get to know, dying."

She laughed. "I always did like you, Lucy. You are so insightful. But too much of a goody-goody, so you can never be successful. You have to be ruthless if you want to be a success."

I gave her my best doe eyes.

"Hell, what could it hurt, because you're right." She snorted. "None of you are going anywhere."

She commanded all of us to sit, then gave orders for her compatriots to bind our wrists and ankles with plastic zip ties. Why were they carrying zip ties with them? The most logical reason would be because they were expecting us.

She said, "The glyphs on the ceremonial shield translate to: 'The Gateway to Paradise is through the Place of Fright'."

And that would be Hell. The Underworld. We had figured out that much without the translation.

"Happy now?" she asked. "You know what the glyphs say."

"Is that all?" Luke demanded.

"That's all I'm telling you."

"And you think the Gateway… is the cenote?" I asked.

Luke, Norman and Moz recognized that I was gaining ground being their spokesperson, and all three decided to remain mute.

Her nod was vague. "Except it doesn't make sense to me." A pause. "How could Atlantis be at the bottom of the cenote? We had a look at it. It is large as far as cenotes go, but it is hardly the size of a continent or even an island. Granted, it *is* deep."

So, she hadn't figured it out. She thought the lost civilization was at the bottom of the cenote that was buried beneath the pyramid of Kukulcán.

I exchanged glances with Luke and caught Moz's glance as well. I swear Anastasie's thinking was skewed. How could an entire civilization get buried in a cenote?

However, she was a fanatic. As bad, maybe even worse, than Moz. Most definitely worse. Moz would not kill us to get to Atlantis.

She retrieved the wooden chest holding the figurines from Diego, and shoved it into her backpack.

How had she missed that mummy and its treasure? Because the only way into this cave was from the Ossuary.

Maybe, in their hurry, they had missed the desiccated body.

She signaled for the men that she was leaving. I couldn't let her go just yet. There was so much I wanted to know. Surely, there was more to the glyphs than just the statement that the Gateway to Paradise was through the Place of Fright?

"Why *that* cenote? Why the hidden one under the pyramid?" I demanded.

She swung around impatiently. "Because, it is the *axis mundi*. The center of the world. Where else would the Gateway to Paradise be? And what could be Paradise except for Atlantis?"

That part made sense. I had come to that conclusion myself.

"You're just going to leave us here?" I shouted, as she gestured for her men to precede her into the tunnel.

"You'll live. For a little while… I may need your help."

"There is no way we are going to help you, Anastasie," Norman growled.

"Oh, I don't know about that." She looked from him to Luke, brushing her flashlight beam from one handsome face to the other. "You both dive, don't you? Well, *I* don't. It will save me having to hire divers that I may or may not be able to trust."

"If you want our help," Luke said. "You had better let us go."

She shook her head. "Better that I know where all of you are." She swung back, and threw over her shoulder,

"Don't worry. I will return."

Their flashlights disappeared inside the tunnel. We sat, lined up against the back wall of the cave, legs bent, hands bound in front of us. Anastasie had left us the backpack and our flashlights after searching for weapons and finding nothing but a switchblade and trowels—which she took—but God knew how long the batteries would last.

"Time to get out of here," I said, my headlamp dipping down to shine on my feet.

"What?" Luke twisted to look at me. "How? She took the knife and anything else we could cut these plastic ties with."

"She didn't take this," I said, fumbling around in the dark. I had managed to retain the chipped obsidian dolphin figurine in one of the gloves and slide it under my bent knees. Anastasie and her henchmen hadn't noticed because of the numerous shadows bouncing around in the mobile light.

Moz leaned over to see what I had in my hands. "That's my girl."

"She is *not* your girl," Norman said, and cursed.

I struggled with the sharp edge, trying to angle it with my bound hands without success. "Now is not the time… Please, Norman. Help me with this."

He didn't need anything sharp to cut the ties from his own wrists. He slammed his fists outward against his chest and the plastic ties snapped.

He took the figurine from my grip, and using the broken end, began to saw my wrists free. I rubbed the sore spots while he cut my ankles loose and then I took the damaged figurine and freed his feet. Then we cut the zip ties on Luke and Moz, and stood up.

Norman retrieved the backpack and shoved it at me. "Time to get out of here before that crazy woman gets back."

"Just one moment." It was Moz who spoke. "I want to see what she saw in the cenote."

Luke kicked the scattered zip ties out of his way and switched on his headlamp. "You think she actually found the secret cenote under Kukulcán? She could be lying."

"I'm positive she did."

"We can come back when we're armed and have our diving gear," Norman said. "I think we should leave."

I wanted to see the cenote as well. What could have made Anastasie believe that Atlantis was at the bottom of the cenote? And what geologic process could possibly have put it there?

"It can't be far," Moz persisted. "I'm going."

Luke's headlamp swung toward Norman. The scowl on his face could have melted iron. "We'll be back in a flash," Luke said.

They vanished into the opposite tunnel. I glanced at Norman. His stare was long and hard, and he knew when I had made up my mind. He sighed. "*Alors*, all right. Let's follow. We won't be doing any good waiting here."

I ducked my head and entered the passage.

Moz had guessed correctly. The passageway was short and larger than the previous one. I could just stand up. The ceiling was high enough that Norman could carry the backpack on his shoulders, stooped. Before we reached the end of it, he pulled me up short by grabbing my arm, and whispered, "Please, be careful around Moz. I mean it, Lucy."

We emerged onto a curving shelf of rock to a startling view. Thirty meters above us was the ceiling, which would be the floor of the pyramid of Kukulcán. We stood on a platform of solid limestone and the pool sprawled before us, about two meters down, a huge circle of deep water. At the opposite end, the tunnel continued… only here, most of it was submerged in the pool.

But what really caught our eye were the paintings on the walls of the cenote. They were ancient, untouched since the construction of the pyramid —or possibly older—and were executed in swirling brushstrokes in black, red, yellow and white pigments.

Luke was silent for a long time, then he said, "It's a creation story, in four acts—"

Moz cut in, nodding vigorously. "Not only does it depict humanity's place in the universe, but it shows how it changed—who the new gods were."

I stared at him. *New* gods? Did he mean the Atlanteans?

My vision returned to the walls. The paintings were executed in the Mayan style. To the east, a four-lobbed shape represented a cave. That much I knew. Two humanlike figures sat inside the cave. Which meant they were in the Underworld. Between the two figures were a set of glyphs.

"They're the same as was on the Mayan shield." Luke pointed. He had a miniature set of night vision binoculars around his neck and set them on his nose, and brought the painting into focus. "Those glyphs, I've seen them before. They're the same ones as on the shield, I'm sure of it."

"Refresh my memory," I said.

"It says: 'the gourd holds the blood of humanity'."

Norman also had a pair of night vision binoculars, and asked me to dig them out of the backpack. I passed them to him and he affixed them over his eyes and fine-tuned the focus. He scanned the entire circular wall and then stopped at the north end. "There—the mountain god, Witz, with the gaping mouth."

"Let me see." Moz stretched out an arm for the binoculars, but Norman ignored him.

Luke passed his binoculars to Moz who eagerly slapped it over his eyes. "Yes, yes. A jaguar, iguana, snakes and birds between plants and flowers surrounding his mouth—the cave. The cave symbolizes the opening to Paradise."

But where was Paradise? I bent my head towards the water and the beam of my headlamp fell over the clear surface. Nothing was visible in the depths except the rippling lights from our lamps. I returned my attention to the walls.

Norman handed his binoculars to me. To the west, one of the images depicted a man impaling his genitals with a sharp blade, an act of ritual bloodletting. This was the Mayan way of negotiating with supernatural powers through sacrifice. Had stories of the Atlanteans been passed down through generations and was it possible that the Atlanteans were considered gods?

The south curve of the wall showed a number of figures that might have been deities. The one that struck me was the man with star markings on his legs, explicitly stating that he was associated with the night. Another image showed a male figure wearing a headdress made from a bloody femur and an eyeball spraying blood. He was definitely connected with death.

Moz shattered the silence. "The fourth day in the Mayan ritual calendar is Ak'bal, the Day of Darkness."

"What does it all mean?" I asked.

CHAPTER 29

A scuffling sound came at the entrance to the tunnel. "It means you should have stayed put," Anastasie said.

Hours must have passed while we were exploring the cave. She had returned. And in front of her was Alessandra Piero with the Sig Sauer pistol in her ribs. Where was Johnny Sayid and Aras?

Before we entered the Ossuary's cave Luke had texted Sayid and Alessa to follow us there. Unfortunately, it looked like they had been ambushed by Anastasie's men. Had Sayid escaped?

Piero had a laptop strapped to her chest, and Anastasie's men were towing diving and portable imaging equipment and extra lighting.

Luke surveyed the activity that suddenly filled the cave, realizing incredulously what Anastasie intended. "This is ridiculous. We have to set up properly if we want to make a go of this. Your makeshift efforts are a waste of time."

Anastasie scowled. "I want to know if Atlantis is down there."

"It isn't." Luke was adamant. "You're wasting your

time. Atlantis couldn't possibly be at the bottom of a cenote."

"But the shield and the glyphs say that it is. And so do all of those paintings on the wall." She gazed at them in something that might be awe. Her right hand tightened on the trigger when Piero thought to take advantage of her momentary distraction, a split second too late. "Don't even think about it," Anastasie warned. "Those paintings surrounding the cenote tell the story of Hell and Paradise. They both lead to the same place but it seems one must go through the Underworld to reach Paradise."

"Matter of interpretation." Luke raised his hands in a shrug. "These paintings represent the Mayan view of the cosmos. And *Hell...* is down there." He pointed with his binoculars.

"And I beg to disagree. I want you and your muscleman"—she jabbed a thumb at Norman—"to go down there. And you are taking Diego with you. He can dive. The rest of your pals are going to be hogtied and killed if you don't return or if anything happens to Diego."

As long as I had known Anastasie—and that might have been around four months—she had always worn long sleeves. But today, due to the heat or maybe because she no longer cared, she was dressed in a tank top which she had earlier revealed by removing the shirt she had tied at her waist. Now little was left to the imagination, not that I was particularly looking, but it was hard to miss the tattoo. Like her sister, Natasha Borg, she had a blue Swastika tattooed over her left breast.

No loyalty between Nazis.

"Did you kill your sister?" I demanded.

She glared at me.

"The fire bombs. Wasn't that you? I mean—your men?"

It was hard to tell if the slight contortion of her facial muscles was genuine emotion. The dim lighting created all sorts of disconcerting shadows, twisting peoples' features like how kids used to hold a flashlight under their chin in the dark while telling ghost stories. But this was far from a ghost story. This was for real.

She suppressed her answer. "You and *you*, sit over there…" She was referring to me and Piero. "You—" she swung around and noticed that Moz was missing. "Where the hell did the other one go?"

Moz was indeed missing. How had he left the cave without anyone seeing?

Anastasie snapped, "Miguel. Tie them up. Tight this time. And make sure they have no weapons." She had brought more men with her this time, and they, too, had guns. They surrounded us. So how had Moz slipped past them?

"You two—" She ordered two of her armed men to go in search of Moz.

That left four to guard the rest of us. I had to hand it to Moz. It would take a miracle to get in and out of these narrow tunnels without crossing paths with anyone else. If he managed to find his way outside to Sayid and Aras, they could help us. But how exactly? We were trapped with Anastasie and her armed hooligans. There was no space to orchestrate a rescue plan.

Alessandra and I were tied, hands and feet at the front. I insisted that we wouldn't be any trouble if Anastasie allowed us to see the screen. After all, her men had guns aimed at our backs. She agreed. We could hardly cause any problems without the aid of our limbs. And with guns at our backs.

Luke and Norman were ordered to gear up with the diving equipment. Fortunately, it was the high-tech stuff the team had brought from the yacht and that Anastasie had confiscated. No way did I trust anything Anastasie managed to scrounge up from the surrounding towns like Espita or Valladolid.

Luke and Norman did a safety check of the equipment. The tanks were full and the gear properly functioning.

When the men were ready, they dived in.

Luke and Norman had cameras on their diving headlamps so we were able to see everything that they were seeing on the synchronized laptop that came with the equipment. Because there were three divers, the screen was split into triple views from the multiple cameras.

It was clear that this cave opened somewhere to the outside. Which was why we were able to receive a signal. A deeper search would reveal where it was, but at the moment, no one cared. The boys had voice systems attached to their regulators and masks allowing them to communicate with each other as well as with the surface. And that was what mattered.

The first thing that surprised me was that there were fish and other creatures that scattered as the divers approached. The environment itself was stark and barren in shades of white and red, as no sunlight enabled the growth of green vegetation. But there were rockfalls perfect for small, marine cave creatures to temporarily hide from larger predators. Not for long, however. Because the big fish had to feed on something. There was one now in Norman's camera. A ferocious-looking head popped out from a crevice and bared its pointy teeth. A Moray eel.

What they found at the bottom of the cenote was unexpected. But it was hardly what Anastasie had been hoping for.

Skeletons, numerous skulls and long bones littered the subterranean lake floor. Luke and Norman hovered over the bones for several minutes while Diego waited impatiently. He had no interest in bones; he was searching for signs of a ruined city or at the very least some sort of treasure.

But there was no treasure. At least not of the gold and precious jewels variety. We followed on the screen as they skimmed toward a strange oblong object. The water was surprisingly clear and we could make out the object quite well. Luke's camera reached it first. The thing was about five feet in length and carved out of a reddish toned wood. A canoe?

Yes, most definitely a canoe.

"How old do you think?" I asked the boys hoping their underwater sound equipment was operational.

It was.

"The preservation is amazing," came Luke's garbled voice. Bubbles fizzled in an upward trajectory with each word uttered. "It might be thousands of years old. Won't know until we date it."

"No time for that." Anastasie scoffed. "I don't care about canoes. Unless you find a ship laden with treasure. Keep looking."

They passed over pale pottery—much of it broken—and jade figurines. But nothing Anastasie would define as treasure. These might have been offerings that the dead people had brought. Were these individuals thrown in here as sacrifices before the pyramid was built over top of them?

The images were stunningly clear. I guess there was little debris or silt to stir up. The bottom of a cenote was pretty much like a clay pot. And unless a current ran through it very little was disturbed—or ever had been disturbed—over millennia. The divers searched for almost a half hour before Luke said. "We're coming up."

"Wait," Anastasie objected. "What do you think, Diego?"

Diego shook his head. His voice came across fairly garbled as he was unaccustomed to speaking underwater. His experience with the newfangled communication device was limited. If he had any familiarity with it at all. Mostly bubbles exploded from his regulator as he tried to speak without getting a mouthful of water. And if it wasn't so amusing, and if he hadn't treated me so poorly, I might have felt sorry for him. "Nothing," he burbled. "The city—is—is not here."

The men surfaced, taking their time, allowing decompression time to avoid getting the bends. When they finally appeared at the top I sighed with relief.

"What else did you see?" Anastasie demanded after the men had stripped out of their diving gear.

"You saw exactly what we saw," Luke said.

"Maybe you didn't see that Moray eel," Norman added sarcastically. "Teeth like this." He made claws with his fingers, and I laughed.

Anastasie looked like she was ready to belt him one. Then Diego said, after a spate of uncontrollable coughing, "They're speaking the truth. Atlantis is not down there."

"Then where is it?"

Luke and Norman shrugged. Although I knew they had guessed, just as I had. While they were exploring the depths, I had observed their approach to the opposite tunnel. The part exposed above water level could be seen from up here. And it appeared the tunnel continued into a winding system of passageways and cenotes. Some of which might actually breach the surface until it reached the sea. How else could those snappers, tarpons, and that Moray eel, have found their way into this underground lake? Granted those fish were very pale so whole generations might have adapted to cave living. That however was neither here nor there.

The point was, the cenote was a way out to the open sea.

"I swear to God, Anastasie," Luke insisted, "you saw exactly what we saw. There was nothing even remotely resembling a lost city. No ruins whatsoever. Only that canoe."

Anastasie gave Diego a quick look. He nodded.

"You're sure? You are absolutely, one hundred percent certain?"

"*Si.* There is nothing but rocks and bones down there and some pottery and jade pieces." Diego had collected a few smooth figurines in a net bag. And now he opened it to show Anastasie the quality. They were quite worn from being rolled in the water, which would devalue their market price considerably. "They may be worth something. *No?*"

She stared at the pieces from where she stood a few feet away from the men, then went over to Diego to examine the jade more carefully. They were traditional and nothing special. Exactly as I had thought. No way near as special as the small chest of game pieces we had discovered earlier with the skeleton in the cave.

"Then what was the ceremonial shield telling me? It led me here." She glared at Luke and Norman who were dripping wet from their excursion in the cenote. "It led *you* here. Why?"

Luke held her gaze with a look as fierce as her own. "Untie my friends and let us get out of this place, and then—maybe we can discuss it."

"No. Tell me what you know."

"I don't know anything for certain. But if you don't let us out of here, I won't be able to find the truth."

"And what *is* the truth?"

The laptop that Piero carried with her suddenly went into a rhythmic chiming.

It was Natasha's. Luke had left it in the custody of Piero and Sayid, then texted them to bring it when they brought the diving gear. Anastasie had appropriated it.

She opened the lid, and made an audible gasp.

"*Qué?*" Diego asked.

"Natasha's terrorist partner."

Cham Nassar. Samar and Rafiq's kidnapper.

She slammed down the lid without answering the call.

"Natasha may have been willing to share the loot with him. But I am not. She's gone. I made no deal with him."

CHAPTER 30

Nazi ideology is aligned with many Islamic extremist principles. Most people do not know this, but during the second world war, Nazi Germany was attempting to promote an alliance with the Muslim world. They presented themselves as a patron and liberator of Islam. They were so successful that they managed to gain the allegiance of Egypt and Iran by putting out a statement that Iranians were racially related to the Germans. The then leader of Iran, Reza Shah, ordered that his country be called 'Iran' instead of Persia. The name Iran being akin to 'Aryan' and referred to the land of the Aryans.

Had Nazi Germany succeeded in mobilizing the Arab world to the extent that he had hoped, the outcome of the war might have been very different indeed. But they had made the effort too late. And in Adolf Hitler's opinion, Germany's Islam policy had not gone far enough.

The Nazi government recognized Arabs as members of a high-grade race which looked back on a glorious and heroic history. They saw Islam as a masculine and soldierly religion. In late 1942, Heinrich Himmler a high-level Nazi official was quoted as saying:

> "(Muhammad) knew that most people are terribly cowardly and stupid. That is why he promised every warrior who fights courageously and falls in battle two beautiful women... this is the kind of language a soldier understands when he believes he will be welcomed in this manner in the afterlife, he will be willing to give his life, he will be enthusiastic about going to battle and not fear death..."

In a way it made sense. This was why Natasha had joined up with Cham Nassar. She believed in the same principles. Even though she was a woman. And Nassar whose extreme doctrine guided every move he made, had taken up with her because he thought her a foolish female, easily duped and ultimately controllable. I shook my head in disgust. I shouldn't even be thinking about her because she was no longer the problem. By now Nassar must know that she was dead, but he still expected his share. Otherwise, Aras' family would die.

The laptop continued to chime.

"We should answer that," I said.

Anastasie glared at me. She had plotted the heinous scheme with her sister from the beginning. She knew all about the hostages. But they meant nothing to her. The hostages were a means to an end. They had brought me and the missing piece of the mosaic to Natasha, and they had got Anastasie released from prison. She cared nothing of Samar and Rafiq's fate. She cared nothing of mine. Unless my life could help her achieve her goals. Such single-minded greed could only lead to destruction. My thoughts were whirling a mile a minute. Had it always been her plan to betray Natasha?

I tried to think back to what I knew of Anastasie. She was as brilliant as she was evil. She had earned a PhD in Archaeology before joining the CIA where she learned the arts of munitions and deception. She was the queen of deception. She had tricked us into believing that she was a dedicated archaeologist, and then, that she was a loyal CIA agent. But she was neither dedicated nor loyal to anything or anyone other than herself. She had even sacrificed her sister. For what? The belief in a historical tale, that even now no one was positive was real.

The chiming of the laptop was persistent. Cham Nassar would not quit. The longer we made him wait the angrier and more vindictive he would become.

My thoughts were with Aras' family. If Nassar's will was defied, he would take it out on the hostages.

"Please, Anastasie," I said. "We need to answer that."

"You want anything to do with that terrorist? Be my guest." She handed the laptop to me but I couldn't take it with my hands tied.

What was I thinking? The woman had no heart. And look at who she was calling a terrorist.

She snatched it back as Luke approached her. The guns of her men locked in place.

Luke stopped moving, raised his hands to show that he was not going to try anything funny. "Let's untie the women, and then maybe we can come to some understanding," he said.

Norman's eyes caught mine before he turned to Anastasie. His first priority was always to keep me safe. Sometimes—oftentimes—that wasn't possible. We did not work in a safe environment. Nor was our work itself safe.

"Do you want to learn how to find Atlantis?" Norman asked. The guns turned on him. Which was exactly where he wanted them. Having been in the military and then a personal bodyguard he was used to being the subject of target practice. "Then listen to Trevanian." He tilted his chin in Luke's direction. "*He* has the means to discover where it is. But if you ask me, I would follow that rogue Interpol cop that you so carelessly let escape. Moz knows more than any of us. He's spent the last thirty years searching for the damn place."

I shot him a fierce look. How could he implicate my father like that? And endanger his life?

But then I saw what he was doing. He was distracting her. Giving Anastasie more to think about. And confusing her with all of the options. Like being confronted with multiple shelves of toothpaste. Which one to choose? Chances are you got so frustrated and confused you left the drugstore with nothing.

Was that what he was hoping for? That she would freeze from indecision?

She needed us, and she must have recognized it. She could have left us behind to die inside this cave. She did not. Her need for Norman and Luke, I could understand. They had valuable skills. What's more, they could dive. And Luke had the means and the resources to find Atlantis. He had a yacht, state-of-the-art equipment and submersibles. All of this she could use. All of this she needed if she was to make a thorough search.

How she thought Piero and I could benefit her was not clear yet, but she obviously had some sort of plan.

"Good idea," she said to Norman. "Where is he? Where is the one you call Moz?"

"How should I know? You were the ones who let him give you the slip."

"Where would he go?" She swung her pistol until it pointed at me. "Tell me now or your bride-to-be is a dead one."

Norman was about to lunge at her. But he would be dead in seconds with five guns aimed at him. Luke stuck out a hand and grabbed Norman by the shoulder. "Easy big fella. Let's think about this."

"I know where he would have gone," I bluffed.

"Where?"

"Cut me loose and I will show you."

Anastasie scowled at me. "What does *he* know that the rest of you don't?"

My vision flew to the Mayan paintings on the walls. East of us was the four-lobbed cave with two human figures on either side of the glyphs—symbol of the Underworld.

Those glyphs were identical to the set on the Mayan shield, and when translated meant 'the gourd holds the blood of humanity'.

Due north was Witz with his gaping mouth. Moz had visibly stirred at the sight of the mountain god, pointing out the jaguar, iguana, snakes, birds, plants and flowers around the god's mouth—again, a cave.

I remembered distinctly his reaction to the picture. *"That, symbolizes the opening to Paradise."*

Where was Paradise? I bent my head at the cenote. And the beam of my headlamp touched the pristine surface. The light rippled from my lamp over the water.

When I raised my head, it was to the west wall.

Where the man impaling his genitals with a sharp blade showed the Mayan way of appeasing supernatural powers through the act of ritual bloodletting. If Moz was correct, the ancient inhabitants of the Yucatán considered the Atlanteans gods.

At the south curve of the wall was the painted figure with the stars on his legs, and the one wearing the freakish headdress—a bloody femur and blood-spraying eyeball. Both connected with death.

Moz had said that the fourth day in the Mayan ritual calendar was Ak'bal. The Day of Darkness.

Tomorrow there would be an eclipse of the sun. Did Moz know this?

My eyes darted briefly at the opposite tunnel. Half of it was above water. A strong swimmer could escape that way. Was it breathable all the way or did the passageway meet with the stone ceiling at some point, forcing the swimmer to take a chance and dive, hoping for a reprieve further along in the form of an opening to the sky?

It dawned on me then. One of the cave paintings had triggered Moz's decision to abandon us. He knew how to find the exact location of the Gateway.

Anastasie poked at me with the tip of her gun, jolting me out of my thoughts. "Wake up, Racine. Tell me what he knows!"

"Atlantis," I said. "He knows how to find Atlantis."

A long silence as she measured my words. But I knew she couldn't afford to doubt my assertion. To be truthful, Moz's whereabouts was as much a mystery to me as it was to her, but I had a guess.

"Cut them loose," Anastasie ordered her men. "But keep your weapons on them. No funny business...

Miquel, Diego. You two go first, then wait in the Ossuary at the bottom of the stairs. No one is to climb to the top and outside, until we're all accounted for. Keep your weapons on them as they come out of the tunnel.

CHAPTER 31

One by one we left the tunnel. And returned to the Ossuary cave. The diving gear we left inside the cavern by the bank of the subterranean cenote. She couldn't be bothered with it. It would only encumber them. And if she made Luke and Norman carry the equipment, they might get the bright idea to use the tanks as weapons and bean someone on the head when they weren't looking. So, she left it—much to Luke's dismay. That diving gear was worth hundreds of thousands of dollars when you factored in the cost of the imaging apparatus and communication devices.

Diego and Miguel were not in the Ossuary cave when I arrived. Odd. But good news. Had they gone to the surface against orders? I glanced up through the shaft where the stairs mounted to the opening. And saw only the glowing nighttime sky.

Maybe Aras and Johnny Sayid had waylaid them. I was the first one to exit, then came Norman and Luke and Alessandra, followed by Anastasie and her remaining men. We were making so much noise we didn't notice any noise above us.

Because Anastasie's men were gone and there was

no one to prevent us from making an attempt to immobilize her, Luke and Norman stood on either side of the tunnel while she crawled out with her gun. Norman kicked her hand and she dropped the weapon, yelping. Luke scooped it up, and Anastasie was dragged out by her arms by Norman who held her out in full view while the others filed out.

"Don't shoot," she screamed at her men. The one in the tunnel tried to duck back. Luke kicked his gun hand, disarming him and Piero leaped to grab it. The other two men in the tunnel were trapped unless they crawled out.

One of them had the gall to fire off several rounds, sending rock shattering down around us. Luke threatened to block the exit with stones and trap the men inside if they refused to surrender. So, they did.

When the men were rounded up Norman sent them up the stairs. He could not care less if they bolted like frightened sheep when they reached the surface. It was likely that was exactly what they would do as we were now in possession of their weapons. The one that had been fired was now empty and useless.

Norman went up after them with a gun aimed at the back of the last man, while Luke followed with Anastasie in tow, and I and Piero took up the rear both armed with the Mexican thugs' weapons.

It was oddly silent as I reached the top.

I paused with my head and shoulders showing. Deep night had fallen. And the moon and stars shone bright, directly on my emerging figure. Outside the brilliance of city lights, it was amazing how the Milky Way creamed across the mauve-black sky. The illusion was perfect. Except for one thing. I was halfway out of the staircase shaft when I looked down below the pyramid. And saw a strange sight.

Each of Anastasie's men lay on the ground at the base of the ossuary, dead. Strangled. Luke and Norman were nowhere to be seen. Anastasie had been spared and was in the grip of a brute of a black-bearded man in army fatigues with an AK-47 in one hand and a knife in the other. He was looking up—in my direction.

"Throw the weapon to me," he said. "And descend, little one."

My heart began to beat thunderously. The voice was unmistakable. It was Cham Nassar's—and it had me shaking.

I had no way to tell Alessa to stay hidden without them hearing me so I tried to nudge her head with my foot.

At first, she simply grabbed my ankle as a warning to stop kicking her. But when I failed to stop, she understood. I could duck back down, but they would only come after me. They knew I was there; they were ignorant of Piero.

I nodded. "I'm coming."

Ten meters below me, the pyramid was surrounded by Cham Nassar's militia. And every one of them had an AK-47 aimed at the summit. I was very tempted to shoot one of them, but what would that accomplish except to send a rain of bullets in my direction. Without giving Piero away, there was nowhere to hide. Or run.

I tossed the FN.57 caliber pistol off the pyramid.

I stood for three more seconds before I could force myself to move. What had happened to Luke and

Norman? I searched the landscape but saw nothing that would explain their disappearance. Had they been startled by the ambush and dropped their guns? That would explain why there was no shooting. But also, they would not risk firing below because that would draw a flurry of automatic fire towards the summit. And there was nothing to hide behind up here. The pistols we had confiscated from Anastasie's men were useless against military-grade assault weapons. And yet, the boys must have gone somewhere.

Something cold, metallic, slid into my waistband beneath my T-shirt. I forced myself not to react.

There were no handrails on a pyramid and the moonlight gave the night topography an onerous form. All of Anastasie's men had been pushed off the pyramid, either before strangulation or afterward. None had been allowed to cry out. The outcome of their fall was not pretty. The steps were splashed with dark fluid. Probably blood. I took my time negotiating the stairs.

Two of the terrorists came to meet me at the bottom. Anastasie tried to wrestle out of her captor's grip. The man's response was instant, his voice deep and coarse. "Silence. Or I will slice your throat."

She immediately went still.

Nassar looked at me, his face expressionless as I was brought before him. These men of the desert were cold, their eyes unreadable.

"Who else is in there?" he demanded, jabbing an elbow at the pyramid.

"No one," I said, sandwiched between my two captors. A pistol was wedged between my ribs and every movement I made caused the gunman to press deeper.

Anastasie was about to speak, but I silenced her

with a glare. These men were not her allies. They had no use for women. Not even a Nazi female.

And had she forgotten? Nassar had killed all of her men. They lay scattered in awkward positions as a constant reminder.

She went quiet but I didn't trust her. Luke and Norman were out there somewhere. And Alessandra Piero was waiting inside the pyramid. It was not likely the terrorists would search it, but if they did, she would know how to hide.

I spoke too soon. Nassar sent three men to the top of the Ossuary's pyramid. I glanced around, trying not to be obvious. Shadows stretched across the historic site flashing and quivering, the pyramids casting their dark forms across the trampled grass like mountains; and the other buildings, just as dark and ominous, rolling across the terrain like hills of stone. So many places to hide. And with their skills in camouflage and stealth, no one had noticed Norman and Luke come and go. They were out there watching. I knew it.

A single man now held me in his grip, arm like a vise wrapped around my arms and chest. They were not going to give me a chance to bolt.

The others returned, spoke in Arabic. It was a long time since I had heard that tongue and most of it slipped by me. I was never very astute in Arabic, but my intuition was flawless. They had found no one else inside the ossuary. Given how short a time they were gone, I decided they had not explored very deep into the tunnel and had missed seeing the cenote.

Nassar issued orders and grunted in the direction of his vehicles. Anastasie and I were zip-tied and blindfolded and forced into separate jeeps.

When the jeep stopped, I estimated we had been driving for thirty or forty minutes. Where were we? Valladolid was my best guess.

I was getting tired of being manhandled, but I was blinder than a mole, and I had to rely on the groping hands to guide me to where we were going.

Finally, I heard the rasp of a key, and then a click and a creak. A door had opened, the smell of unwashed human bodies greeted me. And I was shoved forward and the door slammed behind me. I almost fell flat on my face but someone had caught me.

"Lucy!"

I recognized the voice.

The blindfold was ripped off my head and I blinked into the familiar face.

"Aras! What happened. How did you get caught?"

"I wasn't exactly caught," he said, trying to interpret the expression on my face. "I recognized Nassar's men and they recognized me. I figured they wouldn't kill me if they could use me to their advantage. So, I pretended to be injured so they would take me alive and I could learn where they were keeping my family. Lucky for me, they brought me right to them. They figured three hostages were better than two, especially if one of them was Luke Trevanian's brother."

The blurry image of the people behind him came into focus.

I burst out with joy. "Samar. Rafiq!"

They rose from the floor where they had been sitting and rushed over to greet me. I had only met them once when we were on a mission in Baghdad, which now seemed eons ago.

"Yes," Aras said after they had given me warm hugs.

"They brought my mother and grandfather with them. I planned to ambush our jailors the next time they brought food or water. But they are brutes, and nothing was offered or I would have strangled them." I had no doubt he would have. "But it wasn't one of Nassar's men in the doorway. It was you." He reached for my hands. "Let me get these ties off you. Hold your breath…" He had no knife or scissors to cut the plastic, so he pulled the tie tight and up, pinching my wrists until the teeth released and he could slide it off.

I rubbed my sore wrists, which were scraped and bruised from having been confined three times in one day. "Anastasie Kirsche was captured too. Did you see her behind me?"

"No. Only you and two of Nassar's men. They must have taken her somewhere else."

"I'm worried that she will capitulate if they threaten her. So, we have to get out of here now."

Aras agreed. But there were no windows in this room.

"Do you know where we are?" I asked.

"No. I was blindfolded too, as were my mother and grandfather. They also took our phones and anything we could have used for a weapon."

"No worries," I said. Cham Nassar had seen me discard the FN.57 caliber pistol. It had bounced down the pyramid's stairs to be collected by one of Nassar's henchmen. What he hadn't seen was Alessandra Piero replacing it with this Smith and Wesson.

I retrieved it from my waistband and flaunted it in his face. It never occurred to the beast to search me for a second weapon.

"Excellent," Aras said. "How did you manage to

sneak that by Nassar?"

I passed the gun to him so he could examine it for rounds left. And shrugged. "Sometimes it pays to be a helpless woman."

"You? Helpless?"

I smirked. And he laughed.

CHAPTER 32

The first order of business was to get Samar and Rafiq somewhere safe. We knew we were approximately a half hour away from Chichén Itzá so we must be in Valladolid. We seemed to be inside an abandoned warehouse and this room was possibly once an office. It was formerly painted yellow, but most of the paint was gone and showed the ugly layers underneath. Only a sizeable town would have something like this, as a warehouse would need to be near a transportation route. That boded well for us if we could escape this ramshackle yellow cell. A train, a car, a truck. Anything we could steal or hop aboard. We'd worry about repayment later. The terrorists had stolen our money and credit cards, which wasn't a big deal as neither Aras nor I had large credit limits.

Above our heads was a vent. There would have to be a good system for ventilation since there were no windows in this room.

"Did you try that?" I asked Aras, pointing up.

"Nothing to climb on except each other."

True. This room was devoid of furniture. And if we managed to boost each other up, how was the last person to get up there without help? There was also the fact that Rafiq must be eighty and Samar was close to sixty. Could they make that climb and crawl, God knows what distance, only to find it might lead to a drop that they couldn't manage?

"How often do the kidnappers come to check on you?" I asked.

"Almost never," Samar said. She indicated the corner of the empty room where only a few water bottles and packages of tortilla chips lay crumpled. "That is all we have had since they put us here yesterday."

Something moved among the garbage. A mouse. It carried a tortilla crumb in its mouth and scurried down a crack in the floorboards.

Aras was busy studying the ceiling. He was reconsidering trying the ventilation shafts as an escape route. "Well, since they haven't brought any food or water since yesterday, we probably shouldn't wait for them to show up so we can ambush them. We need to get out of here now."

My hope was that Luke and Norman had followed the abductors back to the warehouse and were waiting for the opportunity to break us out. But I was also tired of waiting. And the vents might be a good option for me and Aras if we could get up there, although it might be disastrous for his family.

Hell, it was worth a try.

Aras agreed. They had been holed up here for hours since his arrival.

The ceiling was unusually high. That made our attempt even more difficult. I could see why Aras had not tried to escape this way earlier. Neither Samar nor

Rafiq could have been lifted high enough nor would they have had the strength to remove the grille cover even could they reach it.

I climbed onto Aras shoulders and sat straddling his shoulders. He was over six feet tall. There remained another four feet of space before I could reach the ceiling.

I pushed at the grille but it didn't budge, then I tried to claw it off with my fingertips but only succeeded in sending a shower of dust into my face. I coughed and shook out my hair. Finally, I noticed that the grille was fastened into place with four screws.

I called down for Aras to lower me to the floor.

"We can only get out that way if we have something like a screwdriver."

Nothing even remotely resembling the tool was available. The kidnappers had cleaned out this room before stashing the hostages inside it.

"So, now what?"

"You're usually the one with the bright ideas," Aras said.

I went over to the pile of refuse and kicked it aside. A couple of more vermin. This time I believe, by their size, they were rats. They found a larger gap in the boards and vanished under the floor.

This decrepid old building was probably never used for anything legal. It smelled of marijuana and some unidentified chemically odor. One thing was for sure, they weren't storing baby booties. But there was no sound beyond the door. That told me this building hadn't been used in years. When it was active however, and if it was a place of illicit activity then they might have had a secret passageway built underground just in case they were raided and needed to escape.

It was worth a try.

"Aras," I said. "I think I've found a way out."

He came to me and saw what I was pointing at. Another rat poked its head out, saw me and retreated.

"I hate rats," Aras said.

I laughed.

We had no tools. Seriously, everything that had ever been in this room had been removed. We might as well have been locked in a box.

Aras walked around the area searching for a spring lock. There appeared to be none. He got down on his knees and I joined him. The boards were all nailed down. I shoved my finger down the hole where the rats had squeeze through and vanished. The opening was about the size of a dollar coin. A Canadian Loonie.

"There is definitely a space down there," I said.

I tried to pull up the board with two fingers but it resisted.

"Let me try." Aras shoved two digits through the hole but it was too small to fit both of his fingers. He tried it with his thumb. And I found a smaller hole on the other side of the board and we tugged in unison. No luck.

"There is one way," Rafiq said. It was the first time he had spoken since we discovered the ratholes. "The wood is probably rotten, like the rest of this place. Smash it with your gun."

"That will make too much noise," Samar objected. She tucked her hijab around her face and rose.

"With your boot then."

Aras tested the floorboard. Rafiq's idea might work. The wood might give and we could learn what was below the floorboards. He handed me the gun.

"Lucy—"

"On it," I said, reading his mind. I leaped towards the door in my rubber-soled Sketchers and planted an ear at the door, handgun tucked against my chest. "So far, so good. No sounds of movement or voices."

"Okay. Hold your breath. I'm going in for the kill."

Aras smashed his booted heel into the wood. It gave. I pressed my ear to the door. Still no noise. I gave him the thumbs up and he hammered the wood floor again. The third time, he leaped on it and crashed through the board, vanishing with a smothered cry.

I rushed to the gap he had left. "Aras?"

His mother and grandfather joined me. "Aras!"

"I'm okay," he said. He rose from where he had fallen, and kicked around with his feet. "So much for the rats."

The shaft was only seven feet below ground and wide enough for a large man.

"Stand back," I whispered. It was imperative now that we make as little noise as possible. "I'm going to clear the sides so no one gets injured on the way down."

Aras backed away from the opening and I used the grip of the gun to shave away the loose splinters of wood.

"*Umi*," Aras called up when I was done, and referring to his mother. "You're first."

She sat at the edge of the hole with her feet dangling. I held her hands over her head as she slid off the side and into Aras' arms. It was a smooth and relatively silent landing.

"Rafiq, you're next," I said.

"No," he insisted. "Ladies first."

"Grampa," Aras called up in Arabic. "No time for chivalry. Lucy can take care of herself. She has the gun."

He grunted and refused to allow me to help him. He got seated by himself and using his arms, lowered his legs first into the hole, while Aras grabbed him around the thighs and eased him down.

"Lucy!"

"On my way. You guys start running! I hear noises out in the warehouse!"

I dropped down and Aras caught me. No way he was leaving before he knew I was following. There was nothing to cover the floor hole with. We had to run.

The passage was high enough that we could jog with backs hunched. It was especially easy for Samar and Rafiq who were a lot shorter than us. I took the lead with Aras and the gun in the rear, and his family in between.

We trotted for ten minutes before I heard voices, and the patter of feet in pursuit. Oh no. We'd never make it. This tunnel had several turns which was lucky; our pursuers couldn't shoot us once we rounded the corners.

But they did try.

Aras only returned fire when his target was certain and in clear sight. We had limited ammunition. We had to get out of here soon. Oh, when was this tunnel going to end?

Finally, I saw a grate. With bars of moonlight streaming through. Please, please, *please* this grate was loose. It wasn't. I grabbed the bars with both hands and pushed, and then yanked. Behind me arms came over and beside my head as Rafiq and Samar tried to help but the space was too narrow.

Then suddenly the grate fell forward nearly taking me with it. And I rose to find a FN.57 caliber pistol in my face.

CHAPTER 33

It hadn't rained in days. Even so, the nearby road where the grate had collapsed outward was damp, and the air humid. But compared to what we had just experienced inside the dank tunnel, the fresh air came as a shock. Two men hunched at either side of the grate with their weapons turned on us.

I recognized their shapes even before I recognized their voices.

"*Merde*, Lucy. I nearly shot you."

Norman pocketed his weapon and dragged me out by my arms and hauled me tight against his chest, my feet inches off the ground. His relief was palpable as his muscles flexed around me. I could only imagine the horror he had experienced when he witnessed me lose my gun. And I started that interminable descent down the pyramid to the waiting arms of Cham Nassar.

They say that the crawling feathered-serpent shadow that decorates the northern balustrade of the Kukulcán pyramid was only visible during the hours leading to sundown on spring equinox. But I swear the carvings in the bas-relief on all of the buildings were crawling just then.

A shiver shook me as I recalled the memory. Norman's panic could not even begin to compare to my own when I climbed out of the Ossuary to the jagged crown of the pyramid. And saw that he and Luke were missing.

"Ça va? Cherie? Are you hurt."

I shook my head, my rapid heartbeats only now beginning to decrease. Any other time I would have demanded he put me down immediately, but I was just so overwhelmed and grateful to see him that I allowed him to hold me high in his arms like a child, the wind raking through my hair.

He kissed me zealously, then set me on my feet. Behind us Luke was helping Rafiq and Samar out of the tunnel. Darkness enveloped us and the shadows of the trees mocked our escape.

"What happened to you two?" I asked, hugging Luke after he had welcomed Samar and Rafiq. "When I didn't see you with Anastasie in the grip of one of Nassar's men, I thought you guys were dead." My gaze swung back to Norman.

"Takes a lot more than a displaced Syrian militia and their half-cocked leader to do any damage to this." Norman tapped himself on the chest and I giggled in hysterical relief.

His voice went serious. "I knew something was up as soon as the first of Anastasie's men reached the top. When we were climbing out of the Ossuary. A large cloud had masked the moon just at that moment making it too dark to see anything. Instinct told me to douse my headlamp. When Miguel and Diego just seemed to vanish into thin air, I did a vanishing act myself. I guess Luke sensed that something was off as well and doused his lamp; and when he came up with Anastasie, she was grabbed and he slipped over the back and down the other side of the pyramid, same as me. They never saw us. Unfortunately, the cloud passed sending moonlight directly on you like a spotlight. Right as you emerged."

Luke and Norman were both trained in tactical, physical maneuvers. Incredible as their escape sounded, it didn't surprise me. They had used the darkness and the shadows—and the fact that Nassar had no idea how many people were emerging from the ossuary pyramid—to their advantage. The only problem was, they couldn't save me. Or even warn me without giving themselves away. So, they had chosen to wait for a more advantageous opportunity. Mercifully, I had managed to warn Alessa, so I was the only one captured. I prayed she had thought to seal the tunnel entrance to the cenote before she fled.

Norman continued, "After Nassar's men left with you and Anastasie, we checked the cave below the stairs and saw that Piero was gone. Fortunately, the terrorists didn't see the laptop that was left behind, so we knabbed it."

Good thing Luke had parked his vehicle down the road away from the parking lot. Which was why they had transportation after the departure of the terrorists. Had Nassar seen the car he would have punctured the tires, leaving the boys stranded. That would have meant several hours delay in making our rescue. As luck would have it, our plan and their plan had coincided.

"Where is Aras?" Samar suddenly demanded.

We were all watching the tunnel but he failed to appear.

There was a loud boom and my heart leaped. I grabbed Samar as she tried to return to the tunnel.

"My boy!" she shrieked.

"Quiet, Samar," Luke warned. "We don't know anything yet. And that compound is lousy with criminals.

She wrapped the end of her hijab over her mouth to stifle her sobs and her father draped an arm around her. "Stop it, daughter," he said. "Aras is a soldier. He fights for the will of God. He cannot be killed."

I wanted to believe it. Aras was a resistance fighter back in Syria. He and his followers had managed to reclaim most of the territory Nassar's men had captured. The jihadists were now confined to the north and held only a small parcel of land. And only one major city. Idlib.

"He *cannot* be killed," Rafiq repeated.

I admired the strength of his faith. Did he mean that God would not allow his grandson to die… or did he mean that he, Rafiq, refused to believe that Aras might be dead?

Still nothing was coming out of the tunnel.

I darted a nervous look in the direction of Norman's gaze. It was obvious where we were. The underground passageway had led us a five-minute, hunched, dash to the main road. Behind us on a low rise was an enclosed compound paved in gravel where several jeeps were parked and a large tin-roofed building like an aircraft hangar. Only it wasn't a storage space for a plane. It was some kind of warehouse. The movement of multiple men was visible, scurrying back and forth in a chaotic manner. Indicating to us that news of our escape had spread.

Norman took a pair of night vision binoculars out of his backpack, and scanned the direction of the compound. "They're armed."

Luke gestured swiftly. "We have to leave. All of you come with me. Or we will suffer the same fate."

But what about Aras? Something was delaying him. He was right behind us. And then he wasn't. Something must have happened.

"He isn't dead, Luke." I desperately had to believe it. Aras was a good man, a great man. His brother needed to know it. But there was nothing but choking dust escaping the black passageway that led from the warehouse to the road.

Luke stretched his hand towards Samar and Rafiq. "To the car. Aras would want me to see you both safe."

That was true.

"Come, Samar," I said. "Rafiq. We must go with Luke to the car. Norman will wait for Aras to appear."

Already he was waving away the last of the pluming dust. If I knew Norman, and I did, he would go into the tunnel to search—if Aras failed to manifest in the next five seconds…

I finally managed to get them to turn and start walking when I heard coughing and a scuffing at the tunnel's entrance.

The fallen metal grate rattled as a ghost materialize in the opening on hands and knees, and clawed it with his hands. Aras was covered in dirt and dust, and his mother and grandfather ran to embrace him as he crawled out of the darkness and onto the tumbled grate. He scrabbled to his feet with Norman's help.

"What happened?" Luke asked.

"I stopped to shoot out the junction and the whole

thing collapsed. Lucky the ceiling didn't land on me. But they won't be coming that way. Better leave though, and fast." He shot a quick look toward the compound and coughed out the last of the dust. "They'll be after us when they see the damage."

Norman draped an arm around Aras. He was limping and there was blood on his forehead, his arm and his knees.

"You're hurt," Samar said.

"Won't be the first time." He grinned and his mother admonished him.

We made it to the car. It was parked in the shadows of some thick-leafed trees, denser than anything found in the heart of town. That told me we were on the outskirts of the city and we had two choices: get lost in the urban chaos of evening markets and restaurants or head for the open road where we might get sighted more easily.

It was a tight squeeze for the six of us. Me on Luke's lap in front and Aras and his family in back. Just as Norman punched the ignition, shouts came from the massive building behind the chain-link fence. Engines revved and shot towards the gate. Fortunately, we were on the other side of the barrier, while they had to stop to open it. If we left now, we would have a small head-start.

We raced down the road and into the city.

CHAPTER 34

The sparkling lights of the town absorbed us. We disappeared into the clots of people, locals and tourists, scooters and vehicles that meandered around the main plaza. A surprising array of colorful souvenir and food stalls, splashy street performers and musicians had set up for evening entertainment.

We decided that Valladolid was not the safest place to hide even with all of these distractions. We also wanted to protect the locals and tourists from inadvertently falling into the line of fire. The terrorists were vindictive; they would not think twice about using their guns if they spotted us.

For the safety of the community, we decided to head back to Espita. The terrorists probably wouldn't think to follow us to such a remote place. Unless Nassar was aware of Natasha's hacienda. And of course, he was. Since her horrific death, it had been in all the papers and on the internet. But—why would we stay in Espita now that her hacienda was burnt to the ground and especially if we were no longer being blackmailed by her? A swift exit to a big city, like Mérida, was the only thing that would make sense to a scoundrel like Cham

Nassar.

Norman made some evasive maneuvers as he was at the wheel, being the most skilled driver among our group. We waited in the shadows of the busy main drag where a row of food stalls backed onto us, until we were certain we had lost them. Then Norman pulled the SUV out of concealment. And drove at a normal speed through the town and onto the highway.

We were back in Espita at the Casa Los Cedros hotel in no time.

Norman and I gave Aras and his family our room as there were currently no vacancies. Tomorrow Luke's private jet would take them home. He had already made the call to his pilot and crew while enroute, and put in motion the passengers' transport. Aras intended to go with them. Meanwhile, after their horrible ordeal among the terrorists, Samar and Rafiq needed food and sleep. Luke made arrangements so they could get access to whatever they needed.

The rest of us headed next door.

We were overjoyed, when we assembled in Luke's room, to see Alessandra Piero lounging on Luke's king-sized bed.

Welcoming grins spread across all our faces.

There was no point in asking how she had gotten inside. For someone involved in criminal activity, no matter what side of the crime you were on, you learned how to pick locks.

"So, glad to see you safe, Lucy," she said. Her hair was damp like she had recently showered. She turned her attention to Luke and Norman. "I would have joined the rescue but you guys left without me."

"Where the hell were you?" Luke demanded.

Norman glared. "We searched but you didn't appear and we didn't want to lose the trail after they grabbed Lucy."

Besides, being an ex-Interpol cop and a member of ISORE Piero was trained to get out of tight places. And I mean that literally. She must have remained concealed inside the pyramid and its tunnels until she was sure it was safe. After all she had given me her gun. It would hardly be expedient to expose herself to a group of armed assassins without being armed herself.

"Where's Sayid?" Luke asked. "Did he manage to return with the helo to the yacht? He obviously wasn't caught by Anastasie. And I'm assuming by your cool demeanor that Nassar didn't get him either."

Piero nodded. "He left as soon as he dropped me and Aras off at Chichén Itzá with your diving gear. You were right about not leaving it in the jungle too long. All sorts of riffraff would like a piece of that bird."

"You mean people would sell the helicopter for parts?"

"Not people," Luke said. "Drug cartels."

Well, now we knew where Johnny was; that was one load off our minds.

"Oh great, you found the laptop," Piero said.

Luke nodded.

"Good thing," I remarked, reaching out for it, and taking it from Luke's grip. "I want to have a look at that shield again. I hope it wasn't deleted." In the absence of the genuine article, the next best thing was the photo of the Mayan ceremonial shield that I had captured when it was still on Natasha's desk. And that we had later uploaded onto Natasha's laptop.

"Room Service first. I could use a big steak—and a

drink." And by drink, Luke meant something stronger than water. We all agreed, and he put in the order. I set the laptop aside.

While we were waiting for the food to arrive, I remembered that Moz was still missing.

"We have to find my father," I insisted.

"He bailed on you," Alessa said. "I told you there was something sketchy about him."

There was something sketchy about her own behavior. She was evasive about her movements since we last saw her, and she refused to hold my gaze.

"Just because he is obsessed with finding Atlantis doesn't make him a criminal," I pressed. "Or even a bad person."

Piero shrugged. She had already formed her opinion of him. And nothing I said would change her mind. Surprisingly, Norman was quiet on the matter.

The hush that ensued was broken by a knocking at the door. "Room service."

Norman rose and let the hotel staff in with the wheeled cart loaded with steaks, chicken enchiladas and cheesy tacos. There was also beer, bottled water and a pitcher of sangria. The last at my request.

We ate in silence for about ten minutes. Only then realizing how hungry we were. For that short time, the only sounds audible were the crunch of tacos and the clink of knives and forks on plates.

Sated, I wiped my hands on a napkin and slurped on my sangria. Why wasn't anyone more concerned over the whereabouts of my father? I brought up the subject of Moz once more.

"We have to find him," I insisted. I glanced at Piero but she refused to return my look.

Luke and Norman seemed unconcerned. "It's possible he escaped through that other tunnel in the secret cenote under Kukulcán. It must have led out to another cenote, only this one must have been open to the surface," Luke said.

Or else he had drowned trying to get out. There was no way to know unless we returned and followed the route. Piero made no comment and without realizing it, I had spoken my thoughts out loud. And still she said nothing.

Not so Norman. "Not a good idea," he warned. "Nassar and his men are bound to return there when Anastasie confesses to what she's discovered. I have no doubt she'll form an alliance with him if it means saving her skin and finding the treasure."

"Treasure?" Piero questioned. She seemed determined to change the subject. "You mean Atlantis actually contains treasure?"

Although annoyed with her for dismissing my concern for Moz, I shrugged along with Luke and Norman almost in unison. The descriptions told of golden statues, ivory roofs, and jewels of every kind. I could do without the ivory. The idea of any culture slaughtering that many animals for their ivory was unthinkable and cruel. But then a people who would demand child sacrifices, would not think twice about killing innocent animals to get ivory to tile their roofs. Yes, I was beginning to build a picture of these Atlanteans and it wasn't all pretty.

"I am not just going to leave him. He might be injured or…" I never finished the sentence.

Luke had risen and clicked on the TV with the remote. It was his way of stemming the tension between me and the team.

There was a news story on about some suspicious incident in Chichén Itzá. The news anchor spoke Spanish, but I understood mainly by the pictures displayed on the screen. The rough gray stones of the pyramid with the temple of Kukulcán materialized. Then the camera panned across the site to the Ossuary with its broken top and its entrance to the bone cave. I shot a glance at Alessa and she nodded, interpreting correctly my silent request for confirmation. She had blocked the tunnel entrance with stones to keep nosy tourists from discovering the secret passageway.

I sighed with relief, but something had caused the hikers to contact the authorities. Although the bodies had been removed from the grounds, the terrorists hadn't bothered to clean up the blood on the steps. It was dawn and despite the fact that the historic site wasn't open yet, some early morning explorers had gone at first light to beat the crowds only to be confronted with the leavings of Cham Nassar.

There was also a gun found on the scene.

"Well, that's that," Luke said. "We can't go back anyways. The site is swarming with police."

At least now I understood where the terrorists had gone when they'd left us alone in the warehouse—back to eradicate the evidence. Where had they dumped the bodies? It was one thing to dispose of a single corpse, but four?

Another story was starting as Luke shut off the TV with the remote. It triggered something in my memory. "Turn it back on," I said.

He did. The story was about the impending eclipse. It was supposed to take place today. Why that was important, I don't know but my instinct was telling me that it was.

"What time is that eclipse supposed to happen?" I asked.

"Just after noon. Why?"

I wasn't sure why except that... "Alessa, can I see that laptop? Does it still have the photo of the shield on it?" She lifted it from the night stand and opened it. The photo was still there.

Inside the borders of the round shield, the turquoise mosaic sea appeared. The two-headed serpent at the bottom with the white conical teeth were actually mountain peaks. In the center of the shield an irregularly shaped golden circle with concentric rings formed an island. The symbol of an island. Or perhaps a continent. And the semi-crescents of mother-of-pearl were boats. From the top, bottom and sides of the shield, pyrite and gold shapes—bridges—radiated from the island.

At least that was my original interpretation. But now I knew them to be tunnels. I had come to see the image as a map; it reminded me of a map. But not a map in the way I had initially thought.

"What's up, Lucy?" Norman asked.

"The ancient Maya were astute in many things. Including their version of the cosmos."

"So?" This came from Luke.

"So... there will be a solar eclipse today. And weren't the Maya capable of forecasting astronomical events?"

"Well, yes. But only to a point. The Maya had no clue as to how celestial bodies moved in space. They didn't know that the moon actually crossed paths between the sun and the earth, blocking the light and casting the moon's shadow over the earth. And so, while they couldn't predict the exact date or time of a solar or lunar eclipse, they could predict eclipse seasons by noting when Venus rose above the horizon just before sunrise."

Everyone had stopped what they were doing, waiting for me to continue. For a moment I was aware that all of their attention was on me. Two years ago, instead of taking center stage I would have been on the sidelines, my opinions unheard or overlooked.

The sound of my voice cracked the silence. "I believe an eclipse had something to do with how the ancient Maya first found their way to the ruins of Atlantis."

"What do you mean?"

"Look at this—" I turned the laptop towards my audience and enlarged the image until we were focused on the golden circle and the four tunnels. "Do you see anything different about the four rectangles leading to the circle?"

"*Je vois*," Norman said. "That one"—he was pointing to the tunnel to the right—"is a much brighter color of pyrite than the others."

I nodded excitedly. "I don't believe this circle is meant to represent an island at all." I glanced up at their confused faces. "Don't you see? It is meant to symbolize the sun and those concentric black circles around it is the eclipse!"

"What are you getting at, Lucy?"

"I know what she's saying," Piero weighed in. "An eclipse is rarely total. It does not block out the entire sun. That rectangle or tunnel or whatever you want to call it is highlighted because that is the one the sun's light strikes just before the darkness passes."

I grinned. "Exactly."

"So, all we have to do is find the right cenote and wait for the eclipse to tell us which tunnel to follow."

"And it can't be the one under the pyramid of Kukulcán because it's not exposed to the sun," Luke said.

Norman added, "That means, the cenote we are looking for has four tunnels leading out from it."

"There are over six thousand cenotes in the Yucatán. How are we going to find the right one?" Luke demanded.

I waved my hands in excitement to draw their attention. "I think we already have. That cenote in the jungle, the one with the petroglyphs. It has four openings. They face north, south, east and west."

CHAPTER 35

As far as I was concerned there was no point in sleeping. It was sunup. But Norman and Luke insisted that we try to rest for a couple of hours. We had a big day ahead of us and a few hours before the eclipse would occur.

I don't know how they did it, but the three of them, Luke, Norman and Alessandra Piero managed to go into snore mode. They called it power napping. I was still trying to master normal sleep.

The three of us had managed to squeeze onto the king-sized bed with Piero on the sofa. They slept. I, on the other hand, was wide awake. I rose without disturbing the boys and went behind the sofa to the window, dressed only in Norman's T-shirt which hung down to my knees, to look out.

The sun was shining. It was still early. Not many people were up, and swimmers had yet to descend on the pool.

I drew the curtains tight and turned to search for my clothes. My eyes landed on the coffee table where Alessa's phone sat. Having lost mine, I reached for the phone to check the time, when I noticed something by

Alessa's belongings. She was sleeping in her tank top and the light cotton shirt she normally wore overtop was next to her phone. The curved edge of a small, grayish stone had half rolled out of the pocket of her shirt.

I stifled my gasp.

A stone pendant. Two inches long and half that wide with a hole at the top, where a leather thong might once have been looped through. Engraved on it was a man in a boat. A stylized image of a man in a canoe. With what appeared to be a fireball bearing down on his head. The man was stained with red ochre.

It was Moz's. It was the pendant Moz had shown me the night before. How did Piero come to possess it?

I glanced up to see her staring at me. She put two fingers to her lips and rolled gracefully off the sofa. How long had she been watching? Her thumb jabbed at the door and I followed her outside onto the terrace.

We stood, staring at one another.

"This belongs to my dad," I accused her, pinching the pendant between my fingertips.

"Apparently."

I scowled, the T-shirt flapping against my torso as a gust of wind swept by. She had guessed that it was Moz's by my ugly attitude. In my anger, I had to be careful not to drop the precious object onto the stone floor where it would smash to a dozen bits. Or lose it in one of the planters filled with rich soil and thirsty plants. There were pebbles mixed in for drainage. "Why didn't you tell me you found this?" I demanded.

"I didn't know it belonged to Moz."

"But you could have mentioned it last night. You knew I was concerned about him."

"Again. I didn't know it belonged to him." Her hands were jammed inside her pants pockets and her hair was unruly. She still managed to look in control. "How did he get it anyway? It's obviously an authentic artifact."

Obviously? Since when was *she* an expert.

I debated on whether to recite the entire tale of Moz's lifelong pursuit of Atlantis. Then decided against it. It would take too long.

"It's not important. Right now, what's important is where did *you* find it?"

It was burning a hole through my palm and I needed her to answer me immediately.

She was about to attempt another diversion when she realized I meant business. She sighed, then explained her experiences of last night.

While Aras, Samar, Rafiq and I were scheming on how to escape the warehouse where Nassar's men had confined us, Alessa had, after slipping me her gun, fled down the tunnel after blocking the entrance. When she arrived at the secret cenote under the pyramid she continued through the half-submerged passageway at the opposite wall, swimming vigorously, until she surfaced at an open-air cenote.

"I got out that way," she said. "Moonlight was visible at the end of the tunnel. Guess I failed to mention it last night."

A very serious oversight.

Because it was obvious that Luke and Norman were unaware of how she had escaped. They, like me, had assumed she had waited for the terrorists to depart and then climbed down the ossuary pyramid and made for the road where she hitched a ride back to the hotel.

"And you found the pendant there?"

She nodded. "Fortunately, the moon was full. I could easily see my way in the night... It was on the bank of the pool, snagged on the branches of a tree... The moon was shining directly on it." I almost thought she was going to say 'like it wanted me to find it.' But that was the kind of thing I would have said, not Alessandra Piero.

"The moonlight made it gleam, and that red pigment really stood out. It was what led me to the easiest path to get out of that hole."

So, she knew Moz must have climbed out following a pathway of stone footholds and tree roots and branches up the steep incline of the cenote's walls. I was amazed they had both managed to escape. Cenotes were often 40 to 60 meters deep. Sometimes deeper.

She realized what I was thinking and her face softened. "Look, Lucy. I don't know what your 'father' thinks he's doing going rogue. But I don't like it."

She had used air quotes with her fingers when referring to my dad, which annoyed me no end.

I clasped my fist around the pendant when she went to retrieve it. "Moz left this for me. He wanted me to know that he had escaped and that he was okay, and that he was thinking about me."

Piero shrugged, then looked out onto the scene of blue swimming pool and green foliage and exotic flowers. "Think what you like."

"Why are you so suspicious?" I demanded. "Just tell me. So, I can understand."

It seemed an eternity before she answered me. Alessandra Piero never lost her cool, but on occasion she might get slightly agitated. This was one of those times. And whenever she got agitated—even slightly—

her Italian accent, which was pretty much absent in everyday speech, reasserted itself.

She measured me coolly. "Ask yourself this. Where is Moz now? *Dai!* He knows where you are staying. Why has he not returned?"

I was silent.

"*Che cosa.* If you ask me, Moz was the one that shot at you the other night when you discovered the petroglyph. He was trying to prevent you from seeing it. And anyone who will shoot at his own daughter is not a father I would want to have."

I clutched the pendant to my chest. "I'm keeping this," I told her.

"Suit yourself."

She gathered her hair up into a ponytail and fetched a coated elastic band from her pants pocket to fasten it into place. She turned and placed a hand on the door jamb while the other sought the door lever. Just as she depressed it to reenter the hotel room, something occurred to her and she spun back.

"Where did Moz get that pendant, Lucy?"

I had half a mind to keep the info to myself; I was so furious at her for accusing my father of being corrupt.

But logic won out. Alessa typically was calm and rational. She had a reason for wanting to know. And maybe if she knew, it would lessen her antagonism towards him.

I answered, "I believe he said it came in a collection of stolen artifacts recovered in a police raid. This one struck him as unusual… and you can see why…"

I raised the artifact to the light and studied the

carving.

"So, he just took it? Doesn't that strike you as odd? That a police officer would steal evidence?"

My heartrate was accelerating again. If she didn't stop goading me... Why was she goading me? I thought she was my friend. Oh crap, I didn't want to get into a lecture on the meaning of friendship... She had her reasons.

"Maybe he signed for it. Agents are allowed to do that, aren't they? It wasn't evidence exactly," I elaborated. "I mean—what was the crime?"

Silence as she let me reflect.

"Theft?" she said, then paused. "Double theft—after he stole it."

I was stumped as to a response. My emotions were clashing. For some reason I believed my father had a legitimate motive for possessing the artifact. On the one hand, I wanted to believe in Moz; on the other I knew Alessa would only be making these accusations if she had good cause.

Moz had taken this object as part of his obsession. Was he so obsessed that he could no longer discern the difference between right and wrong? Was he willing to do anything if it brought him closer to the truth?

Alessandra's head was bobbing as though she were following my line of thought. Her voice came softer when she spoke. "As I recall, there was a modest incident at Interpol regarding some unusual but later declared minor antiquities. Scientists stationed in Antarctica had reported the theft of a small artifact collection, and this piece—I am positive—was included in the manifest."

I frowned. "I thought you and Moz never worked

together."

"We didn't. I came long after he was gone."

What was she implying? That he had returned at some point to steal the pendant? Somewhere in the distant jungle exotic birds began to shriek.

"Are you calling Moz a thief?"

The bird shrieks came louder. "Your words, not mine."

I had no comeback. Moz had almost certainly stolen the artifact.

But that was beside the point. We still had to find him.

"I am going to shower and dress," I said and stormed off.

Why was I so angry? Piero was making me think things I refused to believe about my father.

The men were up when I made a U-turn indoors. Alessandra remained outside, heading for the pool. I watched her through the windows of the latticed door. No matter how miffed I was at her, how could I stay mad? Alessa never made impulsive assertions without evidence to back them up. What did she know about Moz that she was hiding? I would have to get her alone again, and make her spill. She owed me that much. She owed me and Moz the chance for rebuttal. There were two sides to every story. Even if one side might be a bit shady.

Now, what was she doing? I stifled a giggle. Did I not say I couldn't stay angry with her? I wouldn't put it past her to strip off those pants and go swimming in her tank top and underwear.

Which was exactly what she did.

When I came out from the steamy bathroom, clean

and refreshed, Norman informed me that Aras and his family had left in a taxi for the airport in Mérida where Luke's private jet awaited them. I had just missed their departure.

"They wanted to say goodbye," Norman said. "But I know how long you take in the shower. So, I told them to leave. It isn't safe for any of them to remain, not with Nassar on the rampage."

True. If he found them, he would kill them. Extremists had a bent sense of honor. Cham Nassar's reputation *and* his honor had been sullied. He would have no other choice. All the same...

"I wanted to see them before they left. I meant to invite them to our wedding."

Norman gave me a small smile. "Already done. Just don't know that the Eiffel Tower will be free on a moment's notice."

I grinned. Likely not. In fact, they would probably never allow a spur of the moment booking like that again—no matter how rich the billionaire.

Norman took me into his arms and ran his hands down the sides of my body. If only Luke wasn't here. If only there wasn't a madman hunting for us. If only...

A groan came from the other side of the room. Luke was watching the news. The story of the gun and the bloody steps of the Kukulcán pyramid had taken a backseat to the discovery of four bodies in a cenote east of Chichén Itzá.

"We have to double back to retrieve the diving gear," Luke said. "The police have probably left and the site is closed to the public so this is the perfect time to salvage it without being seen."

I wriggled out of Norman's embrace and turned.

"But we have to get to the jungle cenote before the eclipse," I insisted.

Luke twisted to face me. "We will."

CHAPTER 36

Now that we knew the secret cenote's location, it took us half the time to reach it as it had taken the time before. Even with the added weight of lugging three air cylinders on Norman and Luke's backs. The third tank belonged to Anastasie, and Piero had the honor of carrying it. I brought the lighter paraphernalia in my backpack.

I was amazed that this cenote, so close to the hotel, remained a hidden treasure. Almost no one knew about it. And clearly no one had discovered the petroglyph on the south side of the sinkhole, or the cave—which opened to the west. Otherwise, tourists would have long since descended on it. Which in turn would have brought a plague of archaeologists and other specialists to investigate its secrets.

On the opposite side—at the east wall—below the waterline, it appeared that there might be another cave or alcove. And as I had noted earlier, there was also one to the north. I was certain that my eyes, dazzled though they may be by sunlight and shadows, were seeing reality and not illusion.

I pivoted from where I stood at the south side, on

the stone platform, and peered behind the rickety stairs. Was there a cavern just beyond, in the shade of the steps? Or was I focused simply on a very dark shadow?

It suddenly occurred to me. Who had rigged these stairs? If nobody knew of the existence of this virgin cenote, then why were there steps leading to the bottom of it? Yes, they seemed temporary. And that meant something. It meant that this staircase was intended for short use.

Which brought me back to the shooter. At minimum one man or woman was present, and he or she, had shot at us that night. They were determined to prevent our discovering the petroglyph on the south wall. The one of the charioteer Sea god with his winged horses surrounded by dolphin-riding nymphs.

Why?

It could be for only one reason. Whoever our shooter was, he or she knew about the petroglyphs. Did they also know of the other rock carvings hidden inside the westernmost cave?

Piero's accusations against my father doubled back to haunt me. How could it possibly have been Moz? He was on board Luke's yacht. Wasn't that where Sayid claimed he found him? And Alessa was there. She was actually part of Moz's alibi. If he was discovered to be a stowaway aboard the *Madonna II*, how could he be our shooter?

I preferred to believe it was Anastasie.

"Do you suppose Anastasie knows about this place?" I asked Luke.

"She's never mentioned anything that would make me suspect so."

I agreed. I turned to search for Piero. She was

helping Norman check the diving gear. It had not taken us long to return to Chichén Itzá to retrieve it from the underground cenote. We were there and back within the hour.

Equipment was available for three divers. I was a novice, in the process of learning and one dive away from certification. The others were pros. If anyone was going to be left out of the expedition, it was me.

"How soon do you think you can airdrop one of my submersibles?" Luke was on the phone discussing the logistics of transporting one of his lightweight mobile submersibles into the cenote.

Our helicopter pilot's voice come across loud and clear. "Less than two hours," Sayid answered.

"Okay. We'll be waiting. Meanwhile we'll do a quick dive and see what we can see."

"On it."

"We have some time to kill," Luke announced as he disconnected the call.

We stared across the calm waters of the cenote. What appeared to be a log with eyes floated near the east wall. It was so still that I was positive it was a rough hunk of wood until I placed Norman's binoculars over my eyes.

A crocodile. Only its head appeared above the surface. We watched each other for over a minute; not once did it blink.

I passed the glasses to Norman.

"Sure you want to get in there?" I asked.

Norman peered at the crocodile. "They're mostly benign as long as you don't bother them."

I did not want to find out.

Suddenly the croc moved, did an about face and

swam to the east wall.

"Where did it go?" I demanded.

Norman retrieved the binocs from me. "Maybe we should follow it."

"I think we should check out the north tunnel first. Give the old croc a chance to get where it's going." Luke pointed to where a dark opening was obvious in the wall. It was below the waterline but I could see that it was either a passageway or a cavern by the deep shade of the rock under the water, which was astoundingly crystal clear. No other petroglyphs were visible that I could detect.

"Lucy. You stay here and monitor us from the computer. Piero, you might as well stay with Lucy. We won't go too far in since we have limited air remaining in the tanks. Besides, until we know which tunnel we should be investigating, we need to be economical."

Piero scowled, but agreed. I guess she wasn't too thrilled to be left alone with me after our squabble.

It took Luke a good half-hour to set up the computer and synch it to their communication and camera devices. The system fit on the flat surface of a nearby boulder, which I could observe by squatting. Many of the aquifers had been mapped and Luke had a copy of them, but this section of the Yucatán was yet to be covered. In fact, every year new underground rivers and cenotes were being discovered. That meant we were really going into this venture blind.

Another forty-five minutes and the boys finished removing their neoprene suits, fins and masks from the backpacks, checked that all was operational, especially the air tanks, and geared up. I called out after them as they headed to the edge of the sinkhole. "The eclipse should occur in forty minutes. Make sure you're back well before then. And watch out for anymore crocs."

"Aye Aye, *Capitaine*." Norman winked.

Luke grinned, nodded. And seeing no other threatening wildlife, both men spat on their masks, rubbing the saliva over the glass to prevent condensation from forming when submerged, and tipped themselves backwards into the pool.

Splashdown and they vanished into the depths.

After a flurry of bubbles, the cameras on their helmets showed us their progress on the split screen. Norman's view was to the left and Luke's was to the right. Nothing much to see yet except for a small school of startled fish.

My hand absently went to my chest where the pendant lay. I had fastened a shoelace through the hole in the upper part of the pendant and looped it around my neck. It was as though having it close, and on my person, would keep my father from being a mere fantasy. Because in his absence I was beginning to doubt that he really existed.

"Alessa," I said. She was on her haunches beside me watching the screen. "Why do you believe Moz shot at us the other night? I don't see how it's possible if he was with you and Johnny. The three of you arrived at our hotel just as we returned."

She rose and rubbed her thighs before gazing down at me.

"He wasn't with us the entire time. After Johnny brought us in a nearby clearing via helicopter, we made our way to Espita with a rental we had preordered to find your hotel. None of you were answering your phones. And when we knocked at your room doors there was no answer. So, we went to search the neighborhood restaurants and bars. That was when we split up with Moz. I don't know where he went, but he was gone for over two hours. Apparently, he returned just before you arrived back at your hotel—and certainly before *we* did."

Two hours unaccounted for. If a practiced hiker who knew where the cenote was made that trip, it would take less than an hour to reach and even less time to return.

Did Moz know about that cenote prior to my mention of it?

Did he know about the petroglyph before I leaked it to him?

I racked my brain for some memory of his reaction when I enlightened him on not only the shooting but the unusual find. How had he responded?

Evasive? Yes. Evasive. But that could mean anything. Like he didn't think it important.

Or that he did.

Like Piero I too rose to stretch my legs, and gazed out at the quiet turquoise water in front of us. I still refused to accept it. Moz would not shoot at me. Unless he was unaware that it was me, and instead jumped to the conclusion that I was an intruder intent on damaging the evidence.

Except that the bullets had practically obliterated the petroglyph.

Piero's attention had returned to the screen where Luke and Norman were penetrating the black depths of the submerged limestone passage. She dropped to her haunches again. I followed suit. There was nothing much to see even with their headlamps at high, just a cold white light dancing off the rough stone walls of a funneling tube that seemed to continue interminably.

These submerged passageways were dangerous. There was no way to know where they led, how deep they went or whether they opened up to any sort of air pockets or even a gap to the surface. Currents were also a danger, some of them so strong a person could be swept down into oblivion without warning.

"Norman, Luke. I think you guys should come back. You've already used up fifteen minutes of air. Do you see anything?"

"*Rien.* Nothing," Norman said. His voice gurgled through the communication device in his regulator. Some small, pale cichlids swam past and an albino shrimp.

"Ditto," Luke echoed, sending a jet of upward gushing bubbles. "Let's go back. Better to reserve what air we've got left."

They returned in another quarter hour.

"These tunnels are amazingly deep," Luke said, removing his mask and wiping his hair from his forehead. "And there is no way to know just how many zigs and zags there are or how much air we'll require to complete the entire circuit. Or if it's a straight, short run."

"That's why we need to wait for the eclipse," I advised. "No point in wasting valuable air by going down the wrong tunnel."

The boys stripped out of their neoprene suits, dripping water on the warm stone platform, and piled all of the diving gear to the side where it formed a large puddle. We sat down on the rocks away from the wet stone, beneath the shade of the overhanging foliage, some of which were acacias, to cool off as the day heated towards noon.

I handed around bottles of cold water and we drank in silence. The ambient humidity prevented the boys from drying off quickly, although the breeze helped. I closed my eyes to kill time. After a few moments I opened them to admire once more the beauty of our surroundings. A small lizard was staring at me.

Waiting for an eclipse to happen is like waiting for a kettle to boil. It just will not happen.

And then it does.

The lizard must have noticed something too. It suddenly skittered away, down into a crevice between the stones.

Shadows began to creep across the ground, and because we were inside the cenote it seemed even darker. It was as though the plants had grown legs and feet and began moving in a single direction, casting their silhouettes over everything they touched. The clear blue water turned indigo on one side. And then darkened like an artist's brush painting over a canvas. The sky grayed like it was dusk, turned to charcoal night, and only a shaft of sunlight continued over the water, traveling steadily towards the east until the entire pool was dark except for the cavern that was highlighted as though by a spotlight.

The east wall.

Then just like that, it was over. The sun was full and shining and the brief midnight interlude had passed.

We all stared at the cavern, the gateway to Atlantis.

Why had I never noticed this before? Just beyond

the top rim of the cenote, above the cave opening, was a single, solitary pine tree. And past that the peak of a mountain in the distance. Exotic bird cries shattered the silence and an iguana, that at first stood so still it appeared to be part of the rock, hurried away making the plants growing in the cracks and crevices around the tunnel tremble.

"That sub should have been here by now," Luke complained. He glanced at his phone.

"Give him a few more minutes," Norman said.

"It's been over two hours since we talked."

Norman went over to the diving equipment and checked the air in the tanks. Only fifteen minutes left in the two he and Luke had used and just over a half hour in the third tank. "Those won't take us far," he said.

No. We needed that submersible. We were itching to explore the tunnel. Where was Johnny?

Fifteen minutes passed, then thirty. "I'm calling him," Luke said. "Something's holding him up."

Luke waited as the phone rang. His face grew impatient, then worried. "No one's answering."

"Maybe he's on his way," I said.

"He would still answer. His phone has Bluetooth."

"Try Arianna," Norman suggested. "She would have stayed on board."

Luke tried Arianna's number, but it went unanswered. Now, Luke was really concerned. It was unlike his ex-wife to ignore his call. And she hadn't planned to accompany Sayid. Her plan was to catch the submersible on sonar when it emerged from the tunnel into the open sea.

"Try *your* phones," Luke suggested to both Norman and Alessa. "Maybe mine is damaged."

They both tried Johnny Sayid's number and then Arianna's. The result was the same. No answer from either.

"I don't like this," Luke said, leaving the pilot and his ex brief texts.

Norman gave Luke a frown. "Neither do I... I think someone better go back to the yacht."

"I'll go," Luke said. "Two should go and two should stay. In case Sayid shows up. Lucy, you come with me. Depardieu and Piero can stay here."

Norman nodded his agreement, his vision fixed on the large cavern below the waterline across the wide cenote. "If we stay, we will check out that east tunnel."

"You don't have enough air," I warned.

"I'll strap the two tanks with the lesser amount of air on my back. Piero can take the fuller one."

"But what if Johnny shows up?"

"We'll leave the laptop on so he can see where we are."

"But how will *I* know where you are? I don't like this, Norman. You should wait until we bring the submersible."

"That will take hours. Don't worry about us." But he knew that wasn't going to cut it. I was not going to let those two head off on a cockamamie adventure through those endless tunnels without a camera monitoring them.

"Okay, sweetheart. Tell you what." He pulled out his phone and made some adjustments in Settings. He went over to the laptop computer and did the same thing there. "Now, it's synchronized. You can follow our every move." He handed me his phone to show me. "Happy now?"

"A *little* happier." Enough so that I had no excuse to insist on staying. I understood why Alessa and Norman were the right choice to remain. They could both dive. I would be of more use to Luke on the yacht.

I accepted Norman's phone. He moved the headlamp where the camera was mounted so that I could see it was following his every move.

"Okay. Stay in touch," Luke said.

CHAPTER 37

It paid to be rich. As soon as we returned to Espita, Luke was able to get someone to have a boat waiting for us at Rio Lagartos on the northern coast, by which we would reach the yacht. Luke's car was fast and he planned to arrive in forty minutes. There was still no answer from either Arianna or Sayid.

The little village of Rio Lagartos was colorful and quaint. Rows of brightly painted houses and businesses built on short pylons and piers lined the shore. If we weren't in such a hurry I would have loved to visit for a few hours.

There was even a new hotel built on the waterfront with a view of the sea. Those sofas on the patio looked comfy, and would have been welcome along with an ice-cold beer after our hot drive. And did I mention that Rio Lagartos was located in a UNESCO World Heritage Site biosphere reserve? Flamingoes, crocodiles, pelicans and numerous other exotic birds and animals were protected here.

And let's not forget the famous Las Coloradas Pink Lakes.

The privately owned pools were actually

industrialized salt flats. Their high concentration of salt encouraged the growth of a red algae and tiny pink shrimp that fed on it. This was what gave the lakes their characteristic cotton-candy-pink hue. The pools were filled with saltwater as part of the process of salt harvesting. As the water evaporated, the salt, shrimp and algae concentrated.

Fun fact. Flamingoes are pink because these are the very shrimp they feed on.

The surreal rosiness of the water against the cerulean blue sky was reported to be breathtaking. On our arrival some friendly locals insisted it was really something to see. But we had no time for sightseeing.

Rio Lagartos was even smaller than Espita with a population of around 4,000, and was a delightful fishing town. Which was why it was so easy to charter a boat.

While we waited for the captain to board us, I checked in with Norman and Piero. They were geared up in their dive suits and had just descended into the cenote.

"No excitement here," Norman reported. "And no sign of the helo either. We're headed into the Gateway." We had nicknamed the tunnel 'the Gateway.'

It was odd. You would think now that Aras and his family were safely on their way back to Syria, Luke and Arianna would drop the search for Atlantis. But Natasha and Anastasie had started something. And even though the younger sister was dead, we still wanted to beat Anastasie at her own game.

If there *was* an Atlantis, we would find it first.

And it looked like there was. Or something like it. That was so important, people were willing to kill and die for it. I would have been hard pressed to quit even if Luke and Arianna had decided to nix the whole mission. My father, Moz, was somehow involved. Moreover, he was missing.

I had to find him. I believed that wherever Atlantis was, that was where we would find Moz.

I had no idea if Moz could dive. Or even if he could swim. How did he plan to find the lost island? Because I was pretty certain at this point that he had found the Gateway.

I hesitated to say it out loud. But I was worried that, somehow, he had made his way back to the cenote where Norman and Alessa were. Had he also found the right tunnel? And was he even now on his way to Atlantis?

Or was he dead?

"Keep an eye out…" I couldn't bring myself to say it. *For dead bodies.* "And make sure you come back in one piece."

"Don't worry, *p'tite chou*," Norman burbled through his mouthpiece. "If Moz came this way, I will find him."

Astoundingly he always knew what I was thinking almost even before I thought it.

The captain gestured for us to board and Luke took my arm and guided me down into the boat. It was a vintage wooden skiff in need of a paint job but it had a powerful motor.

I kissed my fingertip and pressed it to the phone, then sat on one of the wood benches Luke indicated.

The engine revved and exploded into action. I clicked off the phone and shoved it into my pocket and hung on for dear life as the captain sped across the sea towards Luke's yacht.

It was anchored quite a distance out. And at first, we suspected nothing. The yacht was simply unusually quiet. It was possible both Sayid and Arianna were on their way in the chopper. The roar of the rotors could well drown out the sound of their phones.

The white, streamlined decks, tiered like a stepped, maple-and-vanilla wedding cake showed no movement. The tinted windows were dark and were as lifeless as the eyes of the crocodile I had spotted in the cenote. If not for the stillness of the ship it would have seemed an ordinary day. Blue sky and sharp, pillowing clouds in the background, and screaming seagulls.

I was soaked with sea spray by the time we arrived.

Where was the crew? The helicopter was on its pad at the rear top deck of the luxury craft. The wheelhouse at the front of the ship showed no activity. Under normal circumstances, someone would be standing on the bridge with a pair of long-range binoculars to monitor the arrival of a strange boat.

No people worked or milled on any of the gorgeous teakwood decks. Luke was a purist and while many superyachts had their exterior decks built from synthetic materials, Luke preferred the real thing. It made his yacht stand out among superyachts. The sleek, glossy, rot-resistant wood, polished to its natural glory, was incontestable. It was also slip-resistant but needed constant maintenance to keep its beauty. Which was why we walked barefoot aboard ship.

But there were no barefoot crew today.

Had Arianna given them the day off? When the yacht was berthed and unoccupied, the crew was given time off to sightsee and allowed a few days leave. Even so, Arianna should have been on board, and she was always accompanied by a small crew. The boat was never completely unmanned when anchored at sea.

So… where was she?

Someone should have seen our approach and informed her of our arrival. Pirates were not unheard of. Even in this day and age. And Luke's crew were ever vigilant when in unfamiliar waters. So, this was unusual. More than unusual. But there were no strange watercraft moored alongside or anywhere nearby.

My phone suddenly dinged. I had received a text.

It was from Moz! Not receiving a response from my lost phone, Moz must have decided to text Norman.

I'm okay, it said. *And look what I found!*

Three photos were attached to the text.

The first was of a sinkhole. A virgin cenote showing a tunnel entrance and nothing else. It could have been any cenote. Was it the one with the pine tree above the opening and the mountain peak in the background? The composition of the photo omitted any identifying details. But if it was, he had arrived there long before us and was… where now?

The second photograph was inside a cave showing a petroglyph of a man with stars on his legs. The third picture showed a carved and painted individual wearing a headdress made from a bloody femur and an eyeball spraying blood. Had Moz found these inside the tunnel? The tunnel where Norman and Piero were at this moment?

"Oh, my god, Luke," I said jerking my head up.

"One second," he said.

Luke leaned forward at the bow, drawing the

skiff with him as he bent at the waist and twisted the mooring line around one of the yacht's boarding platform cleats, closing the gap between the two boats. Then repeated the process at the stern. It seemed strange to me at the time that Luke was not more concerned. It was obvious that he was aware of the unusual state of the yacht. But when I tried to query him, he simply gave me a knowing smile. Were we being watched?

Had he dealt with pirates before? Did he have some secret weapon with which to stop them?

And if there was something wrong, why were we boarding?

When the skiff was stable, Luke paid the captain, while we bobbed from the rhythmic waves. He climbed up and squatted to lend me a hand. I popped the phone away and crawled up to stand next to him, and then retrieved it from my crossbody handbag. I was anxious to show Luke the message.

"*Está bien?* All is well?" The captain spoke in a mix of English and Spanish. He remained at the helm looking up at us, the engine cut. Had he too noticed something off?

"*Bien,*" Luke replied.

He didn't sound all that '*bien*' if you asked me. And this made me even more nervous. He took out some more pesos from his wallet, despite the fact that he had already paid the captain, and turned his back to the windows of the yacht to scribble something on one of them with a gel pen. He then scrunched it in his fist passing it secretly as he shook the captain's hand in farewell.

This was more than a well-deserved tip.

When the captain glanced down at the note and nodded, Luke unraveled the bowline from the cleat. And then did the same at the stern, tossing the lines into the skiff. The skiff began to drift away from the yacht. It's motor burst on, and the skiff reversed, and sped back in the direction of Rio Lagartos.

"Why is it so quiet?" I asked Luke, the text and photos abruptly forgotten. I glanced around at the dead yacht.

Luke placed two fingers to his lips. "You still have Norman's phone?" His voice was barely a whisper.

I gripped it uncertainly, gave him a swift nod.

"Text him and Piero to get back here as soon as they can. We've got trouble."

Cham Nassar was holding a phone. He stood on the deck directly above us, with Anastasie Kirsche at his side, looking down. So, they had made some sort of deal. She was working for him now.

Two men stood on either side of them armed with AK-47s. Behind them were others. Out of the corner of my eye I sighted two more armed men, fingers firmly clenched on the trigger guards of their guns, weapons tucked into their chests, slinking down the companionway.

Our only hope was to get a message to Norman.

I was standing behind Luke so Nassar did not see my busy thumbs. I quickly sent the text and dropped the phone down into the coil of rope next to me. The armed men approached.

"Welcome back, Dr. Trevanian," Nassar shouted down from the rail. "We have been waiting for you."

"What are you doing on my boat?" Luke demanded. "Where are my people?"

"Don't worry. They are safe… They are locked inside the wine cellar." This last was said with disgust. Cham Nassar apparently disapproved of Luke Trevanian's lifestyle. And yes, Luke had a large walk-in wine cellar/tasting room, big enough to fit his twelve crew members, his ex-wife and the helicopter pilot. The wine cellar was kept locked. But Arianna had a key. Despite the fact that they were divorced, they still shared some things, and he and the rest of us worked for her as members of ISORE.

Nassar must have convinced Arianna to open the wine cellar with that assault rifle.

"Follow my men up the stairs. We have much to discuss."

I darted a glance at Luke. He shrugged. What else could we do? If Norman and Alessa were here, then maybe… but we were unarmed and outnumbered.

To ensure our lack of firearms, the men frisked us. We were unarmed but they found Luke's phone on him and took it. Good thing I had ditched mine (I mean Norman's). They would have taken that too.

Luke waved me ahead of him. And the twin armed guards followed behind us. When I reached the top, Nassar stood observing me. I had slipped his clutches after he had captured me at Chichén Itzá. I was responsible for him losing his hostages. And his longtime enemy, the resistance fighter Aras. His dark look told me he had not forgotten. And that he would never underestimate me again.

When he spoke, his voice dripped honey. "Ah, we meet again, little one."

The nature in which he addressed me, I was sure, was meant to provoke. "Not charmed, I'm sure," I replied.

His face was olive toned, deepened by years in the sun; his hair, what I could see of it under an olive-green cap, black and unruly. He wore a full beard that showed the bow of his full lips. He was dressed, as was usual for him, in army fatigues, a weapon of mass destruction slung over his shoulder and a holster containing an automatic pistol belted at his hip. He had no need to raise it to me. His men were efficiently doing it for him. Every time I moved the nose of a gun followed.

He looked like he wanted to grab hold of me and throw me off the ship. His cheeks had turned an uncomely shade of purple. I watched the emotions wrestle on his face. Before he seized control over the unwanted feelings and scowled.

"Soon, you will not be laughing. I have plans for you. You have been an invisible sliver in my thumb for too long."

That was putting it mildly. Or maybe it was meant to be an insult. Perhaps he was insinuating that I wasn't worth troubling over. That made him triply dangerous and I regretted goading him.

He continued to hold the phone and now he raised it.

I knew that particular device. It belonged to Moz because it had a distinctive aquamarine silicone protective cover on the back.

When he turned the screen to face me, I realized he now knew as much as we about the location of Atlantis. His problem was how to interpret those petroglyphs.

He thrust the screen forward. "These pictures. I

know they show the way to the lost island. You will show me."

I ignored the accusation. "Where is Moz?" I demanded.

He paused, glared at me. "Who?"

"That phone. It belongs to my father."

A self-satisfied smile spread across his rough features.

Had I made a mistake allowing him to know my relationship with the phone's owner? Or should I have kept my mouth shut?

Nassar's eyes went dark. "And now it belongs to me."

"Where is he?" Luke asked.

Cham Nassar chose to ignore Luke's question as well. It was true that we were hardly in a position to make demands but I wanted to know the fate of my father. He was smarter and much farther ahead than we were in this game. He realized what we were up against. We didn't. He understood things that we did not even know existed.

But at the moment, all I wanted to learn was this. Did Nassar kill him? My heartrate was up; I was beginning to panic. Anastasie must have explained what those pictures on the phone meant. She had solved the puzzle just as we had, albeit through different means.

A pathway into the Underworld and ultimately to Paradise.

Atlantis.

I turned to her. She looked very much the worse for wear. She was exhausted and stressed and very angry. She had never meant to share the secret of Atlantis with anyone. Not even her own sister. And especially not with an Islamic terrorist.

Streaks of dirt-smeared sweat marked her face. Her hair looked fried by sun and wind. Her clothing was greasy and stained. No longer white and pristine. It had been days since she had bathed or changed her clothes.

"Where is Moz?" I demanded of her. "How did you get his phone?"

I was certain she had stolen it. Her goons had gone searching for him. They must have found him. Or if not, they had found his phone.

So how did they know his passcode?

"My men found it near a cenote. After following his tracks."

"Which cenote?" Had he discovered the same one as us? Had she?

"Doesn't matter how I got his phone, does it? The important thing is that I got it. And it brought you to me."

My confusion must have surprised her. What did she want with me? What use was I to her. What she hadn't bargained for was the fact that Norman had stayed behind. Anastasie needed him and Luke to do the diving. And to operate the sophisticated electronics, including the submersibles.

"Enough talk," Nassar said. His words were directed at Anastasie. Eyes fierce, they penetrated her as he spoke. "This is the last clue?"

She nodded. Her vision took us both in and I forced my weak knees to stiffen. Her finger pointed accusingly. A wicked smile stretched across her lips.

"They know the location of Atlantis!"

"Good," he said.

He sent a meaningful nod at one of his gunmen.

Her gaze followed his. Suddenly her mouth opened in horror.

Nassar smiled. "Then I no longer need *you*."

"Wait, wait, wait!" I shouted. "Tell me where my father is!"

Nassar stepped back. Luke yanked me out of the way with one fell swoop. He was too late to save Anastasie. The gunman flipped his pistol on Anastasie and fired three short blasts.

Anastasie lay in a pool of blood on the deck.

I could imagine the thoughts roiling in Luke's head. He had no love for the Nazi archaeologist, but to have her executed on the deck of his yacht was reprehensible. And not just because human life (no matter how deplorable) was no one's right to take. Unless you were given no choice.

Those bloodstains were going to be a bitch to get out.

CHAPTER 38

But this was no time for jokes. Anastasie was dead. Both Luke and I had dropped to our knees to help her. It was too late. Nassar ordered us to rise to our feet. Then turned to his henchmen.

"Throw her overboard," he commanded.

Sooner or later the body would drift to some shore and the authorities would be on it. But Nassar planned to be gone long before then.

The splash made me jump.

I ran to the starboard side. And watched the body sink. Blood bloomed in the clear blue water and fish swarmed in, attracted by the promise of food. In a few days when the corpse began to rot and all sorts of disagreeable gases developed, it would float. Some unsuspecting beachcomber or fisherman would have the unpleasant experience of stumbling across it.

One of Nassar's men had followed me, and now grappled my arms and forced me to return.

"Where is the Frenchman?" Nassar demanded, his eyes twitching from me. Then Luke. Then back again. "Where is Depardieu? I have a beef with him. And he can repay me by finding the treasure."

A year ago, Norman had infiltrated Nassar's stronghold, stolen some priceless statues from him and helped the Syrian resistance reclaim their cities.

"Where!" he barked when we remained silent.

"Gone to get the police," Luke taunted.

Nassar scoffed. "Do you think I am that stupid? I have your wife and your crew locked inside the wine cellar. Am I to believe you are willing to sacrifice them for the sake of a legend? I have nothing to lose, Dr. Trevanian. For the sake of the treasure, I will kill them all."

I tugged at Luke's elbow. "Luke, I think he means it."

Nassar snarled, "Of course, I mean it. I want you to bring the rest of your team here where my men can keep an eye on you all. And then you and your French friend will help me find the treasure of Atlantis."

Silence.

"If the police show up," Nassar said. "Everyone dies." He tilted his head at two gunmen and they went inside the yacht.

"Okay, I was bluffing," Luke confessed. "There is no police. No one knows you've pirated my yacht. How did you get here? Where are your boats?"

"Inside your toy garage." Nassar spat in disgust. Luke's hedonistic lifestyle went against everything the Islamic extremist believed in. The yacht's above-water garage with its portable launch platform contained all kinds of toys like jet skis, zodiacs, two three-person submersibles and three motorcycles. There was more than enough room to add a few more boats since he had left his classic Humvee behind, and two tenders were missing. No wonder we suspected nothing on our approach. He had had the intelligence to hide all signs of his presence after commandeering the yacht.

"We'll help you," I said.

Luke glared at me. I glared back. There was nothing else to do. If we helped him, we could buy time. Enough time for Norman and Piero to arrive.

It looked to me like Nassar had about twenty-five men aboard. I wasn't sure how many we had. Most of the crew had been drilled in dealing with potential pirates, but no one was trained in dealing with terrorists. Was there a difference? Clearly, Arianna and Sayid had been caught off-guard. And because they had been easily taken, I could only assume that most of the crew were on shore. A couple of the tenders were missing.

That was good news and bad. Good because that meant those who had gone ashore on the tenders were safe. Bad because it meant our numbers were small. And most probably disarmed. And without any means of communicating with us. Nassar would have seized their phones.

Luke caught on to my plan and said, "We will help you locate Atlantis and whatever treasure remains there, but first I want to see my wife. I have to know that she and my people are unharmed."

Out of nowhere I heard a gunshot and spun around. One of Nassar's men, who had been on the outside of the circle, dropped to the ground. He was only injured, shot in the shoulder but it was enough to take him unawares.

Everyone dropped to a hunch and crabbed to the rail, guns at the ready. Luke took the opportunity to escape by knocking the pistol out of Nassar's grip. A gunman to his right jabbed a pistol in him and forced him to stand.

Nassar retrieved his gun, and spat on the deck. "Bring him where he can be seen. And if he tries that again, shoot him."

They went to the rail.

It the sniper was someone from our team he would cease firing at the sight of Luke.

I darted a quick look at the water and saw that the shooter was the captain of the skiff. He had returned after suspecting things were fishy.

Convinced that Luke's scribbled note on the extra peso was to tell the boat captain to radio the police, I wished he'd kept going instead of doubling back. Or at least waited for backup. But the men reared on the Caribbean coasts were tough and undoubtedly stubborn. *God bless him for his bravery and please, dear God, save him from being killed!*

No one was watching my movements because I was a woman. And once again Cham Nassar had underestimated me.

I took advantage of the chaos to slip down the companionway while attention was focused on the skiff. Their attention was held in the opposite direction, which was to my benefit, and I rushed to the coil of rope on the platform deck, and retrieved my phone. I shoved it into my pocket, and then raced back by hauling myself up the companionway two steps at a time before I was missed.

My breath labored. And when Nassar turned to search for me, he spied me standing a few feet behind him. Was he wondering why I hadn't taken the opportunity to escape? The thought had fleeted across my mind. But what would have been the point? I could not single-handedly rescue my colleagues. I needed help. And I knew Nassar had no intention of killing us straight away. He needed us. He even needed me. Because if anything would convince Norman to help Nassar, it was me as hostage.

Nassar thrusted his fist seaward at the skiff. "Kill the interloper!" he shouted. His words were in Arabic, but that was my translation.

By this time the sun was low in the sky. Nassar's thugs were hindered by the brilliant red ball in their eyes. Three gunmen hoisted their automatic weapons to their shoulders, and peppered the skiff with bullets until they exhausted their ammunition. These brutes were ruthless. We were in the middle of the Caribbean with no one to hear the screams. The boat captain collapsed inside the skiff, one hand on the helm, dark splotches spattering the bulwarks, the skiff spinning into a semi arc before skating towards land.

"Go after him!" Nassar ordered.

Two men went below to launch one of the terrorist's boats.

Nassar swiveled back to me and Luke. "If you don't want to suffer the same fate, you'll do as you're told."

"What about my wife," Luke demanded.

Had Luke just called Arianna his wife? For the second time? They had been divorced for years.

"What about her?"

"I want to see her before I assist you with anything. I want to talk to her."

Nassar understood that Luke would gladly suffer the consequences and attack him if Arianna was harmed in any way.

Whether he was bluffing or not was anyone's guess. But it appeared as though he had convinced Nassar that he would only help locate Atlantis—even if he aimed a gun at my head—if Arianna was safe.

Lucky for me it never came to that.

He did point the gun at my chest. "*You.* My man will take you to the wine cellar and you can talk to the woman and the crew and report back to your boss."

"Fine," I said.

Luke gave me a promising nod. I followed the gunman ahead of me while a second armed man followed, shoving the nose of his gun into my back.

We arrived at the wine cellar, but I didn't know the code for the lock. Turns out I didn't need it. Nassar had blasted the mechanism and the door was now bolted with a plank of wood screwed into the jamb. For further reassurance guards had been posted at the door.

They unscrewed the wooden board and let me inside.

"You have three minutes," one of the gunmen uttered. "Then I take you back to Nassar."

I slipped inside and saw that only five people were in the wine cellar. One of those was not Johnny Sayid.

I threw my arms around Arianna, and she gave me a brief hug. "Thank God, you're okay, Lucy," she said.

"Thank God, *you're* okay," I echoed. I whispered in case the walls were thin. "Where's Johnny?"

She shrugged. "I don't know. He was supposed to take the helo to Luke at the cenote, and then all hell broke loose when those hooligans boarded the yacht. We never saw them until it was too late. They aren't like regular pirates. They have stealth maneuvers. And know exactly what they're doing."

"That's because they aren't pirates," I informed her. "Didn't you recognize the head honcho? It's Cham

Nassar."

"I recognized him," she said.

I looked around and spotted the chef, the sommelier and the navigator. The other one was a stranger. He was a young man. A crewman. Both he and the navigator had scratches and bruises on their faces. The navigator was clutching his arm like his shoulder had been dislocated. Clearly, they had not surrendered the yacht without a fight.

"Where is everyone else? Where's Captain Jack?"

"I gave them the day off," Arianna replied. "The captain went on shore with them. It was the first time he's been off the yacht in a month. I thought he deserved it."

He did, except that the timing was awful.

"They took your weapons and phones?" I asked the navigator whose name was Lockwood.

"Yes."

I pulled out Norman's phone and activated it. Then saw something that had me horrified.

CHAPTER 39

The phone was still synchronized with Norman's head-mounted diving camera. He was being swept down the stone tunnel in a powerful current, the rushing water blurring anything in his path. It was a wonder the camera remained intact. In front of him I could barely make out Piero's finned feet.

I wanted to scream at him and ask if they were okay. Of course, they weren't okay. I could see their predicament with my own eyes. Besides, the audio was damaged. Not a sound came from the speaker.

How many minutes of air did they have? At the speed they were going, if they crashed up against a stone wall they would be killed.

What I could see, the tunnel looked fairly straight. If Norman and Piero could keep from making hard contact with the rock, they had a chance of surviving the exit.

"What is it?" Arianna asked in a harsh whisper.

"It's Norman and Alessa," I whispered back. Under no circumstances must the guards outside the wine cellar door suspect I had a phone. "When Johnny was a no show with the submersible, they decided to go exploring while we returned to learn what happened to him. They're in trouble." I turned the phone to face her.

Cool as usual in tight situations, Arianna managed to contain her gasp. Her eyes narrowed as she watched for a moment and then she handed the phone to me. "Don't worry. Those two have been in nastier fixes than this. They'll figure it out."

Yes, they would. I knew they would. But still, seeing their lives in jeopardy and being unable to help was the worst feeling in the world. I shoved the phone back at her. "Hold on to it. You can keep tabs on what is happening with them. I can't. I'll be watched. Nassar expects me to return any minute—"

Noises sounded at the door and it swung open. Arianna barely had time to shove the phone into the back of her waistband.

"You," the gunman said, aiming his pistol at me, "Out, *now*." He clawed me by the arm and dragged me out the door.

The door slammed and the board was screwed back in to lock it in place.

We returned to the deck and I reported the state of affairs inside the wine-cellar. Nassar kept a grim eye on me, and I stopped myself from mentioning the fact that the crewman and the navigator had been beaten up. They were alive and able, and the others unharmed; that was all that mattered.

There was not a single jailcell-like place on this yacht, and even the smaller guest bedrooms were huge and luxurious. They also all had sliding glass doors to private decks, and massive scenic windows. If Nassar meant to hold us prisoner. Good luck.

He definitely had no intention of allowing us to be

sequestered with Arianna and the crew.

He finally decided to confine us to the twenty-four-seat cinema. I had forgotten about the cinema. It was one of the only spaces without windows; we wouldn't be able to escape. The doors were pneumatic and only lockable from the outside.

The cinema was as luxurious as the rest of the yacht. The seats were upholstered in plush azure blue with arms and headrests. And a starlit ceiling overhead. The screen was almost movie theater size and the floors were carpeted in white and black fabric mosaics. The room was completely blacked out when the projector was on. Except for the artificial starlight above and some pot lights inset strategically under an elegant decorative architectural overhang at the corners of the walls.

Luke switched on the lights.

It was getting dark. The only access to the outside was through a large glass skylight amidst the digital stars. It was never open—to protect the luxurious fabrics from exposure and the delicate electronics from the weather. If Luke was thinking we could get out that way, he had another think coming. The skylight was more than 15 feet over our heads. The seats were bolted into the floor and not repositionable. Even if Luke stood on one of the cushioned chairs and I climbed onto his shoulders and was able to reach the rim of the skylight, hauling myself up by my fingertips was impossible. What's more, it would be a miracle and a travesty if this beautiful theater was used to store common rope. But—we searched anyways.

The place was clean. Pristine. That's what you got when you hired crew to keep the yacht immaculate. No stray pieces of rope when you needed it.

"Norman and Piero are in trouble," I told Luke.

I reiterated what I'd seen on my phone.

"It's okay," he said. And repeated almost word for word Arianna's reassurances. "Those two are resourceful. Don't worry."

It was hard not to worry. This was my fiancé we were talking about. And in his line of business, I was even beginning to wonder if marriage was the right thing to do.

"We've got bigger fish to fry." He started to pace the floor in the aisle between the seats. "I have to get to the wheelhouse."

"Why? What good will that do."

He frowned. "I wish Depardieu and Piero were here. It would be easier to instigate my plan. And where the hell is Sayid?"

The fact that he was not in the wine cellar was a good thing I reminded him.

"If only I had briefed more people on the new features of the yacht."

"What do you mean?"

"It has a secret I haven't told anyone about."

"It does?" I glanced around. Not that there was anything to see inside the theater. "You didn't even tell Arianna?"

He shook his head. "I know; big mistake. I wasn't sure she would approve… Only two people know. Me and the captain."

"Why?"

"I'm not sure… So much happened since I got the yacht, what with your incident at that castle museum, and you being kidnapped from your own wedding, and

Aras' family being held hostage, it slipped my mind. I only took possession of the new yacht a few days before the wedding… Anyway, it has some fancy bells and whistles."

"That will get rid of pirates?"

He sighed. "Maybe. I don't know… but if I can't get to the bridge, I can't find out."

A tap on the glass over our heads drew our eyes skyward.

Two men appeared in the skylight. Their black shapes were muscular and lean, and sharply delineated against the deepening dusk. Oh crap, did they think we were planning to escape that way? Because we were.

Except like I mentioned earlier. No rope.

We didn't need to have rope. They had it. I saw who it was now. Luke's yacht was enormous. It was easy for a person to hide. If the enemy didn't already know that he was there. The familiar forms of Johnny Sayid and… and Aras?… materialized.

With hand gestures Sayid indicated to Luke that he open the skylight. Luke went over to the console containing the controls for the projector and found the skylight indicator on the touchscreen. I doubt that Luke had ever opened this skylight before.

The glass slid back and Sayid called down in low tones. "You both okay?"

"What took you so long?" Luke asked.

"Was waiting for backup." Sayid jabbed a thumb at Aras who grinned down at us.

I waved, barely able to contain my excitement on seeing the helicopter pilot and Luke's half-brother. "Aras, what are you doing here? I thought you went home with your family."

"I meant to,"—he glanced backwards—"But I saw this guy hitching a ride on the highway and stopped to pick him up. Decided to take a detour and sent my family in the cab to the airport without me."

Guy? What guy? The person he was referring to abruptly stepped into view. Oh my God. It was Moz.

"Too long a story to relate at the moment." Moz glanced over his shoulders, left and right. "Suffice it to say, I found the cenote where Depardieu and Piero left that computer. Let's get you two out of there. Then we can talk."

They sent down a length of rope on which Sayid had fashioned a harness. I slipped into the harness, hung on to the rope as the three men pulled me up. When I was safe on the top of the upper deck, I saw the sky was almost black and the real stars had appeared.

I hugged each of the men in turn. Then said to my father, "How did Nassar get your phone?"

"I left it for Anastasie. To divert her from the actual place. I knew she would send some goons after me... Those petroglyphs were in the cenote I ended up in when I escaped from the one beneath the pyramid in Chichén Itzá."

I lifted the pendent from my throat and said, "Where you left this?"

He smiled. "I knew it would find its way to you. I realized when I ended up in that other sinkhole, and the sun went down, that the key to finding the Gateway had to do with the eclipse."

Like father like daughter. He had come to the same conclusion as me. Minus a vehicle and unable to find a ride, he was walking back to the cenote near Espita (after spending the night in the jungle) when Aras, halfway to the airport, saw him from the taxi.

"Unfortunately, we missed the eclipse... Were you there, Lucy? Did you manage to see the direction the sun pointed?"

"Yes." And the whole horrible incident of Norman and Alessa riding the current through the tunnel returned to panic me.

The conversation had to be shelved; Luke was waiting. The rope was dropped back into the cinema and the billionaire soon emerged. The men helped him onto the rooftop deck and out of the harness.

"How many men does Nassar have?" Luke asked Sayid when we were all gathered in the twilight.

"I counted twenty-five. The two that went after that skiff haven't returned yet. So that makes twenty-three, plus Nassar."

"We are miserably outnumbered," I moaned. "Do you think that boat captain radioed the police?"

Luke shrugged, and seemed nonetheless undeterred. "It doesn't matter. If he did, it will be hours before anyone gets out here. Rio Lagartos is a tiny village with a rudimentary police force and no coast guard of their own. Real help will come from one of the bigger towns... It's up to us to get Arianna and the crew out of the wine cellar... And I know exactly how."

"What about your new bells and whistles," I asked. "The pirate detractor?" I was joking, but he took me seriously.

"With the terrorists in control of the yacht I don't think it will work."

Luke turned to fumble at his pockets and then remembered that Nassar had confiscated his phone.

"If only we had some way to contact her," Sayid said.

My answer came swiftly. "We do. I gave Arianna Norman's phone."

CHAPTER 40

As long as Sayid had a functional cellphone, we could touch base. Both Luke and Moz's devices were in the possession of Cham Nassar. I was glad he had my father's phone. And grateful neither Anastasie nor Nassar had questioned why the phone was unlocked. Perhaps they thought the locking mechanism had malfunctioned when Moz dropped it. Whatever. The terrorist had fallen for the ruse and had no idea where the gateway to Atlantis stood. He needed us alive.

Sayid's phone was fully charged. He sent a text to Arianna. I had had the presence of mind to turn off the sound, so when the text arrived no chime would betray us. Just a vibration. It would be a disaster if either of the guards heard the cellphone inside the wine cellar. I was positive Nassar had impounded all of their devices.

A few seconds later, Sayid's phone vibrated. "She's ready."

The plan was to send the crew to safety on shore, while Luke, Sayid, and I took one submersible, and Arianna, Aras and Moz took the other. The submersibles were already berthed in sub bays, so they were easy to deploy. But first we had to get our people out of confinement.

We had one advantage over the terrorists. We were familiar with the layout of the yacht; they were still learning. It was easy for us to hide.

We slinked along the deck to the lower levels until we found our way to the gun locker. Luke had a slew of firearms, including pistols, rifles, spearguns and automatic weapons. He unlocked it with a digital code and we armed ourselves. Now we had a better chance if we ran up against the terrorists.

Next stop was the crew's galley. This was the least likely place for the terrorists to search for us as it would never occur to them that there were two kitchens on the yacht. I was certain that at this moment they were raiding the luxury main galley two floors above us. It was designed with stainless steel appliances, natural stone countertops and glass cabinetry. Nassar would be drawn there not only because that was where the gourmet food was stored, but because it was there he could inflict effective damage.

The crew's kitchen was one level below the wine cellar, while the main galley was a level above. The crew's galley was also the nearest egress to the sub bays where the submersibles were berthed and to the marine garage containing the inflated Zodiacs.

The dumb waiter led from the wine cellar to both the main galley and the crew's kitchen.

The plan was for Luke and I to take the dumb waiter up to the wine cellar to help the captives escape, while Moz, Aras and Sayid got the submersibles and the Zodiac ready to launch on our arrival.

Then Sayid suggested *he* go in Luke's place. "I might

be needed for the injured."

I had apprised the team of the navigator and the crewman's conditions. But because of Arianna, Luke wished to go himself.

I objected. "You know how to launch the escape craft, Luke. None of the rest of us do. Moz and Aras have never even seen the inside of a submersible before. You're needed in the garage. Johnny and I can handle this."

Luke scowled. "It's a brand-new installment. The dumb waiter hasn't been used before. I'm not even sure the chef or wine guy know how to use it yet."

"How hard can it be?"

He smiled at me. This wasn't the first time I had said those words to him.

He agreed. He explained how the dumb waiter operated and gave us step by step directions, hoping everything had been calibrated to his specifications. And that there were no glitches. Then he and the others left for the garage, and Sayid texted Arianna that we were on our way.

Arianna was surprised that Luke had installed a dumbwaiter on board. The chef and sommelier were aware, but the danger of using it for purposes other than what it was intended was so deeply ingrained, it never occurred to them that this might be a means of escape.

We climbed onto the stainless-steel countertop in the crew's galley and opened the electronic doors of the dumb waiter.

Sayid was a tall, muscular man.

"What's the weight capacity for this thing," I asked. "I think maybe I should be the one to go. And you stay here."

He hesitated. The thing had never been used before and certainly its trial run should not be done with a human guinea pig. But what choice did we have?

I warned him that we were running short on time. And that my weight was less likely to make the thing short out.

He finally agreed. He removed the sliding shelves. Then, helped me into the boxy space. It smelled like new metal and plastic, and fresh machine oil. This was going to be an interesting ride. *Remember*, I told myself. *This is nothing more than a tiny elevator.*

Was it big enough to fit me seated in a crouch? Absolutely, and with room to spare. Good thing—because some of the yacht's crew were larger than me.

Darkness dropped as the doors slid shut from top and bottom. This was blacker than any space I had ever been in. But it was well ventilated. My fingers automatically searched the walls. Perforated vents were everywhere; I wouldn't have to worry about suffocation.

I have to admit it was the most terrifying two minutes of my life. It felt like two hours. If you were prone to claustrophobia, it might kill you.

The lift opened vertically. And I heard low voices as I emerged. Then silence, as I put my fingers to my lips. Too much talking would make the guards suspicious. I unfolded myself, exited with the help of the crewman and the chef, and quickly assessed the captives' injuries as Sayid had instructed.

"What on earth?" Arianna gasped as I approached her. "When was *this* installed?"

Was that a rhetorical question? Or did she really

want to know? I had no answer. Luke never consulted me when he was buying a new submarine. Either way, no time for questions. If there were any lights in the main galley to indicate the dumb waiter was in use, we were in trouble. Nassar could notice us missing any moment.

Arianna nodded. "Okay, let's go."

"You first, Arianna," I whispered.

"God, I hope this works." She removed her shoes, climbed inside, squatting on her haunches with her shoes clutched in each fist, and shut her eyes. I tapped the touchscreen, found the right combination to operate the sliding doors, and touched the icon to descend—and the contraption hummed.

Next went the sommelier, who fortunately was a slight man.

Five minutes later the lift returned. The chef was a little heavier and for a moment I thought he wouldn't fit, but he did. And down he went.

I believe we were all grateful that when Luke had this appliance designed, he had custom ordered something much larger than the standard. I guess some of his parties required the transport of mass quantities of wine and food. And that could be very heavy indeed.

Next was the crewman, a young man who had no problem doubling up. Finally, it was the navigator's turn. Lockwood was the heaviest. He was about capacity, and I hoped he wouldn't damage the lift as I would be the last to escape.

He had trouble cramming in. Not because of his height and girth but because of his injured shoulder. But he was a trooper. He managed to wedge his arm into the right position to fit although I knew he was in excruciating pain. I watched the doors squeeze shut on him. And waited for my turn.

The next five minutes was agonizing, the longest of my life, as I waited for the dumb waiter to return.

Vague sounds come from the corridor, beyond the wine cellar door. If the lift wasn't here in the next minute, I was a goner.

Voices now as the guards discussed something I was too nervous to concentrate on. Then finally, the quiet hum and the dumb waiter's light flashed green.

My ride was here! I tapped the button to open the door, but nothing happened. Had we broken it? Oh shit! I could hear the guards outside now unscrewing the wood that blocked the door. I ran my fingers haphazardly over the touchscreen, and finally landed on the correct icon.

The dumb waiter's doors parted and I climbed in, and perched in a squat. I reached outside and found the touchscreen. My random tapping finally landed on the proper button and I quickly withdrew my arm as the doors slid shut.

The lift began to descend and I could no longer detect any outside sounds.

Suddenly the thing stopped. It was only halfway down. Oh shit. Was I stuck? Was I trapped inside this metal box, doomed to die?

Banging on the doors would only bring the terrorists to my rescue. Only to have them decide to leave me. Or shoot me when they got me out.

My breathing became shallow. My heartbeats ramped up. My mouth was so dry it felt like paper. My head began to swim.

Johnny, please, I screamed in my mind. *Get me out of*

here!

Just when I was about to pass out from panic, the hum started and the platform I was squatting on sank. Five seconds later, it stopped and the door slid open.

"Lucy! You gave us quite a scare," Arianna said.

"*You* got a scare. Just imagine how I felt!"

Sayid helped me out of the dumb waiter and onto the floor. "All accounted for?"

We did a head count, and then Sayid noticed that Lockwood was grimacing in pain.

"We have to go," I warned. "Nassar's men were tackling the door when I got into the dumb waiter."

Sayid approached Lockwood. "One second." He took Lockwood's left wrist and elbow in his hands and slowly brought his bent arm over his head. "This is going to hurt a bit. But I think you'll function better if I fix it."

Then a groan as he returned Lockwood's dislocated shoulder into place.

"How does that feel?"

"Good as new."

A muffled sound came from above as the door to the wine cellar was smashed in. Nassar must have gone to the cinema and found us missing. It was only natural that they would check the wine cellar next.

"Hurry," I whispered. We raced out of the crew's mess and down the corridor to the yacht's interior garage door. Behind us footsteps pounded along the far companionway. Sayid tossed Lockwood a rifle and I unholstered my pistol leading the way with the freed hostages, while the armed men brought up the rear.

At least I *thought* Sayid and Lockwood were bringing up the rear.

We turned a corner and I heard gunshots at our

back. Lockwood returned fire. Then hustled to catch up.

"Where's Sayid?" I demanded when I saw he wasn't with Lockwood.

"He's gone to get the helicopter."

Smart thinking. If our escape had all of their attention, no one would think that one of us would head for the helo.

However. He should have told me his plan.

When we were at the garage door Luke was there to meet us.

"No problems with the dumb waiter?" Luke asked, reaching for the touchscreen.

"*One* problem with the dumb waiter," Lockwood said swiveling through the gap after me. "I don't think it was meant for people."

"No kidding," Luke said. "What happened?"

"We almost lost Lucy."

Luke double tapped the Close button and the doors slid tight. He plugged in the code to lock it and we raced to the boats. The bay doors were already opened to the platform and the Zodiac was ready to launch.

Change of plans.

We might need two spare seats in the subs. So, Arianna, Lockwood and the crew committed to the ten capacity Zodiac, while Luke and I took submersible one, the *Barracuda*, leaving a third seat free. Moz and Aras took the other, the *Tiger Shark*, which also had a third seat available.

Just before Arianna boarded the zodiac, she returned Norman's phone to me. "You'll want this back. I'll use the Zodiac's communications to stay in touch."

The inner steel doors of the marine garage were pummeled with gunfire and the lock broke. A dozen men shoved the pneumatic door open until the gap was wide enough to allow an individual through. He was trailed by his companions, all bearing automatic weapons.

The Zodiac stormed out to the open sea and the submersibles dived, to a rain of bullets. Through the bubble glass I saw the helicopter lights lift into the sky.

Lucky for us, the darkness covered our escape. The Zodiac was long gone before anyone on deck noticed. As for Luke and I, we were submerged and none of the bullets had struck home.

The last thing we saw before heading for deep water were the lights of the *Madonna II* in full beam.

In fact, the yacht's lights were so bright we could see through the surrounding water almost like day.

CHAPTER 41

I had no idea what time it was. Except that it was night. The yacht's searchlights illuminating the water made us a perfect target. We had to get out of its range before Nassar deployed a search party and brought his arsenal with him. Luke sent us plunging thirty more feet. Nighttime under the sea was an eerie—no—spooky—feeling.

The first thing I did was fetch Norman's phone from my pocket. Arianna had charged it in the wine cellar/tasting room.

The picture was out. And nothing was visible on the screen. There was also a profound and terrifying silence. I feared the camera had been knocked off Norman's head and that the audio was lost because of a disengaged mouthpiece. What did that mean? Had they drowned? Was the equipment, along with their bodies, drifting at the bottom of the sea?

The idea was unbearable.

No, no, and no. I refused to accept it. I glared at the phone, shook it. Not that that would do any good.

"*Tiger Shark. Zodiac I.* Do you read?" Luke monotoned.

There was silence and only an electrostatic crackling came over the receiver.

"Repeat. *Tiger Shark*. *Zodiac I*. Are you out there. Respond."

Another few seconds of crackling.

"Do you read!"

"Loud and clear," came Aras' voice. "Everyone okay?"

Luke wiped the sweat from his brow. "Perfect. You?"

"Me and Moz, snug as a bug."

Luke grinned. "Stay close. We're going to do a reconnaissance. Hopefully those third seats will be filled."

"Aye, aye, Captain," Aras mocked. "On your tail."

"Not too close."

Luke allowed himself a small smile then switched to a different frequency.

"*Zodiac I*. Do you read?"

Static. Then silence. Then more static. Before Lockwood's voice came from the communications system. "Copy, *Barracuda*. We're fine. Left those terrorist pirates high and dry. The shooting has stopped. No signs of pursuit. Think they gave up… Headed for Rio Lagartos. ETA fifteen minutes."

"Copy that. We're going to hang out a bit. See what we can see, then rendezvous with you in say forty minutes… Hey, how's the shoulder?"

"Sayid did wonders. Couldn't be better."

"Well, kudos for keeping everyone alive," Luke said.

"Thanks for thinking of the dumb waiter."

"No problem. See you in forty."

Lockwood signed off. And while Luke returned to studying the images on the submersible's main screen, I returned to scrutinizing Norman's phone.

Dammit why was nothing showing on the screen. I was about to tap Luke's shoulder to beg him to do something to find Norman when a red dot began to pulse on the screen.

What was happening? I passed the phone over Luke's shoulder so that he could interpret what I was seeing.

"What is that?" I asked.

Luke took the phone from me and connected it to a port on his console. "It's a tracker."

"You mean we know where Norman is?"

"Yes." He did something on the touchscreen and the red dot started pulsing on a larger scale on the console's wide screen. "We've got contact," he said. "Just no visuals and no audio. They must have suffered damage on the way out of that tube."

"He's alive?"

He nodded. "Of course, he's alive. It would take a lot more than a tussle with the rapids down an underground aquifer to kill our boy."

I grinned. "Is Piero okay too?"

Luke glanced at the screen where a second red dot was pulsating. "I believe so."

"Where are they?"

He touched a few buttons and a map of the underground river system appeared. His colleague had been mapping the aquifers for over a decade. But many were yet to be explored. This map however gave us a general idea of their position.

"They've been spat out to sea."

"Where?" I asked.

"Not far." Luke transposed a topographical map over

the pulsing red dots which delineated the undersea landscape. Coordinates appeared on the screen. "Two kilometers from here."

"And they're alive? They didn't run out of air?"

"I think those subaqueous rapids propelled them down the tunnel so fast, they had more air than they needed. They're at the surface now. We better get up there before Nassar's men find them."

Luke contacted the *Tiger Shark* to inform Aras and Moz of our destination. It took us ten minutes to reach the coordinates.

We doused our lights, and swiftly rose. Seawater streamed off the glass and Luke popped the hatch as we bobbed into fresh air. The temperature was warm and the water calm. The moon reflected on the obsidian sea. A few meters away, another bubble broke the surface and Aras' head materialized as he opened the hatch.

On the far horizon we could see the lights of the yacht.

But where were Norman and Piero?

The silence was deafening, the hot wind felt cold. I was shivering from nerves. We were at the coordinates. Where *were* they? Five excruciating minutes passed before we heard a splash, and a head poked up alongside us.

"*Merde*, it's about time you got here," Norman said. He had discarded his empty tanks to get rid of the extra weight. Steel scuba tanks sank even when empty so why burden themselves unnecessarily. "Piero and I were about to swim to shore."

Alessandra appeared next to him. She too had unloaded her empty tank and had her mask swept up over her hair.

Overhead, an amphibious helicopter hovered, its pontoons ready to float.

"It's Sayid," Luke said. He signaled the pilot to wait. "Your choice. By air or by sea."

"I've had enough of the sea," Piero said with a smirk.

Luke contacted Sayid's radio. And told him to land as close as was safe. The wind from the spinning rotors would send us off-balance. The helicopter made a slow descent about fifty feet away until the pontoons touched the sea's surface. Our submersibles began to rock as waves gyrated.

"Closing the hatch," Luke shouted, "before we get waterboarded!"

Both Norman and Piero saluted, and started to swim in the direction of the slowing rotors. They decided it would be faster to travel by helicopter.

CHAPTER 42

The gang assembled at the new hotel in Rio Lagartos on the comfy couches of the outdoor patio. Arianna had managed to book us rooms but we needed to exchange news. Food had been ordered and laid out, filling every square inch of the coffee tables with traditional foods including tamales, tacos, burritos and nachos with all sorts of creamy and peppery dips. And black bean and corn salads with onions and plenty of chopped tomatoes, lettuces and grated cheese.

As we feasted, having not eaten in several hours, we shoveled food into our mouths in silence. When the edge was off, Arianna informed us that the bulk of the *Madonna II*'s crew had scattered to various resort towns and tourist sites across the Yucatán. They were not expected to return until the end of the week. That meant we would be shorthanded.

Luke got hold of the local police and was apprised that a team was being assembled as they spoke to investigate the strange events going on in the superyacht offshore.

The police had received the mayday cry for help

from the skiff captain, and now he was missing. But the search had to be deferred until first light.

"You mean there's nothing we can do about those thugs that stole our yacht?" Arianna asked when Luke returned from his chat with the authorities.

"Nothing. It's too dark. And needless to say, dangerous. I'm sure Nassar had the sense to douse the lights when they realized we'd escaped their gunfire. The police would be going in blind, and hunting for a group of terrorists on that yacht would be like searching for people in a hotel. The creeps would open fire even before the police announced their presence. They'd be sitting ducks."

Arianna shook her head and made no comment.

"One piece of good news," he added.

She looked up. "What's that?"

"Depardieu and Piero found evidence of a sunken civilization."

There was silence.

It was the news that everyone had been waiting to hear. Though the actual hearing of it in words made it seem incredible.

I was expecting to see the first reaction from Arianna, but I had momentarily forgotten about Moz. He was seated across from her and his eyes widened.

"Where? What is the evidence?"

Luke turned from his ex-wife to locate Norman and Piero. "Show them," he urged. Luke hadn't seen the evidence himself yet. He had taken Norman and Piero's word that it was genuine.

Norman shot a suspicious glance at Moz before he gestured to Piero to hand him something. She shoved a bundle over to Norman. He unraveled the string around it.

His hand went inside the contractable netting, and he pulled a flat nine-inch piece of mosaic flooring from out of the dive bag.

The intricately designed piece of stone floor was made from white and turquoise tesserae and showed a familiar geometric pattern. It wasn't big enough to determine whether it was part of a larger pictorial scene or just decoration. How had it managed to survive under the sea for so long? And still retain its color?

I cupped a hand to my mouth in astonishment. "It's gorgeous!"

"Let me see it," Arianna said and Norman placed the artifact in her eager fingers.

"We landed right on this platform," Piero explained, her voice excited. "It appeared to be the floor of some important building or a courtyard."

"How big was the area?" Moz asked. His voice sounded higher pitched than normal.

"Hard to say," she answered. "But I suspect it goes on for miles. The mosaic floor was peeking out of the seabed and this piece broke off when we shot the inflatable buoy into the rock."

Arianna was unusually animated as she studied the object. "So, we have a marker?"

"We do indeed," Norman answered. "We can search for it on the top of the sea tomorrow morning."

"What else did you find?" she demanded.

"We didn't have time to look around. We were almost out of air and barely had enough for a single decompression. We went straight up after landing on the site."

"No pictures?"

"Our cameras were damaged on the trip out."

No kidding.

"You're both uninjured?" she inquired.

Finally, she had thought to ask. And her eyes went from Norman to Alessandra.

"A little bruised and scratched up, but that's per usual." Norman grinned. "Nothing broken."

Piero raised her arms to show the blue-black marks on her arms and shoulders. "We were lucky that tunnel was reasonably wide and we were wearing neoprene. Otherwise, the damage would have been much worse."

Arianna nodded. "Then I suggest you get yourselves cleaned up. We all need to get some sleep. We have to be awake, and in the water, as soon as the sun's up."

We said our goodnights and went to our rooms. The instant Norman and I were alone I threw myself into his arms. Once again, I wondered if getting married was the right thing to do. "Don't ever do that to me again," I chided him, raising my fists in frustration.

"Stop pummeling me. I've got enough war wounds as it is." He chuckled and dragged me down into his lap as he sat down on the bed.

I examined the strong, sinewy forearms of the man I loved as they locked around my waist. Long scrapes ran from elbow to wrist. His knuckles were scraped too. "You could have been killed," I said, twisting to look up into his face.

"I wasn't."

"But you *could* have been."

He hugged me. Despite his weariness from spending hours floating in the sea his eyes had an almost supernatural brightness. "We found Atlantis."

I exhaled. I felt like I had been holding my breath

since we parted. "You think so?"

"We'll know tomorrow when we go down there with fresh gear. But—I think, yes."

I poked him playfully in the shoulder. "A couple of days ago, you didn't even believe in Atlantis."

"Well, I'm still not sure that I do. All I know is, this has been one hell of an adventure—and maybe I don't *not* believe."

A sequence of raps came at our door. Then a voice. "Lucy? Norman? Are you still up?"

I recognized the voice and leaped to the door. "Moz!"

He stood on the threshold, a smile on his face. This must be one of the only times I had ever seen him smile. I realized we had not had a moment alone together since the team's reunion. There had not been occasion to hear his story in detail after our ordeal at Chichén Itzá.

I gave him an enthusiastic and unabandoned hug.

He returned it. "I just wanted to make sure you were okay."

"I'm more than okay," I said. "Come in."

Moz glanced at Norman seated on the edge of the bed, waiting for a clear invitation.

He rose and waved my father inside. "It's fine. Come in. I was going to have a shower. You can chat with Lucy while I clean myself up."

"Actually, I wanted to talk to the both of you."

Moz came in and although he had not suffered the same kind of physical ordeal as Norman, he also looked beat and out of sorts.

I offered him the only chair in the room, and he indicated for us to sit on the bed while he swung the chair around to face us. His eyes flickered to me.

"I feel like I owe you an apology."

"You already apologized," I said. "You explained why you left Mom and me and Colleen. All those years ago... And where you went to."

"Not that," he said. "Although I guess I owe your mother and sister an explanation, *and* an apology too."

"Then what?"

He leaned forward and saw that I still wore the pendant on a string around my neck, the engraving of the stylized man in a boat with the fireball over his head. He studied it for a long moment and ran a thumb over the stain of red ochre enhancing the figure.

"Where did this come from, Moz?" My voice was soft as I took the pendant from between his fingers. "It didn't come from Antarctica, did it?"

He shook his head. "I believe it came from here. The Yucatán. I just need proof... How it got to Antarctica is a mystery we may never solve."

He had a glazed expression as he lifted his eyes from the pendant to my face. And then his eyes returned to normal. "But that's not what I came to tell you. I wanted to tell you how much you mean to me. I didn't know it at first. Even after I met you at the robbery in the Château in France and suspected you were my daughter, I had no idea how much you would mean to me." He sighed, glanced away and then turned back with a troubled gaze.

What was bothering him so much? Did he feel guilty about abandoning us at the secret cenote when Anastasie ambushed us? If so, he could relax. Any one of us would have done the same had we had the opportunity or thought of it.

"I shot at you in the cenote that night you found the

petroglyph." That remark had come out of the blue, and his eyes sought mine to measure my reaction.

The shock froze my brain. Norman jerked forward ready to throttle my father. I grabbed my fiancé by his right bicep with both hands and yanked him back. "You shot at me? You were going to kill me?"

That, I refused to believe. But here it was. The words had come straight out of his mouth.

Norman's muscles remained tense but he sat back and allowed Moz to talk.

"No. No, no, no. Lucy. I didn't know it was you. Not until later. I was told you were at the hacienda. At the time, I thought you—the three of you—were Natasha Borg's people."

"So—you meant to kill whoever had found your discovery." It was Norman who made the accusation.

He nodded. His eyes left my fiancé and returned to me. A deafening pause descended, meant to detract us from his shame. But it only drew more attention to it. And then he said, "Believe me. I am not proud of myself. But you have to understand. I have been searching for Atlantis *all* of my adult life. I was *this* close—" He pinched his thumb and forefinger together. "I couldn't let someone else beat me to it."

I fell silent—so Alessa was right all along—and I released my grip on Norman's arm.

"I know it's confusing," Moz continued. "But the ancestors of the ancient Maya knew about Atlantis. They made pictorial records of the ancient civilization and documented in pictures the natural cosmological event and subsequent geological catastrophes that sank it."

Norman's head was shaking ever so slightly. He was

holding back, as was I. "So, what is this about? What do you want from us?" he demanded.

"Nothing. I just wanted you to know… well, everything. I don't want any secrets between us."

This answer was unsatisfactory as far as Norman was concerned. "Were you working alone?"

Moz was well aware that everything he had disclosed to me I, in turn, had divulged to my fiancé. It only made sense. Couples told each other things. He must have expected that.

"Always," Moz replied. "I always work alone—*worked* alone—until I met up with you folks."

Norman was still having trouble trusting my father. He wasn't a hundred percent sure Moz was who he claimed to be. Who could blame him?

But *I* wanted desperately to believe.

"Listen to me, Depardieu. This much I know you will agree with… Tomorrow we will start uncovering the remains of Atlantis. This is when the hullabaloo really begins. Between the terrorists, local and national scientists, and the authorities and the ISORE team, who really has the rights to it?"

This was not anything any of us had bothered to consider. People's lives were at stake. That was what had concerned us. But now? Natasha was dead. Anastasie was dead. Their minions were dead. Ryker (Anastasie's CIA partner) and several others had died during a previous search. Who else had been injured or killed because of this obsession?

"When proof of the existence of Atlantis goes viral over the internet, who will claim possession of it?"

"*Pas toi*," Norman said bluntly. "Not you."

There was no need to translate. Like Norman, Moz

was fluent in French as he was in many languages. But Norman did not know that. What he did know, or what he thought he knew, was that Moz had made the search for the lost civilization his life's passion. It was only logical that Moz would stake his claim the same way that the American's had claimed the moon. They were the first to land on it.

"Who owns it?" he asked tersely.

I cut any impending argument short. "Nobody."

Moz agreed with a humble nod. "Simple enough to say. But when it comes to reality, all hell will break loose. When the news leaks—and it will, the internet can be quite unforgiving—tourists and their desire for selfies, and archaeologists and historians who'll want irrefutable proof in the form of artifactual souvenirs will flock to the Caribbean Sea. There will be TV cameras and news people and reporters from all over the world. Every neighboring country will declare it as theirs, including Mexico, the United States, and some of the coastal nations of Central and South America. The UN will be forced to get involved. Work on the site will be delayed for months. Maybe even years. It will be chaos unless we can keep it quiet."

I saw what he was getting at. "What are you suggesting?"

His stare went first to Norman and then to me. "Both of you have the confidence of Luke Trevanian and Arianna Chase. You *have* to convince them to leave it to me. They are too high-profile. If this news leaks, there will be paparazzi everywhere. Don't forget. Cham Nassar is still watching our every move. He won't stop until he gets what he wants. He believes there is gold down there. He may well be correct. But I don't want to see innocent people killed so that he can steal his prize."

"But won't having more people involved deter him? He'll be caught for sure—"

"Lucy. He's a terrorist. Terrorists don't care if they die. And he'll make sure he takes as many people with him as he can before that happens."

"He's right, Lucy," Norman said. "Look at what Nassar was willing to do when it was just us."

"He can't possibly have that much manpower," I argued.

"Are you willing to take that chance?" I could see the wheels spinning in Norman's head. He was standing now and pacing by the window. He had a plan but he wanted to run it by Luke and Arianna. "We can still do an investigation," he decided, turning back to Moz. We are trained to be quiet and discreet—"

Moz shook his head. "Trevanian already made the mistake of calling in the police."

I saw his point, but not before Norman. "Then we'll un-call them."

"We need to get the yacht back," I reminded him.

"We will." Norman busied himself searching his pockets for his phone. "I'm calling Luke right now."

"But first we have to verify the find," Moz insisted.

CHAPTER 43

It was morning and the police were on the yacht. The skiff had been found with its captain dead inside it. If it hadn't been for the death, we might have been able to call off the search. But it was the captain who had radioed in the mayday, and Luke could hardly disrespect his memory when he had been so brave as to help.

They did a thorough three-hour search, sending lights into the deepest darkest corners of the ship, of which there were few. Modern superyachts were airy and designed to be open concept. The thing that frightened me was that Luke's gun locker had been broken into and the remaining firearms stolen.

The terrorist's boats were gone from the marine garage.

That was the good thing that had come out of this whole debacle. But dealing with the authorities had also delayed our expedition to Atlantis.

It was agreed. No word of this discovery was to be leaked. Our official story was that we had returned from a holiday on shore to find pirates had shanghaied our yacht. Luke spent half the day convincing the authorities that he was happy with their response, and since the pirates were long since gone, he thanked them for their help and assured them he could take it from there.

"What about the terrorists?" I asked when the last officer had debarked and we finally had the yacht to ourselves.

"We keep our ears and eyes open… I've summoned all of the crew back. They should be on board by this evening."

"But Nassar has our guns."

"Not all of them. His thugs don't have what we managed to steal away with on our escape. And they left the spearguns behind."

Probably because they were too cumbersome to use on land, and Nassar didn't know how to use them. When would any terrorist go spearfishing?

"The onshore crew have been instructed to replenish our arsenal before they return," he said. "The captain will know what we need. I've spoken to him. And I plan to have every man and woman on the alert. We've dealt with terrorists before, and more specifically with this particular terrorist. I think we can keep a step ahead of him. With a full crew and the coastal police on the alert for pirates, I doubt they'll show their faces again."

I wasn't so sure. But Luke seemed confident. And it was *his* yacht.

He was right about one thing. This was not our first experience with terrorists. Or with Cham Nassar.

Most of the damage was superficial but any major repairs would have to wait. Luke was determined to learn exactly what Norman and Alessa had found.

"I beg of you," Moz said. He was addressing Luke since he had already pleaded his case to me and Norman. "You're making a big mistake. If you start poking around the site now, not only will you lead those terrorist pirates straight to the treasure, you will guide everyone and his camera phone there too."

"We'll be careful," Luke reassured him.

He had been leaning on the rail of the upper deck searching the sea in the direction where Norman had floated the flagged buoy, when Moz accosted him. The flag was invisible from this distance, but if any boats were in the general vicinity, he needed to know in order to divert them.

He turned to face my father. "We won't move the yacht. It stays here so as not to attract any attention. We'll take the submersibles."

"Someone will see you. That marker is literally a red flag."

"Don't worry. I know what I'm doing. This isn't the first stealth op I've overseen." Luke gave Moz a charming smile. "Look, if it makes you feel any better, you're welcome to join me in the *Barracuda*."

"His submersible," I explained, although I was certain he already knew that.

Luke understood my father's concerns, but having led missions to rescue endangered artifacts in war torn countries, he knew the team could handle this discreetly.

But Moz, disgruntled by the fact that Luke refused to leave the exploration of the sunken city to him, turned his back on us. I actually believe he had returned to his cabin to sulk—after all things weren't exactly going his way. It was no more than he could have expected.

Why on earth would Luke Trevanian put him in charge? After I had divulged my father's lifelong search for the fabled civilization—even into the Antarctic ice sheets and the Sahara Desert—Luke, like Norman, pretty much considered Moz a quack.

So, I thought nothing of his disappearance at the time. And was certain that he would reappear at lunch when he got hungry. And for the time being I put Moz out of my mind. This was no longer his obsession. It was ours.

Imaging from the yacht's sophisticated technology had shown that the site Norman and Piero had marked was the site of a sunken plateau where the aquifers beneath the Yucatán drained into a massive undersea cavern.

"That *is* big," Arianna commented.

"But not big enough," Luke responded.

I massaged my head in confusion. "Big enough for what?"

"The yacht."

"What are you talking about, Luke?"

He turned to us and smiled. Now that Captain Jack had returned, he felt confident in handing the helm back to him. "Let me show you."

Even Arianna looked bewildered. Whatever he was about to show us she was not privy too either.

We followed him to the wheelhouse where the consoles for operating the ship were installed. The navigation system was entirely digitized and the largest and most powerful computer was also there.

The screen in front of us displayed a schematic of a superyacht. I recognized it for the *Madonna II*. Luke's new boat. The one we were currently on. He tapped some icons on the touchscreen and the most amazing thing happened. Curving walls slid over to cover the decks and pool and the yacht became an enormous, sleek submarine. It was a Migaloo M7 bespoke mega submarine superyacht built to U.S. Navy standards.

Arianna turned wide, astonished eyes to her ex-husband. "What? This yacht converts to a submarine?"

And no, it would not fit under that cavern in the sea.

He nodded. "Didn't have time to tell any of you. Too much was happening at the time just shortly after it was delivered. It was supposed to be a surprise." He darted a glance at me and Norman. "As part of my wedding gift to the bride and groom I was going to transport the happy couple to their honeymoon destination in style."

In style? Holy crap.

We all agreed that a lot had been happening, but oh my god! This was something.

"I actually haven't had the chance to test it out."

"My fault," I said.

"Most definitely." His eyes twinkled with amusement. "Next time, give a heads up when you're going to be kidnapped."

I giggled. "Roger that. Can we test it out now?"

"Not the best vessel to go exploring in tight places," Norman said.

"Don't worry, Lucy," Luke assured me. "I won't do a test dive without you on board."

The morning was waning. It was time to explore the newly discovered site. We assembled into a scout team. Moz was still absent. It was so unlike him to pass on this opportunity to see Atlantis—or what *might* be Atlantis—up close.

"If Moz shows up," I told Arianna. "Please tell him where we are."

We, meaning Luke, Norman and I, took the three-seater *Barracuda* down to the 160 feet mark. We had spotted the red-flagged buoy easily and followed it straight below to the limestone shelf where the marker had been anchored. A massive black cavern, with several smaller cave openings stacked above it, gave the geologic feature a honeycomb appearance. It was through one of these openings that Norman and Piero had exited after their rapid transit down the tunnel from the cenote. The limestone structure appeared on the far side of the shelf where the mosaic floor had broken off. But what was below that?

We decided to continue on as the undersea cliff dropped to the 1100-meter mark which was the bottom of this part of the sea.

On our way down, the submersible's cameras captured an amazing sight. The subaquatic terrain had the appearance of an once surface landscape, and spread out as far as the eye could see. What appeared to be architectural ruins sprawled in every direction. Foundations, rubble sections of walls and large public edifices indicated by massive pillars and thick stone bricks. Post and lintel construction, parallel wall sections with right angles, all indicated sophisticated design. And something that even looked like the peak of a pyramid.

Whether the layout of the ruins had the circular configuration of Plato's Atlantis was impossible to tell from this depth. We needed an aerial view to take in the entire scene. If only it was possible to temporarily drain the sea!

The lower we got the more obscure the architectural patterns of the undersea landscape became. It would have been an immense privilege to swim among these monuments of the fabled human past. At this depth, though, it was impossible to dive with air tanks. The human body would implode from the pressure. Norman had not seen this part of the site. It was the very first time humans had laid eyes on the city in thousands of years.

It gradually grew clear that we should return to the upper levels where the shelving began in shallower water and where the honeycombed caves were located. The largest cavern was somewhere around 170 feet down. And that was where Norman and Piero had collected the piece of mosaic floor just outside of it. They had not time to explore the cavern itself as they were running out of air.

A school of green and orange parrot fish swam by. There a yellow wrasse. Many more species of fish thrived in the warmer, upper levels.

Luke aimed the sub in the direction of the gaping black hole. He increased the lighting to high and illuminated the dark cavernous overhang.

An invasion of milky particles like a wedding veil drifted across our field of vison as the searchlights pierced the thick darkness.

Illumination swept over mounds of white limestone and glanced off something yellow. These were the remains of an age-old civilization.

One look at the ruins inside told us that we had found the citadel. Somehow it had broken off the plateau during a geologic event and slid under the cavern. Which was why it had never been detected by any imaging device before. The rest of the plateau had sunk to the seabed carrying the bulk of the city with it.

When we sighted the massive statue covered in gold, we knew we had found something special. It was the charioteer, the Sea god, standing in his vehicle with winged horses—and a dolphin-riding nymph on either side. The whole thing had toppled and was lying on the floor on its back. But there was no doubt what it was.

Gold is a unique metal in that it resists corrosion and oxidation. The statue remained strong and beautiful with only minor encrustations.

"Look at the floor," I said, drawing their attention to the white and blue tesserae. "That's a mosaic with a picture on it. We need to get closer."

Luke sent the submersible over the statue and the floor. The cold white light swept over the statue. Surely, it was cast from gold or at least it was covered in a sheet of the precious metal, and the floor it lay on was a mosaic depicting some sort of scene. We used the sub's cameras to record everything we came across. Much of it was covered in layers of crud and algae. But what was exposed was incredible.

Luke's submersible was a science vessel, built to explore underwater archaeological sites. It had all sorts of contraptions that could sweep and scour away sea debris and a robotic arm capable of collecting and depositing samples.

"We need to clean that floor," Luke said. "I want to see what that picture represents."

He sent commands to the sub's scrubbers, and robotic arms deployed to clear the surface of loose debris and gelatinous algae.

What appeared in the cleaned surface had us speechless.

If only Moz were here to see this.

A mosaic of a dark red-skinned man appeared—in a boat with a crown of colorful quetzal feathers and jade discs on his head.

He looked like a Central American aboriginal.

CHAPTER 44

"Incredible," Arianna said. "The statue reminds me of Poseidon and the man in the mosaic is reminiscent of the last ancient Mayan ruler of Yucatán. Why would such seemingly different cultures coexist in the same place?"

"That's why we have to return with a full outfit," Luke said. "And thoroughly investigate the site. From what we could see it is expansive... This has got to be the find of the century. Even if it isn't Atlantis."

"But it *is*," I said.

No one contradicted me.

As we sat on the pool deck having a very late lunch alfresco, I turned to the others at the table. Sayid, Piero, Luke, Aras and Arianna sat with Luke, Norman and I enjoying jumbo shrimp salads and citrusy ceviche with lime, olives and cilantro. And aromatic, home-baked French baguettes. The only person missing was Moz.

"He hasn't returned?" I asked. "No one has seen him? I know he'll want to see what we found on the sea floor. He'll be astounded. And very pleased to know that he was right all along. Atlantis *does* exist."

Again, no one contradicted me, nor did they openly

agree. Good science meant that a site had to be thoroughly investigated before any definite conclusions could be made. But somewhere my inner child was jumping up and down.

Screw the scientific method. We found Atlantis!

Luke had made copies of the photos we had taken with the submersible's cameras. The giant statue of the Sea god in his chariot and the massive mosaic floor with the enormous image of the Mayanesque king in the boat were startling because of the clear cultural differences. We passed around these pictures, our spirits high, even as we ate. Everything would have been perfect if only…

"I wish Moz was here," I said. "This was what he dedicated his life to finding."

"Seriously?" Aras asked. "Your father devoted his entire professional life to hunting for Atlantis?"

Aras' tone, while surprised, was not cynical or smug. He was simply curious, while Luke, Norman and Piero had rather smug expressions. Although for my sake they were trying to keep their feelings hidden. Only Aras, Arianna and Sayid who were ignorant of Moz's extreme efforts looked interested.

I gave them a brief rundown of my father's escapades over the decades. And how this side hustle of his became a fulltime pursuit.

"The search for anything mythical has caused more than one person to become a fanatic," Arianna said. "When scientific curiosity becomes obsession, it can get out of control."

Don't I know it, I mused, reminded of my college ex who had died in his efforts to find Cleopatra's tomb.

"And dangerous," Piero added.

Dangerous? What did she mean?

"How did he leave?" Norman asked, in an effort to change the subject. He could see I was getting upset. He set his fork onto the table and turned to Johnny. "Sayid, did you give him a lift?"

Sayid shook his head. "I was up there—" he raised a hand holding a photo he'd been perusing at the helipad "—giving my whirlybird a tune-up all morning."

Luke popped the last piece of shrimp in his mouth and glanced around. "I had no idea he had left."

I hoped not. "Well, maybe he didn't leave the yacht. I'm going to his cabin. Maybe he's there." I set my buttered slice of baguette aside, dropped my napkin onto the table and excused myself.

At Moz's cabin door, I knocked loudly. There was no answer. I knocked again. Waited long seconds. Still no answer.

"Moz?" I called. It's funny, because although I believed he really was my father, I still couldn't bring myself to call him Dad. "It's me, Lucy. Do you want some lunch?"

When only silence greeted me, I depressed the door lever. "I'm coming in."

The door was unlocked. That was strange. Or maybe it wasn't. None of us had anything worth hiding from each other, so most of us left our cabins unlocked.

Maybe he *was* here. I pushed the door wide and looked inside. The spacious room was empty. The bed was made up with colorful accent pillows. The duvet was neatly spread. No sign of life.

I walked in and glanced around, went to the bathroom door which was wide open. Nobody in there either. I had a disturbing sense that something was terribly wrong, and went to the dresser. I started to open drawers to find clues. Clues to what, I wasn't exactly sure. Moz had been upset with Luke, with me and Norman, when we objected to his request to leave the exploration of the ruins to him. What was he up to?

And then I found something underneath a stack of shirts. I had only seen material like this once before in Syria. A semiplastic putty-like material. C-4. An explosive. It had the advantage of being pliable and could be molded into any shape or over any object. The terrorists used it to blow up archaeological sites out of spite. It was part of their 'scorched earth' policy. Nothing upset the western world as much as the destruction of their own history. And the terrorists took advantage of that.

I was terrified to touch it, but I knew that C-4 was stable and insensitive to physical shock. It could not be set off by dropping it or shooting it with a gun. It could only be detonated when a blasting cap inserted into it was ignited.

I grabbed the still cellophane-wrapped block of gray C-4 and hurried back to my friends.

Norman rose instantly the moment he saw what was in my hand. "Where did you find that, Lucy?"

"It was in one of Moz's drawers."

"What?" A look of horror crossed his features. "Why would he be toting plastic explosives?"

Everyone around the table had a shocked or puzzled expression on their faces. Only Norman and Alessa looked self-satisfied. Hadn't they warned me that he might be a fraud?

Luke called one of the crew over and asked them to check the marine garage to see if any of the tenders were missing.

When the crewman returned, he said, "All of the Zodiacs are accounted for. But one of the submersibles is gone."

How was that possible? When we returned in the *Barracuda*, the *Tiger Shark* was in its sub bay.

Luke rose, outraged. "He stole one of my subs?"

"Some of the diving gear has vanished too."

He must have gone after we returned in the other submersible. He must have been watching and waiting for his chance. Maybe he had even heard us talking about our discovery. And had taken off as soon as we were aboard and out of sight. Everyone else on board was busy with the cleanup and reorganization, and hadn't noticed his activities. Taking the *Tiger Shark* was less obvious than absconding with one of the Zodiacs. By travelling underwater, no one on deck who happened to be admiring the view would spot him.

"I knew we shouldn't have trusted him!" Norman swore.

I raised my hands to fend off any further recriminations. "I'm sure he has a perfectly good explanation."

"*Tabarnac.* His only explanation is that he desired to claim Atlantis for himself. And he plans to use the explosive to hold us hostage, and make sure we let him do it. I should have seen this coming. *Merde.*" The statement was flat and accusing and interspersed with cuss words.

"Listen to what that sounds like, Norman," I objected. "What good will it do him? He just wants to see it for himself. He wants to know that he was right all along. And that there was something to the legend. And that he didn't waste his life and make all of those sacrifices for nothing. If he's gone down there on his own, that's what he's doing. It's not like he can haul up that giant statue on his own."

"Lucy, you aren't listening. He can't go down there in scuba gear. If he does, he will die. The ruins are far too deep. The compression will kill him."

I was startled into silence by Norman's speech. I was a novice diver and even I knew that it was dangerous to dive below 150 feet. Some professional divers could go maybe 400 feet, but they were taking a chance that they would run out of air and not have time to do the proper decompression stops on ascent. The effect of pressure on the body was frightening. Was Moz a professional? There were so many things I didn't know about him.

Oh, dear lord. How desperate was he? The search for Atlantis had been his life's obsession. Now that it looked like we had found it, he wanted no one anywhere near it until he had verified its authenticity himself. How did he propose to do that?

The fact that he was in possession of one of Luke's submersibles meant that he intended to look for the ruins himself. We should go look for him. Now. Before he decided to go down in diving gear. And risk his life simply so that he could touch that golden statue— before he blew it up.

"I'll suit up," Norman said. "If he only goes as far as the cavern, he should be all right. But if he decides to descend to the bottom where the majority of the ruins are and leave the sub to…"

He stopped before finishing the sentence. We all knew what Norman meant.

"Do you think he will do that, Lucy?"

I raised my eyes in despair. I had no idea what Moz

would do. All I knew was that he had spent his entire life searching for Atlantis and he didn't want it turned into a circus. I only prayed that he knew what he was doing.

Norman told the others his plan, then grabbed my hand and dragged me down to the lower deck with him. He knew I wasn't about to just let him go without an argument. At the diving locker, he stooped to remove and check his dive apparatus, making sure everything was functional. Then he stood up and began gathering the gear to load onto the boat.

"I'm going too." I reached for a neoprene suit.

"No, Lucy. You're not." He paused from his task and wrestled the diving suit from me. "You haven't been certified yet… I'll find him."

"But the C-4."

"That's the real reason you're not going. If Moz plans to do what I think he's planning to do, there's no sense in putting us both in danger. We have to stop him… *I* have to stop him."

I insisted. "You can't go by yourself—"

He said nothing and changed into diving gear, then turned to me. "I know when I leave, you will follow me. I just want you to know that that is the stupidest thing you can do."

"Are you calling me stupid?"

"Never."

I suppressed my smile. This was no time for jokes.

"Then let me take you out on the Zodiac," I suggested. "And I'll wait for you there. It means less swimming for you. And you can let me know what's happening."

I went over to the locker. I removed the laptop that was synched to the diver's communication apparatus.

Norman gave me that look he always gave when he was trying to bend me to his will. Only this time he knew it wouldn't work.

"Okay," he said as I returned with the device. "But stay inside the boat."

When he was suited up and we had the laptop, his air tank, mask and fins inside the Zodiac, he returned to reach for one last thing. He took one of the spearguns.

"What will you need that for?" I demanded.

He cut the line that attached the spear to the gun with his dive knife. "Chances are I won't. But there are predators in the sea—barracuda and sharks." Hence the cut line; wouldn't want to be tethered to a shark if you shot it. "My Glock wasn't meant to be used under water." He handed the pistol to me.

We launched through the bay doors out into the open sea.

The engine was idling, and as we throttled slowly around to the starboard side of the yacht, Sayid and Piero were at the rail waving to see us off.

"Be safe!" Alessa shouted. "Hope you find him."

Before either of us could respond, a warning came over the outdoor PA system.

The captain's voice boomed. "Pirates to starboard!"

CHAPTER 45

On the yacht, I saw Luke and Aras join Piero and Sayid at the rail to speculate on the ETA of the pirates. Then Johnny headed for the upper deck to launch his helicopter.

A swift glance over my left shoulder, and I sighted two loaded motorboats headed our way. They felt no need to disguise their approach. They wanted us to know they were coming. They had doubled their manpower. And they were armed.

They weren't actual pirates, although their actions had become piratical. The approaching boats were filled with Cham Nassar and his terrorists, returning for revenge. The extra men he must have recruited from the drug cartels. Had he promised them a share of the loot?

Hauling anchor and setting sail was out of the question. By the time the engines were fired and ready the terrorists would have already boarded. And yet I heard the engines start up.

There was only one thing the captain could do, and it couldn't be accomplished in seconds. It would take several minutes. Norman and I were sitting ducks.

Above us, everyone on deck raced to the nearest entrance. My phone rang.

I fumbled for it and saw it was Luke.

"Where the hell are you two?" he demanded.

"We're in the Zodiac!"

"On the outside?"

"Starboard side."

"Shit. Can you make it back in ten seconds?"

Except via the launching platform, there was nowhere we could climb aboard. Norman urged me aside from where I sat at the helm and took over. He was a better pilot than me by a long shot. He attempted a sharp turn to force the Zodiac back to the bay doors.

We were too late. An alarm sounded giving the ten-second warning. The yacht was morphing into a submarine and we were going to be left on the outside!

"Don't worry about us," I shouted. "We'll be okay."

Of course, we weren't. The walls were curving over the decks and sealing it down. The thwarted pirates tried tossing grappling hooks to claw back the mechanism. But their lines were too short. The hooks and ropes slid off the smooth hull and splashed into the sea, taking some of the pirates with them.

Norman thought our best course would be to get to the other side of the yacht before it dived. It would give us some cover. And then we could race like hell towards the shore.

Well, if I had to die, there was no one I would rather die with than the man I loved.

We had managed to round the stern of the yacht/sub as the hull sealed. The craft became a full-blown submarine. The sounds of gunfire began. With luck the terrorists would expend all of their ammo before they got in range and caused serious damage.

The sub plunged. Leaving us high and dry. Even had Luke aborted the command, it would still take several long minutes to reverse the action and send the sub resurfacing. At least the *Madonna II* and crew, and the ISORE team were safe from the marauding pirate terrorists. There was absolutely no ingress for them now.

Norman had opened the engine full throttle and we were skipping over the waves. But Nassar's motorboats were just as fast and swarmed in close pursuit.

When I looked back, I could see Cham Nassar with an assault rifle on his shoulder.

"Look out, Norman!" I shrieked.

We both ducked, but the shots were high and the bullets missed, skimming off the port bow. "Come forward," he shouted. "Grab the helm. I'm going to try to take a potshot with my Glock."

I wormed my way to the front of the boat and grabbed the wheel. He relieved me of the pistol that I had stowed in the back of my waistband.

He positioned himself in a crouch. And aimed the Glock at Nassar's boat. He took out the pilot, causing Nassar's next round of shots to fly wide. If Norman kept this up, he might cause Nassar to expend his mass-capacity magazine. We on the other hand had limited ammo.

His desire was to take out Nassar next. Then maybe the others being leaderless would retreat. Another rapid-fire of bullets took out our engine. And punctured the PVC skin of the boat.

We were going down if we didn't do something fast.

"Lucy!" Norman shouted. He unsnapped his ballast

belt and shoved it at me. "Take the tank and get into the water."

"What about you?"

"I'll hold him off. Swim to shore. Anything, just get the fuck away from here."

I couldn't leave him, but he was giving me no choice. "Go, Lucy. Dive!"

I rolled the air cylinder towards me and grabbed the mask. No time for fins. The Zodiac was turning into a leaking water bed and if I stayed here, I would sink.

I hip-rolled into the water with the full tank on my back. I yanked at Norman's ankle that was already submerged.

"Don't wait for me. I'll buy you time." He ducked his head behind the sinking motor and fired again. Another man went down. Unfortunately, it wasn't Nassar.

"The stinker doesn't want to die," he grumbled under his breath.

Another round of shots and I jack-knifed into the depths.

Had Norman followed me? We could buddy breathe. But his buff physique was nowhere to be seen.

Then a sudden plunge and sluicing blood. I almost screamed. The regulator burbled in my mouth. I had the sense to clamp down on it before water flooded my throat and poured down my windpipe to my lungs.

The body was dropping, blood streaming behind.

Norman! Had they shot my Norman? I pitched myself after him but a shower of gunfire followed and I had to get out of range. I darted forward to place some distance between me and the raining bullets.

And then I returned to the spot where Norman had sunk. Where was he? For the life of me I could not see him. I dived down as far as I dared. I was a novice diver. I had no idea how deep I was and if I had gone too deep. Too deep meant I would get the bends, suffer brain damage or death. But what did that mean for Norman? I had seen him sink—but how far?

Bubbles escaped from my regulator. If only there was some way to communicate. How was I going to get help? The only help was on board the *Madonna II*, and those pirates had forced her to submerge.

My desperate scan of the vicinity brought no sign of the submarine; visibility went only so far. All sorts of debris swirled and mingled with the blood. And if I remained inert the gore would draw another kind of predator.

I began to rise. I had to catch sight of Luke's sub, flag them. Was there some way they could release a manned submersible while underwater?

Some of the equipment we'd had on board was now drifting into the deep. The laptop computer, bottles of water. The first aid kit and the binoculars. And now came the speargun. I reached out and snatched blindly, the weapon's descent slowed by the buoyancy of the saltwater. High above me I could see by the penetrating sunlight the dark remains of the Zodiac nearly deflated, and dragged down by the weight of the motor. It had long since leaked all of its fuel into the sea.

Damn this terrorist! Was it never going to end?

My first encounter with him had been a year ago in Syria, where he had orchestrated my kidnapping and threatened to sell me as a sex slave. Since then, he had disrupted my wedding in France and now he might very well have murdered the love of my life in the deep green seas of the Caribbean. Enough was enough. I could search until I was blue in the face or I could kill the man who was the source of all my despair. I had to get in touch with Luke's yacht sub, and I had to get rid of Nassar.

No more encumberments. I needed my arms free. I took one last deep breath and struggled out of the air cylinder, spitting the regulator out at the same time as the scuba tank plummeted, barely noticing that below me something had noticed my actions and was also ascending.

I dropped the ballast belt, and shot upward with the speargun in my hand.

Near the surface, I sighted the fiberglass keel of Cham Nassar's boat. Bubbles churned around the stern. The blades of the motor rotated slowly. He was circling the spot where the Zodiac had gone down. All that remained was some wobbling flotsam.

He wanted to make certain we were dead.

I stroked towards the rear of his boat, broke surface and sighted his back. He was at the helm and there were nine other men on board. They were all looking down.

I had eyes for only one target.

I needed something to rest my arms on so that I could position the speargun. The thing came in a piece of bobbling wreckage from the Zodiac. The seats in the Zodiac were made of plastic and floated. I seized the buoyant platform and rested my elbows on the seatback. And took aim.

Seawater funneled down my face, my hair plastered to my head. I used the back of my hand to wipe the sting and blur from my eyes. I had only one shot. One spear.

If only Nassar would quit moving. He was jerking from side to side, searching for us. *If you killed my fiancé*

I screamed inside my head, *I have no choice but to take your life.* The other men kept getting in the way. If I had more spears, I would have speared them all. I was so insanely angry that I had lost all sense of judgement.

"Move!" I finally screamed and the men turned and froze.

Now Nassar was clear in my target. I let the spear fly and released my grip. It struck him in the shoulder and that made him scream.

The ten men in the boat flipped their weapons on me.

"No," Nassar said. "She is mine."

He tore the spear out of his upper arm as though it were a leech. He negotiated his way to the stern of the boat, blood flowing freely down his arm. I was fifteen feet away. Had I been closer, and had my gun rest been more stable, I would have pierced his heart.

I bobbed up and down with the waves. The sea was warm, but to me it felt like ice.

I had no thought to escape. Had I moved, my body would have been instantly riddled with bullets.

"So, little one. You want me dead… I was going to spare your life for old time's sake. But you are a spitfire, and I cannot waste any more time on you." Nassar dropped the spent assault rifle to the deck and raised his semi-automatic pistol.

Norman was dead. I had failed to find him. And even had I found him it was impossible to get him to the surface in time. I was going to die. Would Norman be on the other side waiting for me? Only my belief that he *would* calmed my panic.

I would be brave. I would stare them down. Ten of them against one of me. What cowards terrorists were when it came right down to it!

Disturbed by the actions of one woman.

My eyes squeezed shut. The gun fired. Something lunged to cover me, and a hand clapped over my head and hugged my face to his chest. I felt his grip go slack. There was no tank on his back or ballast belt around his waist. *No. Please. Not Norman.* And as soon as I felt those arms around me, I knew it wasn't Norman.

It was Moz.

He had released his tank and ballast belt to facilitate a quick ascent.

He had stopped whatever plot he'd devised when he heard or saw the assault on Luke's yacht.

And then he had returned to save me.

"Dad!" I sobbed.

CHAPTER 46

He was sinking and it was taking all of my strength to hold onto him and keep us afloat. The bullets had struck him in the back, lodging in his ribcage and his spine. The water around us was growing red. A terrible feeling of foreboding washed over me and the salt of my tears mingled with the salt of the sea.

Nassar took aim again. But suddenly another body catapulted out of the briny depths, and a gunshot dropped Nassar to his knees, rocking his vessel. He was about to raise his gun once more as his men opened fire on us when the strangest thing happened.

A huge, bulging, light-gray mound broke the surface, sending spray into the air and causing a tsunami of rollers that upturned the boat, knocking the terrorist pirates—guns and all—into a waterborne dance.

At first, I thought it was a humungous whale and then I realized it was the *Madonna II*. The sub breached, thrusting the terrorists apart in its massive wake, scattering them. Some could swim; others could not.

A split-second moment of conscience struck me as I

watch the drowning men. But first I had to save my dad and myself. Any minute the blood might draw sharks.

Norman swam over to me and relieved me of the burden of Moz's dead weight. Norman was wearing the air tank I had dropped to the bottom of the sea. And he had stopped bleeding.

"You're alive!" I screamed.

He grinned. "Thanks to your quick thinking. Not sure about this Glock though." He waved the gleaming pistol in the air and it dripped seawater.

Thanks to *my* quick thinking? I had not been thinking at all. What I had done was out of sheer panic.

Thank God *he* was a quick thinker and had been conscious enough to see the tank as it plunged.

I wanted to throw my waterlogged body around him and never let him go.

We both turned to see the massive submarine morph back into a yacht. "Will wonders never cease," I said. "Don't think I'll ever get used to that."

"I could watch that forever," Norman chuckled.

"Not if the sharks get us first. Let's get on board."

Sayid who was a medic as well as a helicopter pilot worked on Moz, after rescuing us from the shark infested waters. He did his best, but it was too late. Moz had too many gunshot wounds and had bled out. He was gone. Norman on the other hand was shot through the shoulder. The projectile had knocked him off balance while the other bullets slammed into the Zodiac fully deflating it, and pitching him overboard.

Fortunately, his deep dive had sent him into cold water and high pressure—effectively sealing off the wound, and reviving him. When he sighted the steel air tank sailing down toward him, he grabbed it. Lucky too that he had had the presence of mind to hang on to his gun.

Luke had sent out a mayday to the coastal police while they were submerged, but they had arrived after the action was over. There were still pirates—alive and dead to retrieve—and the police boats were out now rounding them up. Most of them had perished in the sea and it would take weeks to recover their bodies.

Those rescued alive were taken into custody and processed. Nassar was not among them.

"He's dead," Luke said. "Norman never misses."

From what I had seen, that was true. Norman was a sharpshooter. An expert marksman. One day, in the far or near future, Nassar's body would drift ashore.

While all of this was happening around me, I barely paid attention. Moz's absence had a sharp effect on me. What a powerful presence he was. He was misguided, perhaps. Driven, certainly. And strangely unique. I had only known my father for a short time and now he was gone.

I decided there was only one place where he could be buried. And it was here, at the site of Atlantis. "You found it, Dad," I whispered.

And for the rest of eternity, he would share its riches with the creatures of the deep.

When we searched his body, we found inside a dive bag the C-4 and a detonator which Norman immediately disarmed.

"I don't think he planted any of the C-4," Norman said removing the blasting caps and sealing them inside the magazine designed specifically for their storage.

This rendered the explosives inert. "I think he was on his way down." We had located the borrowed submersible where he had anchored to the flagged buoy. "He must have been in the water with the intention of heading to the ruins—or at least to the cavern where we discovered the golden statue—when the ruckus caught his attention."

"You think he was going to blow it up?" Luke asked.

I said nothing, and Norman answered for me. "I believe the idea crossed his mind."

"Maybe he was right," Luke said.

I glanced up in surprise and this time it was Norman who was speechless.

"You want to destroy it?" I gasped.

Luke laughed. Then he turned serious. "Of course not. What kind of an archaeologist would I be if I went around blowing up archaeological sites?"

"Then what did you mean?"

We were outside on the pool deck leaning on the rail, staring out to sea. Somewhere out there was the lost city—or continent. How large it was and what it contained (other than the gold statue and the mosaic floor) remained a mystery unless we formed a comprehensive archaeological expedition to survey and map it. That would require millions of dollars, the kind of money only a billionaire could afford. But along with that would come unwanted publicity, reporters and tourists, and rival scientists and ultimately government disputes over territory. Was that what he meant?

Right now, this area was largely remote. Here, the waters of the Mexican Gulf merged with the Caribbean Sea. Small villages like Rio Lagartos dotted the beaches. To the east and west there were already too many bustling resorts like Cancun on the Yucatán coastline. The peace and quiet of those villages would be shattered.

Luke rested his elbows on the rail and his cenote-green eyes scanned the seascape. Somewhere out there was a red flag attached to a buoy.

Somewhere below that buoy was a magnificent golden statue of a Sea god, a charioteer, lying on a mosaic floor depicting a Mayanesque king.

"Humankind has been searching for Atlantis for thousands of years," Luke said, turning to face us. "Ever since Plato mentioned it in his writings. Why do we need to find it so badly? If it was a true story, then huge numbers of people died because of it. The gods destroyed it and all of its people because of their greed, arrogance and corruption. And when I say gods, that could be anything from a meteor to an earthquake or tsunami.

"Look at how many people have died this time around for the sake of a sunken city. Natasha Borg, Anastasie Kirsche, Cham Nassar and all of their various partners and followers. Not that any of these individuals were pillars of the community. But maybe, had they not caught Atlantis fever, they would have been better people…"

Somehow, I doubted it. Nazis and terrorists were bad by definition.

"And let's not forget that courageous Yucatec skiff captain," he said. If we and the terrorists weren't searching for Atlantis, he wouldn't have got caught up in this. He'd still be alive."

Norman and I nodded in unison.

And then there was Moz.

Although no one spoke his name aloud we were all thinking the same thing.

"You said that he spent his entire adult life hunting for clues to Atlantis." Luke's voice was flat but not without impact. "And look where it got him. Look at what he had to give up in order to do it."

He was gazing straight at me. I needed no convincing. I never even got to know my dad because I was a baby when he left. And my mom and sister… I can't imagine what it felt like to be abandoned. If anything had killed my father, it was Atlantis.

"Humans are not ready for Atlantis," Luke said.

That afternoon we buried Moz at sea. Interpol had been informed, and after Luke had explained what had happened, they agreed to let former agent Alessandra Piero make the report. No autopsy was necessary. There were witnesses to his death. Me and Norman. Not only that, but the perpetrators were wanted terrorists. It was best to bury his activities along with his body.

Moz's funeral could hardly be called a funeral. We took one of the remaining Zodiacs and loaded his body onto it. It was a solemn and short event. He had lived his life in secret and had no people to speak of. So other than me, Luke and Norman, no one else was present at his send-off. He would have wanted it that way.

I tried not to think of him absent at my wedding. He had promised to walk me down the aisle.

Ironically, before he left Paris to find my kidnappers in Yucatán, he had called in a favor from his boss at Interpol. They had fast-tracked his DNA test and he was identified positively as my father. By his request, the results had been emailed to me, which I accessed through one of Luke's computers.

It made no difference. I almost didn't open the email because I had already decided for myself. Moz was my father. I knew it in my heart and no DNA test was necessary.

I had no flowers to give him. I had only the pendant he had meant for me. But how could I keep it? It was part of his legacy, part of the Atlantis mystique.

I opened the body bag the police had given us. I placed the pendent of the man in the canoe with a fireball over his head on Moz's chest before Norman zipped it up.

The last thing we did before leaving the spot where we dropped the weighted body bag into the sea was to remove the red-flagged marker and its buoy.

Perhaps in another couple of thousand years, humankind would have evolved to something better. Maybe then someone would be ready to find Atlantis again.

CHAPTER 47

"I do," I said.

The Château de la Madeleine was magic. Hovering on the skyline above a swirl of evening mist the gray stone castle poked through the sea of trees atop the rolling green mound overseeing the village at its feet.

White lights were strung throughout the stone structure and garlanded with roses, peonies and hydrangeas. The Eiffel Tower was no longer in the picture. This, the tiny town of Chevreuse, was an even better wedding spot.

It was here I met my dad.

As Norman repeated the same vows under the ribboned arbor, we clasped hands and kissed. The local preacher pronounced us married. The guests flung rice and a riot of colorful wildflowers that caught in my wedding dress, a simple white silk frock made in town by a local seamstress.

We strolled down the flower-strewn aisle to the sounds of a local violinist playing: *You're too good to be true... I can't take my eyes off of you...* A soft wind blowing through my hair and fluttering my dress. With a deep scoop neck and thin straps, it flowed around my body like a sexy summer slip.

As we passed Norman's adorable little daughter Gigi, I kneeled to give her a hug, and unpinned from my loose hair a single pink rose. This I fastened over Gigi's shell-like ear and gave her a kiss.

"*Merci, Maman* Lucy," she said, and my heart melted. This beautiful little girl in the white eyelet dress with the pink piping, gorgeous black flowing hair and inquisitive, sparkling eyes was Norman's cherished daughter. And I was going to be her mama.

The bridal bouquet of pink peonies and white rosebuds wrapped with a white satin ribbon I tossed to Alessandra Piero. I had given her permission to forgo the dress. Instead, she wore white slacks and a matching halter top. With her long brown hair tied into a side ponytail, she looked stunning. I would have given anything to capture the startled look on her face on camera, when she involuntarily caught my bouquet. At least I would have the memory. And that brought a smile to my lips.

She scowled, then returned the sentiment. There was hope for her yet. Johnny Sayid, who stood with a glass of champagne by her side, pretended not to see. But I knew he had.

We wandered through the ramparts and towers, hand-in-hand, greeting our guests. The notes of the violinist following us… *At long last, love has arrived. And I thank God I'm alive…*

The ceremony had taken place outdoors on an airy terrace that held thirty people. This time around we decided to keep it small. The whole event was romantic and intimate; the exact opposite of anything

I had ever imagined. But when I suggested the idea to my sister Colleen, she immediately took charge and made it happen. No way was she going to let me do any planning. She knew if I had anything to do with it, somehow ten things would go wrong. And the ceremony would never take place.

She found the flowers and the garlands and the unique table settings and made it happen in three days. The local bakery and food shops were happy to provide the food.

Everything was perfect. From the filet mignon to the *Dom Perignon*. And the three-tiered lemon-raspberry cake.

Everyone I loved was here. My mom Eleanor, and my stepdad Ted. My sister Colleen and my brother-in-law Shaun, and their precious daughter Maddy. And then there was Norman's mother and Gigi, and her cousin Evie. And let's not forget the ISORE team. They were my other family. Arianna and Luke. Johnny Sayid and Alessandra Piero. And Aras. This wedding was much less formal than our first ceremony. The girls were dressed in light summer dresses and the men in business casual.

So perfect.

Except for the absence of Moz.

I went to the rampart and stared over the stone wall to the road leading to the Château de la Madeleine. The road was named after my ancestor Jean-Baptiste Racine.

Moz was as different from Jean-Baptiste as he could be. While his revered ancestor was a celebrated playwright and dramatist, Moz was an adventurer, living in a time when adventurers and explorers were a rarity. Had he lived a couple of centuries ago he would have been on that African expedition with Dr. Livingstone (I presume).

The two men had one thing in common. They were drawn to fantastical stories: Jean-Baptiste who wrote them and John Mozley who sought the real-life things that inspired them.

I have not yet told my mom the story of Moz. I will. But this was not the time. What Colleen knew I will not even pretend to guess. Somehow, she had made peace with the idea that her husband and her sister lived secret lives. However, no more. We were forbidden to go on missions without her knowledge or permission. And that was fair. Shaun had already decided to give it up, and Norman and I? After what happened I have no plans to search for anymore lost cities.

As I rejoined Norman who was chatting with some of our guests, a strange man came up to me. His manicured hand was extended and I automatically shook it.

"Congratulations on your marriage, Ms. Racine," he said. "Or should I say Mrs. Depardieu?"

I excused myself from my guests and stared at him. He was dressed in a gray summer business suit with a burgundy tie and a pale wine-colored shirt. He was fiftyish and graying at the temples with the rest of his well-groomed coif a salt and pepper.

"Who are *you?*" I asked. I had no memory of this person, so I certainly hadn't invited him. Was he a friend of Norman's or Luke's? I doubted it.

"Is this man bothering you, *ma belle?*" Norman asked, noticing my mental departure and also not recognizing the man.

"So far, no." I patted his arm in reassurance.

"Norman Depardieu," my imposing new husband said, turning to the nicely dressed person who waited patiently. "The groom. And you are?"

"Ian McDermott. Attorney-at-law."

"You're a lawyer?" I asked, surprised.

He nodded. "I represented your father John Mozley Racine before his passing. I am very sorry for your loss by the way."

This was most inappropriate, and Norman thought so as well. I was so taken off-guard that I stood with my mouth half-opened.

"Your father requested that I get in touch with you as soon as possible on his passing."

"If this has to do with Moz's will, surely it can wait," Norman said. "We are celebrating a wedding."

"I realize that. But this has nothing to do with his will. This is something personal that he wanted to give to his daughter."

Ian McDermott handed me a plain white envelope. "You *are* Lucy Racine?"

I nodded. "What is this?" I asked, taking it nervously.

"I don't know. My job was to hand-deliver it to you personally, not open it. I apologize for the inconvenience but it couldn't wait. Your father stipulated in his will that upon the unfortunate event of his death I deliver it to you on your wedding day." He dipped his head. "Lovely location for a wedding might I say."

My gaze spread out over the scene. We were on the upper level where a large terrace had been created when the powers-that-be decided not to rebuild this portion of the castle. The floors were the original stone, cleaned up for the event. The broken walls were high enough to prevent any accidental falls and low enough for a spectacular view of the river winding through the wooded hills and village below. Iron-railed, golden-hued stone footbridges linked the forest to the town.

McDermott shook my hand and Norman's, and then took his leave. I was about to call him back and ask him to stay for some food and drink but he had already disappeared among the crowd.

I glanced at Norman and he shrugged. He gestured at the envelope. "Do you want me to open it?"

I smiled. He had gone into bodyguard mode and was prepared to risk his life for me. You never know—the envelope might be laced with anthrax. But I was joking. Why would my father's lawyer wish me harm.

"I don't think it's anything dangerous," I replied.

I opened the thin envelope and withdrew a sheet of thick, quality paper and a silver key. A key to a safety deposit box.

It was a letter dated on my birth, telling me of Moz's search for Atlantis. And I suppose it was an apology of a sort.

The last paragraph almost broke my heart. It seemed so familiar. I swear not too long ago I had quoted words to this effect myself.

> *... Every one of us is blind to our destiny. We cannot predict the future, only guide it in the direction we wish it to go. Every obstacle that you will face is just a stepping stone to where you will end up. Remember my baby girl, courage cannot be measured by comparing yourself to others.*

Courage can only be measured by comparing yourself to yourself. Only when you face what you most fear do you show true courage.

What demons hounded my father? What fear did he feel he must face? The fact that he might never find Atlantis?

Or that he would?

To accept the consequences of what he had done must have been difficult. What must have been harder still was to know that no one would condone his choices and yet be driven in that direction regardless.

I doubt I will ever possess the kind of bravery or conviction of my father. I know my mother thinks very little of him. But one day I will tell her what he did to save his child.

In the end, he found the courage to place someone else's life above his own.

I won't blame Mom or Colleen if they can't forgive him for abandoning them. But I do know this. I will miss him.

And something else. If Norman and I ever have a child of our own I will never put any obsession I have above them. No matter how sunken the city.

The people you have in your life are precious. It's too bad Moz didn't know that.

And the most precious one? I had, right here, with me now.

I folded the letter and shoved it and the key inside the envelope.

This story was over, but a new one was just beginning.

The sun started to set. I wanted to watch it descend over the village from the turret at the pinnacle of the castle. I grabbed Norman's hand and told him to race me to the top.

If you enjoyed this book, *please leave a review at Amazon*. It will help me to spread the word. And thank you for reading The Fresco Nights saga!

Fresco Nights
(Fresco Nights Saga Book One) – Deborah L. Cannon

Billionaire archaeologist Luke Trevanian and his sexy bodyguard Norman Depardieu seduce museum illustrator Lucy Racine into their shadowy world. Is it the end of her routine life? Yes! These are two mysterious men with dark pasts. She is attracted to both. They have the bodies of athletes, the charm of gentlemen and the alluring ways of con artists. Are they also a pair of crooks smuggling priceless artifacts? Lucy refuses to believe it until Luke whisks her off on his mega yacht to Italy's romantic Amalfi Coast. Their purpose is to dig up Italian frescos. Instead, she digs up his past. That past involves a Black Madonna worth millions of dollars on the black market. Art thieves and Interpol are racing to get their hands on it. Will Luke's name be cleared of the theft? Can Lucy love a man with a shady past, whose ex-wife just happens to be her boss? Or is it the bodyguard she loves? Sometimes the heart doesn't know what it wants. In the heat of the night and the cold of murder, Lucy must decide what she wants.

Pompeii at Dusk
(Fresco Nights Saga Book Two) – Deborah L. Cannon

At a fancy museum gala in Naples, Lucy Racine and boyfriend billionaire archaeologist Luke Trevanian get bad news. The guest speaker has been killed in a plane crash on the cliffside of a small Italian village. The crash victim is not only Lucy's boss but also Luke's ex-wife Arianna Chase! Luke insists that Arianna is still alive. New information suggests the plane was sabotaged because of a stolen Medusa. Arianna is not dead after all. She is the prisoner of a local smuggler. Now Luke is hell-bent on rescuing his ex. Is he still in love with her? Her suspicious behavior points

Lucy to a smuggling racket that trades antiquities for guns. An underground network running from Syria to Pompeii leads straight to Luke's ex-wife. Confronted with the truth about Arianna's shadowy activities, Lucy turns to Norman. He is the only person she trusts, and the man she secretly loves. In this second installment of the Fresco Nights saga Lucy's life is about to change when she uncovers a terrorist plot with roots deep in the Middle East.

**Midnight in Palmyra
(Fresco Nights Saga Book Three) – Deborah L. Cannon**
A mission to Syria turns deadly when terrorists hold two children hostage and destroy the ancient temples of Palmyra. Lucy Racine and billionaire archaeologist Luke Trevanian, and bodyguard Norman Depardieu, join the secret organization of ISORE, the International Save Our Ruins Effort. They must rescue a Syrian curator and her two children from Islamic extremists, and intercept a truckload of artifacts bound for Europe's black market. Norman has sworn to protect Lucy. Can she hide her desire for the bodyguard? When mindless acts of terror are aimed directly at her the threat to her life exposes the heart-wrenching rivalry between her two heroes. But true confessions must wait until Lucy can escape. And the team moves in to reclaim Palmyra's historical ruins—and the lost children.

**Baghdad before Dawn
(Fresco Nights Saga Book Four) – Deborah L. Cannon**
After a horrific museum bombing Lucy Racine follows her heart to the famed city of Baghdad where she faces an enemy that has no conscience. An explosion in the tunnel of the Palmyra Museum has collapsed on top of bodyguard Norman Depardieu. There is hope he survived. A man meeting his description is sighted among the rebels in the desert. Why doesn't he return to the ISORE base? Lucy's love for billionaire archaeologist Luke Trevanian's bodyguard

has her desperate to find him. Before the team can infiltrate the terrorist stronghold, Lucy is inside their camp facing a terrifying reality. Norman has turned to the enemy side. He doesn't recognize her. But—all is not as it seems. Norman is on the trail of a stolen truck bound for Baghdad containing the legendary Winged Bulls of Nineveh. The greatest test of Lucy's strength comes in the thrilling fourth installment of the Fresco Nights saga.

Cairo by Nightfall
(Fresco Nights Saga Book Five) – Deborah L. Cannon
How did she die and where was she buried? Cleopatra vanished without a trace. No archaeologist ever found her body...until now. "Do not scream when you see the mummy." When Lucy's ambitious and dangerous former boyfriend resurfaces after a decade, a mysterious warning appears on her phone. Museum illustrator Lucy Racine goes to Egypt to face a dilemma. Save the reputation of a disgraced Egyptologist and risk losing the love of her life or expose the corruption of a nation. Just as she and bodyguard Norman Depardieu join forces for an ISORE rescue, Lucy's ex lures her into the treasure hunt of a lifetime—the search for Cleopatra's tomb.

Twilight over the Aegean
(Fresco Nights Saga Book Six) – Deborah L. Cannon
When Lucy Racine's boss buys a statue of Helen of Troy, mysterious objects come to light. A stone head at the bottom of the Aegean Sea, a pot shard matching a valuable vase depicting the Trojan war, and an antique necklace worn by Lucy's friend. At the ambassador's villa, Lucy discovers a nearby chapel built from stolen artifacts hidden in 'plain sight', an antiquities dealer falls to his death from a staircase and a museum curator drowns on the beach. Both victims once owned pieces of the statue. To top it off, Lucy learns that her fiancé has one last secret. Is it connected to the statue? Lucy's life is thrown into turmoil as she realizes

that the number one suspect is her friend's husband, the ambassador—a man the police cannot touch...

Sunrise on Cádiz: Key to Atlantis
(Fresco Nights Saga Book Seven) – Deborah L. Cannon

Twin silver doves are stolen from an archaeology dig near the Spanish city of Cádiz, an ancient site said to be the mythical City of Silver. Lucy Racine's fiancé meets secretly with a woman, who turns out to be his sister. She has fallen for a scoundrel and helped to steal the silver doves. When the scoundrel is murdered, Lucy learns that he was a CIA agent on the trail of a neo-Nazi cult operating in the Cádiz area. Why is the CIA so interested in the doves and the silver city? Do the Nazis want to loot it to finance their growing movement? And what does Atlantis have to do with the ancient sites near Cádiz? As the clues gather, Lucy realizes the hunt is on for a turquoise mosaic, an artifact that just might be the key to the mythical island's location. The leader of the cult will kill to possess it—and Lucy is the only person in the way...

Sunset over the Yucatán: Gateway to Atlantis
(Fresco Nights Saga Book Eight) – Deborah L. Cannon

It is the morning of Lucy and Norman's wedding. Lucy has several hours to kill before the ceremony. She goes to a small castle museum outside of Paris. No one is there except her and the security guard who is giving her a tour when three armed, masked men with Spanish accents, swarm them. Gagged and tied onto chairs, they watch helplessly through the windows as a mosaic ceremonial shield disappears into an unmarked truck. When their cries are finally heard, their rescuer looks shockingly like her dead father—a man who died while searching for Atlantis. During Lucy and Norman's wedding ceremony, masked men break in, S.W.A.T. team style, and kidnap the bride. Who are these kidnappers working for and what do they want from her? Being the first to discover the mythical Atlantis isn't the *only thing at stake when Lucy's past comes back to haunt her.*

Acknowledgements

Where is Atlantis? Most archaeologists agree that the lost continent is a fictional place, a figment of Plato's imagination. Others are certain it exists if we just join the dots and hunt harder. From Antarctica to the Sahara Desert, from New Zealand to the Mediterranean, across Spain and into the Caribbean, Atlantis seekers have found pyramids, roads and ruins that might be the lost continent. Unfortunately, archaeological evidence checks some of the boxes for the existence of Atlantis, but never all of them. Although that will never stop the search.

During WW2 the Nazis and the Islamic extremists almost formed an alliance that would have changed the course of the world. Their extremist ideologies made their modern day contemporaries perfect partners as villains in my story. To them, Atlantis was the cradle of humanity, and when an epic tsunami hurled its population across the globe, its culture spread.

The idea that Atlantis might be buried deep below the Caribbean was a location that made sense to me and was the inspiration for this book. To the many authors and organizations who documented the historical and modern-day search for Atlantis, especially Andrew Collins' book *Atlantis in the Caribbean*, a big thank you.

As always, thanks to my readers and supporters who have encouraged me to continue the series, my multi-talented husband for the lovely cover, and my two pups, Luke and Lucy, who patiently wait for me to finish each day's writing before demanding we go for a walk.

About the Author

Deborah L. Cannon is a novelist and short story writer. She writes under three names: Deborah L. Cannon under which the Fresco Nights novels are written, Deborah Cannon under which are published The Raven Chronicles series and her Chinese epic fantasy *The Pirate Empress*, and Daphne Lynn Stewart who writes a series of Christmas romances for pet lovers. She is also a contributor to *Mystery and Suspense* Magazine and the *Chicken Soup for the Soul* franchise. She is a graduate of the University of British Columbia (BA), the University of Toronto (MMST) and the Humber School for writers. She was born in Vancouver and has lived in Toronto, Montreal and Cambridge England. She now resides in Hamilton, Ontario with her archaeologist husband and her two adorable dogs Luke and Lucy, near the Royal Botanical gardens lakeside.

Manufactured by Amazon.ca
Acheson, AB